THE FIRE'S SCAR

BOOK TWO OF THE CRYSTAL MYTHOS TRILOGY

AUSTEN RODGERS

Copyright © 2019 by Austen Rodgers
www.austenrodgers.com
Illustration and Cover Design by Jeff Brown
Edited by Bodie Dykstra
Interior Images by Stacy Sheppard

First Edition: November 2019
ISBN   978-1-950278-03-9   (ebook)
ISBN   978-1-950278-04-6 (paperback)
Published by Hypercube Press
www.hypercubepress.com

HYPERCUBE **PRESS**
SCIENCE FICTION AND FANTASY

CONTENTS

PROLOGUE

Quill and paper always made Shedim feel that his words carried more importance. Taking the time to write letters to the other councilmen seemed to be the only way anything would get done the way he wanted it. A few of the others always loved to put him down and belittle him in public audiences and Council meetings alike, but when he wrote to each councilman directly he could be much more convincing.

He dipped the tip into the inkwell again but paused to tighten the cord around his waist. The cold of his chambers was sinking into his bones, but he wasn't bothered enough to travel to a communal firepit in town and warm himself. That would take too much time, and he'd only grow cold again when he returned to finish his letter to Melech and ask him about the most promising students in his classes.

Just as the message was coming to a close, a booming *crack* like thunder resounded through his home. The sound reverberated off the carved stone walls, and two of the candles on his desk blew out. Before relighting them, he turned to face the person arriving, annoyed.

A hand parted the red drape that covered his doorway to the tunnel outside. Ruchin shuffled into the room, one arm over his stomach. The salt-and-pepper beard that hung to his waistline was in desperate need of brushing, and he was dressed in the black robes and crimson cord of every councilman. He stopped just inside the chamber and looked over Shedim with wary eyes.

"What is it that demands you barge in like this?" Shedim asked. "Someone had better be dead."

"W-Well, no, not dead," Ruchin stuttered as the words came to him. "But it seems that your brother has come back from Earth in less than—"

Shedim stood so quickly his wooden chair toppled over and crashed onto the floor. "Truly? I dreamed of the day I'd see him return, but I almost find it impossible to believe." His mind raced, filtering through all the memories he had of his older brother: playing ball in the market square underneath the Kissum's steps and trying to see if they could throw a rock high enough to hit the cavern's ceiling. His elder brother had gotten into quite a bit of trouble when Shedim was still a boy. It had something to do with a girl, he recalled, but their mother and father had always swept it under the rug and never told him the truth of it—probably because they were worried he would follow in his footsteps —but maybe now he would finally learn what had happened to his brother all those years ago.

"Tell me, when did he arrive and where can I meet him?" Shedim asked. "I have so much I want to ask him."

Ruchin's eyes drifted away for a moment uncomfortably. "Well—" he began, and then Shedim knew he did not have good news. "You should first know that your brother has been gravely wounded. Just an hour ago, he was brought to us, crippled and damaged for involvement in some rather nefarious things, or so she had said."

Grim lines stretched across Ruchin's face as he spoke with gravel in his throat. "Eli fell from a bluff, fifty feet, and it shattered his legs below the knees. Worse yet, he struck his head, and his wits have left him. All he can do is moan and howl in pain, I'm afraid."

Nervousness buzzed in Shedim's belly like flies, sadness spread across his chest, and his strength rushed out of him all at once. He could only recollect pieces of his childhood with his brother, yet he didn't imagine it would hurt any less if he remembered more. He felt like throwing up and turned away from his fellow councilman with a dismissive wave of his hand.

Shedim didn't need to know any more of the details or the name of the person who did this to his brother. He already knew. In a matter of seconds, he went from elation to sorrow, and now he began to brew on revenge.

CHAPTER ONE

A ngela crept closer to the glowing stronghold in the dead of night. An array of knives was concealed under her cloak: two short daggers of crude iron for throwing, a narrow silver blade that reminded her of Michael's, and her skinning knife with its curved edge and leather-wrapped handle. But she kept her ever-favored brass knuckles on her fingers.

A thick outer wall of brown blocks separated the keep from the rest of the plantation. Outhouses, stables, storerooms, and the slave quarters were all left to withstand the salty wind outside the metal portcullis. Short towers watched over the area through murder holes—both inside and out. The bobbing torches atop the ramparts cast shadows on the trampled ground below and gave a better idea of the plantation's size.

The bailey was at least a hundred yards across, which was impressive for a target of no royal lineage. Farcus was gifted with a long life, great strength, and an understanding of the world much deeper than that of the humans he commanded. It was a shame he put so much effort into domination and wealth, and it must have taken him a large amount of determination to build this small empire for himself. Normally, Angela had no qualms with rogues, whether or not they were associated with humans, but Farcus had gone wrong in one simple and clear way: men were not slaves.

She crouched, letting the shrubs cover her up to her green eyes. The earth was moist and spongy under her fingers. No doubt a good place for farming, and with free labor, this plantation was assuredly more profitable than most. Luck was on Angela's side when she heard word of the slaver so far away from home, and now that she was here, it was only a matter of determining the methods she would use to deal with him.

Knives and knuckles offered two drastically different endings, and while Angela always preferred to avoid killing, she wasn't entirely against it, either. She'd killed before, and would likely kill again, and that knowledge bothered her little. The most important thing she would see through was Farcus's disposal and the humans set free. Little else mattered.

"Can we go yet?" a nagging voice asked.

Angela glanced behind her to see Neti crouched low and staring at her impatiently from behind his black bangs, which almost reached the tip of his nose. High cheekbones and a sharp jawline in the faint glow of distant torchlight highlighted his thinness. Shifting his weight onto his knees uncomfortably, he asked, "How long are you just going to look at it? The plantation's not going anywhere, and neither is Farcus."

She huffed. "I'll look as long as I'd like to."

He rolled his eyes and came closer, holding up his loose brown trousers as he dragged his knees across the ground.

"You're not going to find anything new by staying here. Besides, the two of us will be able to get him without a problem." He pointed a thin finger and asked, "See that open door?"

A fire inside the outer walls lit the building with flickering light. Over the top, she could see a second-level balcony with wooden handrails and a chair and table. Through the door, next to a dresser and mirror, green drapes fluttered on the far wall of the room. Angela couldn't believe she missed it; her sight was better than most, or at least she had thought.

"Let's just jump right into that window and get it over with. We'll probably catch him while he's sleeping."

Angela clacked her tongue against the roof of her mouth as she considered it. "Nah. Too easy. And Farcus's men aren't just hired swords. They're slavers, too. We shouldn't let—"

The crash of thunder cut her short, and she didn't have to look behind her to know that Neti was gone. Now his black silhouette was standing in front of the open door on the second-floor balcony, hundreds of feet away. He waved to her just before stepping inside the plantation, and Angela groaned as she pushed herself to her feet.

Why can't you just listen?

She shook her head and went after him, slashing open the invisible barriers that gave Earth its borders—the veil—and thrust herself inside. The space between the worlds was an endless corridor of unfathomable colors. There, she could travel to any place in the three worlds so long as she had been there before.

The sensation was freezing cold and boiling hot at the same time. Time was measurable, but her body never changed and she never took a breath. Yet she could consciously string together sentences of thought and repeat hymns, poems, and stories in her mind for the hours or days that she perceived as she traveled. Her mind pictured the destination and the pushing force of her souls moved her forward. The longest journeys were always the ones when she lost sight of where she wanted to be.

The master's suite filled with the snap of her concussive entry when she broke through the veil again. The canopy hanging over the large bed billowed and threatened to fly free, the fireplace on the far side of the room fluttered out, and a lamp toppled over, spilling black pitch and igniting the wooden floor.

Neti stood with his back to her and his arms raised above his head. Across the room, a grizzled man with scruffy blond hair and wearing grayish-blue nightclothes held a brass gun in one hand and the battery in the other. Sweat was beading on the scar across his forehead. His lip curled as his eyes scanned Angela. "Stay there! I-I know who you are!"

Angela raised her open palms and took a slow step toward the bed. "Put down the gun, Farcus."

The Anunnaki spat. "Just leave. Stay to your own business, why don't you? I have done nothing to garner your attention."

Angela shifted to the side. The fire was spreading across the floor quickly. Farcus took a step toward the door to his side, but his eyes never left her. Shouting erupted from the walls outside the balcony door. Then doors slammed beneath the floor, and the feet pounding up a staircase grew louder.

"Trust me, you don't want to shoot," Angela said. "Just come with me easily and pay your time. Things will get a lot more personal if someone hurts either me or the boy."

Farcus shook his arms in rage. "You don't know how hard I've worked to make this place what it is, and you come here and torch it! The prosecution I've faced—for what? A damned shifter and the freedom I wanted? Yes, I've stepped on folks, but so has everyone else. Curse you and curse the damn Ascendancy."

She shook her head and restrained herself from laughing. "I don't know what trouble you've caused the Ascendancy. They aren't the reason I'm here. The slaves that work your fields are not yours to control. Your superior lifespan, knowledge, and strength give you an advantage this world cannot afford. You've bent mankind to your will far enough."

The door burst inward as two men charged into the room. They carried short swords pitted with rust, held wooden shields with iron bands, and spoke in a tongue Angela couldn't understand.

Farcus responded to the men, then sneered at her. "I've given these people food, clothes, and a simple life that won't chew them up alive and drive their bones to dust. Yes, they serve me—whatever I want, when I want it—but they are taken care of in return. All of their needs are met. Would you have me throw them into the savage wilderness to die? There is no harm here but you."

Angela shook her head and let her arms fall to her side. "You are right. Life is hard, but buying and selling humans like property is despicable." She pushed her fingers through the brass knuckles at her side, clenched them tightly, and said, "Last chance. Throw down the gun and come with me."

His lip twitched as he stared at her down the barrel of the gun, snarling. "I wonder what the Council will give for your head."

Click.

Angela grabbed Neti by his midsection and yanked him down to the floor with her. The pop of steam and the whizzing sound of a flying steel prod never passed over them. Looking over the bed, Farcus shook his gun, cursed, then reeled his arm back and chucked it at Angela's head. She dropped back down, letting the gun soar over her head and clatter against the balcony behind her.

A smile stretched across her face as Farcus shouted gibberish orders to his men. As he turned to leave the room, Angela bounded forward, but the two foot soldiers stepped up and swung at her. She glided back a pace, avoiding them, then raised her fists. The men snickered at her brass knuckles and stepped closer.

Time for a lesson, then.

The man to her left swung downward at her. She twisted, sidestepping the tip of the sword, and pulled on the souls inside her as she brought up her right fist to strike. The extra speed and force her souls' energy gave her would rattle the humans. Brass knuckles smashed into a shield with a *crack,* crumpling the carrier's braced arm against his chest and sending him stumbling against the wall. The wood had cracked inward enough that light shone through it. He rolled his shoulder and muttered something to his partner, who only chuckled at him. Angela assumed they were surprised that a woman had thrown him off-kilter, but they came for her again.

Either brave or well paid, Angela thought. *I don't have time for this.* Her knuckles crashed into the men's shoulders and arms as they slashed around her. When her fist connected with one's chest, he winced and fell back, dropping his sword and clutching at himself as he tried to catch his breath. Another sword came slashing at her stomach, and once the blade passed, she lugged a fist upward, cracking the man in the jaw. His head lolled and he toppled over next to the fire.

As she moved to pull the closest man away from the growing flames, a sound like the tearing of a million reams of linen filled the room. A burst of crystal-blue water gushed from thin air, crossed the room, and rammed into the men. Their swords and leather helms flew, carried away by the force of the stream. In seconds, the flames were extinguished, and Angela was soaked.

Neti was standing behind her with his eyes closed. In the dying light of the fire, his age showed itself: the patchy whiskers on his cheeks suggested he was nearly fully grown. His small pointed nose seemed to keep him young, but his growing ability to harness the energy of his soul was the true indicator of his maturity.

The two humans screamed as they tried to push against the current and save themselves from drowning. They gargled and choked as the water smashed them into the floor, and Angela stretched her mind. Feeling the surrounding veils, she brushed against Neti's mind and found the hole in the world's fabric. It was a good-sized slash that would have taken him a respectable amount of effort to puncture. Together, they began to stitch the barriers back together again. Within a few moments, the room was quiet again, other than the ragged breathing of the men on the floor.

Angela pointed at Neti. "You know you're not supposed to bring the elements out of their worlds."

He shrugged. "I know, but their swords were getting closer to you with each swing, and the fire—"

Angela dismissed him with a wave of her hand. "These are humans. Hardly worth the risk. Now, if they were councilmen coming at us with flame and stone, I'd expect you to retaliate the same, and I would probably even join you, but you must remember the story about the first Dalkhu who killed half their own numbers opening a hole they could not close. We must be... *selective* when determining if it's appropriate to use tactics that weaponize the veil."

"Yeah," Neti said, "but I also don't care. I saved your life." Tiptoeing over places where the wood was too burnt to be trusted under his weight, he crossed the room ahead of her and passed the humans crumpled on the floor. Angela groaned and followed him, the humans watching her step into the hallway with wide eyes. They wouldn't try anything else, for they had far too much to ponder now.

"You know," Angela said in the hallway, "I appreciate what you did and all, but I wish you'd listen better. I don't want to get caught in the middle of one of your *blazes* should you decide that fire is a better alternative. I'm glad that this time I'm only sopping wet."

Neti waved his hand, shushing her. "Can we talk about it later? Right now, we can't let Farcus get away."

Lanterns hung in the hallway, lighting wooden doors on either side. Red and blue rugs and tapestries gave this floor more color than the dark brown wood that was used to build the manor. They glanced in each room and found nothing of interest, then turned to the main stairway. An ornately carved handrail led them down the stairs and into the main foyer, where the front door to the manor was wide open.

"Farcus isn't entirely foolish," Angela said, making her way toward the open door. "He knows his men won't last against us, so he'll either hide in one of the outlying buildings or try to escape."

Cushioned chairs and a large table made up the main

room of the mansion. Through another door, she could see the butcher's slab of the kitchen and cabinets. Even from a distance, she could smell the bundle of garlic hanging over the basin. A closed cellar door faced them from the far side of the room. It was too quiet inside. Not even a single servant at work.

"I didn't see a shifter on him. Did you?" Angela asked.

Neti shook his head. "That's probably stashed in a room behind us somewhere, but I haven't heard anyone breach the veil yet. If we do, we can probably assume it's too late. He'll make for the stables and take a horse."

Angela nodded. "Let's move."

They stepped out of the manor and into the bailey. The yard between the outer walls was about as small as she had expected. Shoddy storage shacks were crammed into one corner, and straw archery targets lined the other. The gate-house door was closed, which, for the moment, made Angela believe that Farcus doubled back and was hiding somewhere inside the keep.

A shout spread over the courtyard from somewhere above. Then an arrow came whistling down and snipped her across the side before it buried its point into the ground behind her. Angela grimaced and held her hand over where it stung, more surprised that she hadn't seen it coming than upset about getting cut. She only had to glance at Neti for him to know what to do. They disappeared from the yard in a blast of air that knocked arrows to the side, then reappeared atop the wooden palisade walls.

They sprinted across the platforms. Neti kept pace and cleared the other side of the courtyard with Angela. Both made their way down the wall, ears ringing with the blasts of teleportation. It only took quick shoves to dispatch the men over the edge. They screamed as they fell. A few might not survive the twenty-foot fall, but she hoped the rest would take it as a learning experience—that what they were helping Farcus do was wrong.

The towers were even easier to clear. From behind their murder holes, the men inside had seen them disappear from the courtyard and heard their partners on the walls scream as they fell. Angela only had to swing a few more fists and they were unconscious. Once again topside, Angela saw Neti climb his way up to face the night sky when a sound of cracking sticks and thumping hooves came from the grounds below. A lantern was bouncing on a horse's ass as it ran full sprint and disappeared behind the rows of birch trees.

"Fuck," Angela said after she appeared next to Neti's side on his tower. "We almost missed him."

"We're going to if you don't hurry it up," Neti said.

Angela grinned but otherwise ignored his comment. "Well, come on then," she said, extending a hand to grab his shoulder.

He glanced at her arm, then back at her smile. She winked and didn't let go.

"No," he said, shrugging her off him. "I don't want to do *the bastion of pain*. I'm always the one that gets hurt."

She laughed and shook her hand. "Come on! It's my favorite! We will lose him if you don't stop whining."

Neti groaned and stomped over to her, then grabbed her by the shoulder to lock their arms together. "You owe me, then."

And Angela teleported them away.

FARCUS HEARD THE CRASHING SOUNDS CASCADING through the forest behind him and spurred his horse to run faster. The animal weaved through the trees as elegantly as it could, plopping up and down on logs and stones and almost tripping several times. Another blast of thunder came from behind him, this one louder than the others, but he glanced back and saw nothing. The forest thinned, and Farcus broke into a clearing. The waxing moon did little to help him see the tree line closing in ahead.

He'd have to return to his plantation at some point to recover his belongings eventually, but he wouldn't dare stay there longer than he had to. Without a doubt, Angela would return to search for him. The blighted woman was no better than him, he swore, but he knew that she wouldn't give up until she found him.

Stories of her and her vengeance had reached his ears before, and he'd seen its effects sweep across the Earth as his contacts stopped replying to his letters and Anunnaki partners he'd known for years disappeared. He'd have to move somewhere far away to start a new life with a new name if he wanted to stay safe. As annoying as that would be, he knew that once he found a place to settle, his life would get better once again.

But then it got worse.

Angela and Neti appeared just a foot in front of him. The concussion stung his eyes and rattled his brain, and their locked arms crashed into his chest. The horse whinnied and bolted for the woods. The boy's grip slipped and he *thudded* onto the ground behind him, but Angela still held onto Farcus's nightclothes and saddle.

He scowled over his shoulder, then reached for a hilt protruding from a saddlebag. But Angela had already raised a fist and swung for his head. The brass knuckles *clinked* against his skull, and a sharp thrum of pain reverberated through him. He grunted, then fell like a tree and smacked onto the dirt below. Everything spun. He lay on his back, grunting in pain as his vision faded in and out.

When Angela found him in the dark, she asked, "Are we done?" and bent to grab him by his shirt. His fist flew at her suddenly and struck her across the cheek. Reeling back in surprise, she let him go and held her jaw where it stung. Beneath her, he smiled from ear to ear like a giddy child. "Were you feigning an injured back?" she asked, incredulous.

Farcus laughed. "I had to get at least one hit in, you bitch."

Angela smiled as she grabbed him by the collar with one hand and formed a fist above her head with the other. Farcus shielded himself and winced, but when she didn't swing, he glanced out from his hands, and *then* she swung. The back of his hands smacked into his nose. He cursed, and she could faintly see the dark blood on his lips.

"What right do you have?" Farcus asked, furious and spitting at her now. "How could you hunt down your own people? We're Anunnaki. We're from the same home."

She shook her head. "Neither of us call Dingir home, and don't act like you hold yourself in such high regard. Just because we come from the same place doesn't mean we are the same kind of people."

Angela stretched her mind inside herself and felt her two souls rotating around one another, fighting to occupy the same space in her chest as they always did. The blue soul, the Anunnaki one she'd had since birth, gave its strength to her easily. The red soul slipped out from her grasp a few times, but she took hold of it with patience. It was never as easy as the other. Maybe because the Dalkhu soul wasn't really hers.

CHAPTER TWO

With the guidance of her mind, Angela pushed her way through the empty space for what felt like the better part of a month. The tingling sensation of fire and ice on her skin never waned, and her eyes never left Farcus's red cheeks, bloody lips, and swollen gray eyes. Carrying his extra weight and the distraction of staring at his battered face was what made it take her so long to finally reach the place she was looking for. A blast of wind whipped her hair around, and goosebumps crawled up her skin.

Farcus gasped for air at the sudden change of climate, his breath tendrils of fog as he whirled about in circles and cursed her name. "Dingir?" he cried.

Angela nodded, gripped him by the shirt with both hands, and hoisted him to his feet. "Dingir."

"Why would you bring me..." He trailed off, and within moments, the crazed look of fear in his eyes was replaced with cold acceptance. "Very well. I won't forget this."

She rolled her eyes and gave him a tug forward. They walked up the brick path of alchemical gold and past bits of broken wood signs, discarded shreds of clothing with drips of blood, and loose stones that littered the overgrown lawn. The front windows of the cathedral structure were barricaded with planks. Sections of stone slabs had been replaced with yellow rock instead of the white and gray of the rest of the building. Some areas were even scorched black with ash. The Ascendancy looked worse every time she saw it: more trash on the ground, more broken windows, and more hopelessness in the eyes of every person she met.

She pulled Farcus to a stop just before the whitewashed steps and dark oak doors she'd passed through a thousand times before. Tipping her head up, she shouted, "Bring me Ja'noel!"

A few moments passed with no sound but the wind.

"Bring me Ja'noel!" Angela shouted again before thinking about inviting herself in, then deciding against it. This wasn't her place to walk into unannounced anymore.

It wasn't much longer before the pallid face of a young Etlu foot soldier appeared from behind the door, saw who was shouting, and disappeared again in a hurry. Then a blast of air pounded against the back of her head. Neti folded his arms around his stomach to try and keep warm as he walked to her. She was so focused on getting Farcus here that she'd forgotten him.

"You know, I kinda wish you would've stayed behind," Angela said.

Neti shrugged. "I know, but I'm here anyways."

Ja'noel and most others wouldn't appreciate a Dalkhu in their city. He'd joined her there several times before, and almost every time she had to shake people off him or pull him back to Earth for everyone else's safety. As the years passed, she occasionally forgot that the Anunnaki and the Dalkhu saw one another as beings of shrouded fire. Even though the difference of their souls had caused her so much hardship in the past, those old wounds had scabbed over. It was only when Neti was around other Anunnaki that she remembered their souls were astral opposites.

The double doors beneath the Ascendancy's steeple groaned as they swung wide open. Down the steps came three men in brown leather pauldrons and cuirasses atop green cotton underclothes. Angela remembered what it was like to carry the weight of their tool belts with the myriad of cables leading to and from the batteries and weapons. Other than a badge of a golden sun pinned on the man in the middle, they all looked the same. Ja'noel stopped front and center with the graying hairs of his chin held out. The wrinkles under his eyes had grown worse since she'd last seen him, and his black hair was a ruffled mess.

They sized one another up in silence until he finally said, "Another month, another captive."

Angela released Farcus's shirt. "I do what I can to pick up the slack."

Ja'noel tilted his head to the side and stared at her in disbelief. "I see no signs of slack here." He raised his arms and motioned to the city around him. "Only too much to do and too few hands to help."

"No. Plenty of hands, just none willing to help. Or maybe the ones who were have already left." She shrugged. "Must have to do with the city's direction, I take it."

His face grew red, and he held up his finger as though he were about to retort, then shook his head and sighed. Defeated, he asked, "What's this one in for?"

Angela nudged Farcus forward. "Other than the usual desertion, Farcus Caim is guilty of enslaving humans, stealing Ascendancy equipment, the extortion of 'hired' swords who used to work for him, and pretty much whatever else you want to put him down for, too."

Ja'noel rubbed his eyes for a moment as he thought. The men beside him shifted uncomfortably, waiting until he finally said, "I take your word for every prisoner you bring me—you must at least give me that much credit—but the prison is full enough to burst. Soon it'll be two to a bed and six to a cell. To be honest, I don't know if we have the means to take him. Holding so many convicts requires extra men to watch and tend guard, and to use fewer would be a disaster waiting to happen if any escaped." His lips stretched into a devilish smile. "I might just have to release Farcus here. Too few hands, remember?"

By the look on his face, Farcus enjoyed the sound of that.

"You'll make room," Angela said sweetly. "Lest you lose all the free labor I provide catching these rogues in the first place. How many soldiers can the Ascendancy afford to lose to the appeal of freedom, of open space to call your own, of everything Earth has to offer? Everyone knows that you don't have the strength to keep would-be deserters in line. You need me to catch your traitors and return them to you or everyone would leave Dingir. My threat is what keeps them in their camps."

Ja'noel snickered and looked away—a sign she'd left a mark on his pride. When he recovered, he clenched his fists and said, "That's Ascendancy property at your waist there. And last I knew, you abandoned your city and your post. Doesn't that mean you fall under that same title? A traitor?"

"But I don't move against you, do I? In fact, I'm an

independent peacekeeper who aids you, remember? Dingir, Kur, doesn't matter where the wrongdoer belongs. If I suspect someone is abusing humans or get scent that an extremist Dalkhu is plotting to rejoin the Anchor and the worlds, I'll be involved. Beyond that, the war between Dingir and Kur is not my fight anymore."

He hummed and tugged the scruff under his neck for a long, silent moment. With his eyes in the sky, she knew he was trying to give them both time to relax, and she respected him for that. He hadn't been the Grand Uri Gallu of Dingir for as long as he had and not deserved it. Angela turned away, too, looking off into the blue distance and breathing deeply. The wind picked up, filling their lack of conversation as puffy white clouds floated in the sky.

Ja'noel dropped his head and looked at his feet, his eyes dark and weary. "What's become of us, Angela? Why can't we work together anymore?"

Angela put a hand on her hip. As much as she wanted it to be otherwise, Ja'noel wouldn't learn if she bent her knee. "Maybe it has something to do with how no one here would listen when I told them I wasn't completely possessed."

"That was just as much my own fault as it was Michael and Kushiel's—may they rest in peace. We thought you were possessed by a Dalkhu, and we had no way of knowing you were still in control of yourself. Dingir has never been good at embracing its spiritual side. It's something we've run from for so long it's become ingrained in our character. Now, you've had your time on Earth, improved many people's lives, I'll say, but it's time for you to come home and help the people who raised you into who you are."

Ja'noel raised his arms above his head and said, "Look

around you. This city hasn't been the same in years. We still have to rebuild the platforms that fell because we don't have the supplies. Every month a new camp is attacked. The tradesmen are asking to use human currency when we've always existed on barter. There's no faith in the Ascendancy or me leading it.

"The point I've been trying to tell you is that I want to be rid of the title 'Grand Ensi.' Managing both the Uri Gallus and the Etlus is too much weight for one person to bear. If you can find the strength to forgive the things we've done and return to aid your city, I will give you command of the Etlus. I swear it. Don't parade around with this boy. Help the people who birthed and raised you. Is it not clear that Dingir needs your aid?"

Angela took a deep breath and swallowed her excitement. "There was a time when becoming a Grand was more than I ever dreamed of, and it is obvious that the city needs help... but I'm not the one who can give it." She watched Ja'noel's expression turn sour once again. "If the Council catches wind that I'm affiliated with Dingir again, I'm not sure how they will react. They might take it as a direct move against them and see it within reason to strike again, and that's the last thing any of us need. I keep balance between Dingir and Kur now, and the Council is finally recognizing that. I won't tip the scales again."

Ja'noel sneered, his icy blue eyes burning. "Fine. If you are so willing to let your city suffer, then I am just as willing to force your hand. I have an old friend of yours restrained by leather straps and a pressure plate on his seat rigged to electrocute him should he rise."

Angela's eyes narrowed as she racked her brain. Eventually, she gave up and asked, "Who?"

His voice was calm and strong. "Donny."

Her knuckles went white as every muscle tightened and fury pumped through her veins. "He's been alive all this fucking time?"

The smile on Ja'noel's face was a sign that he knew how much leverage he had over her now. "Yes, he survived Michael's knife, all those years ago, and we've been holding onto him—until now. After how many tries of making peace with you, it seems the city cannot spare any more time. As much as it disgusts me, I'm forced to use his life to motivate you."

"Let him loose," Angela demanded. "He's done nothing outside of helping a friend that needed it. He's no traitor to the city."

"I know, but we need your help. There's a bigger problem in Dingir than the obvious lack of supplies and declining morale. The crystal shards have been disappearing from caches all around the city, almost like someone has been skimming off the top. Even the stash in the armory is no exception, but we have had no sight of any Dalkhu intruders, so we suspect there is a thief. A fellow Anunnaki would be well beyond difficult to identify, and it would explain why only a few crystals go missing at a time. A Dalkhu would take all the stock in a cache."

Angela crossed her arms and began to pace when Neti approached from behind and whispered in her ear, "I don't know about all of this. He has to be stretching the truth in more than one way. How do we know him saying Donny is alive, offering that you become the Grand Etlu, and telling you crystals are missing isn't all a ploy to get you to come back to Dingir? His desperation is showing."

"I know," she replied. "But that doesn't mean all of it is a lie." Angela walked to the base of the white stone steps, looked up at Ja'noel, and said, "Take us to Donny and we'll go from there."

Ja'noel tried to hide the grin on his face, then stepped to the side with his palms open and motioned toward the door. "By all means, lead the way."

They climbed the steps as the Uri Gallus, dressed in the browns and greens of their role, pulled open the dark double doors to the Ascendancy. As she stepped through the threshold, she saw dings and cracks in the wood, yet the colored glass was still intact or had been replaced recently. The latter was more likely. Inside, the familiar smell of paperwork and dusty air flooded her nose.

The lobby had fewer chairs against the walls than she remembered. Yellow bulbs hanging from the ceiling flickered, and a few were black and dead. The woman behind the counter shied away as Neti walked past her, and the group rounded the corner to the left and set down the long hallway. At first, the people they passed looked away or stared and watched them pass with contempt or fear in their eyes. When they reached the steel door Angela knew far too well, Ja'noel produced a ring of keys, unlocked it, and led the way down.

The spiraling staircase was a crude tunnel; the stone was covered with sheets of metal secured on rods driven into the rock. Loose plates on the steps rattled as they stepped downward, making the journey clamorous with each step. The stairs led them to the T-intersection, and down each hall, cell bars lined both sides. As Ja'noel took the lead down the left passage, she noted the cell she had been confined to all those years ago. That was the place where she had lost hope in the system she'd devoted her life to.

The Grand Ensi wasn't making light of the situation:

the cells were packed with people. Men and women filled three out of four cots, and at least half of them were recognizable. People that she had put there. It was early enough in the day that most of them were asleep and did not notice her, but a few rose to their feet, scowling.

Ja'noel stopped at the last cell in the hall, where a man sat on a metal throne behind black iron bars. Stringy blond hair stretched down to the middle of his torso, his beard almost the same shade. Blood had crusted under his nostrils, his cheekbones showed through his skin, and his eyes were closed.

"Donny?" she asked, taking the iron bars between them into her hands. No matter how hard she looked, she couldn't see that the person in front of her was Donny. This man's wrists were frail, and his frame far too thin. Yet a part of her knew if he was living on only the energy of his soul for nigh on fifteen years, he would lose weight. When she repeated his name, he opened his eyes. She saw the vibrant blue of his irises and knew it was him.

Leather straps and brass buckles secured his arms, legs, and waist to the chair. Cables sprouted from the steel cap on his head and trailed down into the chair, then ran up into the ceiling. Without thinking, Angela shook the jail cell door and almost teleported to the other side.

Ja'noel took her by the shoulder. "Hold that thought. If you try to release him, that chair will give him a killing shock."

The anger in her belly rose again as she watched Donny's eyes flicker, then shut again. His head drooped and he fell back asleep. This was a man who had saved her life and pushed her onward when she had wanted to give up. He didn't deserve to be starved and locked away from a decent life.

It's a ploy, Angela thought. *A test. He wants to give me command of the Etlus, ease his own burdens, and get ahold of the strongest fighter he has ever known in one move, but he can't trust me.*

Was becoming the Grand Etlu something she still even wanted? Did she want to be roped in with people who would complicate her ambitions to protect humans, or could she change Dingir itself?

"The Dalkhu have an inside man stealing crystals right from under our noses," Ja'noel said from behind her. "Every day extremists take another step toward rebuilding the Anchor and rejoining the worlds. New outposts spring up on Earth every day. Their claim of crystal shards is growing, and our destiny of death grows more certain. By not choosing our side in this eternal conflict, you're siding with the Dalkhu."

Neti began to say, "I take offense to that," when Angela cut him off with a finger.

She scowled at Ja'noel and said, "You speak like all Dalkhu are interested in rejoining the worlds, but you should speak, really speak, with Neti and you'll see you're wrong. That's why I can't side with Dingir. You still hold onto your prejudices so tightly, so unwilling to change."

"Soon the scales will tip to where we cannot balance them," Ja'noel said. "If too many crystals go missing, we'll lose our ability to travel between the worlds and the extremists will be that much closer to restoring the Anchor. Find the thief, and I will release Donny."

Angela's lip curled. "Unless the Council brings the fight to Earth, I won't get involved in your war or take part in creating a new one. Get me some more substantial evidence that crystals really are missing and a councilman is actually behind this and I'll have your back, but not until then. You'll think of something to pull Dingir through in the meantime." She spun, took Neti by the arm, and pushed them between the veils.

"A SOUL IS PLIABLE?" SHEDIM'S QUESTION FADED INTO THE darkness of the surrounding cavern, his voice echoless. The torch in his hand flickered as it threatened to go out. He needed to speed things up. "What do you mean?"

Something hard scuffed against the cavern floor behind him. An uneasiness settled into his spine.

The soul is weaker than the son of Dalkhu thinks.

Shedim winced, then rubbed his temples. The head pains were growing worse the more they spoke to him, but he couldn't leave just yet. He had learned more in the last hour than he had in the last ten years, and he was on the cusp of another discovery.

"You mean that Angela taking my master's soul wasn't that big of an accomplishment?" he asked. "Souls can't be as easily influenced as you make it sound. I mean, maybe to you, but not to us."

He couldn't tell if the low grumble that followed was out of annoyance or just a contemplative hum.

Influenced—no. Wrong... tongue of it. More... manipulatable.

Shedim had to keep himself from scoffing. He wasn't going to make any more progress with them today, it seemed; their old dialect was hard to understand, and his head was throbbing.

The strength of a soul, or the lack of a soul's presence, does not matter. It is the manner, the force, that the soul is taken, or given, that kills.

"That would explain humans, I suppose. They don't have souls, aren't born with them... Is there a possibility Udug could have survived without his soul? If we had found his body, of course."

A chance.

The talking stopped for a few minutes, giving Shedim time to contemplate everything. Perhaps humans really were brothers of the Anunnaki and the Dalkhu. They all had the same physical shape. Humans simply were not born in a world with a weyline to give them souls. Maybe there was nothing special or different about any of them; it was just bad luck to be born on Earth.

"Regardless of if Udug is alive or dead, she must have taken her soul back by unconventional methods, then. The spell Udug tried to cast took months of preparation, hours to cast, and their souls were swapped by mistake and misfortune. Neither of them died, either."

Swapped?

Shedim motioned with his hands. "Traded."

A throaty rumble that barely resembled laughter came from every corner of the dark.

A master that cannot cast a spell? Droll. Perhaps the Council of Dalkhu's children is feebler than those we knew in the past. We may not need you ere long, Shedim.

A gust of hot breath washed down the back of his neck, but he did not dare turn around. In the darkness, he had only managed to catch a glimpse of a hand and he was afraid to see the rest of their bodies.

"I wouldn't be so hasty," Shedim said as calmly as he could. "You need me as much as I do you. Spellwork may be your expertise, but the Council excels at walking and manipulating the veils—something I believe you only have rudimentary skill with, considering you are still trapped here."

One of them huffed.

"You wouldn't be able to land a claw on them."

CHAPTER THREE

Thehe clamor of their arrival reverberated off the white-tipped mountains and cascaded through the evergreens. Ravens, bluebirds, and other songbirds rose from the treetops in a great flutter. The sun had nestled between two peaks, and Angela knew the day was coming to a close. They had been gone for the better part of a week, and the smell of crisp pine and the moisture of recent rainfall was welcoming.

Neti's crunching footsteps trailed behind her as she led the way through the forested valley until the sinkhole widened in front of them. She walked to the edge and descended the ladder she had carved into the stone five summers back. Teshub had grown irritated at her and Neti for constantly teleporting in and out and made them swear to never do it again. The sinkhole was more his home than hers, so Angela agreed and dug handles and rungs out of the stone. The treetops of the garden below swayed in the breeze, like they were waving to her and welcoming her home.

After two-thirds of the thirty-some-meter drop, Angela

reached the top of the trees, and the stone walls of the sink-hole angled out and away. Swaying rope with wooden rungs replaced the solid stone. The lower she climbed, the wider the sinkhole grew until she finally reached the ground level.

What light there was at the bottom filtered through the dew atop the trees' leaves, casting sparkles and bits of color on the brown stones around them. The garden was circular, with a small dirt path that weaved past a wooden bench in the center. Of the three tunnels around the edges of the sinkhole, only one was illuminated.

"You'd best leave me to speak with Teshub," Angela said. "The news will upset him."

Neti nodded and walked away at once, but she waited until he'd disappeared into the tunnel that led to his room before she marched her way toward Teshub's. As she followed the tunnel's curve, she sighed at the thought of the impending conflict. Ahead, a black sheet served as a door and covered the opening to his chambers. She pulled it aside and stepped through, then choked as smoke filled her lungs. A small fire of mostly embers crackled in the room's center, barely casting any light.

A mass of darkness morphed and changed shape. What she thought was a pile of clothes spun and lurched toward her. Vaguely, she saw Teshub's wrinkled face in the black.

"Where have you been?" he asked, his old voice cracking and frail, and stepped into the light. In his old age, it seemed like every day his frame grew thinner and his skin thicker.

Angela covered her mouth with her shirt and walked past him. "Open this place up before you smoke yourself out," she said. Pulling pillow-like plugs from fist-sized holes they'd drilled through the rock gave the room some ventilation. The room brightened slightly, and the wind carried the smoke out the doorway.

Teshub grumbled and pulled his cloak tighter. "I'm cold, dammit."

"It's plenty warm out," Angela said, tugging another plug out.

"Not when you're this old," he mumbled. The Dalkhu pulled a stool next to the fire and sat with his hands over the flames. "You have not answered my question," he resumed. "Where were you these last five days, and why did you take the boy with you?"

"I told you. I was going after a lead," she said, tossing the last cotton ball next to the others on the floor. "And Neti's not a boy anymore, you know."

Teshub smacked his toothless lips. "No, he is still a boy. Just because he's nearing the end of his physical maturity does not mean he's an adult. There's still decades of experience and countless—"

"Yeah, yeah," Angela said, cutting him off with a wave of her hand. "We're all kids to you."

The old man grumbled but let it go. "Regardless, what lead are you talking about? I haven't got the faintest recollection that you've told me anything. You two just disappeared."

She put her hands on her waist. "Farcus. The Anunnaki slaver who eluded me two years back, remember? I followed him west, but the trail went cold. This time I got him," she said with a smile.

"And what of him?"

"I took him back to Dingir, where he's been imprisoned for his crimes."

Teshub groaned and rubbed his eyes. "Don't tell me

you took Neti with you to Dingir. He's not ready to see that place, to withstand what they will throw at him."

Angela shrugged. "It wasn't the first time he's been there, Teshub."

The old man shook his fists. "Is there no bit of brain in your skull?"

Angela held out a hand. "Cool your head."

His eyes burned like an inferno. Pointing a finger, he said, "If that boy gets hurt, it will be your fault, understand? Dingir will crush him, given the chance."

"He... No, we will be fine. Dingir isn't the place you think it still is. Not perfect or glamorous in any manner, but not as deadly or volatile. Why are you so upset about this?"

He huffed and rose to his feet. The hunch in his back had grown worse than she remembered. "Besides the fact that you took him to a place he could have been killed, I'm even more irate that you may be teaching him to cast judgment on others."

Angela scoffed. "Please."

Teshub took a step closer and pointed a gnarled finger. "No. I've told you this before. You deal judgment as you see fit, smashing your authority onto the heads of people not too different from yourself, and you never think about where your place really is—where it should be."

She rolled her eyes, and that only irritated him further.

"What's the difference between you and these rogues you hunt?" he asked. "What about Neti or myself? Am I too much of a traitor? I cast myself from the Council and betrayed the trust they had in me. I have killed men, women, and children in order to leave behind a life monitored by laws for one of freedom."

"You don't enslave helpless men and extort them,"

Angela said, raising her arms. "I haven't seen you murder for crystals."

Teshub shook his head and looked away to rub his eyes and pull his hood down to his shoulders. His gray hair seemed to thin by the minute. "It's a matter of principle, Angela. You cannot cast judgment and boss others around like this. Do you think Dingir and Kur will put up with it forever? They will grow tired of it—tired of you—and they will question your role in all of this. When that happens, both you and the boy are dead. Learn your place."

Angela shifted her weight and crossed her arms. The answer was simple: "No, they will learn their place because I give them no other choice."

Teshub pulled at his hair and stormed across the room. He cursed, grabbed a basket filled with books, and heaved it across the room. The leather-bound pages burst into the air as they collided with the wall.

"What about Neti, then?" Teshub blurted. "He hasn't gone through everything you have and doesn't know any better. You've dragged him along on your quest for the last ten years. Look into his eyes, Angela. He has no home, no allegiance. The boy is lost. He does not understand where he belongs in all of this, and you're showing him a future of harassment and controlling other people. Why can you not hold your hand and let history play its own? Stay out of Dingir and Kur, or sooner or later, one of them will end up killing the both of you."

"You've completely lost it, haven't you?" Angela said, shaking her head. "I am a walking example of freedom. I redeem the enslaved and fight for the weak. Instead of pursuing a life of selfish solitude and peace, like you, I deal in banishing the hostile from my world. I rose from the ashes of the fire that your pupil, Udug, cast me into, and I fight in ways no one else does: unhindered and unbiased by the aura of a single soul. Dalkhu, Anunnaki, it makes no difference to me. There is no land on Earth that is up for the taking, no men to manipulate, rule over, or extort, and no Anchor will ever be restored so long as I breathe. So tell me where I fall astray."

Teshub looked deeply into her eyes for a long moment, then turned to stare into the hot coals next to them. She hadn't meant to raise her voice, but sometimes the old man was too forgetful and too stubborn. In her mind, there was no doubt she was doing the right thing and that Teshub was wrong, but she did her best to sigh away her anger and said, "Finishing the story... Ja'noel made me an offer."

"The Grand Ensi? What does he want?"

Angela walked across the room, grabbed a piece of firewood, and tossed it on the ground. "He told me that Anchor shards are disappearing from Dingir. They have no evidence, but he suspects that an Anunnaki is stealing crystals and handing them over to the Council. He wants me to investigate."

Teshub nodded to himself and sat back on his stool with a groan. "Why are you telling me this?"

"I value your opinion," she said, rolling the log onto its other side with her foot. "Even if I don't always do as you say."

The growing fire reflected in his eyes, but his expression was cool and his voice calm. "You have choices to make—that is clear. When you first came here, you told me you fought for humanity's right to live unaffected by higher beings. Now you teeter on the edge of fighting for the balance between Dingir and Kur, and if that is true, sooner or later, you will be pulled into their war. Choose where the line is, and define when you get involved and where you stay back. One person alone cannot end a war. It will go on and on. Many battles will be fought, and the war will change names, places, and dates. It may even lose its original meaning, but it will still be the same war."

Angela considered it in silence, leaning her back against the cold rock. He wasn't entirely wrong, but even with the wisdom of his age, he could not predict the future. "I understand what you're saying," she said, "but Ja'noel has Donny captive. He promised to release him if I find whoever is stealing the shards."

Teshub hummed in thought for a moment. "That Anunnaki is more trouble than he's worth."

"Weren't you two friends?"

He shook his head. "Acquaintances and witnesses to an event uninteresting to you." The old man sighed and looked Angela in the eyes. "Do what you want, but heed the things I've said. Be cautious with what you teach Neti. He does not understand where he belongs in this world. And don't dive into a river stronger than you."

The old man turned to his bed, leaving Angela with nothing but her thoughts. Taking it as a sign that her mentor no longer wanted her company, she pushed herself upright and off the wall, then left the dark room in silence.

The sinkhole garden had grown dark in the mountain shadow, and Neti was slumped on the bench in the center of it, hugging his arms in the night's growing cold. With his chin up, he gazed up at the darkening sky, completely unaware that she had returned.

"Did you hear our conversation?" Angela asked.

Neti sighed and rose to his feet. "Of course. With how loud you two talk, how could I not?" He walked to the rope ladder on the sinkhole's edge and began to climb.

"Was it something I said?" Angela asked, but he

continued climbing in silence, leaving her no choice but to follow him up to the valley floor. She couldn't leave him to brew on things without at least trying to defend herself—or Teshub, if she had to—but didn't think she'd said anything that might have offended him. When she reached the surface, he slipped behind the line of trees and disappeared.

He'd picked up his pace, so Angela did as well. Twenty meters into the woods, she spotted the back of his brown tunic and slowed her pace again. Together, they trampled their way up the valley's side in silence, weaving through the bluish-gray of juniper and pine trees. Neti never glanced back at her, but he must have known she was following him.

As they walked upward, walls of stone grew around them. The path narrowed into rocky outcrops covered with moss and dead branches until the pass between the two mountains widened into a grove. A trickling waterfall had built a pond at the base of a boulder. A thin, leaning tree dangled purple figs over the water, and Neti sat on a stone with his arms propped between his knees and chin.

Just seeing the dejection in his slumped form brought Angela down with him. She stepped to the edge of the pool and fumbled with her tongue. "It's nothing I said, is it?"

Neti only shook his head.

Even though the feeling of guilt faded, she still felt bad for the boy. Something was bothering him. "You know how Teshub is. He sees things that aren't there. Ask him how every tree has a face and he'll tell you their names." She snickered, but Neti only lifted his eyes to the brightening stars in silence. They were beautiful, she admitted. A great black ocean with such tiny pieces that sparkled in the night. She pushed the distraction from her mind and remembered what Teshub had said: *He has no home, no allegiance. The*

*boy is lost and does not understand where he belongs in all
of this.*

"I've always said that you could leave if you want," she
said. "You don't have to stay with me—fight my fights."

"Yeah, it's just..." Neti groaned, and the words stopped
short. Lurching to his feet, he kicked a stone into the pond
and watched the ripples for a moment.

"Do you really feel lost?" Angela asked.

The sheen of his black hair reflected the last of the
sun's light when he turned to face her. "I don't know. I
wonder about my people sometimes: what they think of me
living with you, and how different it must be there. Like
training. How different is Teshub's teachings from theirs?
There has to be a reason they're so different from the
Anunnaki, some major event in their history that steered
them down a different path, and I'll never know anything
about my ancestors or my parents."

The pang of grief struck her again, and she looked away
from his eyes like she always did when he spoke about his
parents. Rising to her feet, she reached out over the water's
edge, plucked a purple fig from the tree, and rolled it in her
hands. As uncomfortable as it was, and as much as she
didn't want to know, she asked, "Are you angry at me for
what happened to your parents?"

Neti sat back down. "Sometimes. Less than I used to
be, though. I don't remember them much, or Kur, since I
was only three. But there are bits and pieces."

She wondered if he remembered the night she killed his
mother. The first bite of fig sweetened her tongue, and the
seeds gave her time to think.

"You told me what it was like for you, back then. The
things you were going through, and I understand that things
were out of control. I can't imagine your home turning into

an inferno and your day-to-day life being filled with pain, but I just wish I knew what I was missing out on. To be foreign to the place you're from is… jarring."

"I'm sorry for what I did," Angela said. "I realize that by taking you here to the sinkhole, with me, I've taken even more from you than just your parents. Opportunities and chances you couldn't get anywhere else, things only your people could give you. And I'm serious when I say you can leave at any time. I only wanted to ensure that you had a fair shot at life, and I wanted to find a way to pay you back for what I took from you."

Neti shook his head. When he spoke, it was almost as though he was speaking to himself as much as he was speaking to her. "I know you meant well, and I couldn't leave. Couldn't go back." He faced her. "My place is with you now."

Angela smiled.

"Besides," Neti said as he rose to his feet, "if I grew up in Kur, there's a chance I'd be on the Council, good as I am." He brushed invisible dust from his shoulder. "Wouldn't want you to beat the shit out of me."

They shared a laugh.

"That reminds me," Angela said through her smile. "I may still need to beat on you. I told you we weren't going to teleport onto that balcony and you went ahead anyway!"

Neti clicked his tongue. "We got Farcus because of me, and I don't know why it matters now, so let it go."

"Because of you? It was my idea to do the *bastion of pain*, and I dare say you wouldn't have come up with anything better."

He opened and closed his hand and mocked her in a high-pitched tone. "I dare say you aren't better than me with a sword."

Angela grinned. "Is that a challenge?"

The cheeky kid eyed her from the side. "Perhaps. Should we take this to the valley floor before the last of the sunlight leaves us?"

She laughed and tossed the remains of her fig into the pond. "We should."

They vanished from the mountain pass and appeared just outside the tree line near the sinkhole. Two white training swords made of pine leaned against the base of a tree, just where they had left them last. They took the light sticks, put twenty meters between them, and faced one another.

Neti held his weapon with two hands raised above his head, taking up the high guard stance he always seemed to favor when he held longer blades. It was typically more of an aggressive stance, so the only question was how she would open her own path to him. The fool's stance would be her best bet, she deemed, and she held her wrists loose and let the point angle toward the ground. That way, she could poke his belly just as fast as he could bring his stick down on her head.

Let him think he has an opening, Angela thought.

"Any rules?" Neti asked.

"Well, let's not—"

He disappeared in a blast of air, then reappeared a second later with his stick swinging down at her. Angela stumbled to the side, brought her own wooden sword up just in time to deflect the blow, and stepped back before they squared up again.

"Aggressive this time, aren't you?" Angela beamed.

Neti shrugged and raised his hands above his head again. He'd tire quickly if he was going to keep that up. "Well, yeah, considering there's ale on the line."

"What ale?"

He lunged at her again, with his feet this time, and stretched himself for a wide horizontal swing. Their swords clacked together loudly when she brought him to a stop.

"You never said anything about betting drinks!" Angela said. She pushed him and stepped to her left before swinging her blade up toward his chin, but he flexed back just enough to avoid it.

"I did just now," Neti said, smiling as he brought the handle to his side and thrust the point at her.

She brought up her sword to meet his, then sidestepped to get closer. With a heave of all her weight, she threw her shoulder into his, knocking him back. His arms flailed as he tried to keep himself off his ass. Angela stabbed at him, but not fast enough; he swatted her stick away and she felt the blade slide in her hands.

That irritated her. She'd had a perfect opportunity to win free ale, but Neti was dangerously fast with a sword. She let him regain his balance and raise his stick above his head before she approached him again; she wanted to prove that she was faster.

"Give up now before I give you a bruise bigger than your head," Angela said. "I'll be nice and only order two beers."

Neti's eyes gleamed from behind his thin strands of black hair. "Well, that's typically all it takes to get you drunk, so—"

Angela teleported only a foot closer to Neti in the blink of an eye and raised the point of her stick, pushing it into his belly. He grunted, but a blow rattled Angela's skull only a second later. They both staggered a few steps back. Her hands cradled the back of her head while he held his stomach tenderly.

"I win!" Angela exclaimed, arms raised.

Neti's eyes grew narrow. "No you didn't. It's a draw at best. I still would've killed you, maybe even survived the poke you gave me. And why did you have to do it so hard?"

Angela laughed. "I wanted to win, dummy. And don't complain. You hit me in the—"

A sound like the crack of a whip pulled her attention to the sinkhole's edge. The wind blew her hair back, and Teshub, in his ragged scraps of sewn robes, strode toward them with dark, tired eyes.

When he was close enough, Angela playfully asked, "I see you can warp in and out of the sinkhole."

Teshub glanced at her with a furrowed brow. Clearly, something was still upsetting him, and Angela wondered just how much babysitting she'd have to do that day.

"Learning what I have today," he said, "I'm afraid something must change. I've harbored the two of you for a number of years, felt both pride and disdain at how you've progressed, as any mentor would, but I must be honest and forward with the two of you. I'm leaving the sinkhole for good, so this place is now yours to call home."

"What?" Neti blurted. "What do you mean?"

"You can't just leave, Teshub," Angela added.

The old man's eyes dropped to his feet for a moment, then rose back to her. His jaw was clenched and his expression steeled.

"You're serious," Angela said with surprise. "How could you leave us?"

Teshub sighed, but he did not look sorry about it. "Do not take it personally. I have abandoned my home many times before, and I likely will again, but my time here with the two of you is over. I can feel it."

Neti was tense, pallid, and his voice shook with fear. "Why are you saying this?" he asked. "I don't understand."

The old man shrugged. "There are times and places for everything, Neti. You might not understand me today, but I hope that you will in time. Our time together has shaped you into the young man you are today, and I would be lying if I did not admit that you are like a son to me."

Neti swallowed and looked away.

"Yet you're going to leave him behind?" Angela crossed her arms and took a few steps closer to Teshub, drawing his attention. "Is this because of what I said?"

Teshub ran his thin fingers over his eyes in exhaustion. "No, it's because you do not heed what I say. All you do is take and use. I have never mattered beyond what I can give you."

"What about our training? I've never been able to replicate what happened in Dingir. I can't harness my souls' energy like I did that day. In the last fifteen years, you've taught me so much, but you promised you'd show me how to manifest my souls again."

While she was certainly better at commanding the souls inside her, there was a barrier she could not pass. A weight on her ankles she couldn't break free of and a power deep inside her she could not harness again. More than anything, she wanted to return to the skies on wings of energy, like she had when she took back her soul.

Teshub pointed a finger at her. "I never promised you anything. Your memory of things is skewed by your own ambitions. Yet again, all you do is seek to use me. You have something inside you that no one else has. How do you expect me to teach you how to use it?"

Angela shook her head. She wanted to grab him by the wrists and shake it out of him. Instead, she said, "You're the closest thing I have to a mentor, Teshub. I need you, and so does Neti."

The ex-councilman shook his head. "No, something tells me you need a Nephilim. The aura your souls give off is strangely similar to what I remember feeling when I was a child. I have given you a foundation, something to build on, but I cannot complete the mansion you seek."

Angela scoffed. "A Nephilim. That's grand. You said they were dead."

"No, I only assume they are and have no proof. It is plausible that some are still alive, hidden away from the rest of the world. They do not age, as far as I am aware, so those who have not willingly chosen death, or have not been dealt it, may still be in hiding."

Angela didn't understand. "How can they not age? Not just every person but every *thing* does."

"Now, Angela, have you forgotten already? I would assume it is their souls. Think on this: our bodies do not require food to be sustained. Why is that?"

"Our souls provide us with all the energy we need."

The old man nodded. "The Nephilim were born in the world before these three, when all the worlds, all matter, and all the aetherical weylines of energy existed in one dimension. They were born with mighty souls that fed them everlasting life, it's said. I read more than adequate amounts of writing on the first mortals in my days as a councilman, so you can trust me on this." He pointed a crooked finger at her. "I even wonder if you possess similar benefits. Given that you have two souls, it is safe to say you can expect to live longer than anyone you've ever known or will meet."

Neti stepped forward, eyes narrowed. "Wait, so Angela could live... forever?"

"It doesn't matter. Just thinking about it…" She shifted her weight uncomfortably. "I'm not sure if it fills me with joy or sorrow. It would just mean I'd have to watch more loved ones pass."

There was a moment of silence until Teshub shrugged and said, "I don't know any of this for certain. I could be entirely wrong."

That was how Angela knew he was likely right. He was the kind of man to keep quiet about the things he wasn't certain about, and he only ever retracted a statement to ease her concern. "Still," she said, "you can't leave us here. There's so much more I need to know. So much you can teach Neti."

A long sigh escaped him. Without anger or guilt, he said, "You will find what you are looking for, with or without me, as it always has been." The seriousness in his eyes was overpowering, and there was no changing his mind. "I'll leave behind some of my things that might aid you. But you won't help me move the rest of my belongings—I do not want to be found once I leave." Then the old man turned away.

CHAPTER FOUR

"F uck!" Neti said as he dropped his mug onto the bar top, then buried his face in his hands.

"Calm down," Angela said. "You're going to piss someone off shouting like that."

Neti's eyes were on fire. "It's a tavern, Angela. People shout all the time."

Angela knew better than to argue with that look and brought her cup to her lips, took a long draw, then savored the taste. Most brews were made with fermented barley and dates and supplemented with honey or something just as sweet. This particular ale had a touch of bitter wheat, but a tinge of fig settling on her tongue was satisfactory enough. What mattered most was that it was cheap, and she wasn't in the mood to care about much else.

If Neti's yelling had disturbed anyone, she couldn't tell. The surrounding patrons sitting on shoddy wooden chairs and benches at large tables continued their conversations without a glance her way. There were families and bachelors alike. A few smelled like sweat and farms, and some were speaking languages she couldn't understand. Only the barkeep kept a close eye on them, and that was just to fill their mugs.

"I can't believe Teshub's leaving us," she said solemnly.

Neti forked another piece of his peppered chicken from his plate, shoveled it into his mouth, then wiped his lips on the back of his sleeve. Even then, they still glistened from the chicken's honey glaze and grease. "I know. A part of me understands that moving around is how he's stayed alive as long as he has, but the other half of me feels like I've just been abandoned."

Angela held up her hands. "Well, yeah, it's clear we're being abandoned when we've spent fifteen years under his guidance. He's become a part of our lives. I just wish I understood why I only mention Ja'noel and Dingir and he flies out of the rookery faster than a starving falcon."

Neti chewed his bite slowly, then said, "He's afraid."

Angela laughed. "What would Teshub be afraid of? Have you seen him when he's pissed? And I'm not talking grumpy—he's always upset about something. I mean truly angry."

Neti took another stab at his food. "He's scared of what you told him: crystals disappearing from Dingir, Ja'noel trying to force you into helping him. He knows you well enough. He's afraid you'll be up for a fight, and that will only bring attention his way." His gaze turned to her, eyes solemn. "Maybe we should be a bit afraid, too. If Ja'noel isn't lying, and what he said is true and trouble is brewing, that can't mean something good is about to happen."

Angela pursed her lips and blew a raspberry. "There's always something brewing, and that's especially true with the Dalkhu. No offense."

Neti shrugged and swallowed. "You know more than I

do about Dalkhu, I'll give you that." He split off another piece of chicken, poked it with his fork, then chewed it for a moment. "So what are we going to do after Teshub's gone?"

"You can do whatever you want. Teshub would probably let you go with him if you asked. It's me he wants distance from, not you." She threw her mug back and drained the last of it, but Neti remained quiet. "You could keep training with him. I'm sure he'd let you."

He dropped his fork, leaned back in his chair, and ran his fingers through his hair. "But what about you, then? What would you do if I did leave with Teshub?"

She didn't want Neti to leave her, but she couldn't go back on all she'd said before. Nodding to the bartender to fill her mug again, Angela said, "Honestly, I'll probably just keep doing what I'm doing now. It's been quite some time since we heard about that sea raider. What was his name?"

Neti raised his hands, palms showing, and changed the subject. "You wouldn't investigate the missing crystals? That seems like it's something worth checking out, even if it's only to see if Ja'noel is lying or not. And what about Donny?"

"I don't know," Angela said as she planted her face into her hands, distressed. "There's no way Ja'noel is telling the truth, and I'm not too proud to admit that I think Teshub is right and I shouldn't get involved with Dingir again. I'll just sneak around Dingir till I can find a way to break Donny out of there without killing him. If I do get tangled up in that mess, the request for favors will never stop."

Neti scooped up his own cup, took gulps large enough to drown a fish, then put it back down half-empty. "You know, I said before that my place is with you, and I meant it. So whatever you want, I'm all right with it."

She smiled and brought the cup to her lips.

"But," he continued, "we really should look into Ja'noel's problem."

Angela groaned. "Do you want the shit beat out of you? You know it'll happen. Dingir is the last place I want you to be. Besides, if Ja'noel really wants to make an ally out of me, holding a friend hostage isn't the way to do it. Because of that stunt, he can figure it out himself."

Neti clicked his tongue on the roof of his mouth, disagreeing. "You saw the same Dingir I did. Well, a less fiery version, but that place is falling apart. What if it's all true and they can't find whoever's responsible? Slowly, the councilman, or men, will steal more and more crystals until Dingir is completely crippled. What if they seriously get enough that they become a threat? Are you going to fight all of them by yourself to stop them from rebuilding the Anchor? You might be a lot stronger, you might have even terrified them that day on Dingir, but you aren't invincible. I've seen you bleed."

Angela shook her head. Neti was making valid points, and she didn't like when it wasn't her idea. "So what are you suggesting, then?"

He planted a finger on the bar. "Think about this: an Anunnaki in Dingir isn't out of place. It's going to be harder to find this thief when he, or she, is surrounded by other Anunnaki. And if it's true that the thief is giving these crystals to the Council, then why don't we go to the place where the thief would stand out? We need to go to Kur."

That put a sour taste in her mouth.

"Think about it," he continued. "It'll be easy for me to spot an Anunnaki—even at a distance—if we're in Kur.

And with Ja'noel tightening the ropes in Dingir, the thief will have to return to his master in the Council before too long."

"Shit, Neti," she said, letting out a deep sigh. "You might be right."

"My safety won't be such a worry there, either, because I'll be a Dalkhu in Kur. Even if someone does know me, there's still the chance they won't straight up try to kill me." Neti brought his finger to his lips, paused for a moment, then said, "But... there will definitely be councilmen who will want you dead the moment you step foot in Kur."

Angela took another drink, then smiled out of the corner of her mouth. "But I'm a bit harder to kill now, I think. Like you said, I scared them enough to send them hiding all those years ago. They don't understand how I did it—or my limits."

Neti smiled. "Coincidentally, you also lack those same understandings, so you'd be bluffing your way through it, essentially."

Angela chuckled. "Yeah, makes it sound stupid when you say it like that."

"But you're serious, though, right? We are going to Kur?"

The eagerness in his eyes made her uncomfortable, and she ran her fingers through her hair and hummed. "I'm not convinced yet. Give me a day or two to think about it, yeah? A lot of bad could happen if we step on the Council's toes for nothing."

Neti nodded and tried to conceal his grin, but she wondered if the reason he was really interested in investigating the crystals was to go to Kur. Maybe he thought he would find something about his parents there or maybe learn something about his people. Either way, it made Angela uncomfortable.

When she finished her drink, she waved the barkeep over and paid him with three silver chips, and they left. With Neti trailing behind her, they walked the streets, passing people crowded around market stalls as they shouted over sheep and handmade tools and argued over daughters and wives of one illegitimate bastard or another. Occasionally, she'd watch seven or eight people cram themselves into a home the size of her room. The homeless would gather around firepits and roast skewered rats caught in the cesspits outside of town.

Tarsus was a busy, dirty place, but the view from the steppes north of town made it worthwhile. Well, that and the ale, but from up there, she could look down over the city and smell the breeze coming off the sea. The southern harbor was busy with fishing boats and galleys at dusk, and it was beautiful when the sun filled the sky with reds and oranges as it settled over the horizon.

Humans never reacted well to people disappearing in a blast of thunderous clamor, so they walked the western road out of town for the better part of a mile. Confident no one was watching them, they slipped off the road and into the brush.

Once over a hill, they trod down a steep decline and into a small ravine where the ground grew softer and the grass was taller and greener. When they felt as though they'd gone far enough, Angela plugged her ears, and Neti vanished from sight. She gave him a few moments, then pushed herself into the space between the worlds.

For what felt like several weeks, Angela imagined the valley surrounding her. The trees waved to her in the breeze. The songbirds were singing their last tunes of the day, and the smell of freshly fallen pinecones was strong. The hazelnut bushes would be ready for harvest in a month or so, too. She could see the snow-capped mountain peaks looming over her, but the picture in her mind did not match what she saw when she appeared on the valley floor.

"Angela!" Neti screamed from somewhere behind the floating red sparks of burning trunks. Black smoke rose out of the sinkhole like a volcano's crater. The blaze in the valley had already reached the feet of the mountains. The dried pine needles that had littered the ground that morning were now black crisps and ash. The air was heavy in her lungs and hot on her face. It smelled bitter and full of dread.

Neti rushed from somewhere around the sinkhole's opening, coming out of the thick smoke with his shirt pulled over his mouth as he screamed for her again. Angela pulled her shirt over her face, too, and sprinted toward the wall of black ooze that rose into the sky. Without stopping, she raced past Neti, to the sinkhole's edge, and looked below. There was hardly any fire left or any fuel for it to burn. Only small fingers of flame danced around the edge of the garden below, and she took that as a sign that their home had been burning for some time.

"Teshub!" Angela shouted.

The opening to every room below was dark and unlit. She pushed through the veils and appeared at the bottom of the sinkhole, then dashed into the tunnel and stooped underneath the smoldering, half-burnt drape that covered his doorway.

"Teshub!"

There were crunchy skeletons of ash where wicker baskets once sat. The covers of scrolls and books smoldered on their shelves, and wooden crates still slowly burned. Pieces of the bed frame had disintegrated into fragments and were too far spread out to be just from the fire. Someone had broken it into pieces and chucked them across the room. A charred figure with an outline of a person lay underneath a charcoal-black piece of lumber.

"Fuck!" Angela yelled and began chucking the searing-hot remains of a bed frame off the old man. She winced as each piece burned her, but her hands were not nearly as bad as Teshub's body; his clothes had burned entirely, and his skin had charred black. It cracked open when she tried to take him by the arm and pull him to his feet. His shriek was weak and pitiful, and blood seeped from the wounds across his body. Her eyes stung from the smoke, and the smell of his burnt flesh filled her nostrils.

"D-Don't…" he rasped. "Hurts… Terrible."

Neti fumbled over debris as he entered the room behind her, then gasped when he saw what was left of the closest thing he had to a father.

"L-Listen, Teshub," Angela said. "We need to get you out of this smoke." She bent to try picking him up again, but more of his skin split open. He wailed and slapped her away.

To Neti, she said, "Get water. Now."

He nodded, then closed his eyes as though he was going to breach the veil and bring it through.

"No, not like that. You'll tear the skin right off him. Find a damn bucket and fill it somewhere else."

Neti stammered, shut himself up, and walked out of the room.

"A-Angela," Teshub murmured.

His hair was gone. The jowls that sagged under his chin were now shriveled to his bones, and he was almost—no, he was—completely unrecognizable.

"W-Who did this?" Angela asked, feeling a tear dribble down her cheek.

The old ex-councilman groaned and spoke with a wheeze: "I don't... know. There were... sounds. Then came a stream of brown... blue fire... unlike anything... Something..."

He hacked up blood, which splattered down his scorched chest, then reached out and took Angela's hand in his. He groaned as he lifted something long and black from the burnt floor and placed it in her hand. It was too curved and heavy to be a wooden piece of debris, and where she rubbed it clean silver shimmered under the dwindling fire's light. It was a sword covered in soot.

"T-Take... this. My son... made it... for me."

Angela almost jumped to her feet. "You have a son? When?" She shook her head and pushed it back to him. "It doesn't matter. Teshub, I can't take this."

A groan escaped him as he shoved the blade toward her and shook it. "No. You... take it." She could tell by the weakness in his voice that he would not survive this, and something told her he knew it as well.

"It should go to your son, not me," Angela said. "I don't deserve your last memento. Where can I find your son?"

"M... My son... son is—" For a moment, he fought, panting to draw in air and catch his breath, but then he accepted his fate. His muscles relaxed, his arms went limp, and his breathing stopped with one long sigh.

Time seemed to pause, until Neti was there, and she wasn't sure how long he'd been standing next to her. Part of her wanted to yell at him for not doing anything, but she couldn't bring the words to her tongue.

"Give it," Angela said, and she took the bucket out of

his hands. Pouring the water over Teshub's body made him steam and sizzle, but he was cool to the touch and she could move him somewhere out of the smoke. There was a moment of silence as the reality of Teshub's end returned. Then she clenched the bucket by its handle, chucked it across the room, and rushed to her feet. "A fucking fire?! Bullshit! There's no way this happened by accident." The burning in her throat got the better of her. She broke into a fit of coughing and crying and stormed out the door. She passed through the tunnel and out into the charred remains of the sinkhole garden. The air was a little clearer, but the burning in her chest remained.

Neti followed behind her, quiet, until he asked, "If it wasn't an accident, what happened?"

She spun and faced him, sweat beading on her forehead. "This was an attack. No doubt. Someone found us, came here, started this fire, and killed Teshub."

His eyes dropped to the ground. He wiped the soot on his cheeks and asked, "But who would do that? Who even knows about this place?"

Angela cussed and nearly threw a fist at the black remains of a tree trunk when she realized she was still holding the sword. It was short, curved, and surprisingly light. The square guard would barely protect her knuckles, but she was sure that, somewhere underneath the soot and blood, the weapon was stunning. She turned the blade in her hand and curled her fingers around the grip tightly. "I have an idea. Teshub might have died, but I know this attack was aimed at me, and there's only one person I can think of that would try something so unprovoked like this. Help me bury Teshub and put out the fires in the valley. Then gather your things and get ready to leave this place."

Neti stepped closer, his eyes nervously scanning her as his whole frame shook. "Where are we going?"

As old has he'd become, she was reminded that in some ways he was still a child. A child that needed direction, lest he stand idly as things fell into chaos around him. He, like many things, required a strong hand to guide him.

"We're going to Kur."

CHAPTER FIVE

Angela screamed before the echo of their thunderous arrival faded. Her voice carried off between the teeth of that cavern and reverberated off the walls and down the deepest tunnels, shaking the city of Kur.

"Shedim!"

Dalkhu men dressed in the gray and brown robes of tradesmen shifted uneasily behind their stalls while women in colorful gowns squealed and clutched their children by their clothes and tugged them to safety. It was the men dressed in black robes, with scowls and tense eyes underneath their hoods, that concerned Angela. Each of them was trained in war—at least to some extent. The color of the cords around their waists identified their skill, but beyond the red of a councilman, she did not know the hierarchy. None of them were Shedim, and that was all that mattered to her.

Once more, she called out his name, and finally a few people scattered like rats and began their climb up the marble steps to the Kissum. The black stone, marbled with veins of white and gold, traveled up to the Kissum's massive set of double doors. Carvings wound their way up the pentagonal sides of the looming capital building, with five bulbous domes and a spire atop each.

Even the market square she stood on was cut and polished from the cavern. Gems of red, blue, and yellow set in the floor marked off sections underneath a clear adhesive that sealed the gems and smoothed the surface. The moss that clung to stalactites on the ceiling cast their colors downward on the finished floor as though a cloudy green sea filled with milky stars was above and below. All of it was a testament to Dalkhu stonesmanship.

They waited at the foot of those great steps for nearly ten minutes as the people shuffled about nervously, steering clear and wide. Barely audible whispers fluttered through the air as civilians began to close their shops and wander into their straw and stone homes around the market. More so than Neti, Angela could sense that she was not welcome in Kur. She was known, hated, and feared.

"Shouldn't we just head up the steps?" Neti asked in a whisper.

"No," Angela said, then pointed at the Kissum's doors. Four figures dressed in black robes and red sashes were gliding toward them. Before they were halfway down the steps, she recognized all but one of them.

On the very left was Ruchin. The sags and wrinkles under his eyes had gotten no better in the years since she'd dealt with him, and his gray beard nearly reached his waistline now. While Teshub had not been forthcoming about the Council and his past life, he had mentioned that he and Ruchin were trained and tested, side by side, when they were children. That meant that he was very old.

And hopefully not as stubborn...

On the far right was another councilman she'd seen before. This man was as pale as bone, and his head and face were shaved smooth. A sharp jaw and a crooked nose were little alarm compared to the tattoos and piercings that riddled his skin. Black designs ran along his scalp and down his neck, but his face was untouched other than the silver ring hanging from his nose and the loops that stretched the lobes of his ears. He'd been on Earth when Kushiel and his men, including Michael, clashed with the Council fifteen years before, but she couldn't recall his name. Maybe she'd never learned it.

To his left was a councilman she had assuredly never met before: a young man with freckles and curled red hair that spilled out of his hood and down past his shoulders. A green jewel encased in a copper pendant hung from his neck, and his face was solid and sharp like a statue, a stark contrast to his bright green eyes, which constantly scanned the world around him.

But most importantly of them all, Shedim glided down the steps next to Ruchin, his chin held high. He lowered his hood, revealing brown hair cropped short and a goatee that he'd let grow to the lump in his throat. The way his smile twisted at the corners when he realized it was she who'd called him filled her with a rush of anxiety and adrenaline at the same time. Angela wanted to laugh at his idiocy—or his boldness—in coming right to her as she had asked.

All at once, the men of the Dalkhu Council stopped on the last step before her.

"Angela," Shedim said, "I see that you haven't brought any new deserters to bleed on the floor, so what brings you to Kur? I'm also concerned as to why you specifically summoned me."

Amused by his demeanor, she nodded politely with a

curt smile, then stepped forward and pulled Teshub's sword from its leather scabbard on her shoulder. Half of the councilmen reached into their robes but paused when she held it horizontally on her open palms to show it to them. Their narrow eyes glanced at her suspiciously, then looked to one another and back at the weapon with the square golden guard in her hands.

"Is this familiar to any of you?" she asked.

By the looks in their eyes, every one of them grew even more suspicious. Not only did it seem as if they had never seen the blade before, but they seemed incredulous that she'd come and asked them about a sword in the first place. The Dalkhu could forge blades, but human craftsmanship clearly inspired this longer, curved style.

"This belonged to a man at least you knew, Ruchin: excouncilman Teshub Naamah."

The elder Dalkhu moved uncomfortably and sifted his fingers through his beard. "It's true. I knew him a long time ago. But... how would you come upon his sword, and what does it matter? You open this old councilman's scars by speaking of that man."

"Before today it belonged to Teshub himself," Angela said, "but now he's entrusted it to me, and I need to know if any of you know why. Don't try to play me like a fool, and I won't waste anyone's time if you give me what I need. But if I discover that any of you hid information from me, there will be a price to pay."

Shedim shook his head, chuckled, and motioned to her. "None of us know anything of the old man's sword. If I remember correctly, he has not held his seat for at least one hundred years, and I doubt any of us know as much about his recent whereabouts as you. He caused a ruckus in his day and fled the Council because of what he did. Am I right, Ruchin?"

"It's true," he answered with a gravelly voice. "Teshub was cold, harsh, and unwilling to bend to the Council's rules. He broke the laws of matrimony, preached folly to the other members, and started rumors of a revolution that would shatter our society. Betrayal after betrayal plagued us until we put him back into his place, and he could not accept his loss and fled the Council and Kur, so how did you come upon his sword?"

Shedim stepped forward. "And beyond that, what does this have to do with the reason you have summoned me?"

Angela matched Shedim and took a step closer, then tried to hide her smile when his eyes glanced nervously at her sword. "It should be news to you that Neti and I have lived with Teshub for nearly fifteen years. Just a handful of hours ago, we returned to our shared home and found Teshub on the brink of an untimely death. But Teshub was too old to cause trouble to anyone, and to be killed after such a long time of solitude is too much of a coincidence. The attack was intended for me, and there is only one person I can think of that would have the motivation and be bold and stupid enough to try." She let her gaze settle on Shedim.

He loosed a nervous laugh and paced away to collect himself. When he returned, sweat beading on his forehead, he asked, "So you accuse me of killing the betrayer? That is more your line of work, Angela, as I have as little care for him as I do for you." He turned and said, "Fellow councilmen, I warn you, this woman is trying to deceive you and shatter the Council's resolve. Do not let that happen."

Angela's grip on the sword tightened. He was feigning bravery, but she could see his lip twitching as he talked.

"Don't lie," she said. "No one but a councilman would possess the skill to try and strike me down, and none of them would have the motivation behind it but you. I doubt you've forgotten what I did to your master—or the piece of him I still carry with me." Angela tapped her chest.

Shedim's fists clenched and his lips snarled. Words formed on his tongue, but he let them fall in a sigh and he shook his head. "I think you seriously misunderstand me. How many years has it been? Tell me what evils I've done since the day you took your soul back from Udug."

"So far that I know, you murdered a man who exiled himself and lived in peace. I told you not to play me for a fool, and you still are trying. We both know the biggest thing stopping you from restoring the Anchor is me, and getting me out of the way would solve so many problems. You could launch Dingir from its skies in a great ball of fire."

He smiled. "Mmmm... As much as it would please me to be free of Anunnaki harassment, I would not wish to provoke you. Besides, the vision of restoring the Anchor and returning all the worlds to one was never my own, I admit. It was Udug's. How was I supposed to deny the offer of a seat on the Council? I told him what he wanted to hear and played the role as his tool for fear of my own life. That movement died with him, I assure you."

Angela shook her head and turned to Neti, looking for guidance. As far as she could tell, Shedim was being honest, but she had to keep pressuring him and thus turned to him again. "I've fallen for your glib tongue once before and haven't forgotten. If what you say is true, then why do you still bear the title 'the Restorer'? The nature of the name goes against what you say."

Shedim rolled his eyes now, annoyed with her. "It's

nothing more than a name given to me by Udug. It does not define who I am or my role in the Council." He crossed his arms and sighed. "I remember how hot-headed you were back then, but you outdo yourself now. You cannot touch me. I am not the one who torched your home. I played no part in Teshub's murder, so go back home."

Angela laughed and said, "I remember you as being a better liar, Shedim."

His brow creased in confusion.

"I said nothing about a fire."

His eyes grew wide as Angela swung her sword and slashed clean through his neck. Legs falling out from under him, his head clunked when it hit the floor.

The tattooed councilman bellowed and pulled daggers from the sleeves of his robes. In an instant, he crossed the distance between them and was slashing at her face. The blades' silver edges shimmered past her nose as she maneuvered around them. He was faster than anyone she'd ever played swords with, and the one she now held in her hands was heavier and made her feel sluggish. Crudely, she parried his attacks as the rage in his bright yellow eyes grew.

Neti was screaming and racing closer to help her, but he couldn't get involved in this, so Angela grimaced and opened a path into the veil. With a push of her souls, she vanished, leaving the councilman stumbling forward when his blade didn't connect with hers. Then she appeared again not half a step behind him. She swung low, slicing him across the back of his calves and sending him to the ground.

A final blow would end this councilman as well, but an outside presence grabbed hold of her like a viper's fangs, and she hesitated. The councilman with the red hair, just twenty feet away, had his eyes closed. Sweat formed on his brow as his mind washed over hers like a lead blanket. While she didn't like fighting the Dalkhu way, she could play the game well enough. Angela snarled and turned away from the bleeding councilman on the floor. Neti stood between them now, and he prepared to strike back.

The mind is the knife, and the soul is the hand that guides it forward and gives it force.

The councilman's mind bit into her like a squid's hooked beak, ensnaring her. He was certainly more skilled than her, taking on strange shapes and always shifting and moving, but Angela had something he could not even try to mimic: a second soul. Brute force was her game. She gnashed her teeth, grabbed hold of his mind, and pried him off her like the snake he was.

His mind warped, trying to flex its way free and strike back. Clenching her fist, she snapped down on the councilman and pushed, smashing him into the veil with a crack. Panic set into his green eyes just before he disappeared. Water gushed from thin air where he had been standing and poured onto the ground like a waterfall.

From that watery dimension, the councilman's mind lashed out at her, frantically trying to injure her enough that she would release him. When he realized it wouldn't work, he tried to pull himself free of her grasp and teleport into another dimension, but Angela held him there, drowning him. As skilled as he was, he could not overpower or escape the strength of her grasp.

The tattooed man with the cut calves was on his feet again, sneering at Neti, who stood between them. Just as he roared and tried to lunge, a haggard voice shouted over the splashing water.

"Stop this at once!" Ruchin yelled. He hobbled forward

and pushed the other councilman's blades down. "Cease this, Maulkatu. You will only get yourself killed, you stupid fool."

Ruchin turned to Angela, his beard swaying as he dropped to his knees. "Please, don't do this. Bring Toth back. He's the youngest of the Council. You can't hold it against him for reacting this way. Nor Maulkatu."

Her eyes were hard and cold. They looked down on him as she weighed Ruchin. She could hold that councilman in the watery world long enough to kill him, but it would cost her souls a good amount of energy. Tears were forming in the elder's eyes as he asked, "Did you come to massacre the last of the Council, Angela? Or did you come for the revenge you have already attained? I beg you: spare these two."

Angela took a deep breath and let the red-haired councilman return to Kur. He collapsed onto the floor, coughing and choking as she closed the hole in the veil, which poured water onto him. When finished, Ruchin hobbled to Toth and pulled his soaking frame to his feet. "Thank you," Ruchin said. "I understand the pain Teshub's death must have caused and have no doubt that Shedim was involved in the attack that killed him, but his actions do not represent the rest of the Council. I swear it." The old man's voice was shaking as he tried to stop the conflict and save his brothers. It was commendable.

Angela lowered her sword but did not put it away. "I'm afraid that's not the only problem coming out of Kur these days. Some here don't want the peace that we have. Considering these moves against me and the conspiracies I've heard, I must be forthcoming and declare that I intend to live in the city for the foreseeable future."

Maulkatu's lip curled, revealing rows of crooked yellow

teeth as he said, "We cannot allow her to stay here, Arbiter. This woman comes into our home, kills a fellow councilman, and threatens our lives. It's clear she means to take hold of the Dalkhu people by finishing off the Council."

"No," the old man said. "If she harbors distrust for us, we must show her there is nothing to fear." Ruchin turned to Angela, his gray eyes shimmering in the torchlight. "This old quarrel is settled, for ill or good. You may stay in Kur, but all I ask is that you promise this will never happen again. Killing a councilman in public will put fear and rage in the populace and harm its confidence in the Council's ability to provide safety. If you create an uprising amongst the others—if you have not already—the entire force of Kur will be upon you, and I will not stop it. But tell me, what do these conspiracies whisper?"

Angela was uncertain how she should take that. Ruchin wasn't wrong; there was a good chance that someone else was working against her as well, but the possibility that Shedim was also the councilman stealing crystals from Dingir was quite high. "Nothing of concern, should they be false. But in order for me to disprove them, I will need access to every area in Kur. Libraries, shops, personal chambers. Everything. Starting with the vault that stores your share of Anchor shards—right now."

Wide-eyed, Ruchin stammered, "Wh... How do you know of the vault, and why would you need to see it? Truly, I feel sorrow for what's happened to you, but that does not change what you have done here today. If you feel you can come to Kur, kill a councilman, and barge your way into people's homes and our most secret places, you certainly are delusional."

Angela scoffed. The old man had a backbone, after all.

"You can either allow me to access it peacefully or we can make more bodies." She motioned to Shedim.

With a wave of his hands, he said, "No, it won't come to that. If you want to be a part of this city for a time, a councilman will accompany you wherever you go, and you will never be alone. I will do my best to temper the other councilmen, but I can make no promise of your well-being."

She nodded. "I understand the position you're in and the difficulty of what I'm asking of you. Thank you."

He snorted, not buying her genuine appreciation. Things could have gone a lot worse if he hadn't stepped in. Even she wouldn't deny that. "I hope that showing you the vault will be taken as a motion of my trust in you, proof that I want a strong peace between us, but I do not think you see the fire you're walking into."

Ruchin's gaze was so piercing that she had to turn to Shedim's corpse on the stone floor. The water had washed away all the blood, and his head had been pushed nearly twenty feet away. Market stands and stalls were packed with nervous commoners who'd just seen more action in one fight than they probably had in all their lives.

"Toth, clean the square and see that our deceased is taken care of properly. Then inform the others of Angela's arrival. A meeting will be held shortly."

The red-haired councilman nodded, and Ruchin motioned for them to follow behind him. Angela thought about asking to be present for the meeting but knew she was lucky enough to be allowed into the vault peacefully. Inspecting and taking stock of the crystals that the Council held would be the first step to discovering the truth of Ja'noel's claim. If the count ever increased without reason, she would know that someone really was stealing shards and that Shedim wasn't the only one working against her.

While Ruchin seemed to be the middleman between her and the rest of the Council—and he genuinely seemed to give a shit about peace—she wondered if it was just a facade. Maybe all he wanted was to know just how much she knew about the Council and its motives. Toth, on the other hand, was too green to be anything serious. Maulkatu seemed volatile and dangerous, but understandably so. There were other Council members as well, but only time would tell which, if any, would move against her.

CHAPTER SIX

Angela followed Ruchin's hobbled steps into the Kissum in silence, tracing her fingers along a carving of a serpent on the massive stone door as they entered the main foyer. Many years had passed since Angela had first come to this place, and the sight of the high, domed ceiling impressed her for the second time. More intricate designs weaved their way up stone pillars and underneath the arched halls to the left and the right. The Kissum was a pentagon. Each corner was a topped dome, and the space was used for different things, though she had never gone beyond the entrance before.

Ruchin's breathing was heavy from the climb up, but he continued explaining some rules. "Teleportation is allowed in Kur so long as you do not leave or arrive inside any structure or in the markets. Sound carries far down here," he said and turned to lead them into a long, arched hallway to the right.

At the end of it, they were underneath a second dome, but this room was stuffed with tight rows of dusty book-shelves. In the center was a common area with tables carved from the same stone as the rest of the building. Between scattered piles of tomes and scrolls, a few people in colored robes saw her first, and then the soldiers in black stiffened and she could feel their tension in the air.

"This is the only public library in Kur," Ruchin said, turning to them. "There are other private ones with selected tastes and topics, but you may have the same rights as anyone. Read anything you wish in this area, but everything must be returned as it is, and you cannot take it from this room. Do you understand?"

Angela and Neti agreed in unison, and Ruchin led them into the next arched hallway, where he produced a ring of keys and unlocked a black door on the left. The hallway beyond it was much narrower than the last. There were no carvings or paintings, and a silver door with black iron lock bars and chains waited for them at the far end. With a different key, the councilman unlocked padlocks and began heaving the bars out of the wall.

The heavy door groaned as it opened, and a faint greenish glow poured out and onto the floor from inside the vault. Stones varying in size from pebbles to coconuts lined the interior walls, casting the color. Stepping inside, Angela crouched next to the closest green rock to examine it.

Ruchin spun and grabbed her by the shoulder. "Don't touch those. Those are rocks that have fallen from the cavern's roof. The moss that grows up there survived and gives the stones their light. Touching them with bare skin will kill the glow and risk your life."

At the far end of the vault there was an altar made of gray stone, unlike the usual black or white marble. Curving lines, roses, and shapes that resembled diamond crystals traveled up the altar's legs to the face of a drawer with a lock and knob. Ruchin produced a third key, much smaller than the others. He released the drawer from the stand, pulled it free, and placed it on top.

Stepping to the side, he said, "Here are the crystal shards of Kur."

Several large leather bags rested in the drawer, filling up most of the space. Angela went to reach inside but paused when she realized that Ruchin was watching over her shoulder, tense. "You may," he said, "but I will remain right here and watch to be sure you do not take any of them. These are the one thing we have that keeps Dingir from overpowering and killing us all."

While Angela didn't particularly agree that her people would outright kill them, she did agree that these crystals were what gave Dingir its military power. Unlike the Dalkhu, who had mastered the soul and the mind, the Anunnaki needed crystals from all three worlds in order to travel between them. Every crystal shard Dingir lost damaged its ability to fight, travel, trade, and survive just a little bit more.

Angela untied each leather bag and poured the contents into the drawer, creating a colorful spectacle with at least four inches of shards. Red, the color of crystals aligned with Kur, was the most common. The blue crystals were aetherically connected with Dingir, and green would lead to Earth. Both formed about equal quarters of the cache. She had never seen so many crystals together before, not even in the Ascendancy's armory.

She lowered her pack to the floor, dug through it until she found her blank book and pencil, then handed them to Neti and told him to write the numbers. He nodded, and she began to count the crystals by picking through the drawer and returning them to their bags.

Some of the shards flashed and pulsed with an intensity

she'd seen before, but others seemed to vibrate the air with life. That amazed her, and as she counted, old memories and myths drifted to the surface of her mind.

In the beginning, a single crystal containing all the aetherical energy in existence held the world together. When it broke, pieces of the crystal shattered across the splitting dimensions and became attuned to the new worlds and their energies as the eons passed. If this story were true, the pieces between her fingers were the remnants of the Anchor. Udug had stolen shards from the Ascendency in the hopes of someday putting the crystal back together and reuniting all three worlds into one, but that would destroy them all.

When she dropped the last blue crystal into its bag, she cinched it shut and asked, "How many?"

Neti took a moment to scribble and add them up, then said, "Four hundred and twenty-seven altogether. Ninety-three blues for Dingir, one hundred and nineteen greens for Earth, and two hundred and fifteen for Kur."

Amazed at the count, Angela almost swore aloud but then she realized how the Dalkhu never lost crystals like the Anunnaki did. When an Etlu died in battle, there was a good chance that his shards would be taken from his corpse, and Dalkhu never carried any on their persons in battle, so they slowly accumulated this great treasure in front of her now.

Yet Ruchin pushed her out of the way and took her place in front of the altar. "Are you sure you added them correctly, boy?"

Neti's eyes narrowed. "Well, yeah. I'm not a dote."

The old councilman shook his head, cheeks turning pink. "That is yet to be determined." He snatched the book from Neti and scanned the page. A minute passed and he handed it back, grumbling as he hastily picked up the drawer and locked it back into the stand.

"What is it?" Angela asked.

Ruchin turned, his gray eyes bouncing about the room. "There seems to be—" He huffed." Something is not correct here. I saw you count aloud, watched you, saw no errors, and rechecked the math, yet if my memory is correct, there should be four-hundred and fifty-one crystal shards, not twenty-four less."

"Twenty-four less?" Neti repeated. "When was that count taken?"

"Not even a year ago. The count was more likely to go up, not down."

Angela's guts twisted like she was going to be sick. "Are you saying someone on the Council stole crystals within the last year?" She laughed and crossed her arms. "I mean, Dalkhu do tend to have sticky fingers, but I'm not sure I buy that."

Ruchin turned red at that remark. "Is it really so hard to believe? You've seen firsthand the wayward ways that some councilmen have adopted." He ran his fingers through his beard and murmured to himself. "This is ill news. I must convene a meeting with the others immediately and put a stop to this madness." He ushered them out of the vault, and Angela remained quiet and compliant as he locked it again.

A declining number of crystals in Kur made no sense. If someone on the Council was stealing crystals from Dingir, why would Kur's stores be shrinking? They should be growing. "Maybe it's possible Shedim was three steps ahead of me, knew I'd be coming here, and stole from the vault just to throw me off."

"That's possible," he said, turning to face her. "Only the

Arbiter and the Restorer have all three keys: one for the door in the archway, one for the vault, and the third for the altar. Shedim is dead," he sneered, "so there's no way to confirm if it was him, besides finding the twenty-four crystals that are missing. I think we can conclude that I am not involved, or at least I hope so."

"What about the other councilmen?" Neti asked.

"For one of the others to get in, it would require three other councilmen. Toth, Maulkatu, Kanu, and Melech all have different keys that are traded at intervals. There are spells at work in this vault, so no commoner or soldier can enter without all three keys."

Angela couldn't confirm or disprove his claim of spells, so she took his word on that, but something didn't seem right, and she wondered if Ruchin himself was involved. He had admitted and shown her that he was one of two councilmen to have singular access to the vault. The whole situation stank. "I want to search Shedim's chambers."

Ruchin turned red again. "The man has not been dead an hour and you want to search his belongings? No, you will wait until the morning. The Council still has burial arrangements to make and a meeting to hold. Undoubtedly, some councilmen have lost respect for the balance of power and the lives of those different from us, but you must give us space now. Trust that most of us do not crave to unite the worlds. Many of us are afraid of it. So please, just come with me in silence. Let us get you and the boy a place to sleep, and we will talk more tomorrow."

She narrowed her eyes in silence and tried to see past Ruchin's guise, but she came up with nothing.

He seems to stand between me and the rest of the Council, but is it because he has something to hide?

BACK IN THE LIBRARY, RUCHIN SORTED THROUGH OLD records until he found a large leather tome with a single cord holding it closed. He took it to a table, shoved scrolls and books aside, and scanned its pages. After a few minutes, he scribbled something inside, sealed it shut, and said, "I've found you a chamber that will serve for now. Follow me."

He led them back through the library's rows and into the main foyer, where other councilmen adorned in black robes with red sashes had assembled near a door that led to the center area of the Kissum. They approached after Ruchin took note of every face in front of them. "Good, everyone is here," he said. "I'm sure you've already heard the news, but let us delay any conversations for the time being." He glanced over his shoulder at Angela, and every councilman shifted his eyes to her. Maulkatu's fists were clenched, and Toth stared at her down his long nose. Only one of them looked skittish and nervous, keeping to the back of the group of six remaining councilmen. There used to be thirteen before Udug upset everything.

"Which one of you would take Angela and Neti to their temporary chamber? It is the seventeenth of the north-eastern tunnel."

A councilman with a scar along his forehead smiled at that but didn't offer his assistance. Another Dalkhu Angela couldn't recognize, his black bangs cut at an angle, stepped forward and removed his hood. "I will volunteer to take her and watch her." He spoke with a smoother voice than she'd expected. "But beyond that, expect little from me. I cannot promise that no one will attempt to seize your lives— tonight or any night. As long as you remain here, I will not aid you, and the rest of the Council will not hold me accountable for that."

Ruchin's eyes grew big and nervous, but Angela let it slide. She'd argued with enough Dalkhu for one day. To ease the tension, Ruchin wrapped an arm around the younger man and turned to her. "This is Kanu, the Lawkeeper. He is simple and calculated about some things, hence his title. But take no worry: I have faith in him."

Angela shrugged. "I'm not worried."

"Well," Ruchin said, "with my part concluded, I take my leave until tomorrow." He bowed and joined the others behind him.

Angela and Neti walked a few paces behind Kanu. The steps in front of the Kissum were much easier to climb down than climb up. At their base, Shedim's body was already removed from the market square, and the activity was much quieter than when she had first arrived in Kur. Their eyes closed, some people sat with crossed legs near where she had killed him, murmuring to themselves in either meditation or prayer. Others leaned against wooden stands with their arms crossed or spat as they passed.

Part of her wished she had the time to justify her actions. There was a time when she was hated back in Dingir, but the implications and situation were entirely different now, not to mention that she never killed anyone back then. Even the Dalkhu. She used to hate it, but now it was inevitable. Some problems always had a chance of returning if she didn't wipe them out completely, she'd learned.

Underneath the green and white glow, they stepped out of the rows of stone-and-mortar buildings and into the outer expanse of the cavern. Fields of stalactites and stalagmites, which had formed over an immeasurable amount of time, surrounded the city from every direction. Angela and Neti followed Kanu on paths through the stone spikes, then up stairs that led to a constructed platform along the outer walls of the cavern. The wood creaked under their weight as they approached the entrance to a tunnel, a single torch glowstone illuminating it.

"I'm beginning to wonder if there wasn't a house any closer to the Kissum," Neti complained as they walked down the long, dark tunnel.

"Probably," Angela said. "But I doubt the Council would want us living among other Dalkhu." She tapped Kanu on the shoulder. "If you're the Lawkeeper, Ruchin is the Arbiter, and Shedim was the Restorer. What is everyone else's titles?"

Kanu glanced back. "Toth is the Virtuoso, and—"

"Virtuoso?" Angela asked. "What does that entail?"

Kanu shrugged. "It's an older way to say spellcaster. Toth is the most skilled at spells, and despite his newness as a councilman, he shows much promise in his endeavor to take us further in that art. Councilman Melech, with the scar on his forehead, is the Teacher. He oversees most children's learning paths, regardless of if they are to be soldiers or tradesmen. Eventually, they reach a point of maturity and move on to another councilman or a teacher of a trade to learn the specifics of their role, but Melech is a very... protective kind of person. Ah. Here we are."

Kanu took another glowstone from a sconce on the wall and motioned to a doorway covered with a blue drape. Angela hadn't noticed it tucked away into the rock, so she pulled the drape aside and entered their room.

"How much does it cost for a door?" Neti murmured behind her.

Angela snickered. The main room was unfurnished

other than a rocking chair and a table with stools. Another blue draped doorway divided the space and formed the bedroom, which had two beds and one dresser. It was a shoddy place, and even though she was grateful they wouldn't have to share a bed, it felt as though something was missing.

Then she realized where she was.

That bastard!

Out of all the homes and outer chambers in Kur, Ruchin had picked the room that Neti had spent his childhood in. The last time he was here, he was a boy. Angela could see Neti's father standing in the doorway, warning her, and Neti's mother, Ardat, crumpled next to the doorway, blood from the back of her skull pooling on the floor.

"What's wrong?" Neti asked, his eyes big and concerned.

"N-Nothing." She turned her back to him and stepped into the bedroom.

He followed behind her quietly, wiped his hand on one of the beds, and sat down on it. "Do you think someone will try to kill us?"

"Me? Yes," Angela admitted. She fell onto her own bed, and a cloud of dust rose around her. When she could manage to stop coughing, she said, "I would be more surprised if no one tried, and I don't believe a single councilman would try to stop it. Shit, some would probably help, so we need to stick together."

Neti nodded and let himself fall onto his back. "You know, why can't we just sleep at the sinkhole and return here during the day?"

Angela had already contemplated it. "Things don't only happen during the day, and as terrifying as it might seem, being attacked would actually be a good thing. There's a chance we could capture them, question them, and find out something else we don't know. Besides, there's the chance that the Council knows where the sinkhole is, anyway."

"Yeah, I guess. But for the archive, I don't like that now we're both bluffing and baiting our way through this." He sighed for a long moment, then looked to her. "Do you really think it was the right thing to kill Shedim?"

Angela bit her lip. "To be honest, I'm not sure. I lost my temper, I admit. But he was involved. That's for certain. The only thing that still confuses me is that Teshub said 'then came a stream of brown... blue fire...'"

"I wonder if it's all connected," Neti said, staring up at the cracks in the ceiling like he would find the answer there. "Shedim, the fire that killed Teshub, the crystal shards missing from Dingir and Kur. I wonder how involved the other councilmen are, too."

Angela faced him. "Me too. I don't know who I can trust, so thanks for coming with me. I know I don't say it enough, but sometimes I need help. This place—this whole situation—is just completely out of control, but I'll do what I can to set it right. No matter what."

Neti smiled. "Not a problem. It's good to admit that, but I've always been curious about this place, anyway."

That made her uncomfortable. This place was something she had taken from him years ago, and it ate her up inside. She pulled herself to her feet and raced to change the subject. "We should put that table in front of the bedroom door, block it off and move the beds around the room. It'll give us some time to react if someone teleports into here."

By working together to lift the wooden table from the living room, carry it into the bedroom, and tip it against the doorway, they effectively barricaded the front door. Then they moved the beds to different corners of the room, but it didn't seem like quite enough, so they reinforced the table with the dresser.

To guard them while they slept, Angela dug around in her bag until she found a brass figurine. She placed it on top of the dresser and took a step back to examine it. It was a ram with a square body and squat, chunky legs. In the green light of the glowstone, it looked more yellow than gold. The horns that curved out of its head were the most realistic part about it, but Angela doubted Michael had been after realism. He'd made her many different animals, even a few people, but now Angela only had a few left, and keeping them close helped her fall asleep. She sighed, missing him, then turned to her bed.

THE RED WOODEN DOOR GROANED AS MAULKATU PUSHED his way through. Behind it, the other councilmen in their seats at the round table glanced at him.

"Finally," one of them murmured. "Our first has returned."

Maulkatu shut the door, walked around the table, and sat on his padded seat on the far end of the room. A low-hanging chandelier with candles filled the room with dim light. Bookshelves lined the walls, and the table meant for thirteen was more than half-empty now.

"It takes time to arrange a brother's burial," Maulkatu said.

Ruchin glanced up from his scroll, nodding. "And how go those arrangements?"

He shrugged. "Fine. The stonesman has sealed the tomb and begun the inscription. It should be ready for the Council's viewing by the time we adjourn." He turned to Daevas, a slim and nervous young man with curly blond hair who had only just come to his seat a year before. It was harder than ever to find capable people, and Maulkatu imagined it would be another year before they added a seventh member. "What did you find?"

Daevas shifted in his seat. "Uh, yes... I searched his chambers but couldn't find anything that would lead us to believe that Shedim was involved in an attack on Angela. I might also point out that there's no way of knowing for absolute certain she was truly attacked, even though her actions and what's happened so far make it seem believable." He sighed. "Other than that, Shedim's brother is his only remaining kin, and with his state, I don't believe it's worth trying to tell him what has happened."

A bitterness welled in Maulkatu's gut. He recalled moments of his childhood when he played with Shedim and his brother. Hazy, wispy memories, but the emotion was still there, buried underneath the rest of him. "Agreed. Let them both rest."

Ruchin crossed his arms and took a deep breath. His old voice cracked when he said, "I want all of you to look around this table. See how empty it is and remember the faces of those we have lost. We must work together to get through this."

Maulkatu laughed. "No one here is going to argue that, only how it's done."

Ruchin's cheeks grew red. "Thank you for bringing me to my second point. The more we bicker, the larger the wedge between us grows. No more sneaking and hiding behind one another's backs. If one of us here is working against Angela, the rest of the Council will know it now."

Nothing but silence filled the room for a long moment

until the door creaked open again. Toth threw down his hood and brushed his ridiculously long hair behind his shoulders. Maulkatu had learned when he was young that long hair in a fight only served to give the enemy a handle to grab onto, so he kept his shaved. Once, he had even tried to tell his fellow councilman as much, but Toth was not one to change his ways willingly. That one was always watching and slow to ruse.

When he was settled in his seat, he said, "Apologies for my tardiness. I see I'm the last to return."

Ruchin looked to Toth. "It makes no matter as long as you bear good news."

Toth shook his head. "I have found no word of suspicious activity around the vault. The missing Anchor shards appear to be a mystery we must still solve. Something—or someone—is yet alluding us."

Melech rubbed a hand over the scar on his forehead. "I suspect either Angela or Ruchin stole the crystals." That was why Melech was one of Maulkatu's favorite peers. Unlike Ruchin, he was quick to the point and wasn't prone to take a knife in the gut before turning it around.

Ruchin and Toth laughed.

"I'm not jesting. Ruchin has all three keys, and it's clear he wants to keep the peace at any cost. What's a few crystal shards to him?"

Maulkatu considered it. "The woman is forceful. She takes what she wants."

Toth shrugged. "But Ruchin is the one who told us that the crystals were missing. If he were involved, he simply wouldn't have told us, and I am also having a hard time believing that Angela would be involved. I believe the Anchor shards are half the reason she came to Kur. Why else would she request to see them not an hour after she arrived? That shows their importance to her."

Ruchin nodded to the redhead. "Thank you for your defense, Toth. I would like it if you would take tomorrow's watch. I want you to appease Angela, show her what she wants to see, and she will be gone sooner. That goes for everyone. That is the plan."

Melech raised a hand. "To be straightforward, it's clear to me that she has killed a councilman. If Kanu were here, he would advise that we push her out of Kur or kill her. With the six of us together, we can do either."

Maulkatu smiled. "Agreed, to an extent. If it were any other Dalkhu that killed Shedim, the sentence would be death, so I vote we give her what the law demands."

Ruchin shook his head. "I would advise the rest of the Council to be wary of direct confrontation. Only half of us were there at Dingir. Toth, Daevas, and Melech replaced more experienced councilmen that we lost. We need caution. She has withstood the push of five of us before, and if she was a problem for men who have spent decades on the Council, she will be a harder foe now with such young members."

None of the others dared question Ruchin's statement; they all knew he was likely right. The elder stroked his beard and said, "I will not cast my aid in any such endeavor, even should the Council deem it necessary. Give Angela what she wants, and she will be on her way with less blood spilled."

"So you suggest we remain idle?" Maulkatu asked, incredulous. "You would rather allow the woman to come into our home when she's injured us so? You would not fight for your people?"

Ruchin's gray eyes settled on him with a steely gaze. "I

am suggesting that we do not rush into battle with the woman. There's a time and place for everything, and today we mourn."

Maulkatu tapped his knuckles on the table. "No, today is the day to avenge. What do the others say?"

Melech, Daevas, and Toth looked to one another.

Ruchin grumbled. "Very well. I declare the commencement of a vote. All those in favor of a direct assault, say so."

Maulkatu rose to his feet. "I am in favor."

Melech raised a hand. "While I am not convinced the woman needs to die, she does need to leave Kur—by violent means if necessary."

The others remained seated and quiet.

Ruchin smiled under his beard. "Of those of us here, and assuming Kanu were present and cast his vote in favor, that is three against three. The vote would not pass. For now, we remain at peace until something changes."

Maulkatu cursed and wrung his hands. He turned to Daevas and Toth across the table. The imbeciles of the Council, no doubt. "You two are too soft and blind to realize what is at stake. Today it was Shedim, our seventh. Which one of us will die tomorrow by this woman's hands?" He turned to Ruchin. "You've grown complacent, Arbiter. Sooner or later, another of us will die. We all know it. Yet we vote to do nothing."

Ruchin rose from his chair swiftly, his finger shaking as he pointed at him. "We have voted for peace, Maulkatu. You can't seem to understand how it's attained. The cheek must be turned. Shedim's involvement in Teshub's murder was his downfall. That is the very thing I'm trying to save this Council from. Appease the woman until she leaves. No more secrets. There is only one way that we will discover who this crystal thief is." He waved a hand over the others of the Council. "Turn in your keys. All of them. If any more go missing, you will know without a doubt that it was either I or Kanu."

Maulkatu threw his down on the table, and while a few of the others grumbled complaints, four keys were produced. Ruchin tucked them into his robe and continued. "To whoever stole the crystals, be it someone in this room or Shedim's corpse below, I say good work. You've only forced her to stay here longer than she may have."

There was a knock on the door, and the room grew silent for a moment. Ruchin sighed and settled back down on his chair. Maulkatu crossed the room and opened it. A man in tattered gray robes stepped in, his hands folded across his belly. "C-Councilmen," he mumbled. "Sorry for the intrusion, but the stonesman is ready for you."

Ruchin nodded. "Very well." He looked over the others one last time. "There was little progress to be made here, anyway. Let us go see our brother buried. Afterward, Toth, when you relieve Kanu in the morning, would you see to informing him of what has happened here? We are adjourned."

The councilmen rose from their seats. Maulkatu clenched his jaw and resisted demanding that the Council sit and discuss the matter further. He knew a few of the councilmen were too afraid to ever agree with him. Kanu would likely vote them to a tie, given his title of Lawkeeper, but Toth was too quiet and too deep in his studies to risk his life. Ruchin was too stubborn, and that meant Daevas, the weakest of them all, would be the tie-breaking vote.

They walked in a small group through the back hallway, underneath the arches and symbols of their ancestors, until they stepped into the domed room in the northeast corner of the Kissum. From there, steps led them fifty feet downward. Walking three abreast, they reached the lower tunnel and passed through two sets of black doors. Beyond the second, the hallway opened wider, and tall pillars were spaced almost as far as the eye could see. Plaques that marked the names of those buried lined the wall.

Passing most of Kur's dead, they headed toward the distant light of a torch deeper within the tunnel and found the stonesman at Shedim's grave. The commoner was silent and only nodded to the Council members in greeting, then left them to mourn their loss. Maulkatu watched each councilman step to the crypt in solemn silence and bow his head, but none of them said anything.

Shedim was no Udug, Maulkatu thought. *He had no vision for himself, so he only became a tool, and he never did care about restoring the Anchor. Only power, survival, and his brother mattered to him.*

CHAPTER SEVEN

Angela attempted to flip over the stack of books so she could read their titles, but she spilled them into an ornamental glass orb and sent them all over the table's edge and onto the floor. Dusty pages ruffled, spines came loose, and glass shattered. Behind her, Toth stared out from beneath his hood but remained steeled and expressionless. Even if he didn't appear offended, spilling a dead man's last belongings onto the floor was probably not appreciated, especially when she was the one that ended his life.

Shedim's chambers were dark, cramped, and stuffed with curiosities and junk alike. There were a few dressers filled with personal belongings of no interest, a single bed larger than most, and a desk that had been carved out of the same stone as the walls and floor. Angela had to direct Neti where to hold the torch so she could see, but when she finished picking up the books, she noticed the carved intricacies weaving along the desk's surface.

"This was Udug's room, wasn't it?" she asked. "I recognize this desk."

Toth's voice was nearly a whisper behind her. "Udug was the Virtuoso before me. He prided himself on his transcriptions of old language, the things he found in texts far older than himself, and kept all of his work here. When I was voted to take his place on the Council, I requested to move into these same chambers, but Shedim would not have it. 'I am the Restorer,' he said. 'My role shall grow more important than yours, so it is imperative that the knowledge stays where it can best serve.'"

"Sounds like you still hold it against him," Neti blurted.

Angela pulled Neti by his sleeve and whispered in his ear. "Don't piss him off by reminding him, please."

Neti smirked. "If anything, he's going to kill you first."

She rolled her eyes and returned to the books and scrolls in front of her. Some were written by Shedim, but most of his work appeared to run off in tangents, only to end abruptly. A few books had fictional-sounding titles like *The Mother Serpent's Dance* and *The Last Giant of Vi'dinor*. Normally that would intrigue her, but these were written in an old Dalkhu dialect and the first pages proved to be dull reads.

The spell that swapped my soul with Udug's is likely buried somewhere underneath this mess, she thought. *If I find it, I swear I'll burn it. No one deserves to go through that.*

She flipped open a book titled *The Sky Wyrms* and the spine threatened to crumble and let the pages loose, but she kept it together and thumbed her way past sketches of mountains with a series of structures protruding from the sides of cliffs. There were crude maps, too, and more scenic pictures of rivers and environments that were unrecognizable. The text was nearly as illegible; the pages were smudged with dirt or charcoal, but as she neared the last quarter of the book, she found a folded piece of parchment tucked inside. Unfolding it, she saw old letters written in red ink. The text was impossible for her to understand, but black letters written below appeared to have translated it into a more common tongue:

Eld Kur, The Mourning City and the Scratched Hall, we left behind. Three days, toward the light we climbed, until in a colossal cavern of black, green, white, and gold we found rest. At his behest, we sent two back down below, and when they returned we heard the news. Two-thirds of us have perished, but no more. They are behind a wall of stone past the red ravine, off the lake, in the deep below. N'er again a claw in our backs, or a child coated in fire. May those—

"Look," a voice behind her said. Neti walked to her side, black cloth in his hands.

Angela furrowed her brow. "You're interrupting. What is it?"

"Robes. Smell them." Neti shoved them up to her face and she pushed his hand away.

"I don't want to smell a dead man's robes."

"No, they smell like ash." Neti brought them up to his whiskers and sniffed.

Angela followed suit, and they did smell like ash. She looked closer at a small part near the bottom, where they were singed and crusty from a fire. "These were the robes he was wearing when he torched our home." A lump formed in her throat, and she chucked the robes toward Toth, who barely reacted fast enough to catch them. "Here's the Council's proof." Even the councilman lifted the robes to his nose and smelled.

She glanced over the page in her hands once more, thought it was a curious thing, and tucked it away between the book's pages again. "Who did Shedim spend the most time with?" she asked, setting it down on the desk.

Toth shrugged and said, "He preferred to be alone, except when the Council demanded his presence. The past year he had become more solitary than he ever did before, and as far as I'm aware, he did not confide in anyone but these pages. Well... and his brother."

"Interesting. I didn't know he had a brother."

The councilman let his head hang as though the weight of something was overwhelming. "Aye... He does."

"We should see him," Neti said. "Can you take us to him, Toth?"

"I can, but I don't think you will gain much."

THEY PASSED THROUGH THE HOVEL'S WOODEN DOOR AND were swallowed by its earthy smell. The stones used to make it were mostly lime, and the mortar that filled the spaces between them was little more than mud, but at least the fireplace kept it warm. The floor was hard-packed dirt and little softer than the rock below it, the bed was straw, and the table was rough wood with bark still around the outer edges.

"He's through here, Anunnaki." The caretaker, dressed in a tunic and trousers blackened by mud, led them through an open doorway toward the back of the home. Without the fire, it was dark, and a steady drip falling from the ceiling had eroded the ground in one of the corners. The first sight of Shedim's brother almost frightened them; he sat on a chair, rocking himself in the darkness.

"He does that," the caretaker said.

"What's his name?" Angela asked.

"Eli." He grabbed hold of the chair and swiveled Shedim's brother around so Angela could see his face, and she recognized it. He used to be savage, she'd heard, but now Eli swung and moaned like a toddler. He drooled and garbled his speech, if he was even trying to speak. The caretaker grimaced when he took a blow in the arm, but he remained patient and stepped away without a word of complaint.

Eli is not all he used to be, Angela thought in disdain.

When she knew him, Eli had lived under the human name of Abrah and was known as the leader of a tribe of horsemen that took slaves and raided villages in the northwest wilderness on Earth. Not until he'd begun making his way toward Tarsus did Angela know of him. For thirteen days she searched the northern steppes for his camp, and in the end, she had taken him in the dead of night, like she did with Farcus. His tent had been on the edge of a bluff, and he struggled against her, hard, and fell over, broke his legs, and fell unconscious. When she returned him to Kur, he was still sleeping, but she had never imagined he would wake up an imbecile.

Have I ruined more lives than I know? Angela took a deep breath, shoved the thought from her mind, and asked, "When Shedim visited Eli, did he ever say anything you might have overheard?"

The caretaker's eyes narrowed. "It might be that he did. What does it matter to you?"

"The late councilman struck a blow to my home and family. I need to know if he ever said anything about what he was trying to pull off. Did he ever mention a sinkhole or his plans to steal crystal shards from both Dingir and Kur? Did he mention me specifically at any time?"

His smile was vicious and smug. "Aye, I heard him

speak about things of that ilk. There was a secret he discovered and shared with Eli. He swore to avenge him, but of those details I will not tell."

Angela stepped up to the man, squared her frame, and looked down on him. "Let's say that Councilman Shedim had planned on gaining his revenge. Did he say anything about what he would do after he killed me? Was there anything bigger or more wicked being shaped? I'm sure you have an idea of what a councilman is capable of, but do you know how I can get what I need? I can take you to Dingir, show you what it's like to try to survive in a world of soul-fire."

A hand grabbed her by the elbow. Neti pulled on her arm and said, "You should leave it there, Angela."

The caretaker's eyes were unwavering and fearless. "The pain you could cause me is nothing compared to what you have given this family." He motioned to Eli. "Terrible things are brooding for you in the darkness, Anunnaki. You don't belong here, and your light is about to expire."

That does it.

She curled her lip and swung her fist into his cheek, sending him crashing into Eli's chair, and both toppled onto the dirt floor. Eli began to screech and shake as the caretaker tried to gather himself. Angela raced out of the house and stepped into the street, the others just behind her, before Neti tried to get involved again. A small crowd of seven commoners had gathered just outside and even looked a little afraid at her sudden appearance.

"That was not a good way to handle that," Neti said, stepping out of the hovel with an angry look on his face.

"You heard him threatening me," she said. "And he knows something. Whose side are you on?"

Neti slunk back. "Yours, of course. I just… I just don't

think that smacking around a commoner is a good idea right now. We don't need the entire Council coming down on us." He glanced at Toth.

The councilman pulled his hood back up over his head and sighed. "I understand what drives you, Angela, but the caretaker was correct: you don't belong here."

JA'NOEL PULLED THE BLANKET UP OVER HER SHOULDER, covering the goosebumps the cold had given her. Sunlight filtered through the blinds behind him, giving the room, and her face, a dim yellow glow. He brushed her black hair behind her ears to see her beauty better. When Kushiel died, he never expected that she would become his heaven, but their partnership had brought something new into his life.

Sarosha smiled brilliantly, and her green eyes glimmered in the light. "You're awake early." She wrapped her arms around him and buried her face into his chest. "Why are you up?" she asked.

Ja'noel hugged her closer, letting her warmth soothe him. "Just can't sleep."

She tilted her head up to look into his eyes. "Well, what are you thinking about?"

He sighed, then rolled onto his back to stare at the ceiling while he talked. It had always been hard for him to look her in the eyes when he admitted to his weaknesses. "Angela."

Sarosha scooted closer and rested her head on his shoulder. "What about her?" Her voice betrayed her worry.

"I was wrong," Ja'noel said. "I don't think she'll help Dingir, don't even know for sure how much Donny really means to her, and with the way things went, I don't know if I can count on her. If anything, holding Donny in secrecy has made the chances of her aiding us worse. Even though the city needs her, she's too upset over what happened after all this time."

"Yeah…" Sarosha's eyes were closed already, yet he couldn't help but kiss her forehead again.

"But I have to do something. I can't just wait and see what happens. The city needs action and real, visible progress, and I won't be remembered as the Ensi who waited too long—or as the last one."

Sarosha only nodded, so he lifted her arm, slid out from under her, and stood. The cold air raised bumps on his nude skin as he walked to the window and pulled a corner of the blind to the side. Trash was scattered along the street. Ice had built up everywhere, and four of the seven windmills supplementing the energy from the boilers had stopped spinning.

"What are you going to do, then?" Sarosha asked from the bed. She was sitting upright, clutching the blanket around the bare skin of her arms.

Ja'noel shrugged. "Dingir has remained in its ways for so long. Even as we face the biggest struggle of our people, we push on doing the same thing, expecting it will work as it always had, even though things are different now. We've tried to hide so much of our ancient past from ourselves over the millennia, and I think that has to change."

He walked to the dresser, pulled the pen from the inkwell on top, and began to write on a fresh sheet of parchment. It took him almost ten minutes and several blank pages to word it well, but when he was finished, he sealed the ink and set the pen down.

Sarosha asked him, "What did you write?"

"A notice to be sealed and put into action." He picked it up and blew over it to help it dry quickly.

"Read it to me."

"As of the twenty-third cycle of Earth's four thousand and twenty-second known year, I, Ja'noel Yishren, Grand Ensi of Dingir, do commence the creation of a new division of Etlu fighters. Apart from the customary chain of command, the Bui'du will serve the city of Dingir as a whole. They will not answer to any person of the title 'Grand,' including in times of peril when an Ensi possesses a majority of power.

"Comprised of four individuals, and never less, though it may be increased by a majority vote of the Grands, the Bui'dus act as they see best benefits the city. They may ask of any resource from the Ascendancy or Dingir's crafts-men, traders, or citizens as they see best suits their fight for a safer city.

"All laws are subject to a Grand majority vote of disproval, where afterward the Bui'dus are not inclined to follow. Every soldier of the force is to be trained in the ways of the Dalkhu. Neither spells, the skills to teleport with one's own energy, nor any ancient knowledge shall be forbidden from them.

"May this mark a shift toward a stronger, more lethal way of Anunnaki survival. Long live the floating city. Signed, Ja'noel Yishren."

CHAPTER EIGHT

"**A**re you sure this is a good idea?"

Angela tightened the green sash around her waist with a smile. "Yeah."

Neti wasn't so sure, but he went along with it and pulled his arms through his own black robe. They had returned to their room outside the city, with Councilman Kanu guarding them just outside their chamber again. Instead of relaxing until it was time to sleep, Angela had come up with another investigative plan. Yellow was the only other colored cord in the dresser, so that would have to do.

"Why are you having such a hard time getting behind this?" Angela asked.

Neti was incredulous. "Well, we don't even know if this color cord is realistic for someone my age. What if yellow is just a step below a councilman? That wouldn't make sense."

She held a finger over her lips. "Too loud."

He groaned but leaned in and began to whisper. "What does it matter? The moment we teleport out of here, Kanu is going to know we're gone anyway. There will be repercussions for this, you know, especially if we get caught while we're out there. That will only make it worse for us."

Angela patted him on the shoulder. "You worry too much. All you have to do is trail Ruchin. See where he goes, who he talks with. If he goes to sleep, see if you can rummage around in his desk. Just keep your wits about you, be aware of what's going on behind you, and find something if you're worried it won't be worth whatever punishment the Council tries to throw our way."

Neti rolled his eyes. "And you make it seem like it's going to be so easy."

A devilish smile stretched across her face. "Don't worry so much. Just remember, meet up back here by morning. Ready?"

He pulled his hood onto his head and shrugged. "I guess."

They counted down with their fingers in unison, then disappeared between the worlds at the same moment. Frost settled over his skin as he traveled, then washed away at the first blast of warm cavern air. Standing on one of the platforms overlooking Kur, he waited until he heard two blasts of teleportation echoing off the walls. One of them was his own, reflecting back to him. The other would have been Angela's arrival. The plan was for her to appear on the opposite side of the city so that their instantaneous appearances would echo so loudly throughout the cavern it would be impossible for them to be located. But only time would tell if the idea was worth a damn.

He vaulted himself over an old wooden handrail, which creaked under his weight, and stuck the landing well enough on the cavern floor twenty feet below. Occasionally, he placed his hands on the wet, cold stalagmites as he passed them. A few times he almost fell, but he reached the city's outer edge easily enough and slipped between houses as the Kissum grew larger over him.

With no idea which way Angela would head, Neti figured the best place to find a councilman was where he worked most often. Ruchin was the Arbiter, which meant his role was primarily debating and settling arguments. While he wasn't sure if that carried beyond the Council's matters and into the private lives of Kur's citizens, he had the best chance of finding him around the Kissum.

When he reached the market square, he strode down one stretch of the perimeter to get a better view of all the people there. A few people behind market stands shouted out to him, waving jeweled necklaces or juggling fruit to entice him into purchasing something, but he turned them down with a motion of his hand and they left him alone. As far as he could tell, there were no councilmen, and he was the only person in black. He couldn't decide if that was a good or a bad thing.

Neti turned and was walking toward the Kissum when he came to a public cookfire just a few dozen paces off the square. Two men sat on padded mats adjacent to the fire, playing dice on the stone ground between them and soaking in the heat. One rolled and the other laughed. Neither had their shoes on. They were both grimy, with dirt caught under their nails and matted into their hair and clothes. Miners, Neti guessed. Simple and happy, too.

He strode to the fire and placed his hands over it to warm himself. From there he could watch the market square as inconspicuously as possible. The men near his feet continued their game for the better part of fifteen minutes before a third joined. Then a woman with a babe in her arms tapped him on the shoulder and he stepped to the side so she could use the fire to heat something in a lidded pot. It smelled like some kind of pork or beef stew, and soon his mouth was watering. Even the men playing dice made a game out of heckling the woman for a taste, but she would not budge and was gone shortly after.

There was something about watching these people that entertained him. For a while, he was enthralled and forgot that he was trying to spot Ruchin. He felt at ease even though he was risking so much, and he was at awe at the simplicity of their day-to-day existence. But something else grew in his chest and troubled him.

I'm jealous of this life...

A fire-tender with a wagon came around and threw a few logs onto the pit, giving it new life within moments. The heat grew, but it was time for Neti to move. He let out a long breath and pulled his hands into his sleeves to savor the warmth for as long as possible, then made his way to the base of the Kissum's long stairs. The building sat up high on its own plateau, and each step was harder than the last, but he made it to the doors quickly enough. Getting a closer look at the carvings etched into the stonework crossed his mind, but when the sound of a dozen sandals slapping against the floor reached his ear, he froze as panic gripped him.

A crowd of at least fifteen men dressed in black marched toward him, coming out of the archway that led to the left, unknown section of the Kissum. He lurched through the door and around a nearby pillar, which reached far above his head and held up the domed ceiling. From behind it, he watched all but two of the soldiers pass him by and walk out through the double doors. The two who stayed behind in the main foyer were councilmen, and they spoke too quietly for Neti to hear. They both bowed, and the one with curly blond hair left out the front while Ruchin turned away and walked through the archway that led to the library.

Neti was already sweating enough that he had to wipe his brow before emerging from behind his pillar to follow the councilman. He watched the old man disappear behind an aisle of bookshelves and thought it best that he step into a different aisle that went perpendicular to his. Between the dusty books, he paused for a moment before sticking his head around the corner, but Ruchin was gone. Puzzled, Neti made a few quick turns and looked out over the library's common area. No one was sitting at any of the tables, and the library was as quiet as could be.

Where is he going? When it hit him, it felt like an iron bar across his chest. The councilman had already walked through the library and entered the northern arched hallway, where he couldn't see him.

He's headed toward the vault!

Neti surged forward, knocked a chair over as he crossed the common area, and dashed past the last section of shelves. By the old councilman's pace, he had expected to see him near the vault doorway. Instead, Ruchin had walked past it and entered the next foyer. Without getting too close, he caught up to the councilman and kept pace with a solid thirty feet between them. Going out into the open again made Neti uncomfortable, but he tried to take solace in the fact that the Kissum wasn't busy at this hour.

This foyer in the back of the Kissum was much like the main entrance: the floor was open, other than for the pillars staggered in a circle. There were locked cabinets against a wall, a few stray crates of mats, and a podium that had been pushed to the side, but where the room differed was the set of stairs that Ruchin descended until his head disappeared below ground. Neti walked to the steps, peered down into the darkness, and had no choice but to follow.

He crept into the quiet darkness, barely able to see his own feet on the steps, and went farther down than he had expected. When two stones embedded into the wall cast their green glow on a pair of black doors, Neti wondered what exactly he had gotten himself into, how much farther he had to go, and where he was headed. It was too late now to give up the chase, so he swallowed and continued on.

Veins of yellow and white traveled up the black marble double doors like rivers on a map, intertwining with pictograms and symbols. Toward the bottom were houses, stalagmites, and detailed figures of people throughout. Even the stone's colors gave the relief's rocky outcrops and cavernous details more depth and realism. In the door's center was an impressively accurate portrayal of the Kissum.

Neti grabbed the golden handles and pushed his way in. The air, almost as freezing as Dingir's, rushed around him when he stepped into a hallway that split off in three directions. There was a door to his left and his right and another double door straight ahead. The torches hanging on the wall in this room weren't fire; they were chunks of the green glowing stones bound and knotted to wooden shafts. He took one from the wall and wandered to the door straight ahead.

When he pulled the groaning door open, a blast of damp and heavy air washed over him. The passage widened into a tunnel not unlike the archways in the Kissum above him. Carved pillars reinforced the cracking cavern ceiling all down the long, dark corridor. He took a few steps downward and saw that, beyond the pillars, there were names engraved into the stone.

Movement caught the corner of his eye, and a man awash with the greenish glow of his own glowstone stepped out from behind a pillar and said, "You don't need to sneak after me, boy." Neti stumbled with his tongue, and the councilman raised a hand. "Nothing to explain to me. Just know that I have nothing to hide. Namtar's son is always welcome, although it is a surprise to see you trailing me. Angela must not trust me."

"No, that's not it," Neti said, trying to throw the conversation off. "I was just wondering what was down here."

Ruchin gave him a suspicious look, his bushy eyebrows raised. "Don't try to hide it. If you are suspicious of me like Angela is, you should say it. Those who speak their truth boldly and stand up for themselves have a strength that's respectable, even if they are wrong."

Neti sighed. "You're right. I am suspicious, but not as much as Angela is."

The old man stroked his beard. "I knew as much, and I would be safe to assume that the two of you have broken away from your guarding councilman to investigate us a bit more privately." He motioned to the cord around Neti's waist. "Yellow is a bit unrealistic for someone your age, but a good disguise nonetheless."

A part of Neti died inside.

Ruchin put a hand on his shoulder. "It's fine, boy. Let's just hope that Angela doesn't cause more trouble. But I wonder if you would like to see your parents again while you're here."

"My parents are here?" Neti asked. Then it struck him: the names on the walls were tombstones.

"They both have a place here, yes. This public crypt is the largest of the Dalkhu people. While there are some smaller ones in the outer tunnels and underneath the ruins of Eld Kur, the Kissum has been around for the majority of our history and houses the most dead. Would you like to take a walk with me? I can tell you about more people as we go."

"I... I would actually enjoy that," Neti admitted.

The councilman smiled, and they began to walk side by side down the never-ending hall. They passed plaques and names for a minute in silence until Ruchin motioned to one. "Telal. One of the four founders of the Council before it was expanded to thirteen members a hundred years after. My memory of him is vague, as he passed just before I came to take my own red cord, but I recall he was a bit of a hard man to please.

"When we first came into contact with the Anunnaki on Earth, he was one of the first to highlight the potential terrors of the Anunnaki. You must remember, back then, we had such little knowledge of the worlds. We had no idea about the weylines, the effects they had on our souls, so we saw the Anunnaki simply as bestial humanoids shrouded in fire. The fact that we shared tongues with them meant little. They hurt us, so we hurt them. Or vice versa, if you wish to believe."

Neti wasn't sure how to respond. There was plenty of justifications on both sides of the war, but Ruchin had to be at least a thousand years old. And that would mean that the Dalkhu and the Anunnaki had been fighting for a very long time. "There's so many names... Is there any order to them?"

The councilman's long gray beard looked green under the light. "There is. The farther you go, the more recent in history the person lived."

"Were you visiting anyone in particular or just trying to get away from me?"

Ruchin smiled, his black teeth melding with the surrounding darkness. "I visit my parents from time to time. They say it's so quiet down here that sometimes you can hear your ancestors whisper guidance in your ears." He chuckled, then trailed off sullenly. "And I came to see Shedim as well... That was not a way for any man to go."

A knot tightened in Neti's belly. A part of him had been afraid something like this would come up. "But it was Shedim's way to go. Nothing can change that now, and I think it's debatable if it was deserved or not."

Ruchin hummed in thought for a moment. "I'm glad you took my advice to heart and speak for yourself, but it does not matter if it was deserved or not. There were better ways to resolve the issue."

"How would you handle a man who meant to kill you but killed one of your closest friends and mentor?"

"I find the older I get, the less I care for killing. It may solve the problem at hand in a much faster manner, a more permanent manner, but later on, it almost always creates more complications that will also require solving. I believe that exile or prison are better options." Ruchin looked over to Neti, his brows furrowed and his eyes sincere. "I also fear that Angela will overstay her welcome and others will die attempting to kill her."

"Angela isn't one to swing first." After he said it, Neti remembered the caretaker and realized he was wrong, but he continued. "If someone tries to take her life, she would be defending herself."

The councilman grumbled. "Sometimes you must look at the entire picture. It does not always matter who swings first if there is still a bloodbath in the end. Both parties and the people in them made one conscious decision after the other to incite more violence. The most important thing is to have the strength to end it. And the only way to truly end it is to turn the other cheek, but no one likes to do that. It isn't a natural thing to do, but if Angela were wise, she would leave as quickly as she could."

Neti stopped in his tracks, anger getting ahold of him. "What do you want, Ruchin? For me to condemn Angela for what she's done to Shedim? To my parents?"

Ruchin sighed. "I confess, I do have need of you, but do not consider me a schemer. I don't intend to turn you against her. I only think you should convince her to quit this search of hers. The more time she spends in Kur, the more likely that blood will be spilled. You are clever like your father was. Even you cannot deny the logic in that."

They stared at one another for a moment.

"It would be easier for your people to welcome you here if she were gone. You could be given the upbringing that the son of a councilman deserves. You could live your own life and shepherd yourself clear of Angela's missteps."

Neti shook his head and resumed walking. He couldn't look at Ruchin again until he thought of something. When he was calm again, he said, "You know, you're right. Angela's made mistakes, but you're trying to undermine what we're here for, and that makes me suspicious. The fact remains that there are people in Kur that want to destroy her, me, and reunite the worlds in the hope that the conflict between Anunnaki and Dalkhu will end. Those people sneak around in the dark, and when you kill one, another takes his place. Kur is a breeding ground for hatred, and that disregards the innocent human lives that Angela is fighting for."

Ruchin sighed behind him and said, "Think what you wish about Angela, but the fever to restore the Crystal Anchor died with Udug, rest assured. In my old age, I only want peace. I am too old to play these games, so all I can ask is that you think about what I've said. Angela needs to leave—and soon."

Neti was silent, unsure if he should trust Ruchin. Everything he'd said was spinning around in his head like a hurricane. So far, he was the most passive and honest councilman he'd met, yet a part of Neti told him to be careful.

They walked in silence until Ruchin stopped and motioned to the left wall. "Here are your parents," he said. "Well, your mother at least."

Neti stepped between the pillars and held his glowstone over the plaques that sealed the tombs. Their names, Ardat and Namtar, were engraved on their own blocks. He couldn't remember much of them: what they looked like, their hobbies and passions, who they were as people. Yet a part of Neti still longed for them, even though he was satisfied at Angela's side. At least she had always been honest with him. She could have lied and kept the truth of his parents from him, but she'd admitted her mistakes when he was younger, and he respected her for that.

"You make it sound like my father isn't here," Neti said.

"Unfortunately, he is not," Ruchin said. "Your father's body was never retrieved from Dingir fifteen years ago. They suspect he fell when a third of the city did, or he was burned by the Anunnaki."

Neti wasn't sure what he felt: contempt, anger, or sorrow. He was confused about his own emotions. There was a compulsion to justify his feelings, to break them down and discover just how far he was willing to let things go and what direction he should travel. His parents had died so long ago he couldn't even remember it, yet it still hurt.

Neti turned away from the crypt. "Thanks for your help."

Ruchin followed behind him, and when he caught up, he said, "If there is ever a time you would wish to learn more about your parents or heritage, perhaps even more of your people's history, you only need to ask."

Neti didn't respond. There was too much on his mind, and he was far too uncertain about Ruchin to continue the conversation.

CHAPTER NINE

B *oom.*

The sound resounded through the caverns, carrying off between the stalactites, through the streets and market square, until it finally returned to her. Teleporting to opposite sides of the city was Neti's idea, and it was a good one at that. Angela swore she'd tell him that, but for now, she had to keep herself focused. Inside her, Udug's soul kept the Dalkhu from seeing her in flames and helped her blend in. Unfortunately, being a woman in the black robes of a soldier would not. Keeping her distance until she found the councilman she was after would be key.

The old wooden steps groaned under her weight as she dropped down them two at a time. By staying off the cleared path into the city, and between the tree-sized stalactites, she was able to creep up to the city unseen. She further decreased the likelihood of being seen by stepping out onto the street from between two homes—until she collided with a wheelbarrow.

"I'm sorry," the man who pushed it said.

As much as she wanted to cuss him out, she looked away to hide her face and kept moving down the street without a word. Children ran and played in the streets while mothers tended to laundry in wash bins and made meals over cookfires. Most men appeared to be working heavier labor: constructing new homes or rolling carts filled with chunks of iron and coal from mines outside the city. It was funny how traditional the Dalkhu were. Roles were more or less assigned. Women weren't soldiers, but even Angela had to admit that the people didn't seem unhappy.

Walking down the road grew harder the closer she came to the market square. If Angela were to put her head down any more to hide underneath her hood, she would have had to drag her face on the ground. That only made her uncertainty worse. Was she standing out by looking down at the ground so much? She didn't have a large bosom, but it would only be a matter of time before someone spotted lumps under her robes.

Maybe they'll think I'm extra meaty.

It was hard to contain her laughter until, just out of the corner of her eyes, she caught sight of a black robe ahead. Underneath the green and white glow of the moss above, a councilman with a red sash stepped out of a home, onto the road, and turned toward her. As he walked, a public bonfire illuminated the scar along Melech's forehead.

The Teacher. He didn't seem very fond of me...

Angela turned around before he saw her. Keeping her pace quick, she walked until the road turned and disappeared around the corner, then slipped between homes to double back and peered out onto the street she'd just been on. A moment passed, and then the councilman did. Following behind him now, she was careful to keep just enough distance between them as he turned the corner and led her to the edge of the market.

From just along the outer edge of the square, Angela positioned stands between them as she pretended to browse wares. Keeping her head down, she watched the councilman peer over a stand displaying tools: pickaxes, drills, and hammers of all sizes made from iron, bronze, and, more rarely, steel. Melech moved to another stand with daggers and other blades.

Within moments, two soldiers dressed in black and a commoner shackled by the wrist, and in little more than rags, approached the councilman. At their distance, their voices were only murmurs, but Melech seemed annoyed and motioned them away with his wrist. The soldiers bowed, grabbed the prisoner by his manacles, and pulled him away.

Angela had no clue what that was about, but when Melech moved on toward the far corner of the market and disappeared into the crowd, curiosity got the better of her and she walked to the stand to find out. With her eyes low and on the array of blades on the market table, she asked, "What did Melech want, and who was he talking to?"

The shopkeeper just stood there, smacking on something in his mouth before he spat on the ground next to him. "The councilman wanted me to tell you this…" He lunged forward, bending over the table and producing a silver blade from behind his back.

A sting in her belly. The point of his short sword pierced her robes, underclothes, and skin alike, but she'd moved back fast enough to get out of the way of most of it.

Immediately, the people around them sensed the surge of activity and gasped. The middle-aged man came barreling over his stand with a shout, the mustache hanging below his chin waving as he vaulted toward her. The shop-keeper wasn't a soldier, but she pulled the brass knuckles from her pockets no slower.

I won't even need them for this.

The knife was coming at her again faster than she antic-ipated, forcing her to spin out of the way. She ducked and weaved as the man, shouting with each swing, slashed with vigor and skill that made her wonder if he was a retired soldier.

A hard strike to drive the brass into his shoulder muscle was enough to send the sword flying from his hand with a groan. Angela grinned; she had put a bit of her souls' energy into that blow to give him a little extra sauce. Judging by his staggering and wailing, she guessed this was going to be an easy fight. At least until a sound like a boulder being cracked in half came from her left.

A pillar of rock came jutting out of thin air not ten feet away, crossed the distance between them, and slammed into her side. The air whooshed out of her as she dropped to the ground with a thud, then rolled out from underneath it before the hole was sealed and it crashed to the ground where she just lay. The shopkeeper was scrambling for his sword.

Shaking, she rose, and the silver blade was dancing around her again faster than she expected it to. Anger bubbled inside her now. There was no one else around dressed in black, but she didn't think that the man in front of her could breach the veils. His eyes hadn't closed in concentration and his mind didn't reach out past her, so someone else had to be around.

When the timing was right, Angela grabbed the man by the wrist and twisted it behind his back before kicking the inside of his knee. A blow to the head put him to sleep, and she shoved him over. "Who opened the veil?" she yelled. Those who remained in the square stood behind stalls and put crates and wares between them, peering out at her as silently as mice. "I asked, who hit me with that?"

"I did." A black robe stepped out. The person's face was covered with taught gray fabric. Eyeholes were cut through the mask, gloves covered the hands, and the colored cord had been replaced with a regular rope. "On behalf of the entire city of Kur, I ask that you leave the city to the Dalkhu." The voice from behind the mask was masculine, young, and smooth.

"I can't do that when my home and I have been attacked, now can I?"

The masked man crossed his arms. "The way I see it, you have limited options: stay here long enough that you're destroyed by vigilantes and commoners, or leave. Just because the Council won't act doesn't mean the people will stand by." A few of the commoners shouted out in agreement, raised their fists, and found the courage to step out with the masked man.

The fact that he had mentioned commoners and vigilantes made her wonder if that was exactly what she was looking at, but she figured that was a false lead. Given the mask, this person was probably a councilman hiding his identity. Though she had been tracking Melech, that didn't mean he had instructed the shopkeeper to attack her, and there was probably no way to prove it was him without ripping that mask off. All she could do was say, "I'm glad you've found the courage to fight me directly, Melech. Let's end this."

She disappeared in a blast, arrived a step away, and connected her fist with Melech's cheekbone and watched him fall onto his back. As she stepped over him, the veil quivered between them for a split second before a gust of air blasted her into the air. Twenty feet farther away and with a lot more back pain, she pushed herself to her feet to see the masked councilman standing there and waiting for her to move.

"First you breach the world of rock, now air?" She smiled. "Two can play that game, but doesn't the rest of the Council forbid you from bringing out the dimensions that way?"

Melech laughed. "It used to be illegal, but now it's just taboo. I made it so."

Something doesn't click. The Teacher isn't a lawmaker… I think. Would that mean this is Kanu? I'll just have to finish—

The masked man disappeared, and if the sound of his arrival hadn't come from her left, she wouldn't have spotted him standing atop a shoddy home's thatch roof. The veil rippled again as another spire came tearing through the air at her, but Angela shifted to the side, felt the rock-on-rock contact shake the ground under her feet, then slashed out with her mind.

Aiming projectiles from the elemental dimensions required pinpoint accuracy. Every point of existence had a fabric to it that could be penetrated on all six axes and every degree between. Angela wasn't talented at this, and the rock she loosed slammed into the wall just below and to the left of the councilman's feet. It pushed its way into the home, crumbling bricks like toy blocks and sending dust and dirt into the air. The roof still intact, Melech was unharmed, and she was sure he was smirking under his gray mask and black hood. It embarrassed and angered her.

A jet of flame burst toward her from the side, and Angela pushed herself between the worlds. Its icy expanse was certainly more welcoming than melting alive, and with all the time in existence, she pondered how she should continue. The councilman was certainly more skilled than her with just about anything involving the veil or the mind, so Angela decided it was best for her to play to her strengths.

Instantly, she appeared just behind the councilman, grabbed the back of his hood, and pulled it down to his shoulders, but the gray fabric had been tied around the back of his head. She reached for the knot, but the roof cracked and caved beneath them. Crashing down onto the home's packed earth floor, the snapped sticks and thatch scratched against her cheeks and hands, cutting her.

I'm lucky I didn't lose an eye, she thought as she fought to rise to her feet in the rubble.

A woman in the corner screamed a high-pitch wail, startling Angela as she staggered upright, but the masked councilman had disappeared. When she ran outside, the only black robe in the market square was hers. The attacker had either already risen and ran out the door, or he'd teleported before they even struck the ground, conveniently leaving her with the mess.

A market stand that had been selling robes, blankets, and rugs was on fire. One rock pillar lay across the entire length of the market, but it hadn't smashed anything. The one the councilman had brought down on her had buried its nose into the ground and smashed its way throughout the polished and gem-laden square.

Angela's stony spire, on the other hand, was still sprouting from its hole in the veil, growing longer and longer as it began to push itself into the cavern's ceiling with a terrible, distant gnashing sound. She watched a massive stalactite rip off the ceiling and seemingly slow down as it fell. The resounding boom when it hit the floor below shook the whole cavern. Luckily, it fell outside of the city and into the stalagmite fields, so she at least had that much going for her.

"What happened here?" An old voice carried loudly from behind. Ruchin weaved his way between the wreckage of a stand, his hands shaking in rage. "You did this? I can't believe what you've done!"

She raised a hand and stepped closer to the councilman. "Calm down. You don't know the specifics. I assure you that this wasn't wanton—" Her breath caught as Melech and Neti stepped out from behind him. Without a word, she lurched forward, shoving her way past Ruchin, grabbing the Teacher by the collar of his robes, and raising a fist over her shoulder. "I see you've re-dressed yourself."

A hand grabbed her by the wrist, forcing her gaze to meet Ruchin's steel eyes. "What is the meaning of this?"

She turned back to Melech but noticed that there was not a single mark on his skin. Surely, he was flush red and sweating nervously, but there was no bruise where she had punched the masked man's cheekbone, and his black robes were crisp and clean. Not a single piece of straw on them. With a furrowed brow, she released him and stepped back to regain her thoughts.

"A disguised councilman attacked me. Right here," she said.

Neti stepped between the shattered remains of a stand and leaned in close to her. "Are you all right?"

Angela only nodded.

Ruchin crossed his arms, but his eyes cast to the floor. "I see."

That was easy. "You believe me?" she asked, surprised. "I'll admit, I was trailing Melech through the city to that stand over there. When the councilman left, I approached it to question a shopkeeper and he attacked me. Next I knew, I was ripping holes in the veil with someone far too fast to not be a councilman."

Both Ruchin and Angela watched Melech's expression change under the scrutiny, but in the end, the Teacher only shrugged. "I am not sure there is anything I can say. Surely, I'm no fan of the Anunnaki, but I'm not a fool. I wouldn't attack her in the market square during its busiest time."

"Did you see behind this mask? See that it was truly Melech?" Ruchin asked. "And tell it true, Angela."

A rock sank in her gut, but she sighed and said, "I don't think it was Melech now."

Ruchin ran his fingers through his beard. "I am not surprised that someone attacked you, but councilmen are not the only ones who can bring forth the elements. We have many skilled pupils who can do so just as quickly, but I don't think you are grasping the situation you are putting this city in, Angela. You have claimed that you want to foster peace between us, but why do you move behind the Council's back and against our requests? Did I not ask you to stay with a member of the Council at all times?"

"You did."

"That is not only for the city's protection, but for your own."

Angela laughed. "I trust every councilman quite little."

"That much is clear," Ruchin said, stepping over broken planks to her. He leaned in and whispered, his breath warm on her ear, "You have no idea what I am trying to hold back, for your sake. One more broken rule, one more trick like this, and you'll have changed my vote." There was a moment of silence before the councilman waved them away and instructed Melech to escort them back to their chamber. Angela did as she was asked and left peacefully so the rest of the Council could begin cleaning up the market. A part of her did feel terrible about the damage. The Kissum and the market square were both made with great stonesmanship, and the Dalkhu were proud of their work.

When they reached the seclusion of their bedroom chamber, Neti leaned in closer and asked, "What now?"

Angela shrugged. "Ruchin knows something we don't, and he's not very telling about it."

"I got the same feeling. I followed him into the Kissum's crypts. I got caught, but we talked about things for a while. He thinks you should leave before things get out of hand."

She smirked. "Things already are out of control, but it's me they are really afraid of, not you. Do you think you could get closer to Ruchin and gain his trust? Make him think that you're meeting with him out of your own will and gather more information out of him?"

Neti nodded.

CHAPTER TEN

Head down, Neti walked around a group of stonesmen with heavy hammers and chisels at their belts, avoiding their glares as best as he could. The looks they gave him almost made him feel as though he was in Dingir, not Kur, all because Angela had smashed up the city in her fight with the masked vigilante. While he didn't blame her for defending herself, he wished she would have just fled instead of making a mess of things. Already, her actions were having a direct effect on him.

A foreman shouted orders at his men and they broke apart before Neti was swallowed whole, revealing the pillars that had made such a ruckus. The damage they had left was hard to look at; the stalactite that had fallen was now an empty, black spot in an otherwise sparkling sea of green and white stars, and the market square was terribly cracked and damaged where a stone pillar still protruded from the ground.

Four councilmen stood nearby, eying it and discussing how to get rid of it. Before Neti could think of something to say, Melech noticed him and pointed him out to the others. Neti gulped, wiped his sweaty palms on his trousers, and stepped forward. He had changed out of his black robes and hoped he hadn't offended anyone.

Ruchin's gray beard was frizzled and uncombed like he'd either just rolled out of bed or hadn't slept at all. "Where's Angela?" he asked.

"I convinced her it would be best if she stayed in our chamber for today," Neti said. "Especially after all this."

Melech laughed and hit Ruchin playfully. "Maybe you should use the boy more often, peacemaker."

Ruchin took a half-step back, holding his shoulder and grumbling, but otherwise ignored him. Turning back to Neti, he said, "That is very wise of you, and I appreciate the notion, but what brings you out today?"

"You said before that if I ever wanted to learn more you would show me around, so here I am."

A smile stretched across his wrinkled face. "That pleases this old councilman more than you know. I'd be happy to show you a thing or two, but if you will excuse me, we were just about to clear these stones from the market. If you could give me just a short amount of time, I'll be with you soon."

Neti bowed his head and gave the councilmen some space to work. During their brief huddle, they argued over what portion of the pillar's weight each councilman would take and where they would make their incisions. When it was all decided, Toth, Ruchin, Melech, and Kanu took their positions around the base of it.

"Is there a way I can help?" Neti asked.

Ruchin smiled softly while Melech seemed to roll his eyes. Putting a hand on his shoulder, the elder said, "No, I don't think that you could help without getting in the way.

We can't leave any area of the stone uncovered or we'll just be ripping a hole in the veil. It takes coordination and an ability to take subtle cues from one another's minds without words, so it would be best if you left us to it."

Neti nodded and stepped back without a word. *He didn't say I couldn't feel how it was going.*

When the councilmen closed their eyes in concentration and Neti knew the work had begun, he stretched out with his own mind as well. Immediately, he could feel their confusion as his mind touched theirs. He was careful to remain back far enough that he did not get in their way but could still feel the details of their process. Between the four councilmen, they cast their minds over the stone and cut through it as close to the ground as they could manage. When they stilled and the pillar was contained in their minds, the veils around them shuddered as they pushed the stone through.

A great blast of air rushed forth, billowing back hoods, scattering loose parchment across the market square, and knocking crates over. Quickly, the councilmen worked to seal the hole, but not before Neti reached in and felt around. They had banished the pillar to a place on Earth he wasn't familiar with. When the torrent of wind calmed, he noticed a circle of brown stone in the floor where they had cut the pillar almost completely parallel with the polished black stone of the market square.

The councilmen had a harder time casting their minds over the second pillar, but Neti couldn't imagine how much each pillar of stone weighed and how much effort it must have taken. A grunt escaped each of the councilmen's lips when the obelisk disappeared, and Ruchin stumbled to his knees, exhausted. Even Toth's chest was rising and falling quickly.

A few hands in the crowd clapped for the councilmen as Neti helped Ruchin to his feet. The old man groaned and said, "Thank you, young Neti. I appreciate you not involving yourself in that, and I understand what it's like to only want to help and restrain yourself." He exhaled long and slow, wiping the dirt off his black robe. "So you said you wanted to learn something new? Well, there are many things I could teach you, so you'll have to be a bit more specific."

Neti kicked at the ground. "I hadn't really thought about it, but one thing I've always been curious about is how different my training might have been from the students of Kur."

Ruchin raised his bushy gray eyebrows. "Interesting choice. I believe councilman Melech has a class awaiting him, is that true?"

Melech glanced over to them, the scar on his brow glistening in sweat. "Aye, I do. You could accompany me if you like."

Neti tensed. At one point, Angela had thought that Melech was the one who attacked her, and he wasn't sure how much he should trust him. Besides, he'd come all the way to town specifically to be with Ruchin. The elder councilman must have sensed it; he hummed and ran his fingers through his beard before saying, "I will come as well, I think. It has been some time since I've checked on those young boys."

Melech shrugged and turned toward the Kissum, and Ruchin and Neti followed, leaving the clean-up to the commoners. The black stone floor would probably always have a jagged circle of brown where the pillar had burrowed, and Neti wondered if that spot would become a historical marker, remembered as the place where an Anunnaki was nearly smashed by a vigilante hero. Angela wouldn't want that, but for now, it didn't matter, and they couldn't stop it, anyway.

Up the steps intertwined with flecks and veins of gold and white, through the double doors, and down the left archway, they reached the farthest corner of the Kissum. Underneath that dome, a group of boys just a handful of years younger than Neti were gathered around a pillar. A quick command from Melech and they ceased fooling around and straightened their backs, then rushed to gather their mats and bags.

The group made its way through a set of doors, everyone chattering as they went into the central dome of the Kissum. Everything about this room was different; the pillars, the height of the ceiling, and the painting were unlike anything Neti had seen. Along its outer edge, the dome depicted a raging sea with long serpents and other creatures he couldn't identify. Animals and humans of different sizes occupied a green land that stretched throughout the middle portion. A blue sky with clouds and a single star in the center of the dome was home to a single, massive bird with talons and teeth instead of a beak. Its eyes were black. As were its wings that stretched from one end of the dome to the other.

Ruchin stepped next to him, his gaze on the ceiling. "Impressive, isn't it? My father once told me that the scaffolds that had to be built to carve this room consumed entire forests for their lumber. If other stories are to be believed, the entire Kissum does not have a single seam where two stones meet, but I think that's folly."

The students piled their bags on the side of the room and knelt on their mats. Melech, standing front and center, first instructed the boys to focus and find the center of their souls in meditation. The boys shut their eyes for a few minutes as he paced back in forth in silence. A part of Neti wanted to join, but he wondered if it would be too imposing.

He whispered to Ruchin, "At what age do their trainings begin?"

"Parents encourage their children as young as a few years old to kneel, close their eyes, and pay attention to how they feel," he said with his creaking, old voice. "This sets a foundation of awareness of oneself, and by the time they are five, they attend their first class. Of course, there is nothing too challenging for them to start, but the idea is to get them accustomed to their souls and have some command of them by the time they are eight or nine."

Neti frowned. "Their path is decided by the time they are two? Or three?" Where was the freedom and, in turn, the passion in that?

Ruchin nodded. "Some have paths assigned to them by their parents for their beginning years, but all are given the opportunity to change course when they reach maturity. It may be because the child is unruly and needs discipline and a strict set of rules to abide by, or the parents themselves were born into the role of soldier and they grew to see the values of servitude and fighting for a cause bigger than oneself, and they want to instill that same feeling in their children. In the end, as long as a child is apt enough, he can move between trades and soldiery as he pleases."

That got Neti thinking. "And what's the Council's thought on women being soldiers? I know it's forbidden, but Teshub never told us the reason why."

Ruchin's gray eyes seemed to twinkle, and Neti wasn't sure if that was because he mentioned Teshub or female soldiers. "That is a topic we have debated innumerable times. One school of thought is that, as a free society, if a woman wants to give her life for her people, she has every right to. The other idea is that women are so vitally important to us, as a culture, that we should not risk their lives. It isn't an attempt to control women but protect them."

"Well, what makes women important to Dalkhu culture? I've never heard such a thing."

The councilman let out a long breath. "Well, there's differing opinions on that, but it comes from a place far older than the Dalkhu or even Kur. In the world before these three that we know now, it's claimed that there was a mother of all mortal life. Of course, the truth of this mother is hard to verify, or even research, when the Nephilim that survived the Anchor Crystal's break are the ones that passed these stories to our ancestors eons ago. For some Dalkhu, the all-mother is still revered and sometimes prayed to." Ruchin let out a long sigh. "But the older I get, the more I find that people hold good intentions on all sides of a debate. What matters most is that there is no harm done."

Neti glanced over at the councilman. "I wish the rest of the Council shared those views. Angela is quick to anger and oversteps her bounds, I'll admit that, but she comes from a good place. She's only worried that someone will try to reconstruct the Anchor Crystal again, like Udug wanted to."

A heavy look settled in Ruchin's eyes as he spoke even quieter. "I will be honest with you, Neti. There are things at work behind the facade the Council puts up. Several councilmen are moving in the dark, and I fear they only wait because I hold them still and I am not sure how strong my grip is. If Angela stays in Kur much longer, someone may move against me—and her again." His eyes flashed over at

Melech like he was concerned he might hear him. "I don't know what they are doing, but it cannot be good. She must leave before things get out of control."

More than one councilman? Neti leaned closer. "Who, Ruchin? Who is moving in the shadows?"

"Maulkatu."

CHAPTER ELEVEN

"**M**aulkatu is missing, huh?"

Neti nodded. He'd rushed into their chamber so quickly the sweat on his forehead shimmered in the light and his hair was clumped. "That's what Ruchin said," he whispered. "But it didn't sound like he was the only one, and he seemed nervous with Melech in the room."

Angela sat on her bed with her back against the cold wall, parted her hair behind her ear, and propped her chin on her knee. "Did Melech have a bruise on his cheek yet?"

Neti shook his head.

"Damn. Well, then we can't say for certain he really was the masked councilman. And unless Ruchin is purposefully trying to lead us astray, we could assume it was Maulkatu."

He scratched the back of his head, eyes on the floor. "See, that's kinda the problem with all of this. We can't really act unless we have proof or the rest of the Council is just going to come after us."

A long sigh escaped her. They had a worse problem

than that. Trying to find the other Council member working in secrecy would be a lot harder than a direct confrontation. She took a long moment to consider creating more ruckus and trying to force them into acting, but she couldn't come up with a situation that seemed worth the cost.

Angela secured the room with the table and dresser, then climbed into her bed. Half of her mind was worried that someone would break through their makeshift barricade or teleport directly into the room, and she stared at the cavernous ceiling in silence until sleep finally took hold of her.

When she awoke, cold and shivering, she lay there trying to stay warm as she formed something of a rudimentary plan. Instead of drawing Maulkatu out of hiding, maybe she needed to go to him. She rose and put on new clothes before shaking Neti by the shoulders and leaving him in the bedroom to wake up. Everything in the living room seemed to be exactly where they had left it the night before, but Angela still looked for the slightest disturbances.

"Is there any water?" Neti asked as he sat in the rocking chair, rubbing his eyes.

"No," Angela said, "but we can get some in town. Since I can no longer sneak around after these rogue councilmen, and I probably shouldn't try to draw him out, I think it would be best if we follow the long trail to truth."

Angela grabbed both of their bags out of the bedroom, along with her sword, and returned to find Neti's eyes closed like he was falling asleep again. She kicked his chair lightly to get him up and moving, and though he grumbled, that was usual. With minimal coaxing, she led him through the blue drape to the hallway and peeked outside. Kanu, the black-haired councilman guarding them, glanced over at her, his eyes heavy with fatigue. She bowed shortly to him and said, "I would like to go to town and specifically the library."

"What is your infatuation with books?" Neti asked, stumbling up behind her. "It's early, and you're better off talking with people."

Kanu nodded in agreement, so Angela glared back at Neti. "I find that people lie more frequently than books."

Neti shrugged. "Fair enough."

"I'm sure you'd like to be replaced while we are in Kur as well," Angela said, turning back to the councilman.

Kanu nodded and extended an open hand, and Angela took it. Once Neti had a hold of the crook of her arm, she reached out with her mind and cut their way into the space between worlds. The trip was over quickly enough, and they were walking down the city's main avenue, surrounded by the smells of the cavern's last millennium of habitation as they neared the markets.

The eyes of the commoners around her seemed more hostile than the last time she was in the city. By now everyone would know what she had done to Shedim and most likely knew what had happened on the day before last. In the markets, they passed between stands until they found someone willing to sell two skins of tea. Angela sipped on hers gingerly as they searched for a blacksmith to hone the edge of her sword, but every person that turned down her business made it harder to maintain a decent composure. Eventually, she gave up and they began their climb up the Kissum's steps. Not until afterward did she realize that asking someone to sharpen the weapon she had used to kill one of their leaders might appear as though she was bragging or showing off. Regret clutched her chest, but it had already happened and she could not take it back.

They passed through the main foyer and its archways and stepped between the rows of shelves. When they came to the library's common area, she saw that Toth was seated among the tables, a scroll in hand. Angela took to a table of her own and unloaded her backpack onto it. As she unpacked, she listened to Kanu take advantage of the situation and ask Toth to cover his guardianship. While the redhead complained under his breath, it wasn't long before she spotted Kanu leaving between two rows of shelves.

With a notebook and pencil in hand, she began to wander between the tomes, looking for specific things at first: maps of the tunnels surrounding the city, trade logs between the Council and the public in the hopes they were actually public, and a record of the counts of Anchor shards. The last two didn't exist. There weren't even any logs that stated what wares had been imported from Earth or exported.

Most of what she found were encyclopedias of flora and fauna in Kur and on Earth and some pieces of either pure propaganda or delusion around Dingir or the Anunnaki. Titles like *The Anunnaki Age: A History of Dalkhu Subjugation* didn't surprise her but still stung a bit. The farther she went, the older the books got. There were plenty of dictionaries to help bridge the gaps between different dialects and languages, but there wasn't anything she could use to try to find a councilman in hiding. Nothing really even interested her until she found a red leather-bound tome called *The First Mortals*.

Teshub had once said something about the first mortals, and the book seemed to beckon. She pulled it from the shelf, and when the pages threatened to fall out of their bindings, she grasped the bottom, took it to the table, and examined it closer. The text was written in an older style of her language and was hard enough to decipher without the crinkled pages and ink smudges in some places, but it was the only title that had grabbed her interest. She tore into it one slow sentence at a time until her head began to ache, and it wasn't until Neti plopped down at the table beside her that she remembered where she was.

"I'm bored," he said.

Angela chuckled. "We just got here an hour ago."

"Yeah." Neti scratched the back of his head. "But it's all so... uninteresting. I want to *do* something."

Angela sighed and thumbed through another page. "Go hit your head against something until you see stars, goat-head. Better yet, you know how to read. Why don't you find a romance story, huh? You could learn something about talking to girls."

Neti's cheeks grew red. "No... I don't want to read anything like that. I don't really want to read anything." He rose to his feet and began to walk away.

Angela had to fight to keep herself from laughing at how uncomfortable he was. *I wanted him to go away, and that did the trick.* She turned back to her book with a wide smile, feeling relieved and giddy at the same time. Within a few more minutes, she finally saw the word she was looking for: Nephilim. With Neti off to explore a different section of the library and leave her distraction-free, she made her way through the scant passage.

Most of what it said was the same as the Dalkhu myths she'd heard from Teshub. The Nephilim were a species that had given birth to the Dalkhu through spiritual means at the dawn of time. They were particularly good with spells and handed that knowledge to their sons and daughters, but most couldn't travel between the veils of the worlds. The book seemed like it wasn't going to inform her of anything new when she stumbled upon other things she recognized: Eld Kur and the Scratched Hall.

She remembered the passage she found in Shedim's chamber, tucked away between the pages of a book:

Eld Kur, the Mourning City and the Scratched Hall, we left behind. Three days, toward the light we climbed, until in a colossal cavern of black, green, white, and gold we found rest. At his behest, we sent two back down below, and when they returned, we heard the news. One-third of us have perished, but no more. They are trapped behind a wall of stone past the red ravine, off the lake, in the deep below. N'er again a claw in our backs or a child coated in fire.

Angela rose to her feet, book in hand, and spun around to see Toth still seated at the table behind her. His eyes met hers as she approached him. Dropping the book on his table and sliding it to him, she said, "This work mentions a place called Eld Kur and another called the Scratched Hall of the Nephilim."

Toth's eyes grew narrow in his otherwise expressionless face.

He knows it.

"What could you possibly want with that place?" he asked coldly.

"So it exists, then?" She smiled. "I want to know where it is. Based on this passage here, it's suggested it's not anywhere near the cavern the Kissum is in."

Toth sighed calmly, then closed the book in front of him. In a low tone he said, "It is hidden from those who need not know its location or what it contains."

"Please, the secrecy of what's there is laughable. There are spells. Big ones." She pointed at the book. "The Nephilim commanded them to carve away the rock and stone and smooth the tunnel so they could scratch down their history and passages into stone. That is where they recorded everything they knew."

Toth's disdain was difficult to see underneath his steeled expression, but it was there. "Tell me why you want to go there."

Something about his cold stare made Angela feel compelled to tell the truth. "Ever since my soul was taken from me fifteen years ago, I've wanted to know what spells the Council has access to," she said, but in reality, her reasoning was much more specific. There was no way Shedim had found their sinkhole on Earth without the help of a spell. He couldn't have just stumbled across them when they hadn't had any trouble or visitors before. They were always highly secretive about where they lived.

If I can find the spell that Shedim used to locate our home, I could use it to find Maulkatu.

Toth's eyes were unwavering as he analyzed her in silence.

Angela sighed and scooped the old book into her arms again. "Look, if you're not going to help me, that's fine. I'll find someone else who will or a map that will—"

"You won't find the Hall on any map, and I will take you there on one condition." He held up a single finger, and Angela stilled. "I admire your tenacity and desire to dig into things and learn, but not a single person beyond you or the boy will know where it is or what it contains. The councilmen before me have kept the location of that place hidden from the public for thousands of years, and that chain will not be broken because of me."

TOTH PULLED THEM INTO THE SPACE BETWEEN WORLDS, AND that familiar, icy chill covered her skin. She helped him by thrusting them forward with some of her own energy, but since she wasn't familiar with the destination, she couldn't help steer. Even with the weight of three people, the councilman finished their journey within what felt like only a few hours. Either she had helped more than she thought or Toth was incredibly focused.

The cavern was pitch-black, and the sounds of dripping water and the echo of their arrival seemed to carry on forever. Toth dropped to his knees somewhere in front of her. Then flashes sparked as he hit flint with steel and a torch flickered to life. They stood on a narrow path clear of the fauna, looking down a cliffside.

Awakened by the torchlight, ancient moss all around them cast yellow and red glows. Giant flowers with orange heads bloomed on the ceiling and lit the cavern like tiny suns. Below, a stream snaked through clutches of decrepit and crumbling buildings beneath the massive flowers, and stalagmites thicker than any tree she'd ever seen had fallen over what might have been a main road in the past.

As Toth spoke, his breath turned to fog. "This is Eld Kur, as it's called now. The ruins of a Dalkhu civilization much different than the one you know now."

He led them to the cliff's edge and down a narrow clearing along the bluff's side. The stone under her feet crunched and threatened to give out, but she followed and listened. "This old city was abandoned nigh on five thousand years ago. Believe it or not, most of the damage is from the Nephilim during the revolt. Some Dalkhu stayed to fight, others fled, and those that survived thought it better to build their own city than repair the one the

Nephilim let them build. It's said that they cut holes in the veils so large that half of the Dalkhu fighters died."

"I'm familiar with the story," Angela said.

"Yeah, but not the part about this place," Neti said. He took a deep breath, then let it out slowly. "Even the air smells old."

"It smells dead," Angela added.

"Well," Toth said with a raised brow, "it is a dead city."

When they reached the bottom, they followed the road into the city. The mortar between the buildings' stones had long since turned to dust. Toth steered them around a stalactite and forced them to climb over broken stones and squeeze their way between fallen homes. Whenever a brick fell or rolled onto another, the sound carried on and on into the distance.

When they came out of the rubble, they turned and followed the stream. It was no more than ten yards across, but it quickly turned into rushing rapids as the ground took on an incline. The cavern's walls and ceiling grew closer as they walked until they reached a tunnel along the rushing river. The path wasn't wide enough for a horse, and the rock under their feet was wet and slippery. At the end, the river spilled into a chasm that stretched left to right. Toth's torch was not bright enough to see how far down it went, but the sound of water hitting the bottom was quiet.

A single arm of connected stone formed a bridge to the other side of the gap. Toth went on ahead of Angela and Neti, testing his weight on the rock. When he motioned them forward, Neti and Angela looked to one another uncertainly but gulped down their fear and followed after him. As they neared the middle, a sound like knuckles on a wooden desk came from somewhere ahead. She thought she was only hearing things, but when Toth paused and so did the clacking noise, she knew it wasn't her mind playing tricks.

"What is that?" Neti asked loudly. Angela whipped around and held a finger to her lips.

Toth was quiet for a moment, holding the torch out in front of him. They could see the end of the bridge, and thirty yards beyond, but not what was making the clicking sound. After a long, nervous moment, he said, "I would guess at least one rimanis—an insect creature two to three yards in length," he answered. "They have antennae, pincers like a lobster, and use sound and vibration to see."

Angela fought the compulsion to gag. "Are they dangerous?"

Toth glanced back. "When cornered." He moved forward slower than he had before and kept his torch high above his head. By the time they reached the other side, the noises had ceased and there was nothing but mounds of rubble and the opening of another cavern. When Toth deemed the path ahead was safe, they quickly entered the tunnel and picked up the pace for a bit.

All seemed well, but still Angela spoke quietly. "So what else lives down here other than moss, flowers, and giant insects?"

"Rats," Toth said. "Smaller bugs. Mushrooms. Bats. Things heard and not seen."

The path widened into a larger cavern, and Toth veered to the right. The sounds of dripping water grew louder, and just as Angela was thinking of asking him how much farther they had to travel, he stopped where the trail ended. In front of them, a cliff of rock rose into the darkness. She couldn't even make out the ceiling. No moss illuminated this chamber.

Toth turned once Neti caught up and said, "This place is

something you should feel most privileged to see. Do not touch the stones with your bare skin and keep everything you find to yourself." Toth leaned in closer, his green eyes demanding their attention. "I am placing a great deal of trust in you. You must swear to keep these secrets safe."

Angela and Neti nodded.

"I'll respect that request on my honor," Angela said.

"Me too," Neti added.

Toth eyed them skeptically for a moment, but he turned his back to them and placed his left palm on the wall and his right on his chest. A light brighter than anything natural flashed from the stone, blinding Angela and Neti. They gasped and staggered back, shielding themselves. When her eyes adjusted to the darkness once more, there was an opening in the cavern wall. An immense hallway of black rock, wider than three wagons, stretched into the darkness in front of them.

Amazed, Angela stepped in front of Toth, forcing him to face her. "How did you do that?" Toth stared at her blankly, and when it was clear he would not answer her, she shrugged and turned away. "I'll find out on my own, then." She was the first to enter the tunnel.

Eventually, the cracks and unshaped stone ended, and patterns began. The farther in she went, the more certain she became that the lines on the walls had been intentionally scratched into the stone. Occasionally there were symbols, but she could not recognize them. Before too long, the markings became clearer.

Dalkhu and Anunnaki wrote similarly other than the use of some verbs, patterns, and punctuation. The old Dalkhu she'd studied in the library was challenging but not nearly as difficult as these symbols. Some were different shapes entirely, with long, trailing scuff marks down the wall. It was surreal. She'd heard stories about the Nephilim count-less times before, mostly in Teshub's teachings—the Anun-naki had hidden themselves from their spiritual ancestors, should the stories be believed—but this was the first, real proof she'd ever seen with her own eyes. At one point in time, the Nephilim really existed.

Two symbols stood out to her: three triangles pointing upward indicated Kur. Not the city, but the world as a whole, she believed, but there was no way to be certain. Another familiar one was a myriad of arrows and a pentagon that meant "stone." She tried reading the rest of the sentence but grew frustrated and moved on.

"Have you made sense of all of these, Toth?" she asked.

He walked past her, taking the light with him. "Some. Most of the writing is annals and accounts of the world before, and they make little sense. There are spells, too, but it is a shame that the largest collection of Nephilim knowl-edge is mostly unreadable. Language has changed and evolved, like a tree sprouting limbs. Even some of these texts are written differently than the others, suggesting that the world before was old and multilingual, too. Deciphering these words is a difficult task that few have bothered to undertake."

Angela moved to the next cluster of symbols. "Can you teach me?"

The councilman turned to face her, his black robe blending in with the darkness behind him. "Teach you what? To read the words or cast the spells?"

Angela shrugged. "Both."

Toth scoffed, and that was the end of the conversation. For the better part of an hour, Angela and Neti made their way down the stone corridor, trying to pick out anything of value. Occasionally they passed small streams of water that trickled from the ceiling and had eroded the writing, making entire passages incomprehensible and useless.

Angela nearly stumbled into Toth's back when he stopped unexpectedly. He was frozen still, and even his breathing was silent.

"What is it?" Angela asked, stepping around him to see his face.

"Another bug?" Neti asked nervously.

Toth shook his head, then let out the breath he'd been holding. "Do you feel that?"

Angela paused.

"The cold?"

"No. There is a breeze here that I do not recall."

Angela squinted as she looked down the dark shaft. There was barely enough wind to move a strand of her hair, but she didn't question the councilman and they continued on.

Within a minute, Neti asked, "So what's the difference between a spell and just projection through the veil? Teshub never taught us anything about spells."

Toth only sighed a little. "Both require the energy of a soul, but a spell needs a deeper kind of mastery of oneself: the ability to contort the soul and mind to one's desire. Every emotion the heart produces, and every urge that the mind creates, must be cast aside. Teleportation is as simple as turning a spigot or pouring a bucket of water over where you want it to go, but with a spell, you must shape the water as it falls and give it intention. Some spells also require a physical component to help bring them to a focus." He glanced at Angela. "Like the spell that Udug cast on you. It required your blood to connect you two together. If that is not enough of a challenge, consider the difficulty of translating these walls if you crave something new or different. Understanding all of what needs to be done and how it's accomplished, that is where mistakes are made. Occasionally, deadly ones."

She'd heard some of that before, but she knew it was important and was grateful that Toth had even agreed to take her here in the first place. Neti and Toth continued their conversation for a while as they walked deeper into the dark hall, but Angela didn't pay too much attention and kept her eyes on the walls around them. She paused when four words caught her eye, her heart skipping a beat: "speak with the dead."

Neti and Toth turned, bewildered at her slack jaw, then walked to her side. "What is it?" Neti asked.

She reread what she could, but even the fragment she could decipher was questionable. The passage could have also meant "the dead speak" and had nothing to do with any kind of communication, yet she hoped with all her heart. *Could I speak with Michael?* Her eyes began to sting.

Angela dropped her backpack and dug out her notebook and pencil, then pointed at the symbols. "Read this to me."

Toth squinted and leaned closer. "Those lost to the energies..." He huffed and got even closer, his nose only a few inches from the stone. "Communicate... Clearer the closer... to... to the proximity of the soul. And then something about a mirror finish and a call." He took a step back and rubbed his eyes. "This is a spell for speaking with the souls of those who have left us."

Her heart was pounding. "Will you show me how to do it, Toth?"

The councilman looked to her quizzically. "This interests you that much?"

"It does," she admitted, "but I can't say why. I'm sure you have lost someone you miss."

"Those that have left me were due to, but it does appear as though this spell is similar to another I'm familiar with. I may be able to guide you, but I will not pave the road you seek. You must be willing to do the work of translating and casting it, of course."

Angela nodded ecstatically. "I am so grateful, truly. To... To think that I can talk with Mi—" She cut herself short and regathered herself, but by the way Neti looked at her, he knew whose name she was going to say. Without touching the wall with her skin, she placed the paper against the symbols and began scraping her pencil against it to get a rubbing of the spell. Within a few minutes, she'd dulled her pencil and had to sharpen it with her knife, but when she was done, she turned to Toth one last time and asked, "Might I return here by teleporting? Or are there spells at work in here, like in the vault?"

Toth shook his head. "There are no spells to harm you here, and you may return as long as a councilman accompanies you, of course."

Angela wasn't sure if bowing was a custom to show gratitude, but she did anyway before they began heading back toward the entrance. Nothing else written on the other side of the hall caught her attention now that her mind was racing with possibility. Even with such little knowledge, Angela knew herself well enough that she could not resist trying to cast the spell. She swore she would find a way and speak with Michael again, if it was truly possible.

WHEN ANGELA AND NETI RETURNED TO THEIR ROOM FOR the night, she was quick to stuff her notebook away in the dresser's bottom drawer and cover it with clothes. With her sword propped against the nearby wall, she dropped onto the bed and let out a long breath. Her head was pounding, and fatigue held her eyes shut, but her heart burned with hope.

Just as the tingling sensation of sleep washed over her, Neti stirred in his bed. "Are you really going to cast that spell?" he asked.

She opened her eyes and rolled onto her back. Neti was lying on his side, his face lit by the dull glow of a moss-covered stone on the nightstand.

"I think so," she admitted. "I know I'm here for Donny and the crystals, but I don't know how I could not try. If I have the smallest chance of speaking with Michael again, I can't pass it up. I have to let him know that I miss him and that he is still the only person with a home in my heart."

Neti was quiet for a moment. "Spells can be dangerous, Angela. What if something happens to you?"

"That's why I've got you to pick up my slack in case I screw up and die." When Neti's expression turned sour, she laughed. "I'm kidding. But... there's no going around this. I have to try."

Neti sighed as he rolled onto his back. "Michael must have meant a lot to you."

She smiled and said, "He wasn't perfect by any means, but he was always there for me. No one has ever cared for me like he did, watched over me, and made me feel safer, like I had a home. I just..." She took a deep breath. "Before I met you and my life was falling apart, I remember dreaming that one day I'd get my soul back and I'd return to him. I fought for the chance to talk with him as the Anunnaki I was supposed to be. Tell him what was really happening to me, hold his hands without the world around me bursting into fire, but I was too slow, and he died. I've forgiven him for what he did, and that's part of the reason I want to speak with him so badly. I've been denied the chance to make things right between us for so long because Udug took that away from me."

"What are we going to do after we get Donny free?"

Angela shrugged. "I don't know. Find a new home, I guess. He won't want to stay in Dingir after everything that's happened. The guy doesn't deserve the time he's spent in that cell, and I'm still surprised he's been alive all this time. Ja'noel never said a word to me."

"I bet he's been holding onto Donny like a playing card, just waiting for the right time to use him."

"Yeah, you're probably right, but I haven't been very aware of what's going on in Dingir, I'll admit. Using Donny to slow me down and get me invested in their fight was a smart move on his part. Ja'noel knows how much he means to me."

"Did…" Neti paused. "Did you ever have feelings for him?"

Angela sat upright. "Who? Donny?" She laughed. "No, nothing of the sort. He was a friend, a great one, but I never felt that way about him. Too… squishy. Both in character and physique." Angela chuckled and lay back down. "I just worry I'm going to spread myself too thin trying to learn a spell and find a councilman at the same time."

JA'NOEL JUMPED AT THE SOUND OF A KNOCK ON HIS DOOR. The clock on his wall told him it was the middle of the afternoon. He rubbed his eyes and said, "Come in."

The oak door creaked open, and Sarosha entered on long strides. Her cuirass was styled after a corset, tight against her body's curves, and thinner than his own. A knife, a tether gun, and a single battery hung on the belt on her waist. He asked her to wear armor weeks ago, and it was funny how all it took to get her to wear it was a bit of flair. Dingir was disorganized, people were desperate for freedom, security was loose, and he had grown afraid for her safety.

She closed the door behind her and walked to his desk, then sat herself on the lip of it. The way she weaved her fingers through his messy hair relaxed him as though he was allowed to breathe for the first time that day. "You push yourself too hard," she said.

"Yet somehow it still isn't enough. A handful of smelters have taken to protesting, refusing to manufacture support beams the city needs until I'm replaced, and I just received word that one of our camps on Earth has declared itself unassociated with Dingir and has seceded."

A sigh slipped between her lips. "Don't worry about the smelters. I have a history with them. You focus on your areas of expertise: the soldiers." Her eyes glanced down at the scattered papers on his desk. A puddle of drool had pooled on a report, and he wiped it up with his sleeve, somewhat embarrassed. "What's that?" she asked, picking it up.

"A list of all the spells and records we have regarding the Dalkhu and their ways," he said. "It's not much, but it's a start."

She scanned the note, then put it back on the desk. "I still don't know how I feel about the Bui'du, Noey. All the time it's going to take for them to train, the resources and investments that we don't have. You're busy enough as is, and projection and spells aren't how Dingir does things, anyway."

Ja'noel tapped a finger on the report. "Did you know there are records in that room that say we are cousins of the Dalkhu? If it's to be believed, our forefathers came from another world entirely, and they are what bind us together. I can't say for humans, but it seems like we stemmed from these Nephilim."

Sarosha rolled her eyes.

"No," Ja'noel said, taking her hand. "Don't disregard it. We have souls just like the Dalkhu, be it that we do little with them, yes?"

She half-nodded. "Yeah, but we aren't Dalkhu. We don't train like they do. To start now would be useless. Maybe when things are better and the city is on its feet again, but not now."

"What if we've been hiding from our highest potential, working without our greatest abilities and against our nature all this time? What if, without using our souls, we're no better than humans?" He searched through a drawer and placed an old brown tome on the desk. "This says that Nephilim lived with us, in Dingir, for hundreds of years after we first came to be. They taught us everything they could in the hopes that we would carry on their memory and destroy the Dalkhu that slaughtered so many of their kind.

"I mean, it's almost impossible to read, but at some point, the Nephilim left us here to forge our own path. We were too young, and resentful, and we stopped tempering our souls and have been set on our course ever since. We never embraced who we are."

Sarosha shook her head. "Noey, I just don't see this working the way you do. You've given four soldiers unlimited power. Do you have any idea how that looks to the public?"

"Yes," he said. "It looks like I'm doing something to change our condition."

Sarosha took his cheek in her hand. "Not to them. It looks like you're locking down."

Ja'noel sighed, then rose to his feet and wrapped his arms around her waist. Her forehead was warm on his lips. "I understand your concerns, and theirs, but I have to act."

"But you can't get this off the ground without someone there to help them get started. They can't train themselves. Dingir will fall from the sky before a Dalkhu would help, yet the Bui'du still need a teacher to show them the way."

Ja'noel took a step back and scratched the scruff on his cheeks. "I've been exploring the texts with them."

"That's not going to be enough," Sarosha said. "What about Angela?"

Ja'noel laughed.

Her brown eyes narrowed. "What's so funny?"

"Angela wouldn't slay a councilman if he held a knife to my throat. She's turned her back to Dingir... but I don't blame her. We moved against her and didn't listen when she needed help. The only hope we have is the Bui'du."

CHAPTER TWELVE

Angela rubbed her temples as she read. This was the second time that day she'd been through *The Art of Spellwork: A Compendium of the Simple*, and it was getting a little easier to understand.

A convergence of the mind and the soul, bent to the will of the user and known by some as spells, can achieve a myriad of different effects. The simplest methods of meditation can lead to the simplest results, while complex spells may want physical components and will wane the caster's energy further. Some theorize that most objects and items are unnecessary and only aid the mind's focus, but there are schools of thought that suggest it works.

Intent and desire bestowed and brought into life through willpower is what determines the spell's effect. While giving the soul's energy an intention or purpose beyond its own force is difficult, most newcomers to the art have the hardest time finding the balance between their mind, heart, and soul first. To best control those energies, one must be relaxed and at peace with oneself to achieve the best results. Do not think of it in terms of—

Angela thumbed that page over and flipped through the book until she reached the index near the end. She understood the basic principles well enough, she thought, but only a test would tell the truth. In her chair, she twisted to look at Toth seated behind her. His red hair spilled onto the desk and his green eyes twitched as he read his own book.

"Is there a place that you would recommend I start?" Angela asked. "What spell should I try first?"

The councilman sighed and looked up at her, annoyed. "Did you finish the book?"

"Yes, and half again."

"Then we should start at the beginning." He rose to his feet and stepped to her side and flipped to a list in the book. Pointing, he said, "That one. Follow me."

Spark of heat.

Angela closed the book and rose to her feet quickly to follow after him, but she paused when she remembered that Neti was browsing in the adjacent rows. She found him clutching a scroll to his chest with one arm and the other hand struggling to grab a black book on a shelf far above his head.

He swallowed, and when she asked if he wanted to come with her, he said, "No, sorry. I'm in the middle of looking into something."

That got her curious. She leaned in closer, trying to peer at the book he was struggling to reach, then jumped and plucked it for him, but he took it from her before she could read the cover.

"It's a record of all the councilmen who ever served, and this scroll…" He trailed off for a moment as something caught in his throat. "This is a genealogical tree of… my family."

Angela stammered, the guilt rising up in her. She'd cut

him off from that history so long ago and wondered if she would ever forgive herself for what she did to his parents. That was something she would likely struggle with all her life.

"I want to put the pieces together, see where my lineage meshes with the Council's most esteemed members. Ruchin told me about a few of them, but I figure there must be something about Shedim and Maulkatu in one of them. Maybe something that will lead us to them."

He wants to know his people's history and where he belongs in it. Who am I to deny him this?

"Okay," was all she could muster. "Maybe it will even turn out to be a good thing if we tread different paths."

They both smiled, and even though hers was half-forced, the smile he returned was genuine and warmed her a bit. They swore that they would flee any trouble they ran into before engaging a threat, then wished each other well in their search.

Angela knew that finding Maulkatu with spells would be more direct, but she wasn't sure if it would be any faster than Neti's method. The only way to find out would be to jump right into it and hope for the best. With the possibility of dire consequences for failure, learning spells was a risky gamble, but it was the decision she'd stand by despite her fears.

Toth waited for her just outside the library's rows of brown shelves, leaning against a black pillar with his arms crossed. They passed through the archway, headed farther back into the Kissum, and stopped in the next domed room. It was an open floor, and voices in the next room over echoed down the halls. Facing one another, they sat on thin mats of weaved reed.

The councilman twiddled a small stick between his

fingers. The bottom half in his hand was smooth pine, but the section that protruded from his fingers was brownish and rough like it had been rolled in dirt. "We call these shi," he said. "They are as they appear: small sticks dipped into an animal-based glue, then rolled in a ground mixture of different minerals known to be quite combustible. I want you to ignite it without breaching the veils and bringing out the flames of that elemental world."

Angela took the stick from him and stared at it for a moment. Maybe things wouldn't be as easy as she'd hoped.

"All things in the world are alive with energy: the air we breathe, the rock we sit upon, but the souls inside you are a great well of it. This energy can be converted to heat quite simply and is considered the best starting task for new apprentices."

She nodded eagerly. Surely she had at least as much skill as an apprentice. Teshub's trainings had given her reasonable control over her own souls, at least. "All right. How do I do it?"

Toth spoke softly, his voice deep and relaxing. "Close your eyes, and first focus on your toes. What do they feel like? Are they cold or warm? Shift your attention to the back of your head. Is your skin crawling with pin-prickles? Now, I want you to feel your breathing. In and out. Each breath you take in, you borrow the world's air and give it back. Look deeper and envision the souls inside you."

Angela breathed slowly as she did. They were blue and red orbs in her mind's eye, and they spiraled around endlessly.

"Feel them pulse with life. Their energy electrifies the air around them. You are a part of them, and they are a part of you. A symbiotic bond. They are alive and filled with emotion, but they answer to a hand that is strong yet kind.

Your hand. Focus on the end of the shi between your fingers. Feel the granules come free of the glue as you rub the end of it."

She did. The mineral coating fell free under her fingers.

"Now, I want you to connect those two points: the energy of your souls and the tiny particles on the shi. Your energy is life, electricity, the vibration in the air. Transfer that into the granules, give them that same vibration, and you will create the heat to ignite it."

A minute passed in silence. Then another before the sound of someone coughing down the archway distracted her and she lost her concentration. "Dammit," she cursed, dropping the shi and running her fingers over her head, frustrated. Before Toth could either take pleasure in her anger or direct her to keep trying, she picked the stick back up, breathed deeply, and reached out with her mind once more. She stared at the end of the shi this time rather than closing her eyes again.

"Channeling your energy into the shi's particles isn't enough to create heat. You have to give your energy the intention of creating heat. Think about rubbing your hands together and maybe—"

A spark flared between them, sending them both reeling back and shielding their eyes. In an instant, the shi had ignited and burned out in a flash. Angela laughed and tossed the stick on the ground. "I think I can handle it."

Toth raised his eyebrows. "Confident, and it did not take very long, either. You have every right to be proud, but I hope this exercise opens your eyes. Vibrating granules of flammable minerals may seem like a very precise thing to do, but I assure you that this is only the beginning. Things only grow harder from here." From the floor next to him, he handed her a handful of shi and rose to his feet. "I want you to continue to practice with these until it becomes as easy as blinking. When you're finished, there's a book you'll want to peruse before we move any further, and I have to find it in the library. I will be checking on you periodically, but can I trust that you won't run off if I leave you here?"

Angela was surprised that he was giving her that much freedom. "Of course."

TOTH COULDN'T HELP BUT SNEEZE AS HE RUFFLED THROUGH the book's pages, throwing dust into the air. *The Dead Weylines* was not the manual he was searching for, but it was still an interesting read. Maybe Angela should read this as well. *Well, I can simply paraphrase this one.* He tucked it away and moved farther down the bookshelf. There were other generic spell books as well, even some old theories on what the world was like before the Anchor Crystal broke, but on his mind was a specific one that he knew would help her cast the spell she wanted.

He rummaged for a short time until *Scrying with Your Mind's Eye* made itself apparent on a shelf above his head. He tipped it back by the spine and pulled the book down. There was no need to look through it; he remembered it well enough to know it was what she needed, so he walked into the common area and found Neti. With a stack of books on both sides of him and a scroll rolled out on the table, he had devoted his full attention to his study. The councilman approached the boy from behind and read over his shoulder for a moment before Neti almost jumped out of his skin.

"Sorry," Toth said. "I didn't mean to frighten you."

Neti exhaled slowly to calm himself. "It's all right. You're too quiet. You frightened me, is all." His eyes narrowed, and in a serious tone, he asked, "Where is Angela?"

He pointed. "She's in one of the training foyers, practicing her first spell. I left her to find this book." Toth stepped around the table and put it down. "I see that your selection is mainly on the Council's members, but I wonder if it's by your choice or Angela's command."

"I'm looking because I want to."

Toth chuckled. "I'm sure. I did not mean to offend you, Neti. I was only curious, as we both know how determined —and demanding—Angela can be." Neti eyed him cautiously, unsure what angle Toth was getting at, but he was speaking truly. "Those traits are her strengths, as they are her weaknesses, but it is admirable."

"Yeah…"

He was suspicious of him, so the councilman simply bowed his head and said, "I will leave you to your readings."

The boy remained silent as Toth walked away and disappeared into the shelves again. When he broke back into the foyer, he saw Angela down the black and gold archway, still knelt on her mat with a shi in her hand. The two of them were quite close, Toth knew, but he wondered what the limits of their relationship were. He knew where their histories first connected, what had happened to Neti's parents, and what Angela had been through before even that point in time. Surely, Udug trading souls with her drew upon his sympathy for her struggles. He couldn't imagine what that would be like.

"Don't you remember she tried to drown you?" a voice asked. Melech was leaning against a black pillar. Underneath his hood, the white light of moss stones on the walls illuminated the scar across his forehead. He was staring at Angela, watching her. "I heard what you said to the boy. It seems that you have taken a new opinion of her. Why is that?"

Toth thought for a moment before speaking, knowing he had to tread lightly. There was no denying what he said or his actions in training Angela, so he shrugged. "I don't deny it. No matter what book I throw at her, she devours it. Her eagerness to learn and her willingness to fight for what she believes is right reminds me of my days before the Council. I think, if we all look hard enough, we can find common ground with her. This doesn't have to end in violence."

Melech scoffed. "Okay, *Ruchin*. All I see is how forgetful you are. She's a danger to us all. The more she learns, the closer she gets to Maulkatu and the closer the trap is to springing."

Toth's eyes narrowed. "Melech, you know more than you let on. Are you keeping secrets from the rest of the Council?"

Melech laughed, his smile hiding something as he said, "We all know more than we show, don't we?"

ANGELA ROSE FROM THE GROUND WITH A GRIN ON HER face. *Thirty minutes, maybe? That doesn't seem too long for a dozen shi, I think.* She brought one of the burnt remnants to her nose and sniffed it. *Urine?* She shook her head and almost gagged, wondering what kind of mineral made it smell that way.

Heading back to the library, she found Toth and Neti

leaning over a chart spread out on a table. They spoke quietly and traced lines with their fingers as she approached.

"What do you have there?" Angela asked, dropping the shi in front of them.

Toth's brows rose as he glanced up. They were looking at a map. "This is some of the lower caverns around Eld Kur. Neti wanted me to show him approximately where his great-grandparents would have lived before the city was destroyed."

Angela tipped her head. "This old map tells you that? I'm surprised records reach back that far."

"I wouldn't bet my life on these. They are little more than hearsay, but I would trust them enough to point out an area."

Neti shuffled his feet. "It's not that I want to search for it or anything. We have better things to do, but now I know how to cross-reference these old records and these maps."

She knew he was trying to hide his interest in his lineage, and she wouldn't dare dissuade him from that.

"I see you've finished," Toth said, motioning to the burnt remains on the table. "How did you fare? Did it get any easier for you as you went?"

Angela smiled, remembering what he had said. "It did, but not as easy as blinking, I'm afraid."

He shrugged. "It wouldn't be fair to expect my first Anunnaki student to be perfect, would it? Besides, if you were cutting corners, you'd only be hurting yourself when you actually try a more moderately challenging spell. Now, I'd like you to go through this." He retrieved a green cloth book from the table behind him and slid it to her.

Scrying with Your Mind.

"If you remember," he began, "I mentioned before how

the spell you found in the Scratched Hall seemed similar to one I already knew. This book contains the basics for that spell. Scrying is a way of linking your mind to your soul and detaching the former from your physical being to see beyond the veils. Of course, it's not as simple as looking through a window. You must become hyper-aware of the aura of souls, and you must touch and feel your way through the worlds with a sort of blind sense. Primarily, it can only function to find other souled people. As long as you are familiar enough with the aura of their soul, you can find it."

Angela's jaw dropped. This was it. This was how Shedim found her, and she could use it to find Maulkatu as well. She wanted to squeal in giddiness. It couldn't have been any easier than this! What a break! She grabbed the book and plopped onto the chair, ready to dig into it, but Toth put his hand on hers and drew her gaze back to him.

"I will forewarn you before we begin. This spell is not like the last. There is a risk that you could slip too far away from yourself. If the soul loses grip and the mind wanders free, you will become detached from your own body and become lost and unconscious. Eventually, even the soul will slip away, too, and you will cease to be."

Neti shook his head and waved his arms side to side. "No. I don't like this, Angela. The risk seems too high, and you've only just cast your first spell."

She grinned. "It'll be no problem. If there wasn't motivation before, there definitely is now. I won't screw this up."

"Good," Toth said. He put down another stack of books and slid them closer to her. "Once you've finished reading that book, you'll use these to translate your rubbing. I hope you didn't think I would do that for you."

The spine of the old spell book creaked as she opened it. "Not at all."

The councilman left her to her studies while Neti tried to talk her out of it for nearly ten minutes. But her mind was made up. After he let her be, the hours passed quickly. *Scrying with Your Mind* spoke briefly about how scrying the living and the dead were similar, like Toth had mentioned, but she learned that the former required a much higher amount of energy since she might need to push herself into another world entirely. Keeping the link between the soul in her body and her wandering mind grew harder the farther it was from her.

She wondered how vital her concentration was to staying on target and if her mind would take her to Michael automatically, just like having a clear picture in her mind aided her when she teleported. Angela thumbed her way forward through the pages, skimming a few that seemed to be lingering on the nature of souls. She'd heard all that before and assumed she was at least beyond such fundamental teachings.

While the spell book was thin and easy to read, it was much more difficult to use the thick dictionaries Toth had left her so she could translate the rubbing she had taken from the Scratched Hall of the Nephilim. By the time she was finished, she was paranoid that she hadn't done it right. There was no way to tell what would happen if she were to mess up any portion of the spell. She understood the basics of both spells in her head but had no practice using them.

She remembered how Udug had failed to cast his spell as he intended it to be. He had wanted to possess Angela's body entirely, but they ended up trading souls. While the dead councilman was better able to hide it from his people, Angela couldn't. Knowing that the Virtuoso before Toth had failed made her even more afraid. There was something terrifying about projecting herself out of her own body, and she was afraid that small details could have slipped past her.

If she failed, she could only hope it wouldn't kill her and anything less would be fixable. She took a deep breath and rewrote the last symbol in her notebook. A quick double-check satisfied her that everything she'd written was an exact match to what was on the wall. Now, the only question was if she could translate them correctly. But she straightened her back, knowing the foundation of her spell was correct.

What she had thought meant "mirror," or "a mirror-like finish," was really more along the lines of a replicate image. And based on the context of the sentence, she assumed it was trying to tell her to picture Michael with almost impossible clarity. Her mind would be the mirror.

She smiled and stretched in her seat, feeling that she'd done everything she, or anyone else, could possibly do to prepare. The only thing now was one final check, and she rose from her chair. The library had grown empty and quiet without her noticing, and the stiffness of her back and legs made her wonder how long she had been at it.

Neti was asleep in a padded reading chair on the outer edge of the common area while Toth rested his head in his hand over a book on the table. His eyes were fluttering, but he looked up when she approached.

Opening her notebook to a page, she held it out to him and said, "This is as far as I can take it, but I think I've got it."

The councilman raised an eyebrow. "That is very confident of you." He took the notebook from her and skimmed the page quickly before flipping it over. In less than a minute, he closed the book and handed it back. "Looks good enough."

"I'm not stupid, Toth," she said. "I know you might not give a damn if I fail, and I understand that, but if I succeed and find who's behind the missing crystals, that's one less thing keeping me in Kur. You want to do your part and protect your people? Help me do this."

He let out a slow breath as he pondered that. "You ask me to give you skill beyond your experience. Are you a natural at this? Perhaps. But there is one thing you're lacking for that spell."

Angela tilted her head. "You said it looked fine. What could I be missing?"

Toth raised a finger. "Not necessarily a thing. But before I tell you, I wish to quiz you."

Angela shifted to the side, suddenly nervous that maybe she had missed something. She nodded. "Ask away."

The councilman ran his fingers through his red hair and shoved it back behind him. "What happens to a soul when a person dies?"

"It leaves the body behind and returns to the weylines."

"And what are the weylines?"

"Streams of energy—pure and simple."

He snickered. "You will find there is more to it than that. But I digress. Where are the weylines?"

Angela bit her lip. "Well, I'd assume they leave whatever world the person died in."

"The realm between the veils is vast and unpredictable. It is not just one direction a person travels in, but many. There are twists and turns, and it never ends. Weylines reside in that space."

"So you're telling me that all this time I've been teleporting around, I've just been blind to it? How come I've never seen a weyline or felt one while I was teleporting? I'm sure there would be something, wouldn't there?"

"The void between the worlds is a place of nonexistence. You cannot measure distance or time like you or I understand it. The veils as we understand them are barriers that keep the worlds apart, but the worlds overlap one another. Where we stand right now may very well be underneath the Earth's surface or out in the middle of Dingir's blue expanse. Based on relative coordinates, we could be in three places at once. The veils are what hold us in our separate worlds and force us to expel great effort to breach them. Understand so far?"

Angela nodded.

"There are places in every world where the veil is exceptionally weak. It makes it much easier to push beyond the barriers while expending less of our limited energy. From a place like that, you could search the void far longer for the weyline that holds your loved one, maybe even break through a second veil and find someone alive on another world."

Angela felt uneasy. "And you know where one of these places is? A place with a weakened veil?"

Toth made a *tisk* sound. "Don't be greedy, Angela. Make me a promise and I may show you." He grinned devilishly.

She shrugged. "All right, name it."

"Promise you will not kill another Dalkhu during this investigation of yours. No matter what you find."

Angela laughed. "I can't promise that."

"But you must—I insist. The place I might show you is another of the Council's great secrets, passed down from one to the next through text and old rules. Is trading the ability to talk with a lost loved one whenever you wish not worth this small compromise?"

"Fine," Angela muttered. "If I have to, so be it. But don't think I won't injure the bastard when I find who's responsible."

Toth grinned. "I wouldn't expect you to bring them in with hugs and kisses."

CHAPTER THIRTEEN

The morning after was quiet. Thoughts of Donny's safety and finding Michael's soul resurfaced in her mind all night, keeping her awake. In the darkness, she rose and carefully pushed aside the table barricade and settled into the rocking chair in the living room. She pondered her notes for a few hours and wished that she could reread *Scrying with Your Mind*, but Toth would not budge or let her take it to her chamber.

He had also demanded that they sleep before trying to cast the scrying spell. He retired for the night, and Melech the Teacher took guard in the tunnel outside their room. Not until Neti came swaying out of the bedroom with bloodshot eyes did it come time for them to leave. As they walked through the weaving tunnels, she couldn't help but feel uneasy with Melech watching behind her. Something about the way he looked at her, or maybe his scarred face, made her feel uncomfortable.

When they stepped out of the tunnel's confines and into the open cavern that housed the Kissum and glowing moss above, she spotted Toth leaning against the old wooden handrail. Approaching him, she said, "Are you ready for me to show you how it's done?"

Toth laughed, a grin peering out from beneath his black hood. "I think so. Are there any pressing questions you have before I take you there?"

"Let's say she does manage to separate her mind from her body," Neti said, crossing his arms and stepping forward. "Would it help if I reach out to her and keep a hold on her, too?"

The councilman shook his head. "There is little that anyone can do to help her once she slips away, and that may also lead to undesirable effects. What if you're the one that becomes lost? Or what if her mind loses touch with her soul and falls into a panicked frenzy, then pulls your mind out of your body as well? These are the dangers of spells. Just because one person failed in one way and had a certain effect doesn't mean that it can be replicated or stopped, even. Everyone is different, and there are no guarantees."

Angela bit her lip and wondered if she really was ready to put herself into a situation like that. Anunnakis weren't spellcasters to begin with. Her people had shied away from those sorts of things so long ago, and maybe it was for a good reason.

She shook the thought from her mind. Finding Michael, then Maulkatu, was more important than her. "I'm ready. I understand the risks."

Toth tilted his head to the side. "Very well." He reached into his robe and produced a bundle of hide cinched shut by string. As he untied it, the fur fell away and revealed a jagged glowstone large enough to fill his palm. He took her hand and Neti grabbed hold of her elbow, and together they vanished in a blast of air that resounded through the cavern.

When reality snapped back around her again, she stood

there in awe. They were inside another cave, this one much smaller but also more marvelous than Kur. The stones were smooth and looked like they were made of wax, yet tiny fragments shimmered and reflected the glowstone's light. All around her, the colors changed from blue to purples and dark reds. One corner was intensely green, and the opposite was yellow. In the distance, glistening light carried down a crevice in the cavern, illuminating a single stalagmite hanging from the ceiling, displaying all the shades and colors of the cavern like the layers of a cake.

Angela walked toward it and examined their surroundings for a while. Toth and Neti followed behind her until they stood in the light. She asked, "There's no tunnels out of here. How was this place found?"

Toth shrugged. "By accident, most likely."

"Is this even a part of Kur?"

"No one knows for certain. It could be considered a different world entirely."

"And what about all of these?" She walked to an outcrop just outside the light, the stone crunching like gravel underneath her feet. People had scratched into the cliff's rock, filling the wall with at least five to ten square feet of words.

"It's tradition to carve the name of the person you are searching for. Helps concentration, they say."

Angela glanced back at the councilman. "Sounds superstitious to me."

"It could be," Toth said, "but it doesn't hurt."

Angela bent and picked up a glimmering rock from the ground. "Well, just because I'm the first Anunnaki here doesn't mean I'll break that tradition." She smiled and began to look for a good place to write a name but paused when she found her own etched into the stone. Then a second and a third. The more she looked, the more she spotted her own name in the sea of names. It was infuriating and terrifying.

"Someone's been watching me…" she muttered.

"Are you surprised? How else do you think Shedim found your home? It is unsurprising compared to your assumption that you'll be able to cast this spell. Entertaining, really." Toth grinned.

"Doesn't sound like you want me to succeed." She turned back to the wall and scraped her stone against it. The rock crumbled and broke apart like it was made of bread.

"Your success is mine, Angela. I wish you the best, but I simply do not think you are prepared."

Angela shrugged. "I've never been prepared for anything in my life, yet I seem to get by."

She stepped away from her carving that read *Michael*. "You know, I've seen a bunch of places, but this has to be the most beautiful one I've seen. Does it have a name?"

Toth smiled. "The best-hidden things have no names."

"Fair enough." She sat cross-legged on the floor, took a deep breath, and stirred her souls awake. Neti came and sat in front of her, his eyes darting as his nerves took hold of him.

"Are you sure you want to cast this?" he asked. His boyish features glimmered with sweat. "Is it worth risking what we have gained? You and me, our relationship, just to talk to Michael again?"

That hurt her a bit. She treasured Neti like a son, watched him grow into the young man he was, and now he was questioning their bond. "I want you to trust me on this, support me in it. This is the best path we can take. The sooner I find Michael and know I can scry without losing myself, the sooner we can find who we're looking for and get out of Kur. Things can go back to how they were once Teshub is avenged and we can be sure that there's no threat to any of the worlds."

Neti's eyes dropped to his fingertips. He fidgeted for a moment and said, "If you think it's best," then rose to his feet. He walked out of her sight, and Angela wondered if she had said something wrong.

Toth's smooth voice echoed through the cavern behind her. "This spell could lead you nowhere, leave you drifting through the void between worlds for eons. You could even become entangled with someone else's soul, yet you move forward with it. I'll be honest with you, Angela. Few people have this bravery to set off into unknown territory and try to catch a glimpse of pure, unfiltered life as we know it. I admire it. Take solace in that searching for someone dead is easier than finding someone alive. Stay in the void and you'll be all right."

Angela twisted around and looked Toth in his green eyes. "Thank you for your insight today and before. I mean it."

He simply nodded. "Keep your thanks and uphold your end of the bargain. My people's well-being is my only interest, not the war between you and the Council or between your people and mine."

Angela chuckled and faced forward. "Yet another councilman claims to be peaceful. Either I've been wrong about most of you for a long time or you're all fantastic liars."

ANGELA SLAMMED HER PALM ON THE FLOOR. SWEAT dripped down her forehead and puddled on the stone. As she was resting on her knees, her lungs pumped air and her heart raced. "Dammit! This is impossible!"

Neti came up to her and placed his hand on her back. "We should stop this."

Toth laughed from somewhere behind her. "No, I don't believe it is. Spells are simply a rather unnatural way to use one's soul and mind. Making the effects intentional is hard for every beginner. I told you that you were not experienced enough."

Angela scowled. "If it's so easy, why don't you show me how to do it?"

"Bitter, bitter, Angela. You are doing yourself no good by getting upset. Should we call it a day?"

She straightened her back and took a deep breath, shrugging Neti off her. "No, I'm fine." Breathing slowly helped her frustration subside. If Toth was right, her anger wouldn't help. "The sooner I get this over with, the better." Neti's eyes were full of fear, but she ignored him. He didn't understand what Michael had meant to her. She had to see this through.

"Agreed," Toth said. He circled around her, stopping in front to hold up a finger. "Just remember: you must be balanced between the mind, the conjurer of thought, the soul, the source of energy, and the heart, the fountain of meaning and intent. The reason the Council holds my own abilities so highly isn't because I have a particularly sharp mind or my soul is stronger than most. It's because I've found balance at a young age. My biggest challenge was controlling myself and not allowing my emotion to interfere.

"You must look at yourself critically and determine what must change. If I were to guess, it would be your heart, too. You have much of it. Surely you know that when it comes to projecting yourself or others through the veils, emotion gives a spark to the soul and pushes it to give its entire effort, but it does not give you more control over that energy. Take my word for it. I *am* the best Virtuoso, even though I'm the only one alive." He smiled smugly.

"What is this new Toth?" Angela asked, astounded. "Making jests? Not sure I like him too much."

He shrugged and his smile faded away. "Try again." He turned his back from her and walked out of the light.

"I was just trying to make light of it, Toth."

"Doesn't matter. Try again."

She sighed. *He really doesn't know how to have fun.* But Angela did her best to clear her head, and the spell began again with a humble trance. She closed her eyes and simply listened—not with her ears, but with her mind, soul, and heart. The mind was quick enough, sharp, and the heart strong, but the souls inside her were two very different things.

Hers was content, happy to be alive, and a part of her, but Udug's soul, the Dalkhu part of her, stirred and created a torrent inside her chest. It raged against her Anunnaki soul, wanting nothing more than to be free of its confines. She stirred them both alive with her mind, waking them from their slumber and drawing out their energy. A warm feeling spread throughout her body, and all of her fatigue washed away.

With her mind, she begged them to apply force, to push her own mind out of her body. Slowly, she felt the pressure build, and her mind pushed against the veil all around her. It was a soft, gentle shove that broke her free. Like a subtle wink, she drifted away from her body. Panic gripped her as she lost all physical feeling, and she almost lost touch with her souls immediately. Thoughts of Michael kept her together. She had to keep his curly brown hair, his tall and slender frame, and her love for him on her mind.

Her pushing souls gave her motion forward and into the space between the worlds. It was hard at first for her to concentrate on keeping in touch with her own souls and Michael at the same time, but it grew easier as she went. As long as she felt their propulsion, she knew that she was still all right.

She remembered walking with Michael along Dingir's outer edge, the way he smelled and his gentle touches, but more than anything, she recalled who he was. The husband that fought to give her anything and everything she ever wanted. The guy who guarded her ferociously and never let her feel alone. He had wanted a child, but Angela never did. She wished she'd had considered it now.

With his image in her mind, she screamed, *Michael!*

The shout seemed to drift on and on through the endless expanse. She kept pushing herself onward for what seemed like days, even weeks, and when she thought she couldn't give any more, she did. It was quiet between the veils, and it seemed like she was the only one walking down those blank halls.

Angela begged her souls to push her harder, demanded that their energies carry her voice farther, to wherever Michael's soul was waiting for her. She *needed* him and craved, more than anything, to hear his voice again and feel his presence. Ever since she'd seen the spell carved on the Scratched Hall, he was all that she could think about.

Then there was something unusual: a faint brush against the furthermost edges of her mind. She concentrated on it, and the picture of a blue orb, glowing bright in the great expanse of nothing, appeared in her mind's eye and jittered side to side.

Michael! she screamed. It was him, without a doubt. Just the way he *felt* was familiar, reminding her of lazy mornings in bed next to this very feeling. He relaxed her, gave her confidence and peace. There was a greatness to his aura that she could do nothing but adore and love. The Michael she remembered was right in front of her.

It's me, Angela. I'm here. Please, say something.

The blue orb hovered there, as clear as day, and shifted excitedly. The emotion of joy washed over her. Michael *was* joyful and happy at her presence, too.

Michael... While she could no longer feel her body, she didn't doubt that she was crying. She had missed him so badly and grown desperate for his presence in any form.

I love you, she thought.

And she felt his love in return. She wanted to fall over and bawl or get up and wrap her arms around him, but she couldn't move. Either she would snap back into her body or she'd lose it entirely.

Do you remember when you told me you wanted a child? Angela asked. *I wish I would have seen things your way and we had one.*

A feeling that Angela did not expect emanated from Michael: confusion.

Don't you remember?

There was silence. And then his soul slipped away and began to fade into the distance.

Michael, don't you remember?

The void grew quiet again, and she could barely feel his presence anymore as he seemed to pull away from her. She cried out for him again and took off in his trail, but he did not respond. The glow around his soul dimmed as Angela pushed herself after him.

Michael, she called. *Don't go anywhere. I need you.*

It grew hard to keep pace with him. Every second she urged herself faster, the more likely it became that she would lose touch with herself. But luckily for her, he grew brighter again, and she closed the distance between them. His picture became clearer, and she saw that something else was in the void with them. A large black mass hovered all around her.

Strings of energy tethered him to an ocean of pure black. The energy flexed, flowed, and shifted. She felt it travel down a tendril, through Michael's soul, and out another tendril like he was a small piece in this great sea of energy. Cautiously, she reached out to it and felt that the black stream was made of souls.

Michael dove deeper into it, the blackness swallowing his soul. Something about it was not right. She felt danger and malevolent intent seeping from all the entities around her. And then the black pulsed and throbbed. Angela pushed herself in, determined to pull Michael from whatever was swallowing his soul, but the more she burrowed her way through, the more the black fought her until it was almost an unbearable pressure on her mind.

There were eyes everywhere in the black, staring at her. Staring *through* her. She felt the sea tense and close in around her like it was going to crush her and trap her there. It raced along the edges of her mind, following her consciousness back. Eventually it would find her souls, she knew, and coil around her like a snake. The black was vile, and it was going to kill her.

Angela raced to retreat, and Michael disappeared from her vision almost instantly. She begged that her souls pull her back into her body as the imposing black presence came closer and closer to her. It was going to hook her by the mind and rip her out of her own body.

She jumped when her mind returned to her body and reality snapped back together. Her hands were shaking, and she lurched to her feet, desperate to move anywhere away from there. Neti was there, trying to grab her and console her, but she couldn't hear him until her panicked breathing caused her to faint.

When the black subsided, she saw Toth and Neti looking down on her. As he cradled her head, she sobbed.

"What happened?" Toth asked. He crouched next to her, but Angela turned away so he couldn't look at her face.

"Something has him. It was big, like a sea that could move and think. It was absorbing, pulling him into it. I tried to go after him, but it tried to *kill* me."

The councilman narrowed his eyes as he looked down at her between strands of disarrayed red hair, confusion in his eyes. "He's become a part of a weyline, Angela, one of the streams of energy where all souls are born from and return to."

She grabbed hold of his arms and shook. "No, this wasn't something like a river or a stream. I mean, it was, but it was like it had *thought*. Intention, purpose. Between all the rage and anguish and the way it came after me, I could tell that it wanted to pull me from my body. Squash me like a bug."

Toth let out a long exhale. "Where are you, Angela? Considering the amount of stone here, it's likely we're in a dimension close to Kur or the stone elemental plane. Would it not make sense that a majority of the souls in that weyline would be particularly attuned to Kur? And if so, would the weyline not try to push you out because you are half Anunnaki? Maybe it would even try to kill you because it does not know your kind, and perhaps it does act like it has a mind of its own. Some of the elder Dalkhu claimed that souls give us characteristics and nature. They are alive and unique."

"Then why is Michael in a *Dalkhu* weyline? He's an Anunnaki, and he died on Earth, not Kur. What's he doing there?"

Toth contemplated it for a moment with a finger on his lip. "He might have died on Earth, but isn't that considered to be in the middle of all dimensions? His soul could have wound up anywhere, don't you think?"

Angela raised her hands. "I don't know. You should be telling me."

"I'm sorry I don't have more for you. The weylines have never been actively studied."

She rose to her feet, furious, and grabbed Neti and Toth by their clothes and prepared to teleport them back to Kur, but she paused. Suddenly, she was afraid that there was something out there, between the veils, that wanted her dead.

"I believe you," Neti said. "We both do."

That gave her little peace.

Toth rested a hand on her shoulder. "I assure you, Angela, with all the experience I have, Michael is safe. And so are you."

"I hope you're right," Angela said. "Let's... call it a day."

CHAPTER FOURTEEN

Neti leaned his shoulder against the chamber wall. The candlelight alone was barely enough to illuminate Angela's face as she rocked on the chair and chewed on her nails. He wished he could help somehow, but it seemed like her fear was something she would have to overcome by herself.

"Are you sure you don't want to come with?" he asked. "Maybe Toth can get you a few more books that will help you find Maulkatu. Once we find him and either prove or disprove that he's the one that stole the crystal shards, we can leave Kur and focus on rebuilding our home. Maybe even move somewhere else and start new."

Angela tucked her hair behind her ear and sighed. "I don't know if any of that is possible anymore, Neti." Tears were forming in her eyes, but she wiped them away. "You have no idea what I saw. What I felt. There's something out there, and just thinking about reaching into the veils to look for Maulkatu is terrifying. I-I don't know if I can do it again."

Neti walked to the chair, knelt, and put a hand on hers.

"You're right. I don't have any clue what it was like, but I believe you even if Toth doesn't. Maybe staying behind today and just resting is what you need."

Angela grabbed his wrist softly. "No. I don't want you out there alone anymore. This place is… It's chaos. Councilmen working behind each other's backs, the secrets, the lies. It's not safe here for either of us."

"I'll be all right," he said, gently pulling her from him. "I'll keep to the Kissum and markets, and if someone tries anything, I'll come back here. There will be nothing to worry about."

She shook her head. "If there's one thing I've learned about Kur, it's that there is *always* something to worry about. If you feel you can get us a step closer to getting out of here, so be it, but please be careful."

Neti rose to his feet, and her eyes followed him upward. "I will," he swore.

The thinner councilman with curly blond hair, whose name he could not recall, was standing outside their chambers. They exchanged a brief nod to one another, but the man let Neti pass by without a problem. He was grateful for that and felt bad that it was Angela they didn't trust to be alone.

When he walked fifty paces down the tunnel, he slashed the veil with his mind and stepped between the worlds. The cold overtook him and froze his breath until he arrived again just outside the market square. His loud arrival startled an older woman on the side of the street. He apologized promptly, but she waved him off.

The long tread up the black stairs wore him out more than he liked to admit. He couldn't count the number of times he'd gone up and down them over the past week, let alone how many steps there were. Through the Kissum's massive double doors, he spotted a few councilmen, their hoods up, just inside the main foyer. He couldn't tell who they were and didn't care to stick around long enough for them to notice him, so he continued toward the library.

There, he dug up the old genealogical histories of councilmen both alive and dead, then brought them to a table in the study area. There were a few soldiers, dressed in black robes with green and yellow cords, there with him, but they paid him no mind. That was a benefit of being dressed in a tunic and breeches. He probably looked more like an apprentice stoneworker than anyone of importance.

Considering that Maulkatu was their priority interest, he began with a scroll of the Hazi family. It was a thick tree, full of lineage that was traced back to before the Dalkhu uprising against the Nephilim, or so the scroll claimed. Branches broke off from branches until the entire thing was a confusing mess of lines and names. Finding Maulkatu was hard enough, and it was disappointing to discover that the scroll was so outdated that he wasn't even listed as a councilman. Since Angela had met him on Earth, at least twenty years must have passed since it was last updated.

With such a large family, how did no one take the time to update these?

Neti pushed the thought from his mind, ran his fingers through his hair, then pressed his hands into his face, distraught. *Where is this going to take me? I'd be better off trying to find him the old-fashioned way.* But physically searching for him would be just as pointless, to a degree. When a councilman disappeared, he did so for a reason, Neti assumed. Knowing that Angela was in Kur, he wouldn't be around the Kissum, wandering the city streets, or even in his own home.

If I was a councilman who felt that his people were

being exterminated, I would try to find a place or a way
that I could ensure that my people would be safe from
whatever was currently threatening them, even if it meant
breaking traditions or laws... Just like Udug tried to do
with Angela.

Neti rose to his feet, irritated and impatient. He knew
what he needed to do and who he needed to go to, but he
hadn't wanted to admit it. After scooping up his things and
putting every book and scroll back where he found them,
he left the library and walked down the black and white
marble archway, toward the Kissum's main foyer. For a
time, only soldiers passed through, but eventually, Ruchin
entered.

The elder councilman noticed him almost immediately.
"Neti," he said, his long gray beard swaying as he hobbled
to him. "What brings you here today? And without Angela
again, I see."

Neti nodded. Out of all the councilmen, he trusted
Ruchin the most with the truth. "Angela isn't feeling like
herself today. She's staying in the chamber until
tomorrow."

Ruchin stroked his chin. "Toth told me what happened
yesterday. It seems she could not handle the might of the
weylines, but it is impressive she's cast a second spell in
such a short time, I admit."

"We have Teshub to thank for her grasp of the funda-
mentals, I believe."

"I suppose so," the councilman said, his expression
turning sour.

Neti felt guilty. "I'm sorry. I forgot you two used to
know each other."

"We more than knew each other. Teshub was practically
my brother. I loved him like one, but he was a damned fool

and threw away his position on the Council and betrayed me behind my back, all for a woman he could not seem to leave behind."

Neti's eyes narrowed. "Are councilmen not allowed to marry?"

"No," Ruchin said, "but it does not matter. I hate bringing up those old scars. Let's move on, shall we? Is there something I can help you with today?"

Here it goes. Neti swallowed. "Is there someplace we can talk more privately?"

The councilman's bushy eyebrows rose. "Well, yes. Come with me."

Ruchin placed a gentle hand on Neti's shoulder and gently turned him toward the arched hallway behind him. Ruchin led him left from the main foyer and they walked through the training areas used by soldiers and teachers. The councilman produced a key from his robe and unlocked a dark oak door that Neti hadn't noticed before. Once inside, they settled into a smaller, more private library with a large round table and thirteen chairs.

The old man groaned as he sat. "What is it you wish to talk about?"

Neti was nervous. He could feel the sweat on his palms and wiped them on his breeches. *Be assertive,* he told himself. "I'll be honest, Ruchin. Coming to Kur and learning more about my people has been eye-opening, but I also have to be upfront and say that our patience is running thin."

Ruchin's gray eyes weighed him cautiously. He stroked his beard in thought, then said, "You say 'our' as in both you and Angela?"

"I speak for both of us, yes. I need you to understand something and tell the other members of the Council. It's clear that we see things differently, but the Council needs to know that Angela doesn't want to be here any more than you. Give her what she wants."

The councilman grumbled. "You mean give her Maulkatu. Don't play me for a fool, boy. You can try to coat your tongue in snake oil but you are not a councilman. I see through it."

Shit. Embarrassment rippled through Neti, but he steeled himself. "You're right. I'm asking that you hand over Maulkatu. She doesn't want to be here, but until she feels that no one on the Council is stealing crystal shards, she won't leave. She's too stubborn for that."

Ruchin rose to his feet. "We have opened our doors to her—and to you. Given you a place to sleep and shown you secrets that only we know. Yet she is still unhappy with our transparency. She cannot stand the idea that she is not in control here, that she cannot deal justice as she sees it, without reprimand. I have heard whispers in the Council that Maulkatu is poised and waiting for her to act. If you were wise, you would do something for yourself, boy. Leave her before she brings his wrath down upon herself."

WITH A WARM CUP OF TEA IN HER HAND, ANGELA reflected on times when things were simpler. Her notebook on her lap and her eyes staring at nothing in particular, she rocked the morning away and tried to relax. She thought back on the time she'd spent with Neti and Teshub, the sinkhole in springtime, Tarsus, and the things she'd been fighting for, but more than anything, she tried to make sense of what she'd seen between the veils.

Could the weyline truly be a living stream of souls? If so, why was it so malevolent?

The air shook, filling her chamber with a blast and slamming against her eardrums. She was on the ground on her hands and knees as her cup flew across the room. Recovering, she threw herself upright and lurched toward the cloaked man, fists clenched. It was him. Black robes, an undyed cord, but this time, the fabric concealing the face underneath his hood was red.

There was no time for words and no need to speak them. Angela threw a hook with her left, then jabbed for the masked man. Each swing, he bent and twisted away until his back was against the wall. He chuckled behind his mask, and a rush of air blew her hair into her eyes. As she stepped back and cleared her vision, another man came growling out of the bedroom, dagger in hand.

Something *cracked* into her ribs. Pain exploded in her side, and she toppled onto the floor. The masked man was on top of her, gripping her throat before she could realize where the blow had come from. He raised a fist and smashed it into her lips and nose. Uselessly, she raised her arms, but he pushed her down and struck her until all she could see, smell, or taste was her own blood.

Her memory lapsed. There was only pain and blood for a time. Voices were muffled and indistinct. Then she was on her knees and she couldn't remember how she had gotten there. Every cough rattled her side. A pair of sandaled feet were at her head, and she looked up at the masked man looming over her. Through the holes cut into the gray fabric, she could see that his eyes were a yellow as bright as a candle. He twisted a curved, silver knife in his hand, letting the light shimmer off it.

Something was holding him back. She could feel it. If

he had wanted her dead, he should have done it already. *Who is he?* A councilman, for sure. One with ties to the five soldiers that surrounded her. For a moment there, her life was in his hands, and he didn't take it. *But why?*

As the masked man contemplated what he was going to do next, Angela chuckled. "Okay."

Her mind ripped open the veils beneath his feet. The ground rumbled as a fissure split open. The stone and flames from another world created a wall between them. Angela rolled backward and staggered to her feet. The fires touched the cavern's roof and instantly made the room blistering hot. The heated ceiling began to turn red as cracks stretched the room's length. The deep sound of the stone ceiling breaking above her was terrifying.

The soldiers came at her with their knives. She caught the first to swing by the wrist and twisted her way behind him. He screamed as she took his own knife and buried it into his back. When she tossed him to the ground, the others paused, but only for a moment. The masked councilman had extinguished the flames and jumped over the fissure, unharmed. Angela wrung her fingers through the brass knuckles in her pockets, a grin on her face as the unnamed assailants assaulted her.

She took the first by surprise, striking his shoulder, then his throat, leaving him gasping on the floor. The last three surged at her from the left. Ducking and weaving, she sidestepped behind her chair as her mind raced out and latched onto one of them. He disappeared and reappeared in a fraction of a second, fast enough that there was no concussive blast of air. He was burning and screaming for a second more, then dead on the floor. It only took a moment in that fiery world to kill him.

The other two were on her, slashing for her face and

abdomen. Angela couldn't tell if it was blood or sweat that soaked her, but she kept moving, landing blows when she could and relying on the strength of her souls to keep her moving.

She conjured pillars of stone the width of a fist from the veil, but her focus was stretched and her aim was off. The councilman stayed in the back, watching eagerly and closing each hole that she opened in the veil. That irritated her, and she meant to do something about it when one of the men came slamming into her side. He wrapped his arms around her, hugging her arms down at her sides. She could feel the heat of his breath on her cheek as the others moved in.

Angela and the soldier disappeared from the chamber with a crash. There was a great chance that his silver knife was pointed directly at her, but she could not turn her head to see when she was between the worlds. Frozen, and despite his best efforts to push them back into Kur, she bought herself some time to ponder things. The moment they broke through, he'd plunge his dagger into her unless she thought of something cunning.

Teleporting them into an ocean would be pointless; he would still stab her. The dimension of blustering winds would likely rip her arms off as much as pulling him off her. Falling through the sky in Dingir wouldn't help, either. She was running out of ideas.

What about Earth? The dimension of rock and stone?

Stone. That was it.

Angela set her mind's eye on her chamber in Kur, particularly the outer wall of the bedroom. There was no furniture there, and she imagined arriving with her shoulder nearly leaning against the wall before making the final plunge back into reality. She bolted to the side as the atmosphere pressed against her and the soldier appeared *inside* the wall. The edge of his dagger sliced her cottons and the muscle on her lower back. She bellowed as the ground rushed up to meet her. Flashes of lightning shot through her right leg.

Two limp forearms, wrists, and dangling fingers protruded from the wall. Thick cracks spiderwebbed throughout the rock, blood emerging and dripping down to pool on the ground.

More than anything, she wanted to lay her head back on the ground and sleep. Her souls waned, but she pushed to her feet and grabbed the sword from her bed before stepping into the living room. The masked councilman and last soldier turned around to face her as she emerged from the bedroom. She had only been gone seconds to him, but for her, it had been weeks. She was exhausted, but she pulled Teshub's sword from its scabbard and took the fool's stance. He chuckled once, then disappeared from the room in a blast of air.

Just like that, he was gone, and other than the crackling sound of cooling stone, silence settled over the room. With a sigh, Angela walked into the outer tunnel. The councilman who was supposed to be guarding her was gone. Tipped off or maybe even involved in the attack. To her misfortune, she couldn't even remember who it was. Everything was a haze, and the rush of battle was leaving her numb.

She retreated inside the room and sat back down on her chair to rest until the sound of sandals slapping against stone came from the hallway. Ruchin stepped through the blue curtain first, eyes wide and his beard swaying from side to side as he first noticed the fissured, broken floor. Then he noticed her and gnashed his teeth.

Neti entered behind him, just as bewildered, then rushed to her side.

"You're hurt," he said, taking a handkerchief from his pocket and offering it to her nose.

Silent, Angela pushed his hand away as Ruchin stepped forward.

"What happened here?" He pointed at her like she was a dog to be scolded.

Her blood boiled, and she rose to her feet, shaking from the pain. "Someone. Attacked. Me. So think twice before you come in here with that attitude."

Ruchin frowned. "Who was it?"

"I don't know, and I doubt I'll be able to find out, unless you can identify hands."

"Hands?"

She motioned to the bedroom. Toth, who had entered shortly after Neti, poked his head through the doorway and gasped with a hand over his mouth. The councilman entered no farther and only shook his head.

Ruchin turned back to Angela, a solemn look in his eyes like it tore him deeply to say, "You shouldn't have come here, Anunnaki. All you bring with you is death and a game that some councilmen are too eager to join you in." He looked to the floor. "I fear I've failed my own people by allowing you to be here as long as I have. You should have known this was going to happen again. Those who move against you, they want this. Strife will give them the revenge they seek. You know it."

Maulkatu and Melech?

Toth removed his hood as he stepped closer, his green eyes glimmering as he said, "I agree. Finish your business, Anunnaki."

That angered her even more. Whatever friendship they

had developed was instantly crushed by that remark. The only reason he brought her race into it was to remind her that she was something different here. Something shameful.

Her lip curled as her body tensed. "You'll have to get used to me," she said through gritted teeth, "because my investigation is now a hunt. Maulkatu will be mine."

CHAPTER FIFTEEN

S he was sitting on her bed cross-legged when Neti stormed back in, carrying the smell of ash from the living area with him. The curtain between the bedroom and the living room was nothing but burnt scraps now.

Through meditation, she'd been channeling some of her souls' energy into her body for the better part of an hour. Teshub had told her once that a body invigorated with soul energy would heal faster, and so far, it seemed true. The pain from her broken nose had subsided and the cuts on her stomach had scabbed, but when she stretched her legs out in front of her, one of them tore open again.

"I know you're mad at me," she said, holding her stomach for a moment. "You have hardly said a word."

Neti sighed as he sat on his own bed, fiddling with his thumbs before he spoke. "A little. I don't understand how we keep getting into this position. Well, actually, I do. It's just... Why are we always involved in the fighting? Does it come to us naturally... or are we asking for it?" He stared at the floor as he thought, afraid to make eye contact with her.

It was a valid question she didn't take offense to. She had spent many years pondering that herself, only to discover that when something needed to be done, it didn't matter. "You know I wouldn't be here any longer, fighting like *this*, if I didn't believe that there was something serious going on." She motioned to the fissure she'd created in the ground. "Crystals and councilmen missing can't be good."

Neti crossed his arms and gauged her for a moment. He was being cautious and taking care to form his thoughts.

Out of fear of my response?

"What if the whole 'crystals are missing' thing is a ploy?" he asked finally. "Maybe Ja'noel just wanted to get you concerned enough to fight for Dingir again. He wants to trust you, so he gives you a goose to chase after. Once you're back, he gives you the Etlus like he said he wants to, and Ruchin is just too old to trust his memory. Sure, Shedim killed Teshub. We know that, but we got our revenge. We could be finished here, get out while we can. Dingir, Earth, I don't care. We can forget this ever happened."

Angela shook her head, even though she wished he was right. The chances were just too small. "I can't do that. You should know me better. This councilman, Maulkatu, is a direct threat to me. He's trying to show the rest of the Council that I don't have the strength to withstand them, keep them in check. I can't just walk away from a challenge like that. If I do, someone will become a wise guy if they haven't already, and before we know it, we'll have another Udug on our hands, and I won't let that happen."

Neti lurched to his feet, pointing at the ground. "We already have another Udug, Angela. We *have* to leave.

We're going too deep, and I'm afraid, okay? I'm afraid we won't come out of this alive if we don't stop pushing. This isn't our home. We can't control it!"

Her blood boiled. "You are the one who convinced me that we needed to come to Kur in the first place. Why the change of heart? Whose side are you on?"

He paused, his eyes drifting away from hers. "Ours, of course... I just want what's best for us."

Angela rose to her feet, pulled Teshub's curved sword from the bedside, and carefully slung it over her shoulder. When Neti finally looked at her again, she said, "I'm going to go find Maulkatu and end this. You can come with me or not. Like I've always said, you're free to go and do whatever you want. I won't hold it against you."

He swayed on his feet, unsure how to react, but when Angela began to walk out the doorway, he followed. In the hallway, she found Kanu at his post. His eyes glared out at her from underneath his black bangs, but she walked to him with her chin high, ignoring his expression. Taking his hand and Neti's, she teleported them through the veil and appeared just off the market square in an alley.

The smell of earth mixed with braising meat at a cook-fire at the edge of the market, and the commoners paused only for a moment as they passed. Up the stairs, they climbed behind Angela. No matter what the cost, she would end all councilmen who worked in the shadows. A lick of treachery was all it would take. No one would restore the Anchor, and every last one of them would stay off Earth if they knew what was good for them. Even the Anunnaki. They would all have to piss off now, she swore.

When they reached the final third of the long trek to the Kissum, a voice behind her said, "It's not too late. We don't have to do this."

She turned on the steps. Neti had stopped below her, his arms folded across his chest. "I feel like something terrible is going to happen if we poke the bear one more time."

Angela shrugged. "Can't you see that I'm *forced* to take this further? Ruchin has said that every soldier and councilman that attacks me is a rogue. He says that he can't control those that attack me, my home, and my friends, so I will step in and control them for him." She turned her back to him and continued up the steps, blonde hair swaying behind her.

"This isn't our place," she heard Neti say, but she ignored him and carried on.

In the Kissum's library once more, Angela settled at a table and studied. She scanned book after book and scroll after scroll for hours until she felt that she fully understood the similarity between communicating with a dead person's spirit and scrying someone that was still alive.

Like the dead who have long left us, I have found myself capable of finding those still alive. The closer they are to me, the easier it is. It is my personal opinion that anyone who wishes to try either has two things: a mental image of the target with a "mirror-like" reflection on your mind and a familiarity of the target soul's aetherical resonance. The former is obtained through seeing the person before, to focus the mind, and the latter is acquired with the brushing of minds and souls.

Angela closed the book, then her eyes. Deep breaths calmed her racing heart as she remembered the hungry blackness between the veils. The weyline terrified her, if that was what it truly was, but Maulkatu had to be stopped now. She would not tolerate him and his attacks, his pestering and his humiliation of her. The last thing she would be seen as was weak. The time was now, she knew.

It was simple, matter-of-fact determination that gave her mind leave of her body.

The veils around her flexed under her pressure, but by sharpening her mind, she slipped through unnoticed. The void between worlds was a kaleidoscope of hallways, stretching on into infinity with nothing to be seen. Silencing her own thoughts and picturing the councilman in her mind, she moved forward.

She remembered his tattoos, big black tribal designs that traveled from the top of his scalp and down the back of his neck to his fingers. His piercings were silver and black studs like thick toothpicks in his brows, and his earlobes were stretched with loops. Most importantly, she recalled the feeling that his soul gave off. His aura. His resonance. Distantly, she could feel his vibration travel through the veils like a pebble dropped into water. Slowly, she found the ripple's center and pushed herself through the veil once more.

It was Kur; that much she could tell just by the feeling the world gave her. She was in the same cavernous chamber as him. It was larger than most. By the distance she had traveled, and the aura of her own soul radiating from above, Angela knew she was far below Kur. Even in the ruins of Eld Kur and the Scratched Hall, she guessed.

She was close to him now. So close that she could feel the overwhelming voice of his soul pounding against her mind. It was so loud she almost missed the stirring of another soul there with him. Then another became apparent until there were five altogether. These new souls were hearty and thick compared to Maulkatu's, their auras a stew compared to his soup. It reminded her of her own soul somewhere up above.

The forefront of her mind brushed against his soul. He

hardened, like an orb, then relaxed ever so slightly as though a strain had been released from his shoulders. Maulkatu moved a few steps away, then vanished, along with one of the four heavy souls she did not recognize. A moment later, she felt his aura come from above, from Kur.

And faintly, she heard a signal from her body reach her mind: *boom.*

Angela returned to her body as quickly as she could manage, and once physical sensation returned to her, she rose from the table without a word. Neti glanced up from his book, concerned, and then the muffled *boom* came from somewhere beyond the library. It was distant, but Angela had never heard the crash of teleportation in the Kissum before now. She began to walk.

"What's the matter?" Neti asked from behind her.

Angela didn't answer. She didn't know.

As she left the rows of books behind and paced the archway to the Kissum's main foyer, another blast of teleportation carried down the marble hall. Then a third, louder than all the rest, but the queerest thing was that the pitch seemed lower than normal and the volume so much louder.

Neti and Kanu came up beside her as she entered the massive, domed room. Ruchin and Toth rushed through the mighty doors to the city, dragging a limp corpse inside with them. The body was cloaked in black robes and a red sash. His wrist was limp, and his hands riddled with tattoos. They flipped Maulkatu onto his back violently and loomed over him.

With his hood cast down, his bald skin glistened in sweat and his eyes fluttered as though he was about to fall under, but he didn't appear hurt. His chest rose and fell quickly as though he'd just about overexerted himself doing something. She wondered what it was when a sound like rock being crushed under a mill's stone wheel came from outside. Then something *bellowed* out in the city. Not a horn or a shout, but an animal roar.

Ruchin grabbed hold of Maulkatu by the collar of his robe with one hand and slapped him with the other. "What have you done?"

Angela walked to the front doors of the Kissum and looked out over the city below. The glowing moss on the stalactites above and the torches on the streets below provided just enough light for her to see a beast the height of a horse in the market square. It slunk along on four legs, head low to the ground like a cat prowling. Six claws scraped against the stone with every step it took. Horns grew from the top of its skull, and spikes traveled down its hunched spine.

A young couple dashed from beneath one of the wooden stands, screaming as the creature's neck stretched to four feet in length, opening its hideous maw to snap countless hooked teeth at their ankles.

Then its black eyes locked onto Angela, head twisting like that of a confused dog. It twisted its massive frame, muscles flexing underneath its scales as it shifted its weight. The creature yipped almost as though it was excited before it took a step closer. At first, she wanted to doubt that it was really interested in her, but by the time it crossed half of the market, its eyes never leaving her, she knew the truth. It shifted its weight to the back legs and towered at least fifteen feet tall, roaring as black wings unfurled from its side. The torchlight against the thing's chest made its fish-like scales glimmer a dull reddish color.

Angela took a step backward.

Ruchin was yelling at Maulkatu behind her. "What were you thinking, carrying the Nephilim here?"

A second one, pale green in color, jumped atop a house's roof in a single leap. Its shorter and thinner size was a comfort at first, but when a mirror image of the same color jumped up next to it, Angela trembled. Both of the green twins ruffled their necks when they saw her and leapt down to the market square. The count was up to three.

Maulkatu struggled to lift his head off the ground and pointed with a shaking hand and said, "She is the biggest threat to our people. Last, it was Shedim's life she took. Tomorrow, it could be you, Ruchin."

Ruchin slapped him across the cheek once more, then rose to his feet with clenched fists. "No, I'm quite sure it's you."

Maulkatu laughed as though he hadn't felt a thing, his breath returning to him. "Not after today." With a groan, he sat upright, then climbed to his feet on weary legs. He smiled when Angela stared him in his yellow eyes—the same color as Udug's. "I knew you couldn't resist looking for me. Couldn't keep your nose out of it once, even to save your own life. So I picked up the pact that Shedim left behind and waited for you to find me." He smiled from ear to ear. Angela wanted to punch it off his face.

"What pact are you talking about?" she asked.

The councilman staggered like a drunk but spoke in a clear, vindictive voice. "I was ready to turn my cheek, Angela. Let go and forget what you did to Shedim, but you couldn't keep to yourself *once*! This is not your place, and the Dalkhu people are not yours to command! If the cost of getting rid of you is Nephilim rule, I say let it be so."

A gust blew her hair into her eyes. Shielding herself, she turned toward the sound of heaving lungs. An elephant-sized Nephilim with glittering, golden scales landed on the steps in front of her, its talons the length of her hand. Its great weight shifted on its bones as it heaved itself up the stairs toward her. The mouth was large enough she could climb inside, and maybe even a horse's torso would fit. On the edges of its wings, the gold scales transitioned to a shade of rusted iron. Its eyes were black, just like those of the other three, but as big as her fist.

You.

Angela clutched her head and staggered back into the foyer. It spoke *into* her mind. The Nephilim's eyes never left her as it entered the Kissum's double doors, just barely fitting through. Its neck was at least eight feet long, and every breath was low and rumbling. When it halted in the middle of the domed room, it loomed ten feet over her.

Something most familiar, with you. Met sometime before? What name?

Every word rattled her head with a sharp pain. It was hard to catch her breath. Everything was spinning. The Nephilim were real, and that meant everything about the world before and the Anchor Crystal was, too.

Speak, it demanded, its booming voice clashing against her mind again.

"A-Angela."

I took name Basmu, son of Mir'asku. The Nephilim motioned its great head toward Maulkatu. *That one told me you claim to own ours, by right of strength.*

Angela clutched her head. "I don't know what you're talking about."

Shedim is the son of Dalkhu who found us below, but word from Maulkatu is that you slew Shedim. The beast grumbled from deep within its throat. We *reforged our pact with Maulkatu. Your blood for freedom. Our first attempt failed. You left your home before we arrived. So we burnt everything.*

"You... Nephilim killed Teshub... Shedim brought you to the sinkhole to kill me."

Yes.

Angela shook her head. "But why would Shedim make a deal with you after we've had peace for so long?"

Maulkatu stepped forward, raising his hand. "I can answer that. You brought someone very special to him here two years ago. A rogue from Earth. Do you remember who it was?"

Guilt rippled through her chest to match the pain in her head. "Shedim's brother... Eli."

Basmu's presence brushed against her mind and soul, feeling her in a way she was not familiar with, as if he was soaking in the aura of her souls like a sponge. His voice bellowed in her mind. *Must say, at glance and touch, you do give the feel, the aura, of Nephilim.* His golden head tilted to the side. *But I see where we differ. You are two separate halves in one vessel. Not whole, like us. Interests me.*

The green and red Nephilim entered the chamber and crouched low to the ground with eyes locked onto Angela as they flanked Basmu. The two green ones took to her left, and the red one shifted to the right, moving closer to her flanks with every step. These smaller ones were skin and bones, their rib cages looking sickly.

Maulkatu's smooth voice echoed off the marble walls. "There are liars, murderers, and crazed men and women in every realm of existence. Earth. Dingir and Kur. It doesn't matter where one looks. What all those people bow to is power and strength. It is ever the strong who dictate the fate of the weak and uncivilized. Under the Nephilim, may we find unbiased prosecution and protection. For Shedim and his brother, the councilmen, and others dead at your feet, I pledged myself to them, and in return for their freedom and the ability to travel between the veils, they to me." He crossed his arms, yellow eyes unwavering. "I will finish what Shedim started. Do it, Basmu."

The golden beast roared, his tree-trunk legs shifted, and his jaw reached out to snap her in two. Terror pushed her into motion. It was fight or fly, move or die. One of the green Nephilim turned its attention toward Ruchin and Toth. Someone was going to get hurt, and she had to ensure it wasn't Neti. Drawing Teshub's blade from her shoulder sheath, she *pushed* and reappeared twenty feet in the air a second later. Howling, she dropped from above, sword over her head.

The blade connected with the green creature's neck as she landed, flashing sparks as the edge deflected off the scales and the handle came bouncing back at her. She staggered away. The Nephilim yelped and skittered sideways with a grumble. Her blow cracked a spiderweb in the green scale, but there was no blood, and the creature crouched with its rear legs and snarled viciously.

Shit.

She brought the sword back up in a defensive mid-stance, ready for the thing to come snapping for any part of her body. As the beast readied to pounce, she prepared for a thrust at its mouth or eyes, but the Nephilim came in low, ducking its head to the floor and snapping at her legs. With glancing thrusts, swings, and quick footwork, they repeated the dance until they were in the middle of the foyer.

Every blow seemed useless and more annoying than harmful against its scales, and the thing was too quick for her to hit its black eyes. In the corner of her vision she saw the red Nephilim prowling the outer edge of the room between the pillars and the wall. It roared and began to run and flank her. As she turned to face it, something golden tightened around her waist.

She watched the ground sink away from her feet, then rush up and slam into her. Her body flailed. Everything spun around her. The sword flew from her hand and she slammed into the stone again as she tried to pry Basmu's tail off her. The sharp edges of his scales drew blood.

He flicked his tail and released her, sending her twirling through the air and ramming into a pillar. She could *hear* the sound her ribs made when they snapped, the air rushing out of her chest, and her legs crashing to the floor, numb.

The world oozed and danced around her like a sea of gelatin. She spat the copper from her mouth and nearly fell over when she rose to her feet. Everything hurt. As she cleared her head and wiped the blood dribbling down her lips, Basmu's golden head lowered. He straightened his neck and opened his maw, revealing rows of teeth and a drooling, forked tongue. A sound like crunching rock came from his chest, and the Nephilim shook and convulsed as a thick brown liquid projected from the back of his throat. Hot fire trailed the end of the stream.

It's blue... She remembered what Teshub had said.

It felt like she was living in slow motion. The stream splattered against her shoulder and neck and trailed down her left arm until the fire *whooshed* from her fingertips to her jaw in an instant. She flailed and beat on her shirt, but the liquid had already soaked through and saturated her skin. The flame's heat sent her writhing to the floor, but as quickly as the fire ignited, it faded, too. Only seconds had passed, but it left behind lesions, boils, and a reddening scar with patches of wet, pink flesh from hand to neck.

She tried to push herself up with her right arm, but even the slightest movement hurt the other more. On her knees, she saw that Neti was wide-eyed and terrified. Maulkatu was holding a knife to his throat. Toth was missing, and Ruchin was cowering behind a pillar, but all she could think about was the pain and Neti until Basmu's tail cracked against her head and her eyes closed.

CHAPTER SIXTEEN

Neti watched Angela's head hit the floor. He heard the *crack*. She was out. A shout escaped him, but every muscle in his body refused to move. *Is it over?* He felt weak and dizzy. Maulkatu laughed, his iron grip relaxing when he stopped trying to run to her. A foot to the back of his leg dropped Neti to his hands and knees. When he tried to crawl to her, Maulkatu kicked him in the ribs, and Basmu's golden tail lifted Angela to rest her on her knees, head wobbling. They were doomed, he knew. With the Nephilim holding onto her, he couldn't teleport them out of Kur—to safety.

"Ruchin," Maulkatu said as he sauntered toward him. He glanced back at Neti on the ground, his eyes tense.

The bearded councilman was shuddering behind a stone pillar, but he came out slowly when Maulkatu called. Suddenly, fists were flying. Swiftly, Ruchin's nose was broken, and the weeping man was dragged into the open foyer beneath the golden beast's shadow.

Maulkatu put a knife in Ruchin's hand and smiled. "You have irritated me for years innumerable. Only briefly, with Udug's campaign, were you ever sensible to action. Your recent motions to veto every actionable thing that comes to our table is beyond aggravating. Through Melech, I know that you and Toth have become defensive of her. He even went as far as saying that you had befriended the boy."

"No," Ruchin said, his eyes glimmering. He brought his hands together and begged. "Only lies have reached your ears. I only meant to save us all from—"

Maulkatu slapped Ruchin. "*I* have done that already. You forget who you are and where you come from. You don't stand beside an Anunnaki in her *defense*, no matter her strength and threat. Your lack of loyalty is disgusting. You have done nothing to save anyone yet, so I must ask that you finish this." He pointed to the knife. "Earn your place again."

Ruchin's hands trembled. He shook his head. "I've said before, Maulkatu, I disagree with this path. Do what you think you must—you hold our people's future in your hands now—but don't expect me to carry out your deeds."

A sneering look of disgust stretched across Maulkatu's face. He reached out and drove his thumbs into the old man's throat, lifting him from his knees. The elder coughed and choked as his windpipe was crushed.

A surge of courage compelled Neti to act. He gripped his dagger tighter, then pushed himself into the veil and arrived a foot away from Maulkatu. He slashed. The tip of his blade caught the councilman's robes and cut through to the skin underneath. Maulkatu let go of Ruchin, but a torrent of hurricane-like wind lifted Neti and sent him crashing onto the ground a moment later.

After Maulkatu examined the cut on his abdomen, his

eyes turned to Neti. "Basmu, would you please dispose of the boy?"

The golden creature's forked tongue tasted the air hungrily as it shifted its weight. *I can.* Neti flinched at the Nephilim's voice.

Ruchin coughed and choked as the air returned to him. His eyes glanced at Neti, then back to Angela, as his mind raced to make his decision. Weakly, he said, "No. I'll do it."

Wise to allow history, Basmu said.

Maulkatu smiled cruelly, like he was pleased by Ruchin's pain. "Basmu, we can leave the boy be. Ruchin has made his final decision. Now or never, he will prove to me that he cares about his people above all others."

The old man's eyes dropped to the dagger in his hand, then rose to gaze at Neti. Genuine sorrow flooded his eyes. He mouthed the words *I'm sorry*, then rose to his feet and stepped forward. The Nephilim lowered Angela, who slept securely wrapped in his tail. Her arm was crusted with burns and blood dribbled slowly onto the black marble floor. She looked weaker than Neti had ever seen her before.

"Don't do it," he said. "Please. I-I'll give you anything if you let her live."

Ruchin ignored him and grabbed Angela by the hair on the back of her head. With his right hand, he pointed the dagger to her chest. He looked over her soft, peaceful face for a long moment, and his hand twitched forward to plunge it into her. Its edge stopped short, and he dropped the knife. "I can't, and if you think that rule by force brings peace, you have certainly failed to see the outcome of the last time the Nephilim ruled our people."

The councilman's eyes rolled back in his head and the

Kissum began to rumble. Pillars of stone erupted from the veil like meteorites, slamming down through the dome above and crashing into the floor. The vibrations sent Neti sprawling to the floor, his limbs like jelly. Spears and rubble alike cracked the polished floor and filled the air with dust. In a matter of seconds, the room was a maze of spires jutting at all angles, interweaving and slamming and smashing into everything around them.

Basmu shrieked horribly when stone tried to pierce his scales and shoved him to the ground. The scale cracked like shattered glass, but the creature rolled before it was driven through. His neck stretched out quickly, like a snake's strike, and his hooked teeth sank into Ruchin's torso. The councilman wailed as blood soaked his robe from the waist down. The Nephilim flicked his neck and sent him into the air, entrails flinging as he spun. Ruchin's screaming stopped when his head collided with a pillar and his upper half rested on the floor.

Maulkatu's brow was furrowed and sweat glistened against his tattooed scalp as the stones came crashing down from above. Pillars were disappearing with blasts of air. Neti had to move fast. He pushed into the veil, arrived next to Angela, and scooped her into his arms; Basmu had released her when he was hit. The red Nephilim saw what he was doing and vaulted over pillars, voraciously roaring and clawing as he fought to reach him. Neti curled his lip and spat. Then they disappeared.

Pulling her through the veil took a toll on him. His soul waned and tired. His mind replayed Ruchin's expression of pure terror while the echoes of the horrid screeches the Nephilim made rattled him to his core. It all distracted him, filling him with feelings of dread and even worse thoughts. And then there was Angela, cradled in his arms. Her sleeping face staring up at him was peaceful despite what had just happened. He hated that. Staring at her for what felt like an eternity only made him angry.

Why didn't she listen? I told her… But she would not hear me. I told her, and she was just too stubborn.

When eventually he did manage to pull them back through the veil, they collapsed into muddy ash. The scent of rain was still in the air, humid and damp, but the sink-hole's garden was now a muck-filled wasteland. His muscles ached as he dragged her through it, the soot sticking to the burns along her arm and her backside.

Inside his chamber, he covered her with scraps of clothing and left her on the cold stone floor. He was only gone for a few minutes before he returned, a new woven blanket and straw pillow in hand. Then he disappeared back to Tarsus and stole other things from market stands and homes alike. A small glass bottle of a greenish salve, bandages, new clothes for when she awoke, a bed frame to get her off the floor, and food for the both of them. He washed her burns with jugs of water from the mountain pass pond, then applied the ointment and wrapped her tightly. He took a seat on the floor and watched her as he ate.

It's only a matter of time before they find us again… How much do I risk nursing her back to health here? Can Maulkatu scry? Find us how Shedim did?

He sighed, hoping not.

Sleeping through the aftereffects of what you've wrought on us…

A SHARP PAIN WAXED AND WANED OVER HER HEAD LIKE THE tide. The more she awoke, the more she felt it and just wanted to fall back asleep. She was warm and dry, to her waking surprise. There was nothing but soft sheets under her back, and she wore nothing but her underclothes. It hurt to move, but she willed her neck to turn toward the sound of someone sobbing. A small fire in the center of the room was all the light there was, then lightning flashed outside and she heard the rain.

Neti lifted his head from her bed. He was on his knees at her side, black hair a mess and tears leaving streaks through the soot on his cheeks. He sniffed, wiped his nose, and asked, "A-Angela?"

"Wh—" Her voice cracked. "How—"

Neti held up a finger, quieting her. "No, don't. I'll get you some water. Just rest for a moment, okay?" He ran his fingers through his hair and sighed exasperatedly, then rose to his feet. Before he left, he paused, looking down at her. "Thank the worlds you're awake."

Angela slowly rolled onto her side. Her neck fought her every inch of the way, but she watched him get a cup of rainwater from a bucket across the room. When he returned, Neti lifted her head and held the cup to her lips. As she drank, he said, "Your heartbeat was so weak. I was scared you'd taken too hard of a hit and were bleeding in your skull."

She choked, and when the coughing stopped, she asked, "How long have I been asleep?"

"A day and a half, at least. At first, I was hesitant to return here, but I think we're okay for now."

"Why wouldn't we—" Angela stopped short. Every memory rushed back to her all at once. "Oh *shit*. The

Nephilim." Panic gripped her, and she began to rise from the bed, groaning in pain.

Neti gently pushed her back down. "No, no, no. You stay there. You aren't in any shape to deal with them."

"I have to do *something*, Neti. Lying here is not an option."

He pushed down on her harder. "You're not going to do anything like this. You can barely get out of bed."

She raised a shaking finger, pointing at him. "You've seen how terrible those things are. We need to figure out how to stop them."

"We will later."

Angela shook her head. The Nephilim were powerful. Just thinking about the presence of their souls filled her with fear. They had to be stopped. "No," she said. "We have to face this now, before it's too late." She shoved his arm off her and heaved herself up.

Neti slammed his fists on the bed, teeth gritted as he shouted, "Dammit, when will you stop? Don't you realize how stupid you're being? You have to leave this alone right now. You're going to get yourself killed, and you're lucky you aren't dead right now."

Angela paused. Neti had never struck anything in anger before.

"I get it," he said. "You want to help people and uplift them. Humans, Anunnaki, and even the occasional Dalkhu, and the Nephilim are going to do the opposite. But can't you see when it's time to back away from it all and take care of yourself?"

Angela shook her head and struggled to her feet. "I'm not charging into battle. I'm looking for information. We need a plan. It's just too bad Ruchin or Teshub aren't around to tell us what they knew about the—"

Faintly, at the edges of her mind, she felt something brush against her. It was cold and concentrated and an aura she could not mistake for anyone else's. Maulkatu had reached through the veils and found her, as she had done to him in Kur.

Terror froze her lungs. The cold sweat that beaded on her skin dripped onto the burns on her arms and neck, adding to their sting. The combination of her souls' energy and the poultice Neti had put on her had helped heal her quickly, but it still hurt to move when she grabbed Neti by the arm and shook him. "We have to leave. Now."

His brow furrowed. "What? Why?"

"Maulkatu is coming for us."

CHAPTER SEVENTEEN

Maulkatu stretched his back before rising from his chair. The last two days had robbed him of sleep and kept him awake while he negotiated with fickle Nephilim and councilmen alike. The beasts wanted more, and the councilmen were reserved and cautious. Toth had always been quiet, but neither he nor Daevas had spoken a single objection until things calmed down, and while Melech had seemed concerned at first, he was now fully committed to his plan. More than likely it was out of fear.

Still no sign of Angela or the boy, Maulkatu thought as he pushed his way through the wooden door and out into the Kissum's archway. *Surely, I would have expected her to act in some manner other than running away like a frightened child.*

He smiled.

Perhaps the Nephilim are a bigger threat to her than I could have hoped.

Soon, he'd have to call for the last of the Council's

deliberations, and the others would be required to make their final declaration of where they stood. They could support Nephilim rule or be exiled, although he hoped he could convince them to side with him. But either way, a speedy resolution was of the essence. The Nephilim enjoyed their taste of freedom and would promptly want more.

Right now, the rest of the Council was his safety net and his reins on the Nephilim. As long as the creatures believed they could die by projection at any moment and that Maulkatu would teach them to travel between worlds when Angela was gone, he could manipulate them.

If he lost the other councilmen, the chance that the beasts would move against him and that Angela would go unslain, would grow exponentially. So far, they had not killed who they weren't instructed or clearly allowed to, which was superb news, but it would take a fair amount of facilitating for Maulkatu to see success. Both the Council and the Nephilim would have to be his tools if things were to go how he and Shedim had once envisioned it. He had to keep the plan in motion before either of them grew anxious and uncontrollable.

Maulkatu weaved his way through the rubble in the foyer. Rather than waste his own time and energy, he had instructed stone workers to break down the pillars that Ruchin had conjured. The holes in the domed ceiling, through which he could see green and white twinkling moss in the cavern above, would be the hardest to repair. That would require extensive scaffolds and weeks of work.

Once he stepped through the main entrance, he saw Basmu's massive golden body lying in the stalagmite fields outside of town. The others, green and red, lay around him; the reflective colors of their scales were hard to miss.

As he walked to where they lay, the Nephilim raised their heads but remained lying down. "I wish to speak with you, Basmu," Maulkatu said as he stepped between them. "I do believe there's a conversation to be had between you and me."

The beast took a deep breath, nodded his huge head, and shifted his body upright. *I wish to talk also. Curious to me how the woman has an aura similar to us. Last of us will never have Nephilim children. No more can be created with world how it is.*

Maulkatu wondered if Basmu was speaking out loud so the others could hear him. Or maybe only he could hear him. "Yes, you first mortals were born in a world unsplit and whole, where there was only one weyline: Kur's and Dingir's combined. Angela simply has taken on a second half, a Dalkhu soul. It's no surprise she has an aura similar to yours, but I wouldn't concern yourselves with that. She'll die all the same."

The creature's head tilted to the side. *You sons of Dalkhu know so little of the worlds before these, but that is a discussion for another time. The woman... I'll know when to be troubled. Can she manifest her energy?*

Maulkatu struggled to understand his choice of words at first. Then it clicked. "You mean bring out the energy of her soul in a physical form? I believe she has once. A long time ago."

Then I am troubled. So familiar the woman feels. I see a distant face but have no name to put.

Maulkatu raised a brow. "Her name is Angela. You know that."

The beast shook his head and huffed. *This one. But forget. She is not a serious threat, but not without challenge.*

"I am certain we will take care of her, forever, and you will be free to roam the skies of any world you wish. For now, rest. We will try to find Angela again soon enough, but I think she'll be on the move for quite some time. Patience will be key to catching her…" A smile flicked across Maulkatu's face. "Or perhaps we should pull her out of hiding with some bait?"

A deep purring from several of the creatures surrounded him, a sign of their approval.

Maulkatu bowed his head. "Very well. I'll work on something and speak with you soon. For now, I must return to the Kissum and continue to handle things on my end."

Basmu returned the motion, dipping his snout almost to the ground. *Until then.*

The walk through the streets back to the Kissum was quiet and somewhat pleasant, to his surprise. Their conversation had gone better than Maulkatu had expected; the creatures seemed entirely content where they were for the time being, and that relieved much of his stress. Hopefully, they would keep it up and the people would feel confident enough to emerge from their hovels again and business would resume as usual.

It was only a matter of time, he presumed, until Angela was dead and the Nephilim were free to travel between the worlds as they pleased. Once they were proficient in teleportation, he doubted they would have much to do with the Dalkhu. Why would they want to fly in cramped caves littered with leaking ceilings and stalactites when they could fly in the warm air of Earth or, better yet, the seemingly never-ending expanse of Dingir.

Maulkatu smiled to himself as he entered the library's rows of dusty books, the smell of them filling his nostrils.

Once they are free, they won't have much to do with us. They will harass the Anunnaki and the humans, and we'll have more peace than we'll know what to do with.

As he stepped into the open common area with tables, chairs, and stray books, a man with a porcelain mask painted black caught his attention. The stranger leaned his back against a row of shelves. His eyes were hidden behind small holes, but Maulkatu was certain they were staring at one another. The stranger wore a gray tunic, leather riding pants, and sandals. The way the stranger dressed and carried himself was unfittingly human...

Maulkatu stopped where he stood and asked, "Who are you?"

It was only the two of them in the library, and the stranger was almost as unmoving as Toth was. When he spoke, there was something strange behind his dark and brooding voice, like two voices were speaking from the same mouth. "Maulkatu, isn't it?"

A chill traveled down his spine. "Yes... How do you know me? And you didn't answer my question. I'd like to know your name."

The stranger uncrossed his arms and stood straight, then took a few steps closer. "I have instructions for you. Stop this folly with the Nephilim. Time in a stone cell has not changed them. They are evil creatures that know nothing but betrayal and slaughter."

Maulkatu laughed and stroked his chin, a smile stretching from ear to ear. "And how am I supposed to take your instruction seriously if I don't know who you are?" He leaned closer, peering into the mask. "Is that you under there, Toth? Daevas? Don't tell me you're Teshub, still alive and eager for revenge."

"You can call me... Mother, if it pleases you."

The councilman rolled his eyes. "I'm about through with this conversation. What do you want, Mother?"

The stranger stepped closer to him, removed a glove, and extended a wrinkled hand. It was gnarled and assuredly a man's hand, not a woman's. It took every ounce of his restraint not to laugh at the absurdity of the situation.

"Take my hand," he, or whatever gender this Mother was, said. "I will show you what I require and who I am, the pieces you are missing to this puzzle, and a picture far larger than you could imagine."

Something deep inside Maulkatu told him that this person was entirely serious and should be taken as such, regardless of the ludicrousness of his name. Yet the councilman didn't feel he had anything to fear. He was more than capable of defending himself. When Maulkatu's curiosity got the better of him, he placed his hand in the stranger's.

An energy, stronger and faster than anything he had ever felt before, flooded his senses and embraced him. It crackled through his veins like lightning and gripped his soul, then his mind. Pictures, emotions, and eons rushed past him like he'd been there to see it all. Then it disappeared in a flash.

Maulkatu toppled onto his knees, clutching the hand he'd touched the stranger with. Everything felt like fire and ice as Mother's lingering touch still burned in his soul. The presence was ecstasy. Already, he'd forgotten what he'd seen, but he knew the implication, what was about to happen, and what he had to do.

Mother nodded slowly as something clicked in his mind. "I understand what your intentions with the Nephilim are now. It is quite inspiring, and I'll allow you to continue so we can see how this ends. I've also given you a gift. Use it well."

Maulkatu lifted his head, his green eyes fading to black as he said, "I... I am yours."

CHAPTER EIGHTEEN

J a'noel took a deep breath and held it there for a moment, and with every exhale he allowed his mind to bloom out around him. Another inhale, and he pulled himself back together again. Despite having spent half an hour every day exercising and stretching his mind, he still couldn't reach any further than he could before. He needed it to come naturally, to become a part of him and as normal as his need to breathe.

Someone coughed, and Ja'noel opened his eyes. The Bui'dus, his newest squad of soldiers, sat around him on mats like his own. Each person was handpicked from the Etlus and Uri Gallus based on merit, time of service, and the array of his or her skills and proficiencies.

Gabe, the one who coughed, tucked his mouth in his elbow and wheezed once more. When finished, he ran his fingers through his blond hair and scratched the back of his head and apologized.

Jezreal shifted on her knees and closed her eyelids again. "No matter."

"Distractions are good tests," Ja'noel said. He flipped a

few yellow pages in the book on the ground in front of him. The crude symbols were slanted across the page—a sign it was written by hand. "Change the exercise?" he suggested.

Gabe nodded. "Yeah, let's do that, please."

Ja'noel smiled. It was a rough first week, to say the least. He was probably the last person to be teaching people how to use their minds and souls as weapons, but until someone else took his place, all he could do was keep them moving forward. Together, they would have to find a way, forge their own weapons, and blaze their own path. Maybe it would take them years to do the simplest of projections or become independent and toss aside their shifters, but the goal was worth pursuing. Dingir needed to change its course, and it would be stronger for it.

The door to the record room swung open, the knob slamming into a shelf behind it. Twisting around, Ja'noel faced an Etlu dressed in leathers and brass stood in the doorway. "S-Sir," he said, throwing up a salute. He had buzz-cut hair, was gaunt in the face with jutting cheekbones, and had muscular shoulders, but his frantic eyes gave him away. He was new to soldiering.

Ja'noel groaned as he rose to his feet. "What is it?"

"Sorry for the intrusion. If you'll step out into the hall with me, I've received news you'll want to know."

Ja'noel motioned to the Bui'du behind him. "These men and this woman in front of you are the future of the city. If there is something I need to know, they do, too."

The soldier eyed each of them for a moment, then nodded and closed the door behind him. "There's been a sighting, sir. On Earth. I have a report of a man with long gray hair walking about a jungle southeast of the human settlement of Memphis."

Ja'noel narrowed his eyes.

Samuel scoffed from his mat. "A man with gray hair? So what?" A smile flashed across his face. "There's plenty of those anywhere you look," he said, motioning to Ja'noel.

The others laughed, and he couldn't help but smile. Every day, it seemed they understood more and more what their success meant. They needed to work as a team, and it was already beginning to take shape.

The young soldier shook his head. "No, you don't understand. He was wearing Anunnaki armor with a bright gold patch on his chest."

The room grew quiet.

"A soldier by the name of Durian captured the individual and is holding him at camp. While the prisoner won't speak, he believes the man is Kushiel and requests your presence."

Every muscle in Ja'noel's body went weak. "Kushiel? Grand Etlu Kushiel—alive on Earth?"

The Uri Gallu shrugged. "They seem to think so."

Ja'noel scratched at the scruff on his chin and paced. "Well then, why don't they bring him here already?" He laughed. "Tell Durian I say, word for word, 'Bring him here at once, you daft excuse for an Etlu.'" A few of the others in the room chuckled with him as well.

The messenger stuttered, lips trembling in fear. "That's not possible, sir. You will have to go to the camp if you want to see him. It appears that Kushiel has no soul. He won't be able to make the journey to this world."

Fifteen years and Kushiel is alive on Earth with no soul? "How is that poss—" Ja'noel held up a hand, cutting himself off. "Don't waste my time trying to answer that. I'm just having a hard time swallowing this." He took a deep breath and scanned the shelves around him. There were many secrets locked away in that room, but none of them could have prepared him for this. His options were limited to only one.

"Thank you," Ja'noel said. "You are dismissed. All of you, too."

As he walked toward the door, Jezreal rose and said, "Sir, you don't mean to go there by yourself, do you?"

Jezreal reminded him a lot of Angela, which was probably why she was the only woman he'd chosen for the Bui'dus. She had the hardened face of a soldier who had seen her fair share of strife and auburn hair just long enough to put into a ponytail but still appear female at a glance. Just the way she stood and carried herself, wide and proud, gave him more hope for her than any of the others.

"I do," Ja'noel said. "You will all stay here. Even if I pass, here and now or on some distant world, your mission will stay the same. That is something you will have to learn to value above all else. Regardless of who is in charge of the city, Dingir is your priority. Right now, your progress is more important than me or Kushiel. For Dingir's sake. Do you understand?"

One by one, each of them nodded, and there was nothing left to be said.

He left the room and walked the Ascendancy's white halls at a quick pace. Dirt and dust were piling in the corners and on the tops of brass doorway plaques. Normally he would call for someone to clean, but today he did not care. His only concern was Kushiel.

Ja'noel knocked three times before helping himself inside the small office. Sarosha was sitting at her desk, overlooking a stack of papers. Her eyes glimmered and she wore a warm smile. "What do I owe this unexpected visit?" she asked.

Ja'noel glanced over his shoulder at the young soldier

behind him. "Leave us and find the three most seasoned Etlus in Dingir and bring them to me."

The boy nodded frantically and slipped from the room, shutting the door behind him.

"Etlus?" Sarosha asked.

"Yes…" Ja'noel said as he mulled on how he was going to tell her he was leaving. With a heavy heart, he walked to the chair across from hers, but he did not sit. Instead, he shifted his weight uncomfortably until Sarosha broke the silence.

"Why do you need three seasoned Etlus?" She leaned her head on her hand, eyes narrowing. That stare drove him crazy because he knew she saw everything. Sarosha had no fancy for beguile and always wanted it straight. Unfortunately for him, he was too inclined to give it to her.

He sighed, giving up, and said, "A report has come in of a man matching Kushiel's description. It appears he's alive and soulless on Earth."

Her smile vanished as she sat upright. "Kushiel? How? We know he fell from the city, don't we?"

He shrugged. "Yes, but a soldier from a camp gave me a message that was quite convincing. If there is the slightest chance it's him, I have to go. You understand the immense amount of pressure that would take off of me—off of us. I need someone to take over the Etlus. Someone with experience, guts, and leadership."

Sarosha tapped her lip. "How long do you think you'll be gone?"

"It depends on if it really is him or not, and if he doesn't have a soul, I don't know what we'll do, but it's clear that he needs me."

"You're needed here, too. By the city and by me."

It was a feeble attempt to get him to stay, but he knew

she only said it because she loved him. "Sarosha," he said, reaching across the desk to take her hand. "I owe it to Kushiel. We all do. I won't be wandering out in the wilds, just stopping by a camp. No danger. I promise."

She pulled her hand away and crossed her arms. "You are not apt for Earth. I've told you, I never want to see you anywhere near the front lines again."

"You're not wrong…" Ja'noel stood and walked around the desk to her, placed a hand on her shoulder, and looked into the hazel eyes he loved so much. "It's a risk. This'll only be the third time I've ever been there, but I'll have Etlus with me at all times. If anything changes, I'll let you know immediately, and I'll be back. I promise."

"Just don't do anything stupid, Noey."

He smiled and kissed her. "I love you, too," he said, and he walked back into the hall.

WHEN THE YOUNG SOLDIER CAME INTO VIEW, WALKING toward him with three seasoned Etlus trailing behind him, Ja'noel's anxiousness grew. It had been so long since he'd seen Kushiel that he wondered if they would naturally fall back into being friends and old partners again or if Kushiel would be changed by what had happened.

How did he fall from Dingir and end up on Earth?

The soldiers told Ja'noel their names, but his mind was racing and he didn't hear them. With a quick instruction, they powered on their shifters and took hold of each other's shoulders. The circle they formed glowed blue as their devices powered up, and they vanished.

One of the soldiers led the way through the veils, and they appeared on the edge of the seaside cliff. The water expanded out into the horizon, a dark blue with crashing waves beating against the boulders below. The smell of salt on the wind was heavy. On land, a forest sat on the horizon.

One of the Etlus was first to spot the trail down the cliffside. It was only a foot and a half wide and weaved its way toward the sea below. Occasionally, they had to press their backs against the walls and shimmy across narrow rock. Luckily, none of the stones were loose.

Then the path stopped short. A dead end over the water below, or so it seemed initially. By peering over the side, he could see that fifteen meters below there was a lip of stone that jutted out almost another five feet. With great care, he and his men swung their feet over and dropped to the edge below.

The mouth of a cave, illuminated by dozens of lanterns and a bonfire in the center, opened up in front of him when he landed. An Etlu stood with his back against the cavern wall, facing the seaside, and jumped in fright at Ja'noel's sudden appearance from above and threw a salute across his chest.

Other soldiers inside the cave sat on barrels around a small wooden table with coins piled in the center. They all held playing cards. All Ja'noel had to do was clear his throat and one of the men noticed him. He threw his cards down and jolted upright to salute him, but Ja'noel only crossed his arms.

The soldiers picked up their things in a hurry and stumbled as they moved the barrels and the table under the pressure of his gaze. He watched them until an Etlu with a bald head and crooked nose approached from a tunnel. Unlike the other soldiers, his armor had been polished recently. He smiled nervously and asked, "What brings you here?"

Ja'noel extended a hand, and the soldier took it. "I've

come to see Durian," he said. "There was a report from this camp that I'd like to follow up on personally. I'm sure you know what I'm talking about, so don't play dumb." Ja'noel eyed the patch of a yellow arrow on his armor. "And, Captain, you really should see about disciplining the men better."

The captain stuttered, cheeks turning red. "V-Very well," was all he said before leading them farther into the cave.

The tunnel widened on both sides, and they passed small alcoves the size of closets. All were stuffed with crates. The wood had been branded with labels like "leather," "batteries," "blankets," "wires," and a plethora of other tools of the trade. Ja'noel wondered if all of Earth's camps were as heavily stocked as this one. And if they were, he would have to order some of the supplies be returned to Dingir.

The path broke into three, and the bald captain led them into the left one. The light in this chamber was dull and yellow from sparse candles and full of bunks with sleeping soldiers. When the captain found the sleeping man they were looking for, he shook him awake by the shoulder.

"Durian?" Ja'noel asked.

The soldier groaned as he threw his legs off the bed and sat upright. "That's me..." He rubbed his eyes for a moment and blinked a few times before he seemed to realize it was Ja'noel standing in front of him. "My, not a usual day that the Ensi makes a trip to the Adrift."

Durian stood from the bed. His face was meager skin and bones and scarred from a fire below his left cheek. His eyes were shifty, but Ja'noel shook his hand anyway. A twitch had developed in the soldier's wrist.

"Well," Ja'noel said, "it is not a usual day when I hear

that Kushiel is alive and well. Please, take me to him and tell me everything in your own words."

He nodded and led them out of the room full of sleeping soldiers, rubbed at his temples, and sighed before he began his story. "Well, you see, I didn't get the best look at him at first. There's a set of woods a few miles off the coast. I'm sure you saw it when you got here. Part of our daily patrol is making a pass along a river that runs through there. Well, in the middle of my patrol yesterday, I stopped to relieve myself in the stream and I see someone on the other side. There's a man peering out from the bushes, but I can only see his face just staring blankly at me.

"At first, I think, my gosh, that's a pervert trying to catcha glance at me. Well, I put my thing away and warp across the river. This guy's already on the run, but I can see through the shrubs he's wearing our armor. I can't help but think to myself, now why would someone in our armor be running away from me? Let alone peeping? Wouldn't he just teleport?

"So I think to myself, I'm the only one out on that particular patrol, so something is wrong here. I give chase and end up shooting him. He never teleports, does nothing to attack me—just screams and runs. One look at him and I realize that this could be my old Grand. I try to talk to him, but just standing next to him, I see he just doesn't seem right. You'll see. I had to drag him back here, and since he ain't talking, we put him in here."

Durian stopped before a sheet of nailed boards that blocked the tunnel ahead. He grabbed the makeshift door by rope handles and lifted it out of the way to let them pass into the prison. Iron bars had been driven into the natural stone of the cavern and gave the camp two small cells. Inside the closest one was a thin, pale man with wrinkles.

Lying on the floor, he was barely clothed. Gray hair ran down his cheeks in tufts that looked like dirty snow. A panicked look spread across his face as Ja'noel walked closer to the cell.

He knelt before the cell and said, "That is not Kushiel."

The man was old and almost identical in body shape and hair color, but his blue eyes were wrong. Kushiel's were copper brown. Just to be certain, though, Ja'noel reached out with his mind and touched the man. It was true; the man had no soul.

Ja'noel sighed as he stood. "He's human, too."

Sweat glistened on Durian's forehead. "I wondered as much, but that makes it even more confusing as to why he had those." He pointed to a table against the wall, where a full set of Etlu armor lay folded.

Ja'noel crossed the room and examined each piece. Blood had been splattered all along the front of the cuirass, and there were scratches and a few holes in other places. There was not a single battery, knife, or tether gun left. He imagined that the human had likely sold or traded them. But the Etlu insignia on the chest of the cuirass, embroidered into the leather with golden thread, gave him hope.

Ja'noel tapped the armor, a smile on his face. "This armor is Kushiel's, though. Only a Grand's armor would have a golden seal." He motioned to his own, then turned to the graying man in the cell. "Where did you find this?" he asked.

The human only scooted farther back against the wall, mumbling something Ja'noel did not understand. He groaned in disappointment. *The human speaks a different language...* Why couldn't it be easy? Ja'noel spun to the captain and said, "Find someone who can speak to this man. Either from this camp, the next one over, or Dingir. I don't care, but when you do, bring both the translator and this human to me, wherever that may be. No exceptions and no hesitation."

The balding Etlu nodded. "Very well, sir. I'll begin right away," he said, taking off into the tunnel.

Ja'noel turned to his soldiers. "Until we hear from our illustrious captain, we'll need someone to head to Dingir to inform Sarosha of our discovery and my intent to commence a search for Kushiel. I'll require another six men, at least. And, Durian..." He turned to the ragged soldier. "You will take us to the exact spot you found this human."

CHAPTER NINETEEN

*T**hwack! Thwack! Thwack!***

Angela swung the ax again, harder this time. The head of it sank into the wood, and the tree cracked and groaned its last before breaking free and thudding onto the ground. The tree was shorter than the last one, but it was still straight and thick enough for pikes.

She wiped the sweat from her brow and let the cool breeze flow up her shirt for a moment. The sun was high, and she watched the way the wind blew across the meadow grass like a wave in the ocean. Jagged mountains stood tall around the valley's edges, and everything felt peaceful for the first time in a long while.

"Head on the ground please," Neti said. He bent, hatchet in hand, and started clearing branches off the tree. The skin on the back of his neck was red and sunburnt, his hands scratched and dirty, too, but Angela knew she wasn't looking any better.

"Sorry," Angela said. She stooped and joined him.

They worked together, clearing the branches off the tree in silence, sweat dripping in the miserable heat. When they had split it into two shafts and they worked on sharpening separate points, Angela stopped and asked, "Do you want to talk?"

Neti shook his head and swung again. "There's nothing to say that hasn't been said already."

Angela wanted to say something but went back to rolling and shaping her log. Slowly, she turned it into a giant toothpick half her height as she brewed on Neti. He was mad, but she wasn't sure why he wouldn't speak to her.

Maybe it's just the plan. He's worn out. It's been weeks of labor.

As the two of them slung their finished spikes over their shoulders, the sound of hooves came up from behind her. Neti grimaced, and she knew who was coming. The only thing she didn't know was what her human neighbors from the other end of the valley wanted this time. Dropping the log onto the ground, she turned and saw that it was the village children approaching on the backs of donkeys. Even better.

All seven were boys, and she guessed they were anywhere from four to eleven years old. Yet even as young as they were, most carried clubs and short bows with blunt arrowheads. Their eyes were narrower than those of most humans, and the eldest, with long black hair tied into a knot at the back of his head, held up a hand to stop the party.

Angela held out her palms and said, "We've been through this at least a dozen times. Stay away from this end of the valley."

The eldest boy turned to the round boy next to him and said something in another language. They smiled widely and shared a laugh.

"How long's it been, huh? A month? Two? You know I

don't understand whatever language you're speaking. Can any of you speak what I do?"

The larger boy leaned forward on his donkey, looked straight into her eyes, and shouted as his face turned red.

Neti pulled on her elbow lightly, and she met his gaze. "Pick up your log. Let's go. They're just being kids." The sincerity in his eyes and caution in his tone suggested that he was trying to keep her calm, and that only irritated her, but she knew he was right and they weren't worth the time.

She bent, heaved the log onto her shoulder, and turned to leave the valley children behind her when something sharp cracked against the back of her head. Angela bit her lip to restrain herself from cursing and kept walking until she felt a second sting, and then she spun back around. The kids giggled as they reached into pockets and saddlebags and threw handfuls of pebbles, but they didn't damage her skin as much as they did her pride.

"Get out of here," she screamed, stepping closer to chase them off. The stones continued to fly. Neti told her to ignore them when something wet struck her cheek. The children exploded into laughter and nearly fell off their rides as Angela wiped her face with the back of her hand. Her fingers were brown, wet, and stank.

"You threw shit?" Angela's mouth hung open.

She dropped the log off her shoulder and dashed forward. The donkeys reeled and the children screamed as they fumbled for their bows and clubs. She bent, scooping up one of the rocks, and chucked it with all her might. The gray stone spiraled through the air and crashed into the eldest boy's head—the one she swore through the feces.

Neti cursed her name behind her, but she didn't really hear it. The boy's eyes flickered as he fell backward off his mount and thudded into the grass. The other children pointed and shouted at her. Nostrils flared and curses were yelled from both sides, even though neither could understand what the other said. Two boys helped the eldest to his feet and onto his donkey again. He wiped at the blood that trickled from his forehead, spat, then turned his donkey around. There were a few more curses and gestures from the boys, but the others followed.

"That's right," Angela yelled as they rode over the top of the hill. "Get your sorry asses back home. Throw shit at me again and next time will be worse!"

When the last of them disappeared over the hill, she lifted the log back to her shoulder and faced Neti, a sour, cross expression on his face like he was disappointed in her. Angela didn't care. She picked up her ax, touched her forearm to his, and shoved them through the veil.

Screw discretion, she thought as she drove them through the space between worlds. Appearing again, a gust of cold air blasted against them. Neti almost tripped on a rock and cursed at her; he hadn't been expecting her to teleport them. He sneered and turned to storm his way up the windy cliffside pass.

They could have carried their spikes—their temporary home wasn't too high up the mountain—but a part of her wanted the humans to know that they were dealing with someone extraordinary, and she hoped they would leave them alone now.

A little canyon of rock and the stumps of trees they'd felled led them to the mouth of their cave. The clearing was large enough for Basmu and maybe one of the green ones, but no more. And because of the confined space of the cliffside pass and the canyon, the Nephilim would have to fly to reach them.

Through the opening, and before she was five steps in,

Angela had to weave herself around a dozen wooden spikes they had made from other trees. The back of the cave was just large enough for two straw and fur beds on the floor and crates with their belongings. They had tools, a few weapons, and even a little food for Neti. He dropped his log, letting it clatter on the stone ground and dropped onto his bed. Fortifying the cave was her idea, and Neti didn't seem to oppose it at the time, but she wondered what was bothering him now.

Without a word, she rummaged through a crate and found her hand drill, then left him in the dim light that reached the back of the cavern. There was work she would see to with or without him. She cranked the drill by hand, the barbed metal spike grinding the stone down.

Angela pumped her arms diligently for nearly an hour until the hole was deep enough for one of the two new spikes. It was more vigorous work than chopping trees, but she felt safer as they put up more spikes. She'd hoped they would reach a point where anything larger than a person wouldn't be able to enter.

As she inspected her work, Neti approached from the back of the cave, arms crossed. He leaned his back against the cavern wall. Shadows covered most of his face, but Angela was sure he was still upset.

"I shouldn't have thrown that rock," she said, shifting on her knees to begin drilling the second hole. "I know. I messed up."

Neti scoffed. "You think I'm here to scold you? I just wanted to see how you were coming along. You do what you want. It's always been that way."

She paused, eyes narrowing. "Is this what's bothering you? You think you never have a say in what we do? Shit, Neti, we practically went to Kur for you."

"Don't try to twist things," he said. "What I said eased you into the idea, but Teshub's death was the final straw."

"So this is what's bugging you."

"No."

"Then what is it? For real this time. I can't defend myself or try to make things right if you don't tell me what I did wrong."

Neti laughed. "I think we both already know what you did wrong." He stood upright. "You blew it. All of this. I told you we needed to leave Maulkatu alone, and you couldn't listen to me once!"

Angela pushed down on the drill harder, giving it more bite. "I listen to you all the time, Neti. We were, and still are, under Maulkatu's gaze. With the crystals going missing, what else was I supposed to do? Turn away?"

"Yeah, I think so. You brought the Nephilim onto us. Onto all the worlds. Admit it: you don't know what you're even going to do. That's why your digging holes in the ground right now. 'Fortifying.'" He laughed. "Wooden spikes aren't going to do anything."

Angela gnashed her teeth, unable to make eye contact with him as she cranked the drill harder. "What else am I supposed to do? It's just a matter of time before they show up. I won't lose again, so you'd better get off your high—"

The drill bit snapped in her hands and her blood turned into fire. It was the last one. She chucked it and listened to it clatter against the back of the cave. A moment passed as she calmed down again.

"Good work," Neti said sarcastically as he turned back to his bed.

With all her willpower, Angela bit her tongue. Losing her temper and throwing that rock was what started her bad mood. The only thing she could do was keep moving forward, despite how hopeless it all felt. She rose to her feet, dusted off her pants, and walked out of the cave.

With a quick thrust of her mind, she teleported down into the valley plains below the cave. The blast of her appearance bounced off the shaggy hills, and the wind helped muffle the sound. She was only a short jaunt from the human settlement on the far side of the valley. Somehow, she would have to convince them to give her another drill, even after what happened earlier.

Angela froze. The clomping sound of hooves came from the left, but all she could see was the blue sky and the tall tan grass. For an instant, she was afraid that the villagers had mounted their steeds and were barreling toward her end of the valley to put her down, but instead, there were antlers bobbing through the prairie grass atop the hill. The sound of her arrival had startled the animal.

Instinct kicked in. She plowed through the veil, thinking that if she couldn't talk her way out of trouble, she could at least try to buy it. Entering sight again just above the running deer, she drew a dagger, fell on top of it, and drove the steel into its side.

The deer bleated hoarsely and tumbled, throwing Angela into the soft grass. She lost it for a moment, then found it struggling to get onto its feet. It was easy for her to put it to rest. Gutting it was, too. She'd done both numerous times before. When the blood flow slowed, she slung it over her shoulder, knowing it would be impossible to keep the blood off her clothes, so she didn't bother trying.

By the time she saw the small village just beneath the base of the mountains, Angela wished she'd have turned around. There were small wooden homes with thatch roofs. The donkeys were all corralled near the center of the settlement, and children were playing on the packed dirt road that ran through it. There weren't any adults, yet, but she guessed at least fifty people lived in the village.

As she reached the village's edge, a child squatting in the street pointed her out and yelled. It wasn't long before a man rushed out onto the road and shooed the younger ones inside. Then more men stepped into view. Angela walked until she could see the whites in their eyes and dropped the deer on the road. Most of the humans had black hair that hung to their shoulders or was wrapped in buns or ponytails. They wore robes with long sleeves and different colored sashes, but all of them gave her the same cautious look.

A man pushed his way to her. "You've come again," he said. The hair on his chin reached the base of his neck. He was at least forty years old, and the apron he wore was covered with soot. The town's blacksmith was the only one who could speak with her. Even through his accent, Angela knew he was upset.

She brought her hands together and held a bow for a long moment. "I bring you this deer in hopes of a trade—and as an apology."

The blacksmith crossed his arms. "The children tell me you struck one of them, and Asu's son comes to us with a gash on his head."

She kept her eyes at her feet and said, "I returned a stone they threw, I admit. I let my temper take control of me, but I would not have retaliated if the children did not provoke me."

The man frowned, seemingly unconvinced. Angela knew that her best bet for keeping the peace was to acknowledge what she'd done but not regret it. Honesty would see her through it.

She straightened her back and motioned to the deer

again. "Hopefully this will bridge whatever gap I've created and you will come to understand that I do not wish to harm you or your children, but I will do what I must to defend myself."

The blacksmith translated to the others, and they spoke for the better part of a minute and examined the animal closer. Finally, he said, "It is a great size, so the others are willing to consider your apology and trade. Tell me what you want, and we will decide."

Angela was happy with that. "I could use another drill," she said.

"Are you sure that is all?" he asked. "I have several in my shop, and it's a cheap thing to ask for. We could feed the entire village on the deer tonight."

Angela bit her lip and thought about it. "That and a promise. Keep your children away from my side of the valley, for their own safety. There have been two... families of bears roaming around. I wouldn't want any of them to get too close."

The blacksmith tugged his facial hair, then turned to the others. One by one, all the men shrugged or nodded. He turned back to her and said, "They know a good deal when one arises and say 'very well.'"

Within moments the deer was hauled away by its legs, and the blacksmith was off to fetch her drill. It hurt Angela to get so little out of the deer, but she hoped that it would help fix the damage she'd created. When he returned to her with the drill in his hand, he handed them to her quickly.

"I am grateful for this deal," the man said. "Thank you, good hunter."

Angela bowed and said, "Until next time," then turned to leave. She wasn't ten paces away before he called out to her.

"Wait." He raised a hand and walked closer. His cheeks were growing red, and he fumbled with his words. "I-I must ask. What brought you to the valley? Two moons now, yet we do not know your name. Why are you here?"

Angela shook her head. "You don't want to know why I'm here."

The man smiled awkwardly. "Why, that is not true. Perhaps the village sups together and you join us tonight. A beautiful woman should not live in the mountains alone."

She couldn't help but smile, and now she fumbled with her words. "I-I'm sorry. I can't. Just please promise that you'll keep your people away. I don't want anyone getting hurt."

The blacksmith's gaze dropped to the ground. "Very well." He smiled and bowed. "Until next time."

The sparks of giddy awe and affection faded as she walked away from the village. He had surprised her with that comment, and while she enjoyed his attention and compliment, she knew there should be nothing between them. More than anything, she needed to protect them from the things they did not know.

When she was far enough into the valley, she slipped into the spaces between the worlds and brewed for quite some time. Weeks, it felt like, and by the end of her journey to the clearing before the cave, Angela was no wiser.

It was too late for her to take back what she'd said to Neti. The damage was done. They were both pissed at everything, and toiling away with preparations wasn't helping. Their problems couldn't be solved with words alone. They needed a better plan, and they needed change. Maulkatu would eventually come for them again.

But the Nephilim were fearsome. Their eyes and the

spaces between their scales were their weakest points, but those were also the hardest to reach. Ruchin had scolded Maulkatu for bringing them to the city, confirming her suspicion that the Nephilim could not teleport through the veils. That eased her mind a little, but she had read in Kur's library that they were the grandmasters of spells, and the energy she felt from their souls was frighteningly strong. She ran her fingers over the hardened scars on her arm as she thought.

Angela cussed under her breath as she weaved her way through the wooden pikes. When she reached the back of the cave, she paused to look over Neti, who was sound asleep on his bed.

Why do I feel like we need to hide and wait? If Maulkatu wants to play a game of cat and mouse, why should I not move ahead of him?

The Nephilim were only serving Maulkatu for his knowledge. They wanted the freedom to travel between the worlds. In return, Maulkatu wanted her dead. But if she took Maulkatu out of the picture, she wondered if the Nephilim would lose interest in her.

No matter how much she debated her course of action, her role, and if she meant to be a force that fought for balance between all three worlds, she had to liberate the Dalkhu from the Nephilim. There was no place for those ancient creatures in this—or any—world.

Angela dropped to her knees, took Neti by the shoulder, and woke him slowly. When he rubbed his eyes and sat upright, she said, "I have never once wanted to put you in danger, so I have to ask that you leave. Go somewhere safe."

His eyes narrowed. "Why?"

A long sigh escaped her as she contemplated it one last

time. "I'm going to finish this. I'm going to scry Maulkatu."

Thinking about thrusting her mind into the void again was terrifying, but she knew it needed to be done. She remembered the weyline, how it had tied itself to Michael's soul and tried to trap her, too. What if her mind's eye wandered and took her straight to it again? No. If she didn't think about it, it wouldn't happen. The only thing she would do by thinking about it was frighten herself.

She said, "Killing him might slow the Nephilim. They'll be stuck in Kur for at least a little while longer, hopefully until I can find some way to beat them."

"No, I don't think it will," Neti said. "If anything, Maulkatu is holding them back."

Angela rose to her feet. "I guess I won't know until it's done. Either way, Maulkatu has to go. I'm sorry I get so mad, and I'm sorry I've ruined so much." She turned and began to walk toward the entrance to the cave.

Neti cussed. "Don't be stupid. I'm telling you, Angela, you can't do this alone."

She smirked over her shoulder. "We'll see."

CHAPTER TWENTY

A ngela's mind returned to her body and she toppled onto her hands and knees on the sparkling floor. Succumbing to the fatigue, she lay on the ground, motionless, as she caught her breath. That had been her third time trying to scry Maulkatu. No matter how hard she tried to keep her mind focused on the aura that identified Maulkatu, everything slipped away and she wandered the void aimlessly.

Angela tried it four times before she considered giving up, but she tossed that notion aside and decided it might be best to look inward before trying again. Toth had said that spells required balance between the mind, heart, and soul, and only when she examined herself did she realize that she was afraid. Erring on the side of caution was holding her back. She needed to commit.

With a sigh, she pressed the souls inside her chest to push her mind free of its confines. Slowly, they did, and all physical sensation left her. The mind was free, floating in its own space but tethered to her souls. She sharpened the forefront of her mind to a point and pushed into the veil. Like water, she slipped through as though it was a net. It didn't hurt or tear the veil, and it didn't hurt her.

On the other side, in the void between worlds, she shifted from side to side so she could touch the veils. By focusing on Maulkatu's aura, and with her soul pushing her forward, she felt Kur's veil brush against her mind. Compared to the veil in the unnamed room, this one was particularly strong—and harder. It pushed against her as hard as she went through it.

Once her mind broke through, a strange sensation filled her. Judging by where she had entered this world, she knew her mind was just above the Kissum's domes. Her mind could feel the auras and vibrations of souls bouncing off the cobblestone shacks and fields of stalagmites below her, giving her a sort of blind sense of her surroundings.

All people in Kur filled the air with their specific vibration, adding to the chorus and creating a mixture of auras. The Nephilim's tone was deep, like hers, and scattered throughout the city, while the Dalkhu's pitches were higher and louder and covered more octaves. Even in all the noise, and the distance and the stone that separated them, Angela could feel Maulkatu's soul somewhere down below her.

Without a conscious thought, her mind traveled downward like a serpent from the heavens, weaving through stalactites on its way toward the Kissum's doors. By the time she wandered the Kissum's stone halls, she'd realized that Maulkatu was not anywhere inside the building. He was *far* below it.

She guessed about how far he was, then pushed her mind back into the void. Not knowing where else to try, she reentered the dimension outside of Eld Kur's ruins. The ring of Maulkatu's soul was strong enough to follow. She weaved around the crumbling buildings and the stone spires, then slipped through the stream's tunnel and gradually sank lower. It almost felt like she was following Toth a second time, and she wasn't surprised when she found that Maulkatu's soul was the loudest inside the Scratched Hall of the Nephilim. The best part was that he was alone.

Angela retraced her steps to her body and settled back into her skull. Slowly, she could feel the cold stone beneath her and smell the musty cavern air when she took a deep breath. The light from the torch she brought filled the rainbow-colored walls with sparkles, but she couldn't take it with her. Angela snuffed out the fire with her boot and felt for her brass knuckles in her pockets. It had been too long since she had used them last. The calluses on her fingers had already faded.

One last deep breath and she pushed herself between the worlds, letting the void freeze her skin. She ignored it and kept her mind focused on Kur as best as she could. The blast of her arrival resounded off the scratched walls and carried down the tunnel to her ears, which rang in pain. Just down the long, black hallway, she saw the light of a torch move. His bald head turned to face her. He squinted in the dark and smiled.

"Angela!" Maulkatu exclaimed. "Is that you? My, this is an unexpected visit if I may—"

"Quit it." She gritted her teeth, clenched down on the brass between her fingers, and disappeared into the veil with a howl. Less than a second later, she appeared ten feet closer to Maulkatu, then vanished again. Again and again. *Boom. Boom. Boom.* Each time, she arrived nearer and nearer until she was close enough to swing low for the councilman's belly, but Maulkatu jerked to the side, pressing his back against the wall at the last second. His teeth glistened in the torchlight when he smiled.

"Come on, Angela," he said. "You're sluggish today."

She went for him again. Each swing, whether at his head or abdomen, and every attempt to grab him was feeble. Every move she tried, he reacted a second too soon, and he hadn't even swung once yet. Something told her that Maulkatu could have ended it whenever he wanted. He was faster than she remembered. He was toying with her.

It wasn't until she vanished and then reappeared immediately behind him that she was able to change the dynamic of the fight. She grabbed him by the hood of his cloak, struck him in his lower back to give him something to think about, and pulled him into the veil with her.

At first, she had him at her will while the pain in his back dazed and preoccupied his mind, but their pace began to slow before she could take them where she wanted. Distracted by his sudden resurgence, Angela found herself losing. Her two souls, when they worked together, had always been at least a third stronger than everyone she'd ever tangled minds with. Yet there, in the space between worlds, an unusual strength surged from somewhere deep inside Maulkatu's soul. He had not been this strong when they scuffled in the market square or when he first brought the Nephilim to Kur. Now she could not overpower him.

They snapped into a dimension, and she was greeted by the crash of cold water against her. It pushed against her skull, froze her to the bone, and tried to shove its way into her lungs. In the crystal blue expanse with no clear up or down, she fought to hold her breath.

Maulkatu let go of his snuffed torch, then drew two knives from sheaths in his robe. Even slowed by the drag of his clothes in the water, the councilman still moved fast. All Angela could do was twist and push backward to avoid the edges of his blades and wear him out. She had to exhaust his body's energy, and his soul's, but he kept coming at her. Before he showed any signs of slowing, her lungs burned for air, and every bubble that slipped from her lips terrified her.

With a shove, she grabbed hold of him, and they burst through the veils again and arrived outside the Kissum. The streets erupted into shouting and screaming as the two crashed onto the hard market square. A bellowing roar echoed from somewhere farther off, but that didn't hold her back from cracking her brass against his chin.

Finally, a decent hit.

Maulkatu's lip curled as he jabbed the knife at her face to force her back. Then he flexed his jaw and sneered. A second screech echoed across the cavern as the green, winged Nephilim took flight. Its head bobbed and weaved through the stalactites with speed and grace, and the others from elsewhere in the cave bellowed as well.

I need to end this soon.

Maulkatu must have sensed her worry. He smiled. "You really think you can stop me? Stop the Nephilim? Stop this *revolution?* Can you not feel it in the air, Angela? *Change!* It's come to the worlds in a way you must feel. Have you not craved balance between Dingir and Kur? I have! For many years, and we are so close to achieving it."

Angela steeled herself as the Nephilim came bounding closer. "Your anger and desire for revenge have blinded you. This is not the way to peace between us."

He laughed. "Is that the same lesson Teshub tried to tell you?"

Angela pounced like a wild cat, crossing the distance

with a fist held out to strike his cheek, but he caught her by the wrist and wrapped his arms around her. His aura washed over her, and his push was strong. They disappeared before the Nephilim could get close enough and then reappeared in the stalagmite field outside the city. For a second, it felt like she was just above the ground, but as gravity pulled her downward, she realized that she was on the cavern's *ceiling*, not its floor.

As they dropped, she reached out for the nearest spire and grabbed hold of it just before the end of the spike. Maulkatu hung onto her leg, laughing as he looked up at her. Angela kicked his nose. He flinched and let go. Blood appeared on his lips. One of the Nephilim screamed. A flash of gold from the edge of her vision grew closer, and Angela knew it was time for her to leave.

How soon did Basmu crash into that stalactite after I disappeared? How close was I to death?

THE MOON CAST THE ROLLING, BREEZY MEADOW IN ITS eerie glow. Sitting there atop a hill below her mountain, Angela waited. Guiding her souls' energy into places she'd been bruised and cut helped them heal faster. It was the best way she could pass the time until his presence brushed against her again. This time, he was coming to her.

A *boom* cascaded down from the mountains to her left. A man in a black robe contrasted against the white snow-capped peak, and the giant golden beast next to him craned its neck and roared.

Shit.

Maulkatu disappeared for a moment, then reappeared on top of another mountain with the red Nephilim. Then, on her right, he came back with the green twins this time, and all the Nephilim were accounted for. One last time, Maulkatu appeared a dozen feet in front of her, gasping to catch his breath.

"How do you sleep at night knowing that you're holding an ax above everyone's head? You might not mean to drop it, but in the end, you'll kill everyone by letting them free," Angela said.

He wagged a finger, standing upright as he gasped. Carrying all that weight between the worlds wore him out. "The Nephilim are not the beasts you're trying to make them out to be. They feel fear, love, and lust for a spiritual connection. They want to be given purpose, but they also crave freedom. Just like us. You can't hold their nature for violence against them; they come from a world so unlike ours. So cruel and savage they had to become this way in order to survive this long."

"They will slaughter humans like animals, and I can't control them."

Maulkatu laughed. "You're right about that. Even I have had a hard time controlling them. But humans are the *epitome* of meaninglessness. They aren't worth your time. Trust me. I've seen the truth and came out changed. We both have a role to play in the destiny of the worlds, and your time is coming."

With a wave of his hand, Basmu bellowed from up high. By the time she looked, he was already in the air, racing down toward her. The green twins and the red Nephilim began their descent as well. Angela pushed herself to her feet and drew her dagger.

"The ancient past from a world long gone has reawoken, it seems," Maulkatu said. "Good luck."

Basmu's claws dug into the earth, creating deep ruts in

the grass as he landed before her. A grumbling sound came from his golden throat as his voice permeated her mind. *A rumor I heard: you bring about your energy as wings, yet still I have not witnessed it. Like Maulkatu, I doubt you are capable of manifesting your souls' energy in physical form. Let me show you.*

The other Nephilim hit the ground around her, trapping her in a circle as Basmu began to concentrate. A low growl escaped his maw and plates of yellow light appeared around his scales. Like armor, they curved around his shoulders, along the spikes on his back, and down his nose while forming perfectly around his eyes and nostrils. The energy from his soul illuminated the area around him, and the grass that touched him burned.

Angela reached out with her mind, felt the strength of his soul, and wavered. There was no way she would win this if she couldn't repeat what happened fifteen years ago in Dingir. The souls inside her—both of them—belonged to her now and no one else. Ever since she took back her own from Udug, there had been no more visions of fire in any world she visited. Everything about her was balanced now, or at least she had thought.

She gritted her teeth, heart racing. Her muscles flexed and her mind sharpened. It was time to end this once and for all. For humanity, the Anunnaki, and the Dalkhu. The strength that had escaped her for the last fifteen years was hers, and she'd find it again even if it killed her.

Angela bellowed, raised her dagger, and tapped into her souls, filling her body with energy. Her legs responded to her will as she urged herself to a sprint, leaving a wake in the reeds. A thrust with her mind and the ground erupted beneath her feet. Lifting upward on a stone spire, she launched into the air. Flipping the knife in her hand, she aimed for Basmu's eye and threw her arms down as she fell past the creature's open maw. The tip of the blade nicked just below his eye and glanced off harmlessly.

Negating the impact, Angela rolled underneath the creature. The glowing soul-armor didn't protect his underbelly, and she thrust up at a crease between two scales, but Basmu twisted at the last second. The tip of her dagger submerged into the yellow glowing light, and the energy pushed outward, forcing the weapon back at her. The blade emerged red-hot, glowing with heat.

A clawed foot, large enough to cover her entire torso, smashed into her chest. The impact took the breath from her lungs and a talon skimmed across her forehead. Grass and earth crashed against her when she fell, but she was quick to stand again. The other Nephilim were moving closer. She tightened her grip on the knife and pushed herself into the space between worlds.

They are so strong, she thought. *Basmu is hard enough to kill with just his scales, so how am I supposed to get close enough now?*

She could try to shove the Nephilim into an elemental dimension, but she doubted she'd have the strength, considering their weight and the strength of their souls. If Basmu's energy could nearly melt metal, she wondered what it would do to her flesh.

The blast of her arrival rippled over the green plains. Airborne and falling, she crashed onto the green Nephilim, grabbed a spike on its spine, and held on for her life as it screeched beneath her. It writhed, bucked, and tried to whip her off with its tail, but she held strong and lifted the dagger above her shoulder.

They might be stronger than me, but they aren't faster. I can fight all of them at once.

The creature looked up at her to meet her gaze, and she slammed the dagger downward, only for it to glance off the bridge of his nose. The Nephilim chuckled like a hyena and snapped down on her forearm, its teeth tearing deep gashes as she reeled back.

Angela jumped off the creature, then warped a hundred feet closer to the cavern. When the Nephilim realized where she was, they began barreling toward her on wide strides. As fast as horses, the smaller ones were almost on her again in moments. Basmu unfurled his black wings. With a run, he took to the air and roared. Maulkatu stayed where he was, arms crossed and smiling away like a child at a jester's show.

Again and again, she warped back another few hundred feet and drew them closer to the end of the valley. The clearing outside the fortified cave stood out in the forested mountainside. She just had to lure one of them in and trap it inside so she could finish it, and she was almost there.

Basmu grumbled from above the valley. His neck straightened and he shuddered. Vile brown retch flew from his throat and came down toward her and ignited. The wind caught the fire and threw it to her side, creating splotches of falling blue flames broken up across the meadow. In seconds, the grass around them was burning. It had been too long since the last rain.

Angela planted her feet as smoke began to fill the air, waiting until the green Nephilim emerged. Before it tramped her, she twisted and snagged a horn on its neck. Pulling herself up with a jump, she planted the dagger into its black eye.

A roar filled the air and the beast shuddered. Its wails

grew louder as she plunged the knife deeper. Holding on with her legs, she stabbed the other eye, then a third and fourth time until the creature dropped to the ground with a *thud*. It moaned and fumbled around blindly as Angela pried the tip of her knife between two scales on its neck and finished it. When it stilled and she removed the blood-slick blade from its skull, relief washed over her.

They can be killed.

Something boomed in the distance, followed by another crash only a dozen feet from her. The grass parted from the blast of air, and Maulkatu pulled his hand from the red Nephilim's scales and smiled.

"A gift," he said, and the Nephilim shuddered.

A stream of flaming black liquid spewed from its maw. Angela dove, narrowly avoiding another serious burn. The red beast growled as glowing blades of red light protruded from its talons. A spear of light at least a foot long extended off its tail like a scorpion's stinger. Angela wasn't sure what was better: soul-armor or weapons.

Anshar! Son! The red Nephilim's voice wailed with grief in her mind. *You will regret this, Anunnaki!*

The beast's claws tore into the dirt as it launched toward her. Angela bounded backward and tore at the veils with her mind, trying anything to keep it away from her. A wave of water the size of a house opened up between them, blasting the creature and Maulkatu back, but the beast quickly clawed its way out of the rushing torrent.

Coming around the stream, it pounced for her, forcing her to cease knitting the hole in the veil. Angela rolled and lashed out with her mind once more. This time, she bridged an opening to the elemental plane of stone, creating a wall of jagged rock that slammed down on the beast. The impact shook the ground. The red beast screamed as it pressed down on its back legs and hips.

Angela gripped the knife in her hands and raced toward the creature, hoping to end it, when a foreign presence came around her. Stronger than anything she'd ever felt before, it wrapped around her and pushed down like it was going to smother her, but it did not push her through the veils. The weight in her chest and on her arms made it impossible to move. The more she fought it, the more she realized that the force that froze her body was also constructing a barrier between her mind and her own souls. She could do nothing.

The wall of stone she'd created ceased rumbling, the water stopped flowing, and Maulkatu approached her with a smile. "Why the pause, Angela?" he asked smugly, tapping his lips with a finger. "Come on, finish Lahmu the Red."

She tried with all her might, yet her body would not move willingly. Sweat beaded on her forehead, and the little air she could muster did not satisfy. Every inch of her body was filled with leaden veins.

Maulkatu walked around her in a circle. "Oh, I see," he said. "Those Nephilim, as craven as they are, do have their uses. Do you know what's happening to you? Blink twice for yes."

Angela didn't blink.

He lifted his head and bellowed in laughter. "It's a spell. A rather grotesque use of one's own soul and energies, but it is useful. Was it you, Basmu?" Maulkatu turned to face the golden beast in the air above them, the meadow fires illuminating his golden scales.

Aye.

"There you have it." With a flick of his wrist, Maulkatu

pushed the wall of jagged stone through the veil. The impact of air coming back together pounded against her eardrums. She wasn't sure where he sent it, but the red Nephilim staggered back to its feet, then lurched for her like nothing had happened. Maulkatu was yelling at the top of his lungs, but Angela couldn't make it out. The beast jabbed the spear of light on its tail, cutting through her clothes and piercing her gut like hot iron.

It flicked its tongue as Angela smelled her own flesh burning. Then it removed its weapon. Before it could stab her again, Maulkatu teleported next to the Nephilim in a blast, anger rippling across his face. "Do not kill her yet, Lahmu!"

The creature growled. *You want her dead but do not let me do it. My son, dead. You have no command of me, son of Dalkhu.*

Searing pain bloomed in her chest as Lahmu stabbed her just below the clavicle. It carried across her shoulder and made the world spin around her. The feeling reminded her of how it used to feel when a Dalkhu touched her. It was more than just a burn or a cut; the energy dissipated into the fiber of her being, ripping and destroying her in its wake. Her legs felt weak, but the spell would not let her fall.

This is my revenge.

"No!" A cry came from the reeds nearby, and the sound of rushing feet followed. Out of the corner of her eye, Angela could see Neti sprinting closer.

A scream escaped him as red and orange fire erupted from the air between them, jetting toward Maulkatu. The councilman sneered and held out a hand as though he was going to stop it. And he did; a wall of black as dark as an unlit sky materialized, deflecting the flames with ease.

Angela's heart skipped a beat. She had never seen a councilman do anything like this before.

This is his soul's energy?

With a quick command, the remaining green Nephilim had come around and pinned Neti to the ground with a clawed hand, and the stream of fire was stopped. Maulkatu reached for Lahmu the Red next, placing his hands on the creature's head and forcing it to look him in the eyes. The Nephilim shifted. Its eyes fluttered. It relaxed and pulled its light from her chest.

A-Apologies, my—

Maulkatu waved a hand, cutting him short. "Do not forget your place again." He sighed in disappointment as Lahmu bowed his head and stepped back. "These beings are so primal and full of passion and strength yet undeniably restrained by knowledge and power greater than their own." He smiled. "You've done well this fight. Much better than the last. Take pride. You are the first person in a millennium to kill a Nephilim, but don't think I'll let you die now.

"I want you to grow stronger, get so close to your own redemption you can almost taste it, and fail. You will know what it feels like to walk on shards of glass, afraid and unsure that, one day, you or a loved one will take a wrong step and draw blood. I will follow you, haunt you, terrorize you. No matter where you go or how far you run, how much distance you put between yourself and those you cherish, someone will die because you were completely powerless. Like how Shedim felt about his brother." Maulkatu smiled. "We'll start with Neti, how about?"

Angela wanted to scream, lash out, and hit him, but every second drained her a little more. She wondered if she was bleeding internally.

"In the biggest order of things, there is no cost too high for peace. I'll see that you burn. And Neti and Dingir, too, eventually." He turned to the sky. "Basmu, release her."

Slowly, the weight lifted from her mind and body, and she dropped to her knees. The souls inside her were already weary, but she demanded that they give her their energy as she directed it to her wounds. Everything seemed so hopeless. She wondered if it was even worth fighting anymore.

How can I even get Neti out of here?

Maulkatu stepped forward and said, "Like a weed, the more I cut you down, the bigger you'll grow back to be, and in the end you'll see that, even at your best, you cannot save those you love—or yourself."

I have to try, for Neti. Angela reached out with her mind, but when she touched the edge of his mind and soul again, she was reminded of his newfound strength. Something about his soul was *wrong*, and not how she remembered him feeling. His eyes were as black as night, like his pupils had stretched over the whites of his eyes. She knew he had found a power far more fearsome than his own.

Maulkatu must have sensed her touch and her hesitation; his smile spread from ear to ear. "Go on. I'll hold onto Neti for you. If you die now, you are no challenge and unworthy to see his end. But if you do, may your soul find peace once it has returned to the weyline."

Knowing that she might only have minutes to live, Angela squeezed every last drop of energy she had left in her and vanished into the veils.

HEAVY RAINDROPS SPLATTERED AGAINST THE cobblestones, filling the night air with humidity and a thrumming chorus. The sky above was full of black, bubbling clouds in the darkness. She fell face-first onto the road, uncaring if humans spotted her teleporting into Tarsus. Her heart and lungs pumped furiously. If she didn't get help, she would die.

The sound of the pattering rain against the road and wooden rooftops muffled her weak yells for help. Shadowy outlines of people carrying lanterns moved farther down the street, yet they did not hear her and disappeared around a corner. Everything felt weak, and her skin tingled as a gust of wind blew her soaked clothes.

On her hands and knees, she rested her forehead on the ground and cried out again. The pooling water beneath her was tinted red, and she wondered if she'd lie there all night or find the strength to move.

An arm reached underneath her own and pulled on her. Just bending her knees out to shift her weight onto her feet was a challenge. Standing was a sudden exertion that brought everything to a spin, despite the stranger's help. She placed her arm over a shoulder, and they began to walk.

Every sense seemed to be flooded like the city street. Through her soaked hair and the droplets that got into her eyes, she could see the blurred twinkling of torches ahead but not the face of the person next to her. A hood at least half a foot above her blocked out the rain and the light, making it impossible for her to see a face, but she was confident it was a man.

He walked her two blocks down the road and brought her to face a two-story building. Its lumber front was old and rotting, and the iron hinges on the wooden door had rusted. Vaguely, she could make out the word "poultice" on a hanging sign above the door. He guided her up a single step, produced a wooden key, and inserted it into three holes about a foot apart. One by one the pins inside the door released, and the stranger walked her inside.

The far wall of the room was lined with shelves full of books and a door leading into the back. Glass bottles, some with bones, mixtures of different colors, and dead bugs sat in cubbies on the opposite wall. Three beds without sheets or pillows were spaced equally apart, each with end tables next to them. The place reminded her of the infirmary on Dingir.

The stranger led her to the straw and wood bed farthest on the left, then placed a flickering lantern on a table. She couldn't remember him carrying it but quickly forgot about it as he stooped low to wrap his arms underneath her thighs and lift her into the air. She was too tired to fight and let him place her on the bed.

"Thank... you," she mumbled. He pulled his arms free from under her and took a step back. Even inside, out of the rain, everything still swam around her. The lamp next to the bed shimmered, and the shelves seemed to wiggle and move. As her eyes grew heavy, the hooded man spoke in a gravelly voice.

"Don't fall asleep yet." He disappeared in the room's darkness and returned a moment later with a bottle of brown liquid in hand. He uncorked it, brought it to his nose to smell it, then placed it against her bottom lip. "You need to drink."

"I'll—" Angela turned her head and coughed, then nearly vomited as bloody phlegm came up her throat. She wiped at her mouth and said, "I'll repay you for this," and took the bottle in her own hand and drank without worry. No matter what the potion did—stave off infection or dull the pain—she had no choice but to trust him. As she drank the bitter tonic down, the stranger's face became clearer under the flickering lantern's light. He was old and wrinkled with a heavy pair of ice-blue eyes and a white stubble beard surrounding his toothless mouth. When the drink was gone, he took the glass from her and stood upright again. The world only swam for a second more, and she closed her eyes.

CHAPTER TWENTY-ONE

I t was dark when her eyes opened again, and the sound of the heavy rainfall still thrummed against the shop's wooden roof. A numb feeling had taken hold of her, and while she did not want it to fade, she wanted to be awake. The night was colder than she remembered, and when she went to rub her shoulders and arms warm, she realized that her clothes were missing and that the stranger had wrapped her wounds with bandages.

"Hello?" Angela croaked. Even though the lantern next to her still flickered, her gaze could not pierce the darkest corners of the place. "Anyone there?"

The gray-cloaked man returned to the room from the doorway leading to the back, a book in his hand. He closed it and placed it on the shelf before standing at her side.

Feeling drunk and tired, Angela let her head fall onto the pillow. "Thank... Thank you so much. Might I know your name?"

The old man nodded and said, "Kuda, and do not thank me. I think we both recognize that the world is safer with you alive. I cannot let you die."

Angela raised an eyebrow but couldn't seem to find the strength to lift her head again. "What… are you talking about? How do you know me?"

"I hear things," Kuda said. He tapped his sternum. "I feel them, too."

Angela took a hard look at the man in front of her and tried to see what his blue eyes were hiding. She reached out with her mind, brushed against him, and felt that he did have the aura of a soul, yet she could not say he was a Dalkhu or an Anunnaki. "You—"

He placed a wrinkled finger on her lips and shushed her. "*You* must rest. Pushing yourself will kill you, and you cannot die with the Nephilim threat so fierce."

As she struggled to speak and ask him what he knew, Kuda picked up the lantern and walked to the wall on her right. His pointer bounced between vials and jars until he settled on another brown bottle. He plucked it up, uncorked it, and held it out to her again. She could tell by the smell it was the same potion as before. It would numb her and make her sleep.

"You are safe for now," Kuda said. "Trust me when I say that I am a friend."

Angela's eyes narrowed. "A st-stranger who keeps secrets does not seem like a friend."

Kuda shook his head and took her by the chin, pressing the bottle against her lips. "You need to rest. We will discuss this later. Your left lung has collapsed, and I will try to reinflate it while you sleep. You may die if I don't, and we must leave this place before dawn. So if you would kindly take this potion, I can help you."

Her head rolled like a dropped spud. "This… This isn't your shop?"

"No," the old man said. He grabbed her by the nose,

tipped her chin back, and poured the draught into her mouth. She choked the bitter drink down and fell asleep within a minute.

ANGELA'S HEAD POUNDED WITH EVERY BEAT OF HER HEART, and her left lung ached. The smell of fresh straw and the sound of something bubbling filled the air. Flickering light cast dancing shadows across wooden beams on the ceiling. It wasn't the same ceiling she remembered. It was higher up and brighter than the last time she was awake. Even the bed she was lying on felt different.

She lifted her head and realized that she was wearing a new green tunic and brown trousers. They were men's clothes, but she would not complain. It was a small home, furnished with little beyond a table, a second bed, and storage cabinets. Antlers and pelts lined most of the four walls, and two windows let in the daylight. A kettle hung in the fireplace, and a single door was the only way out.

A new prick of agony exploded in her chest as Angela took a deep breath and tried to sit up. She groaned, lay back down, and realized that the stranger who had saved her was seated at the table. He rose and approached with a smile on his wrinkled face. "You're awake."

Shallow breaths helped lessen the pain. "Talking hurts," she mumbled.

Kuda rose from his seat and walked to the fireplace. "I expected as much. I had to reinflate your lung. It will be some time before it feels normal, if it ever does."

She exhaled slowly as she forced herself to sit up. "I'm just happy… I can breathe. Where are we?"

"A safe place. I rented this cabin for the night, but it

won't provide us with cover for long. I haven't got the coin for a lengthy stay, and we must keep moving." He crossed the room, then returned with a steaming bowl of stew in his hands.

"But... *where* are we?"

Kuda gave her a long look before saying, "We aren't very far from Tarsus. A day's journey, if you must know. But we have much farther to travel. Now, eat." He handed her the food.

Angela smelled the stew. Chicken and beans. She hated beans, but the old man wasn't looking away from her and she felt obligated.

"You need every drop of every kind of energy you can get," Kuda said.

She grumbled, but the warming sensation that flowed down her throat was soothing, she admitted. When she was halfway finished and she'd grown too uncomfortable with the stranger watching her eat, she asked, "You told me your name... but not who you are."

Kuda shrugged and walked back toward the table. "I am who I am. I listen to the voice in my soul and do as it says. It's what led me to you."

The thought of his soul reminded her of what she felt when she reached out to him. She did so again and found his presence just as confusing as before. He didn't feel like a Dalkhu or an Anunnaki, yet he was graced with an aura similar to a soul. Kuda seemed to notice her touch and turned to face her.

"Sorry," she said. "I should've asked for permission."

"You should have, but I won't get after you about it." He scooped himself a bowl of stew and sat down at the table again.

The fact that he could perceive her touching his soul

made her believe he had at least some kind of training. Yet as he sat in front of her and ate his stew, Angela couldn't help but think that he was still human. A human with a soul, and an old one at that.

"Have you... always been this way?" she asked.

Kuda smacked his lips and swallowed. "No. I first heard the voice speak nigh on ten years ago, and I've been its servant ever since."

Angela raised an eyebrow. "I don't understand."

The old man cackled. "No one does. I have been doubted, betrayed, and abandoned by loved ones, all because of my belief in the voice that guides me. I cannot explain it, only obey it in hopes that someday it will reward me for my service. Given eternal peace, maybe." Kuda sighed and stared into the distance for a moment.

What kind of human not only has a soul but also claims to hear a seemingly conscious voice from inside himself?

"So," Angela began, choosing her words carefully, "the voice told you to find me... Has it told you more?"

Kuda snapped back into his mind. "No. The voice only comes rarely, but when it does, I hear it loud and clear. When I saw you on the street, it came to me and said that I must help you and take you far away from Tarsus. It said I could not allow you to die." He groaned as he stood, walked to the other bed, and searched through a pile of bags and packs on the ground. When he turned, a bottle of brown liquid in hand, Angela put her bowl on the nightstand.

"I don't want... any more of that," she said.

He sighed as he knelt before the bed, his ice-blue eyes falling softly on her. "I know who you are, Angela. You're lucky most humans are dumb. They thought your arrival in Tarsus was nothing but a rumble of thunder in the rainfall, but I know better than to let you expire before your time. Can you walk? Run? Bend and sprint? What about a leap? Or can you hold your breath for over ten seconds?"

Angela creased her brows. To show him she was capable, she lifted her feet off the bed to swing them to the floor but cringed when she twisted and pain seized her.

Kuda stood and uncorked the bottle. "I thought not. If you cannot handle yourself, you need to be resting so that you can recover as quickly as possible. The worlds need you on your feet." Something about his eyes broke through to her. This old man, as confusing and mysterious as he was, genuinely wanted her to be well.

"I know that it's hard, but you must trust me and the voice that guides me."

Angela took the bottle and sipped the vile-tasting drink. "How much... of this stuff do you have?"

Kuda shrugged. "I cleared out the store's wares. It will numb the pain, keep you sleeping, and fight infection, but you'll need more and more of it as your body grows accustomed to it."

Angela drained the rest of the bottle at once, figuring it would be better to just get it over with. She trusted Kuda enough to believe he meant the best for her, even though his reasons and talk of an inner voice were completely unbelievable.

"How long... before I can walk?" she asked as the potion first took away the feeling in her fingers.

The old man eased her onto her back and said, "Not soon enough."

FOR A WHILE, ANGELA COULDN'T TELL IF HER EYES WERE open or closed. Blurry white lines twisted and turned, grew brighter, then dimmed right in front of her. She wondered if the specs of light were little dancing spirits that dragged their ghostly tails behind them. They disappeared entirely a few times before she realized that they were just the stars in the night sky above her and that she was in the back of a wagon. It was not moving, and the only sounds she could hear were crickets chirping and frogs croaking. The smell of a campfire's smoke rolled over her.

As the control of her muscles returned and she was better able to will her hands to move, she feared that it was only a matter of time before Kuda would return with another dose to force her back asleep without giving her a chance to fight back. It was terrifying to think he could trap her in an endless loop with brief moments of mental clarity yet still leave her physically paralyzed.

Angela sat upright, bringing her head to a spin. A sharp pain reminded her that her chest was still healing. A myriad of gnarled trees with teardrop-shaped leaves surrounded her. The flashes of lightning bugs filled some of the darkness around her, giving her some sense of depth, but beyond what the flickering campfire illuminated, there was little to see. Kuda sat on a small barrel with his hood drawn over his head, warming his hands over the fire.

Carefully, she swung her legs down from the wagon and lowered herself to the ground.

Kuda looked up and said, "Finally awake…"

Her heart was racing, and her lungs burned, but she feared taking deep breaths and did her best to keep calm. "How long have I been asleep?" she asked.

"It has been a week since last we spoke."

Angela's hands were shaking. "A week? I-I can't keep doing this. No more sleep. I'm done. I'll be fine."

The old man rose to his feet in a smooth, fluid motion and tilted his head to the side. The fire's yellow light bathed his skin in a warm tone. "I know. Why do you think you're awake in the first place? I stopped feeding you the drug." He grumbled as he flexed his stiff joints, then walked over to Angela. His hands reached out and tried to grab her shoulder. She pulled away from his touch and held back a hand to swat his wrists aside.

His expression grew sour. "May I remove the bandages, or would you prefer to? There's nothing under there I haven't already seen."

Angela turned her back away from him and said, "I'll do it myself." She felt slightly guilty for threatening to smack him, but she had forgotten about the bandages and he could have at least let her know what he was doing. She unbuttoned the tunic and pulled the bandages free by slowly picking and peeling away at the animal glue that held them secure. Once her chest was bare, her fingers searched her shoulders, stomach, and just underneath her clavicle for scars. The wounds Lahmu had given her were large, but Kuda used glue to reseal them.

"My lung still hurts when I breathe deeply," she said as she buttoned herself back up. "But it is a great deal better... and I know that I probably wouldn't have survived without you, Kuda. So thank you."

He sat himself back down on the barrel next to the fire and said, "It will likely hurt for at least another week, but I believe you're well enough to carry yourself the rest of the way."

Angela settled herself on the ground next to him, basking in the fire's heat. "You're leaving me, too, huh?"

"Is it a surprise?"

Angela shook her head. "Not entirely. Just sooner than I thought."

"The voice bid I save you and point you in the direction you must go. One of these I have already done, so now it's time for us to separate. Your quest to defend us from the last of the Nephilim is destined: those first mortals have no place in this world or any other. The voice has spoken."

Angela raised an eyebrow. "You are a very interesting person, Kuda. I wish I knew more about you and this voice."

The old man chuckled. "I believe the voice is in all of us. We only need to listen to our souls."

She bit her lip. "You do know you're the only human I've ever met with a soul, right? You speak as though everyone in existence has a soul when that's not true."

Kuda cleared his throat and held his cloak tighter. "You know what I mean, and there are others who have a much better understanding of the great scheme of things than I do. It's them you are seeking, I believe. I can guide you no farther than this: continue north on this road until you find the city of Anyang. I cannot say what you're looking for, but you will be a step closer to freeing the Dalkhu."

Angela wondered if he was speaking about Neti or just the Dalkhu in general. Thinking about Neti filled her with grief. It was all her fault he was captured. If she hadn't attacked Maulkatu, thinking she could end it, the councilman wouldn't have come hunting for her on Earth.

Kuda groaned as he stood up from his barrel, lifted it over his shoulder, and walked toward the wagon.

"Will I ever see you again?" Angela asked, rising to her feet.

The old man dropped the barrel in the back, pulled out a

lantern, and lit it. "I can't say for sure, but a part of me believes that we see what we look for. Maybe tomorrow, or in a year, we'll meet again just like this. Perhaps in a millennium with new faces, new walks of life, and new purposes."

He pulled a burlap bag from the wagon and handed it to her. She opened it and saw her extra clothes and gear. "What's that supposed to mean?" she asked.

"Maybe after we die our souls will be reborn in a new body and we will meet again." He smiled a somber smile and pulled himself up onto the driver's seat of the wagon. Grabbing the horse's reins, he urged it forward and disappeared behind the trees.

CHAPTER TWENTY-TWO

As the sun was breaking over the horizon, lighting the forest and the road weaving through the woods ahead of her, the birds sang and the breeze picked up the scent of cherry. Despite all the forests Angela had explored, this one had a sense of serenity beyond all the others. The mountains in the distance, the creeks that babbled quietly to themselves, and the way the light flickered through the dew-covered pink flowers in the trees took her breath away.

The road led her upward until she came out of the woods and stood not five feet from a drop-off. Down below, a river snaked into the distance, cutting its way through stony bluffs. The water was almost completely clear. A school of fish bobbed at the surface, and she could see straight to the riverbed. The drop-off was only a dozen feet from the trail, and Angela wondered how any drawn cart could make the journey to Anyang. If anything startled the animals, it was only a short jaunt off the road and the cliff.

The road led her up and down the rolling hills as the

soil became rockier and rockier. Trees grew thinner, replaced by tall, hardy reeds and green grasses, giving the land a harsh contrast against the gray and brown stones the river's path had revealed in the cliffsides.

Before the day ended, Angela found a village nestled between the curving river and a cliff. Some houses extended over the water, and fewer were built into the side of the bluff. Tiny carved figures of animals sat on red wooden arches where the roads led into the town. Men thrusted off from a wooden dock by pushing long poles against the river's bottom, nets in their sampan. The village was bright and warm yet secluded and peaceful.

She hoped it was the right place and followed the well-worn path down the cliffside and passed underneath the red archway. Chimes hanging in front of wooden homes tolled lightly in the breeze. Sharp, angled roofs were layered with clay plates of reds and browns. As she walked the street, Angela realized what an odd sight she must have been.

All the women wore flowing gowns with sashes, kept their hair up, and eyed her cautiously as they worked while the men stopped what they were doing, crossed their arms, and whispered to one another. Angela couldn't understand a single word they said, but she recognized the language as the same one spoken in the village in the valley.

If only I knew what I was looking for. Why couldn't Kuda be specific? And who was he, even?

The road led her to the wooden platforms suspended over the river. She was wondering where she should begin her search, or what exactly she should look for, when she passed a man on his knees. He was busy scraping the hide of an animal she did not recognize.

He was old and had a long, thin mustache and balding head. His clothes were covered with soot. The stranger rose to his feet with a groan, put his hands together, and bowed. Angela returned the gesture, but his words were nothing more than noise to her. She shook her head, pointed to her ears, and said, "I don't understand what you're saying."

The man's eyes widened like he understood the situation. He scratched at his head as he mumbled, then pointed at the dagger at her waist. When Angela pulled it from its scabbard, he clapped his hands together like a child, flashed his rotting teeth with a smile, and took it from her with scarred hands. Rolling the knife in his hands, he examined it from every side and thumbed its edge to test its sharpness, then clacked his tongue and shook his head.

"I know. It's dull," she murmured more to herself than to the man.

He smiled and sat himself down on his stool, laying the blade on his lap. From a leather bag on the ground, he retrieved a flat stone and wetted it with yellow oil. Pointing the weapon away from himself, he began to scrape the blade and sing. The stone rang against the metal in beat with the song, falling into the rhythm as though he had done this a thousand times before, and it captivated Angela. His voice carried long notes like it was a meaningful song about war, honor, or something, but Angela didn't really care. She was content to just watch him work, savoring the music and this man's uniqueness.

It was over quickly, though. The man wiped off the excess oil with a cloth, then thumbed its edge once more before handing it back to her. The dagger gleamed under the sunlight when she held it at the right angle, and she thumbed it to test his work. Satisfied, she slid it away in its scabbard and bowed to the man politely, but when she turned to leave, the man mumbled and grabbed her by the elbow. His other hand was open, asking for something.

Angela pulled her arm free. "I didn't think you'd ask me for money. It didn't take five minutes, and you just did it without being sure I understood what—"

The old man grumbled as his face turned red. His hands trembled, and Angela was afraid he would swing at her.

"I will pay him," a smooth voice said. A woman dressed in a gown of elegant colors bowed curtly. Most of her black hair was tied back, but her bangs hung just over her thin brows. Angela wondered how she hadn't noticed the woman approaching, and she smelled like she'd grown from a cherry blossom herself.

"You... No, you don't have to do that," Angela said as she threw her bag off her shoulder. She bent to her knees to search for a spare coin but knew she had none and only wanted to appear modest.

The woman produced a single copper-looking coin from a fold in her gown. Her fingers were dainty and thin, face lightly powdered, and Angela realized that she was stunned by the woman's looks.

"If I had known he wanted money, I wouldn't have given him my knife in the first place. I thought he just wanted to look at it, considering it's foreign, but—"

The woman's smile was enough to cut her off. "His name is Gao," she said. "His trade is metals and hides, but he tries bows at times. Don't buy one. But take heed: he never does anything for free." She handed him the coin, and he sneered one last time at Angela before turning away.

Angela rose to her feet when he was gone and said, "Your Akkadian is a great deal better than anyone else's around here. Really good, actually."

"Thank you," the woman said. "I spent years of tutelage in the west. My name is Liu, and might I know yours?"

"It's Angela."

Liu's smile made Angela's heart beat faster. "It is very nice to meet someone from such a faraway place. I wonder if things have changed in Elam."

Angela shrugged. "I'm sorry. I don't know. Elam is quite a bit away from where I'm from."

Liu's emerald eyes caught the light and shimmered. "And where is that?"

"Tarsus."

She placed a thin finger to her lips and tapped. "Haven't heard of that town. Is it anything like Anyang?"

Good, I found Anyang, Angela reflected as she glanced around. "No, not the same. Tarsus is on the edge of a much larger body of water. You can't even see the other side."

"Oh," Liu said with a smile. "It must be beautiful."

Angela knew she was a fool for thinking, *No, but you are.* It was an unusual thing for her to be smitten by a woman, and she wondered why Liu made her feel that way. Was it the way she smelled? The grandeur and grace she possessed? Angela wasn't sure. "Tarsus is all right. The sea and the mountains are pretty, but it's not as green and doesn't have as many flowers. I'd say Anyang's country-side is hard to beat. I'm glad I've gotten this far to see it."

Liu smiled. "If you have come from beyond Elam, it must have been a very long journey. I wish to know why you've come to Anyang."

Angela bit her lip. Even she didn't know what she was here for. *Am I looking for a weapon or knowledge that will help me? An ally like Neti?*

"I'm afraid I'll only be passing through," she said, and Liu's eyes darkened. "But I may rest here for a day, maybe two, or even a month if I have reason and means to. Is there a place I could stay the night?"

Liu dipped her head. "You may follow me."

A short way down the wooden platforms, closer to the cliffside that loomed over them, where the ground returned to sand and dirt, they stopped at a home. Liu knocked at the door. A woman answered, and they spoke for a few minutes in their native language. Throughout the conversation, their expressions changed, but eventually, Liu said to Angela, "You may stay here, with Ah Kum, a mother widowed twice."

Angela took a half-step back, jaw dropping. "No, I can't intrude like that."

Liu shook her head. "It has been two years since her husband passed, and Ah Kum is glad to take you in, although she does not speak Akkadian at all, so I'm afraid you will likely have to serve your own food and water."

"Well, that's no big deal, but why do I feel like I'm intruding?"

Liu gave a dazzling smile. "Maybe you speak the language of hearts, Angela, and know that Ah Kum is repaying a debt by allowing you to stay. Don't let it bother you. Everyone shall benefit from it." Liu bowed low one last time and said, "May we meet again, Angela."

THE FOLLOWING MORNING, ANGELA SLIPPED OUT THROUGH the latticed door before her host saw her. The woman had seemed nice enough and even gave Angela her own room to sleep in, but their inability to speak with each other made the entire visit awkward. Knowing that the woman was hosting her to repay a debt didn't help, and Angela couldn't shake the feeling that she was intruding on a mourning widow.

As the sun broke over the bluffs above and the clear

river sparkled, Angela, seated on a bench on the side of the road, watched the town wake up. The blacksmith, Gao, gave her a dirty look as he walked past her, immediately infuriating her. She had half a mind to steal that sharpening stone from his pocket and clack him on the head with it, but she knew the man was only old and grumpy, and the language barrier between them made things worse than they probably really were.

The better part of two hours passed as she watched the town. It was quiet, peaceful, beautiful, and full of children and happy people. But slowly, Angela felt out of place. Even though everything was new and wonderful, the looming dread of her failure hovered over her. Thoughts of Teshub and Neti, and even the people she had lost before that, haunted her. This place was too peaceful for her.

Is it peace or chaos that I truly thrive on?

She walked to the end of the docks, took off her shoes, and sat with her feet overhanging the edge. The water felt like ice, but it was refreshing. Long-legged birds with feathers as white as snow stopped by to sit on the river, but they were gone again when a small fishing raft came from up the channel.

Neti was right. I was so caught up trying to control the Council that I created this whole problem, and now he's paying for my mistakes more than I am. But what happened to Maulkatu?

Thinking about the councilman made her shiver and feel uneasy. The strength he possessed was overwhelming now, and then there was his Nephilim.

Where did his new power come from? she wondered. *And how can I make this right when I don't even know where I belong? What is even worth fighting for anymore?*

Angela brewed there until she grew angry with herself

again. She rose, turned back toward the town, and nearly stumbled off the dock in fright as she walked into Liu.

"I'm so sorry," Angela said, grabbing hold of Liu by the shoulders to make sure that she didn't fall into the water. Her bubbling laugh lifted Angela's spirits a bit.

"No, I scared you," she said.

Angela noticed the woman was holding a basket full of clothes. A bar of soap sat atop the pile. "Would you like to join me?" she asked.

Angela smiled and almost said yes. The bluffs, the river, the town, this woman, all of it was too beautiful to be real, yet it was. Angela couldn't take it. Staying here meant risking every person in the village, and she remembered what was worth fighting for: people. Those she knew and those she didn't. Becoming stronger, more versatile, and more resilient was important, but it didn't compare to the feeling that Angela had when she first signed up for the Etlus.

Taking on missions to Earth and defending her city, protecting other people who needed her, and fighting for something bigger than her, despite all odds—*that* was what she thrived on. It was the beauty of life that she fought for and everyone's right to enjoy it to the fullest. Humans, Anunnaki, and even the Dalkhu were important. But those who had been with her through thick and thin wouldn't benefit from this fit of self-pity. This wasn't going to get her anywhere.

Angela shook her head with a smile and said, "I'm sorry. I can't join you."

Stasis could mean the death of everyone, even me. I have to move forward, find a way to fix this.

Liu dipped her head. "Very well. Perhaps another time

then." She stepped past her, and Angela left her at the edge of the dock.

Back in town, Angela took everything in—the sights, the smells—as she looked for the smallest sign to point her in the right direction. She scanned the fronts of houses and shops, the roads, and finally the bluffs around the village. The cliffs surrounded them, shielded them. She spotted the road she'd come in on and two more that weaved up and out of the canyon.

No matter what she looked at, nothing stood out to her. It was a human village, nothing more. She rattled her mind, replaying what Kuda had said to her, trying to catch a riddle or something she must have missed. But nothing came to her until she saw Gao, the blacksmith, meditating in the sunlight outside his home.

Maybe it's not an object—like a weapon—that I'm looking for. Maybe it's a person.

For the next three days, Angela watched the people. Gao would meditate three times a day: once before he began his work, once after a break in the afternoon, and once before he retired for the night. Or maybe he was praying. Angela wasn't sure. Humans and some Dalkhu believed in mysterious higher beings that could only be contacted by thought, but not Angela and not the Anunnaki.

The fishermen followed the same day-in-day-out ritual as well; they gathered down by the docks in the morning and helped one another gather and repair nets before heading out onto the river until they returned at night. Women moved to and fro, handling the household's duties and tending to children.

The entire village was a massive clock with a hundred tiny little pieces that seemed to give the same face every day.

A man with a strange hat and a thin golden chain on his neck would exit his house every morning and meditate in a small flower garden to the side of his home. Afterward he would take a bucket from inside his home and carry it up the nearest cliffside before disappearing over the ridge. Angela wasn't sure what the bucket was for or where he went, but every day he would return at midday and seemingly do nothing else.

Upon seeing the man in the hat begin his climb again on the fourth day, Angela wondered what he was doing with that damn bucket. It appeared empty when he left and empty when he returned, so what was the point of carrying it and where was he going? Maybe it bugged her because she'd spent the last three days watching humans' boring lives, but Angela spontaneously decided that she would follow him.

She sprinted as fast as her feet would carry her up and down the bluffs and hills that surrounded the village. Even though the desire to teleport was hard to resist, she had to stay out of sight. By the time Angela reached the path she'd seen the man traveling up, he was out of sight.

Angela sprinted down the path to the base of a hill, then up it, cresting over it just in time to see the white pointed hat with small slashes of red to her left. The man had broken off the road and taken a thickly overgrown game trail used by animals.

Sticking to the shrubs and tall grass, Angela trailed him for the better part of an hour. Luckily, the man wasn't in a hurry, so she followed him up another bluff at a rather leisurely pace. She watched him weave his way through until the trail seemed to end in a wall of tall grass. But as he stepped past the threshold, he disappeared in the blink of an eye.

Angela strained her eyes, focusing on where she'd seen

him last. The grass wasn't *that* thick. The reeds didn't even rustle or move around as he entered them. He just disappeared as though he had teleported away, yet there was no concussive blast of air or any sound at all.

She climbed the last of the game trail, shoving her way through the overgrown grass and bushes, until she came to the spot where he had disappeared, and she stopped to examine the wall of reeds in front of her. There was something unusual about all of this, and that meant she had to go after him now. Angela held her breath and extended her arm. Her hand disappeared.

An illusion similar to the Scratched Hall, she thought.

Exhaling slowly, she stepped into the weeds, but once she was through, there were no weeds at all for her to stand in. The path through trees and overgrown grass instantly changed into a trampled hillside, like a herd of deer had bedded there the night before. Even the hill she was climbing had changed. It sloped upward into a peak where two hills connected with one another. Up above her, and still heading upward, was the man in the white hat.

They had passed through some illusion spell's threshold that appeared to cover the entire area around the mountain. Angela was most definitely intrigued now. She picked up her pace, following after the man up the steep hill. As she walked, she guessed by the trampled grass that the illusion was at least half a mile wide.

About halfway to the top, there was a flat bed of stone, worn down by wind and rain, where the mouth of a cave sat. The human she had been following was standing there before it, his hand digging around in his bucket. Faintly, over the wind, she could hear him speaking to himself. Then something struck her.

I've touched minds with every human in Anyang, and

he's clearly a human. So how did he cast such a spell without a soul? And if he didn't, how did he know about this place, and who did cast the spell, then?

There was movement just inside the shadow of the cave. Something large came forward, stepping out into the sunlight. A spectacle of purple hues reflected off its scales, casting color on the stones all around. It was a Nephilim.

CHAPTER TWENTY-THREE

Angela bolted forward, screaming with a sudden fury that startled even her.

What am I doing? she thought, remembering her last fight. *Am I strong enough for this?*

In a single fluid motion, she lunged, drew the knife with her left hand, and thrust it down upon the creature's claw. As she rolled, the paw withdrew into the darkness of the cave and the beast grumbled from within. The man in the pointed hat was yelling angrily at her, but Angela ignored him and pulled him away from the ancient being.

"Get back!" she demanded.

Then came the spiny head and neck of the Nephilim. Its purple scales cast hues all around as it lumbered from the cave in heavy strides. It shook its neck and stretched as the sound of an avalanche rumbled in its throat. It loomed over her by at least six feet, matching Basmu's size or maybe even beating it. The human she had saved was screaming something she couldn't follow, and the Nephilim cocked its head to the side and spoke into her mind:

He wants me to kill you for finding me. Should I?

Angela scowled at the man over her shoulder. He did not understand what kind of monster he was facing. She tightened her grip on the dagger and said, "You can try."

The creature grumbled, almost as though it was happy. *Much time has passed since I've seen a different face. Does this one have a name, too? Mine is known as Gor, Keeper of Fae, as they call me.*

Her mind raced, and she blurted the first thing that came to her: "Angela, Two-Souled Slayer of Nephilim."

The beast raised its head, curious. *Who?*

Angela wondered if she misunderstood but continued: "Anshar."

Gor swayed to the left and then the right as he thought. *I don't know Nephilim by that name.*

"He was the son of… Lahmu, I believe."

Ah… Lahmu I have not seen in a long time. Angry is his fire, like the color of him. A son of his you killed? The beast took another step closer, shaking the ground, and in a low voice it asked, *Tell me, how did you do it?*

Her heart beat so hard she swore the thing must have been able to see her shaking. It would be coming for her soon. "I drove this blade through his eye two weeks ago."

He rumbled deep in his throat again. *Do you mean to kill me, then?*

Angela shrugged. "I-I haven't decided yet."

Neither have I. His lips stretched back like he was smiling. *So we are equal on terms then. Tell me, why make your presence known?*

She narrowed her eyes and motioned behind her. "I thought you were going to hurt this man."

Ku? No. Gor's purple tail lashed out and struck the bucket, knocking it over. Bloody slabs of meat plopped onto the ground. *Ku is a friend who comes here in search of answers I cannot give him. But to be honest, I enjoy the company and sustenance, so I allow him to believe I know more than I do.* Gor grumbled like he was laughing.

Angela stood there, mouth open and incredulous. Something told her that this Nephilim was harmless. "I need to think for a moment," she said, and she walked to the edge of the flat stone away from the cave. Staring at the creature for a moment, she thought, *Is it Gor I was searching for? Did Kuda send me here to find him?* She let out a sigh and looked over the rolling hills, back toward Anyang. *What else is there to find here?*

Ku was speaking with Gor again. She wasn't sure what either of them were saying, as the Nephilim's voice didn't permeate her head. Angela was a little jealous that Nephilim could have unheard conversations with each other. It would have saved her countless awkward encounters.

A mind brushed against her soul and soaked in her aura, and Gor's voice filled her head: *Tell me what you came for.*

Angela took a few steps toward him and shrugged. "I'm trying to figure that out myself, honestly."

He lowered his head. *There have been many nights I've lain alone and thought that this life has given me everything there is to offer. I do not hunger for blood or knowledge or power, have no companionship other than Ku, whom I will outlive. You would not be wrong to assume I am of little wanting, and over the years I have gained insight into you smaller beings. I know what you want.*

"Yeah? What's that?"

Knowledge. Truth. Just by the aura of you, something confuses you. Your fight was hard, but it isn't over yet. You want to know how to kill Nephilim without challenge, don't you? You want to control those souls inside you, too.

Again, Angela wasn't sure how she should respond. If she said yes, would he get upset that she might kill off the rest of his species? Or since he had stayed secluded here on Earth for so long, did he even care?

"I do," she admitted.

See? I knew it, Gor said. He turned his great head to Ku, who then nodded and began to leave, but not before sneering back at Angela as he walked.

Sit. I will tell you a story of a time long gone. Do you know how the world before this one, the Nephilim's world, Vi'dinor, was destroyed?

Angela hesitated but sat on the ground with her knife on her lap. "Not with any certainty. There was a war, wasn't there?" She scratched the back of her head. "And how is it that you, the Nephilim, are our ancestors? We're nothing alike—physically—at all."

His great purple head dipped low to the ground in a nod, and he too lay down in the warm sun. *You mistake how your species came to be and even how ours was created. There were greater beings and worlds before even ours. Spiritual creatures like the Nephilim create new life by the melding of souls, but that is not what you came to learn about.*

A mere few hundred years into my life I came to find that some Nephilim were abusing the souls given to us. At first, they manipulated their souls' energies into physical manifestations in secret, bringing their energies out of their souls and bending it into any shape of their will. Such a tactic was judged natural and was allowed, as they were not warping themselves, only projecting their own inner energy.

But upon discovering the powers they had, they delved further and found that they could give their energies intent and purpose, and they birthed their first spells. Slowly, the number of those Nephilim who hid in the dark to practice grew. In secret, they eventually found that they could even break off pieces of their souls and imbue weapons and trinkets with their energy and will.

Angela shuddered. "They shattered their souls?"

Indeed. They gave up parts of themselves to give an object an effect, and it forever damned them.

She crossed her arms and thought in silence for a moment. Was it possible that Maulkatu had such an object? That would explain his sudden, newfound strength. "What do you mean by 'effects'?"

Think. A spell is a soul's energy given precise direction with extreme willpower. When a being separates a part of itself and infuses an object with his will and the energy, that spell carries on into the item.

"Is it possible that one of these ancient items could have survived the Anchor's breaking? And could it have the ability to amplify one's own soul?" she asked.

Gor lifted a great claw and scratched at his neck. *It is possible, as I know some do survive. Even outside the body, a fractured piece of soul continues to generate energy. If it has remained unused, the artifact would gradually create a deep well of power to fulfill its purpose.*

Angela bolted to her feet, exclaiming, "That's it! Has to be." She began to pace back and forth. "That's where Maulkatu is getting his new power. How can I destroy such an artifact?"

The giant beast rolled his shoulders like he was shrugging. He grumbled and said, *Destroy it? Why? Better to be stolen, no?*

She bit her lip. "It would be, but I doubt I'll be able to

sneak up on him. Tell me everything, please. So much is at stake."

I know that it will not be as simple or easy as you think. Does one know what the object looks like?

"No," Angela admitted. "But what can I look for?"

What you seek could be anything. Would it not be a better-suited plan to meet him in power rather than subvert him?

Angela couldn't help but laugh. "I can't reach that kind of strength. You said it yourself: this artifact could have been generating energy for thousands of years. There's no way I could find something just as powerful in the kind of timeframe that I need it."

Gor tapped a claw against the stone beneath him. *Even so, there is a finite amount of energy to everything. It will run out, and this person will have to use his own. You forget the power inside yourself. It will return to you after each fight, and could you not project the energy inside yourself? Bring it out in physical form?*

Her heart sank. To this day, she did not understand how she had once flown on wings of lightning. Angela threw up her hands. "There must be a faster way. I barely have days. Just tell me how to destroy the artifact and I'll leave you alone in your cave. This… *All* the worlds are at stake."

Gor purred. *Everything is always at risk of falling apart. Empires built across the ages fall in a day. I will not tell you how to destroy it, only point you toward a tool which might help you rise up to your challenge.*

Angela disagreed with Gor in every way. No one should ever have access to a well of energy and a handful of Nephilim companions. Maulkatu had enough power—spiritual, physical, *and* political. But all she could do was try to best him by whatever means necessary. She took a deep breath and said, "Very well. I'll do as you say and try to preserve the artifact, but you must tell me how I'm supposed to win."

The purple creature snickered. *The energy some Nephilim and other souled creatures project can melt and penetrate most armors—even scales. I suggest you find a way to manifest your energy. To do that, you need balance, but to attain balance you must first see what is upsetting it.*

Such a task would take far too much time. Many do not look deep enough because what they see frightens them. To look and examine means to acknowledge the things that are wrong. In you, I sense no balance. No harmony.

What would normally take years of retrospection may take seconds if one owned a token a friend of mine once had. It is an amulet of lesser power, but its effects grant a peculiar boon. It helps you distance yourself from yourself. It puts down emotion and gives you the insight to see truth in any form. You can use it to dispel illusions or focus it on yourself so that you may uncover things that even you don't know about yourself. That knowledge may give you the control over your energies, like you so desire. If you can find it.

Angela let out a long sigh. Another step that she didn't have time for. "And where could I find this amulet?"

Last I knew, a wise Nephilim by the name of Asbateel carried the amulet into Kur when the world broke apart. When the fighting first began between Dalkhu and Nephilim, he was slain, and I imagine the Council took the relic for themselves.

She chuckled. "It couldn't be easy, could it?" But as she contemplated it, a mysterious thing returned to her mind and she remembered what happened when Toth showed her the Scratched Hall of the Nephilim. He was reaching for the amulet on his chest.

When my turn came to protect my world, I was too afraid, Gor said. *I waited too long to fight and lost my home. It rarely is easy to make great strides to change history.*

Angela thought about that, and a plan was already forming in her mind. "I think you're right. I have to find a way to get myself back to where I was. I have to balance myself somehow. If this amulet is the way to do it, then so be it. On this note, it's time I leave." She bowed to the Nephilim. "Thank you for your insight and guidance. I'll see that your time was not a waste."

Do you not wish to know how we destroyed our world? The story is not complete.

Angela shook her head. "I'm afraid that will have to wait."

The purple Nephilim bowed once more and said, *Until you return,* and she pushed into the space between the worlds.

EVEN THOUGH WEEKS HAD PASSED SINCE THE FIRE RAVISHED the valley and sinkhole garden, it still smelled like ash and smoke. She spent a few hours picking up the singed lumber of broken furniture and teleporting it out into a pile in the valley as she formulated the rest of her plan.

She picked nuts from hazel bushes and buried them in the garden and all around the valley. Pine trees wouldn't do in the garden, so she took a fig from the tree in the mountain pass and planted it below, along with red flowers from outside the valley. The soot-covered earth would give rise to a good spring, she knew.

In her old room, she bent before the charred remains of her trunk. The hinges groaned as she threw it open, sending dust into the air. Her armor lay neatly on top. There was blood and dirt, wrinkles, and cracks in the leather. The batteries in her belt were drained, of course, but she still felt the urge to test her brass knuckles. When they did not spark, she set them on the ground and dug a little deeper until she found her old shifter.

The brass tube was heavy and cold. She squinted through the viewport and found it was empty, then set it down. The leather bag that used to hang at her waist was empty as well, even though she swore that she'd held on to at least a few crystals. But she wouldn't have denied the possibility she'd traded them, either.

Then she realized she was waiting to act again. Her fear of failure and the likelihood that Neti was already dead was making her indecisive. She was letting all of it hold her back.

Angela cussed, threw everything back into the trunk, and slammed it shut. If there was anything left to accomplish before she died, she wanted to apologize to Neti.

Angela stood on her feet and pushed herself between the worlds. While the icy expanse gave her plenty of time to think, she still wasn't sure when she arrived. The glowing moss gave the cavern little light to see by, but she didn't need it, anyway. There in the colors of the unnamed cavern, she sat and began to scry.

While it wasn't, and likely never would be, a normal feeling, she had at least somewhat expected the lack of sensation as she slipped from her body and burrowed herself into the veil. As she suspected, she felt his presence in Kur, buried beneath the auras of the Nephilim.

Basmu's, in particular, was the loudest. His resonance came from the halls of the Kissum. Lahmu the Red and Kishar the Green, father and daughter by Angela's knowledge, were off along the outer edge of the city's stalactite field. Their positioning would work in her favor, she knew, because underneath the Kissum's antechamber, her target's soul resonated quietly, almost as though he did not want to be found. There was no anger, no fear—only pain and determination.

If by chance the Nephilim detected her arrival, Basmu wouldn't be able to fit down in the tunnels. The others likely would, but something told her that she would probably become the victim of another spell before they came down to find her themselves.

Angela returned to her body, took a deep breath, and teleported to Kur.

CHAPTER TWENTY-FOUR

The ancient dust that billowed into the air was older than Angela could guess. She coughed, then dashed into the tunnel as quickly as possible. Ten feet in, she hoped beyond hope that the Nephilim wouldn't investigate the boom of her arrival, which now echoed across Kur. Basmu wouldn't have been able to fit, but the others could squeeze in. It wasn't until she was a hundred feet in that she was confident they weren't coming after her.

A short distance more through the weaving tunnel and she came to the first doorway and peeked inside. The chamber was completely empty, and she realized that the colors of the drapes signified the status of the room and continued on. After another few minutes of walking, she found the red drape of a councilman's room. Taking a deep breath, she asked, "Toth? Are you there?"

A moment passed, long enough for Angela to doubt that she'd arrived at the right place. Finally, a deep voice on the other side said, "Come in."

Furniture filled his living room. Every wall had at least one shelf and cabinet. Books overflowed onto the floors, and carved wooden figurines of Dalkhu men and women lined the shelves. Some were of better craftsmanship than others, but the sheer number of them impressed Angela, and she wondered if they were his.

Toth sat in his robes at a circular table with only three chairs, a pen in hand and an open inkwell next to the parchment in front of him. He placed the pen into the pot and leaned back when he saw Angela entering his home. His hair was a red mess that resembled a bird's nest. Dark rings had settled under his steel eyes, and his cracked lip was crusted with blood.

"I did not expect to see you here again," he said, crossing his arms. "Maulkatu told the rest of us that you were hanging on by a thread."

Angela stepped to the table, eyed what was in front of him, and tapped on her bottom lip. "Seems we both may have a learning deficiency. Am I right?"

He smiled and looked away in embarrassment or shock that she'd brought it up.

"I'll admit I do," she said. "But I think that my stubbornness has been more of an advantage than a disadvantage."

Still, Toth was silent, but she didn't have time to waste. Maybe it was his pride holding him back.

Angela scratched the back of her head. "No cracking your shell, huh?" She sighed. "Remember how I told you when we first visited the Scratched Hall that I would find out how you revealed the tunnel? Well, I think I know how you dispelled the illusion."

He returned his eyes to her, suspicious and curious

enough to talk again. "I don't think it's hard to guess that a Virtuoso of the Council is good with spells."

Angela snickered. Toth was playing coy. He didn't want to be the first to admit it and wanted to be sure she knew all on her own. She obliged him: "No, you used a trinket, a soul-powered artifact from the world before." Toth's eyes grew wide, filling her with satisfaction. Before he could ask, she said, "A Nephilim named Gor told me. The copper and emerald necklace you always wear allows you to see past illusions, gives you a different perspective and a deeper understanding of things."

"I haven't heard of Gor. He isn't one of the Nephilim out there."

"Yeah, that's because I found him hiding out on Earth. Long story, but he knew a lot about Vi'dinor—the world before."

Toth looked wide-eyed and incredulous, like she'd just told him the most amazing thing. "After I replaced Udug as Virtuoso twelve years ago, I was barely allowed to peruse his notes. Shedim always fought for his chambers. So I began my own research and stumbled upon archives that mentioned that necklace. I searched the ruins of Eld Kur for a month, trying to find it on a Nephilim's bones."

The councilman shook his head, letting out a half-suppressed laugh that made his green eyes shimmer. "It's ironic, really. He knew you would be coming here for the amulet." He grabbed the collar of his black robe and pulled it down, revealing the pale skin of his neck and chest. Disappointment ripped her in two. She wanted to scream. Toth didn't have the necklace. Maulkatu did.

"No, no, no..." Angela muttered, burying her face in her hands. That was her hope. Maybe all the hope in existence, and Maulkatu took that, too. "When did he come for it? How could he have known?"

"I do not know, but he came a few hours ago and asked for the amulet. When I first refused to hand it over, he hit me and threatened to do worse." Toth paused, running his hands down his cheeks slowly as he thought. "There was something about his eyes and the way the air felt *alive* around him." His eyes focused back on her, and he trembled as he said, "Something in him has changed."

A groan escaped her. She couldn't hold it against Toth for giving up the amulet rather than facing Maulkatu's wrath. Even she was afraid of him. Afraid of what she knew was going to face her now. He was playing with her, but she had to find the courage to face him.

"I guess there's not much else for me to do here besides ask if you'll help me in this fight," she said. Toth remained cold, calculating, and unemotional. She threw her hands up and stood. "I have to keep moving. Stay here in your chambers, leaving the Nephilim to destroy your people and everything, if you want, but Neti is running out of time."

Toth closed his eyes and rubbed them for a moment, considering something until he took a deep breath and said, "The only aid I can give you is my confidence. This fight to free the worlds from the Nephilim is one I could not lead—or win. Perhaps you should consider that destiny exists, Angela, because no rational part of me believes you will win, yet I know in my heart that you cannot lose."

ANGELA SHIVERED WHEN THE COOL, DAMP AIR OF KUR'S lower caverns rushed against her skin. The sound was loud and echoed throughout the hall in four directions. A moss-covered glow stone sat in a sconce. She took it and cast its green light down each of the passages beneath the Kissum but saw nothing but darkness and carved stone. Minutes passed as she contemplated which to take, until she heard dripping water in one passage and scratching down another. She took the latter, figuring that the scratching was a better sign of life. He was nearby and had to know she had come for him.

A set of stairs led her farther down and into another black corridor with empty storage chambers and intersecting hallways that seemed to go nowhere. Her heart thumped loudly, but she pressed on until she came to a closed wooden door with torchlight flickering from the other side.

Angela placed her ear against it. There was a sound like two pebbles rubbing or scratching together. A sharp smell like onions or sweat reached her nose, and then someone behind the door coughed.

She slammed her shoulder into the old door, and it cracked. Black iron hinges tore loose as the door fell to the ground. This room had a full fireplace. A long countertop of carved stone sat on the far wall and was covered with various beakers and vials topped with corks. A mortar and pestle, alembics, and other alchemical tools sat front and center as though someone was just using them.

She stepped inside, treading cautiously, and searched the room. There were no parchments or secrets to be found other than the mystery surrounding the substances in the glass containers. She lifted a few with powders and liquids and one with bright pink chunks that seemed to shimmer under the light of her torch. The liquid in the mortar was a reddish-brown, its scent unpleasant.

A door she hadn't noticed creaked and shut. Angela

froze, but nothing else happened. Once her breathing settled, she heard something shuffling and went to it. Her hand shook as she reached out and swung the door open. Rusted iron bars sectioned off the room into prison cells. But unlike the last room, this one was occupied.

Smiling, he was sitting on a wooden stool, a silver dagger across his leg. When she entered, his mind brushed against hers for only a moment, like he was dipping his toes in the water. He didn't say a word; his smile was enough. What was of more importance to her was Neti, who was secured to a wooden frame by caltrops at his ankles and wrists. He slowly lifted his sagging head. Bloodshot eyes looked out from beneath his sweat-drenched hair. His nose and lips were crusted with blood.

Freeing him would be no easy task. The wooden frame was attached to the stone wall by iron spikes, which meant the shackles would have to be released. His notice of her had also been a bit delayed. Based on the previous room's alchemical concoctions, Angela didn't doubt that Maulkatu had drugged him.

Smooth and calm, the councilman stood and placed the tip of the dagger on Neti's side like it was everyday business, dashing any hope of her being able to strike the councilman preemptively. His eyes were black orbs underneath his hood, reflecting the light. "I've been waiting for you," he said. "I knew you would come, so he is *mostly* lucid. I wouldn't want him to miss a single thing."

Angela had to refrain from scoffing and keep him listening and interested in hearing what she had to say, but she also had to force him to respect her or things would turn sour. "How generous of you," she said as smoothly as she could. "Keep it up and I might forget what a monster you are."

His eyes grew narrow, and Angela wondered if she'd already taken it too far. Then he bellowed in laughter, almost falling over.

Angela crossed her arms. "I'm serious. I want to make a deal, Maulkatu. You have one of the most important things to me at your knife's edge."

He shook his head, draining the joy from his face and replacing it with genuine surprise. "Well, that's the last thing I suspected you would say. I'll play along. What would I gain out of this deal of yours?"

"No matter how much time passes, I will vow to never strike you or another Dalkhu. I'll return to Dingir and take on the title of Grand Etlu, as was promised to me by Ja'noel. In charge of Dingir's attacking force, my focus will be on converting the city's policies to reflect an isolationist state. I will call every soldier from Earth and no Anunnaki will dare strike your people so long as I live."

Very slightly, Maulkatu's knife hand relaxed. "I won't lie, Angela. It pleases me to hear that." He clacked his tongue on the roof of his mouth for a moment, thinking and looking her up and down. "What are the terms?"

I've almost got him, she squealed inside.

"The Earth can be yours to roam on two conditions. First, you will let Neti go and agree to never pursue him or lead your people against any Anunnaki or Dingir itself. Secondly, you will give me the amulet you took from Toth. Thirdly, you will not allow the Nephilim to leave Kur." As each requirement rolled from her tongue, she watched Maulkatu's interest fade.

The councilman chuckled and held the knife a bit firmer. "I'm sorry, Angela. I know you are sincere, but do you actually think that I would be satisfied with that? The Nephilim would eat the common folk alive if I don't teach them how to walk the veils. I have already promised it. Besides, you're ignoring what I want out of all this. How about this?" he said, pointing a finger in the air. "I've been watching you quite a bit these last few days. Tracking you. There was a conversation I seem to remember…"

Angela clenched her fists. "What conversation?" She didn't need to ask to know he was referring to her conversation with Gor.

But how could he have eavesdropped? You can't hear anything when you scry… Unless Gor is with Maulkatu, but that would mean that Kuda was, too, and that wouldn't make sense. Both Gor and Kuda helped me, pointed me in the right direction. But how could he know?

Maybe he had more tricks up his sleeves than she could have imagined.

The councilman's smile was sinister, yellow teeth reflecting the torchlight. "It would be much more simple if you chose between what you think you need more: the amulet or the boy." He raised the knife's edge to Neti's throat, but he was too drugged and restrained to move or realize what was happening.

Angela's blood boiled. The whole reason she'd come back to Kur was now in Maulkatu's hands. She clenched a fist and wished she could use it. "I'm sick of playing your games, Maulkatu. Just take the deal before I end you now."

She was bluffing, and he knew it. "We will play my games until I've had my fill. Besides, the final, bloody battle is still on the horizon. It's not quite time yet, I think. We have to let fate take its course."

"You're talking crazy. There's no such thing as fate. Only the directions we point our lives toward matter. The rest is luck."

Maulkatu snickered and shrugged. "I'm of the belief that both of our hands are forced by destiny, but we will have to agree to disagree. Now, you forget who is in charge here. I extend my offer once more. Pick whichever matters most to you: the relic you so desperately need to defeat me and the Nephilim I've arrayed against you, or Neti's life."

Angela gnashed her teeth. His strength was more than she could handle, but now it boiled down to killing him or saving Neti. Weakly, she said, "The amulet."

"Are you certain?" Maulkatu asked, an incredulous smile on his face.

Angela nodded slowly. "Give me the amulet."

"Oh my... Did you hear that, Neti? It is never a dull moment with you in the picture. But I think you love it, honestly. And you've always interested me. An Anunnaki woman who's turned her back against her people to protect humanity. It is an honorable notion, no doubt, but when they die so easily and pointlessly, your efforts, too, mean nothing. Yet you say you will give up this boy's life for your crushing desire to defeat me?"

"Yes." The words were like poison slipping from her lips.

Neti lifted his head to look at her, tears forming in his eyes. "You... You can't... be serious?"

A lump formed in her throat. He was conscious enough to hear her, and that killed her inside.

Maulkatu snickered. "Cruel words. He'll die hating you for everything you've ever done to him, you know. Not just for this, but for fighting by your side for so long and you giving up on him at the end. What else would be a bigger waste of his time?"

She had to fight back a tear at the distress in his face,

the pure horror, but it didn't change what had to be done. "I'm sorry, Neti. I have to find a way to beat this. *Everyone* is at stake if I don't do this. You understand, don't you? If you were in my shoes, you'd do the same. You know it."

Neti looked away, quiet.

"Do you want your prize?" Maulkatu asked with a smile. "I am still in disbelief, but this is a fair deal. I accept, and here it is." He dipped his hand into his robe, pulled out the copper and emerald necklace, and threw it across the room.

When Angela caught it, she turned it over in her hand and stared into the gem. She didn't feel any wiser or any better about what she'd done. There was nothing but guilt when she turned back to the councilman and watched him raise the dagger back to Neti's throat.

"I'm sorry, Neti," she said again. "I have to do this."

Sweat was beading on Maulkatu's tattooed scalp. He smiled, hands shaking in excitement, and pulled the dagger across Neti's throat. It sliced his skin and she covered her mouth and sobbed when she saw the blood. But it wasn't enough; the wound only dribbled.

Maulkatu dropped his arm, eying her in some strange sense of serenity and peaceful amazement. "You really would let him die for that. You didn't even try to stop me." He glanced at the amulet in her hand, then back up at her. "You're afraid, aren't you? Afraid to know what it is inside you that's holding you back. Even more afraid that you'll have to give up everything to win. Maybe even your life."

Angela clutched the amulet tighter and reached out to touch it with her mind. Maulkatu was playing with her, holding the fate of her friends and the worlds over her head. The emerald was warm and alive, like a bubble full of a thousand fireflies. All she needed to do was pierce it and let it in.

Maulkatu laughed. "Do it, Angela. Use the amulet, strike me down, and free your poor Neti."

It almost seemed like a request, and that made her suspicious of what other tricks he had planned for her. Slowly, she became more aware that all of this was just some sick test of her limits. He sensed her hesitation and smiled.

"Let's agree to settle this another day. Here," he said, tossing her an iron key from his robes. He reached behind the wooden stand that Neti was restrained to and threw her a familiar-looking sword. By the square, golden guard, she knew it was Teshub's. "Take the boy and that sword, too," Maulkatu said. "No more games—just one final fight, one last chance to find out if you are worthy to see this to the end."

Hands trembling, Angela was too afraid to question what he was saying. He was sounding insane.

Worthy to see what end?

"If you defeat me, I swear on my honor as a councilman that I will bend a knee and you can finish me. I won't run, so long as you swear to do the same. I want you to *earn* what's in store for you. Can you agree to that?"

What choice do I have? She could only nod.

Maulkatu was relaxed, unfazed, and more diplomatic than she had ever seen him before. He spoke coolly. "And there we have it: the answer I wanted. When a person accepts that they have nothing left to lose, they fight harder. Your defeat will be crushing, Angela. To everyone." He held up his fingers and said, "In three days' time I will find you, no matter where you are, and we will settle this once and for all." He flashed a smile, then vanished from the room in a blast of air.

Other than Neti's harsh, uneven breathing, it was quiet for longer than Angela was comfortable with. Even though they were alone now, he kept his eyes to the floor and didn't ask for her to release him from his manacles. Where could she begin? How should she feel? How did Neti feel? Angela was angry, for sure, at Maulkatu's infuriating ability to be one step ahead of her this whole time. Even prior to releasing the Nephilim, he'd known what she was going to do before she did it.

But her anger did not overpower her guilt. An apology was called for. Neti kept his eyes hidden behind his black bangs as she removed the shackles that held him to the wooden frame. When the last one was free, he stumbled forward. Angela caught him by the arms and pulled him to his feet. "Come on," she said. "Let's just—"

He pushed her away, standing on wobbling legs. Still keeping his eyes hidden behind his bangs, he said, "I'm not going with you. I'm through with this. I'm through with *you.*"

That hurt. She could feel his soul tense as he prepared to teleport, but she had to buy time. He needed to talk with her so she could keep him from leaving. "I-I'm sorry, Neti. For all of this. I know that I don't say it often enough. You have to understand that this amulet could be the key to finishing this. I had to stall—get as much out of him as I could so I know what I'm up against. If I was in your shoes, I wouldn't expect you to pick me over the—"

"I know," Neti said, holding up a hand. He turned to face her, his wet eyes shimmering. "But this could be so *different.* You act as though you were the only thing standing between humans and the Anunnaki and Dalkhu.

The only person trying to hold order and balance between the worlds all these years."

He threw his arms in the air, temper growing. "You're blind to everyone at your side! And now I realize that you always have been. Maybe instead of holding onto the past, onto *Michael*, you could have realized what the people right in front of you are feeling."

He slammed a fist against his leg. "Do you even know what it's like standing next to you right now? For *years* now, you've dragged me around the world on your quests for order. I just wish I would have seen all of this sooner. You literally ruined every chance of me having any semblance of a relationship with my people. Now *and* when I was a child. I hate you for that, Angela. I admit it. I *hate* you."

Guilt rippled through her, making her heart ache. "I-I don't know what to say other than I'm sorry I've hurt you —in more ways than one—but I've tried to make it right. After your father died, I tried to find you a relative to stay with. I really did, but your grandparents had already passed. You would have gone to an orphanage, so I did everything I could to give you the life you deserved.

"In the last fifteen years, you've become the most important person in my life. If you want to leave, I understand. You will always be important to me. I'm just sorry I'm not good at showing it."

He shook his head and sighed. "Just... Just go. You have your amulet." He readied his soul again.

She grabbed his wrist, unable to let him leave like this, and made him look into her eyes. "I know it seems like I traded you for the amulet, but I know that I need you just as much as I need it. I need everyone: all the people I've pushed aside and disregarded. I may never be able to make it up to you, and I can't thank you enough for everything you've given up for me, but I need your help. I need you *now*."

Neti shook his arm from her grip, keeping his eyes cast to the ground. He sighed under his breath. "Just shut up, Angela. All my life you've taken away my choices. I'll give you one last fight, but that's it. After this, I'm on my own."

CHAPTER TWENTY-FIVE

Angela walked behind Neti, following him up the Ascendancy's white steps. The sunlight warmed her back just enough to stave off the wind's bite, yet she couldn't help but feel cold inside. This wasn't a happy visit to a place she'd called home long ago. This was feeling more like a funeral for their relationship. After this, she would be dead to him and she would be alone.

He grabbed the iron handles to the dark double doors and swung them open. When they reached the lobby desk, two Etlus came rushing down the hall with their hands on their guns. Angela shoved Neti behind her, but she pushed a little too hard. In his unsteady state, he staggered as Angela launched herself between him and the soldiers. She raised her hand and said, "Back off. My name's Angela Ma'at. The Dalkhu is with me."

The soldier shifted his weight and sneered. He was wide, muscular, and heavy. A fighter, if Angela ever met one. "I know who you are," he said, looking her up and down with glaring eyes, "but you might want to put a collar on him." The Etlus pushed past her without another word.

When they disappeared around the corner, she saw Neti's jaw was clenched, and she grabbed him by the arm. "Come with me," she declared. "We need to get you out of sight and resting. There are beds in the infirmary. We can see about getting someone to look at your neck, too."

He rolled his eyes as he trudged next to her. "Who would that be, I wonder? I think Dingir is quite short of Dalkhu practitioners."

Angela couldn't argue. They walked through the white-brick hall, under the yellow glow of flickering bulbs, in silence. And it was an unusual silence. The last time she'd been inside, it was a hell of a lot busier. The Ascendancy had always been bustling, and she knew this *stillness* wasn't a good sign.

Angela led Neti past the locked record room, Kushiel's old office, classrooms, and old storage rooms to a door marked with a plaque that read "Infirmary." Inside, she pointed him to a bed and arranged his stay with the healer on duty, who was incredibly uneasy at the notion of taking care of a Dalkhu. But by the end of it, she quelled the healer's worries and left Neti to rest.

On the other side of the Ascendancy, she found Ja'noel's office and knocked twice. When there was no answer and she tapped again with no reply, she tested the handle. The door was unlocked, so she pushed her way inside. There were only chairs and a desk full of papers, none of which were interesting enough for her to peruse, so she walked back across the building, past the lobby again, to find that Kushiel's office was empty as well.

Growing frustrated, she marched to the front and approached the man behind the counter. He was young, thin, and wore black-rimmed glasses. She had to tap the marble countertop to get his attention from the box of files in front of him.

"Hi," Angela said. "Do you know where Ja'noel is?"

"No, sorry, I don't," he answered and resumed his filing.

A loud voice carried down the hall. "He's on Earth."

Sarosha walked closer with swinging strides and her chin up. She was dressed in some variation of a soldier's armor: bracers, greaves, green cotton underclothes, and a brown leather cuirass that resembled a corset and didn't protect the shoulders. It was unusual to see her clad in any armor, as she overlooked no combative aspects of Dingir's management, yet she wore a tether gun at her waist. Two Uri Gallus following closely behind her were even more armed. Angela was right. Something was wrong here.

"Sarosha," she said, extending an open hand.

The darker-skinned woman glanced down at her hand but did not take it. She said, "I heard you were around— and that you brought a Dalkhu with you."

Angela crossed her arms. "He's with me, for at least a brief while longer, and resting in the infirmary. It won't be an issue, will it?"

Sarosha shrugged. "As long as his stay is short. But I'm more interested in why you've returned to Dingir and not your true home."

Why is she so cross with me? Angela wondered. *They had never been friends by any means, but Sarosha had never been this rude before.*

She shook her head, disregarding Sarosha's attitude. "I need to speak with Ja'noel."

Sarosha's face hardened. "He's…" She looked away for a moment and swallowed hard. "You'll have to talk to me."

Angela frowned. *So whatever happened involves Ja'noel.* "Let's head somewhere private, then."

Sarosha nodded and raced past her, leading her until they entered Ja'noel's office. She pushed reports on the Ensi's desk to the side before seating herself in his chair.

Angela sat across from her. When Sarosha had regained the strong composure she was known for, Angela asked, "What's happened around here?" Curiosity was getting the best of her.

As Sarosha tried to form her thoughts into words, her expression melted into sorrow. Her lips drooped, her eyes grew wet, and she buried herself into her hands. "Ja'noel's gone missing. He went searching for Kushiel on Earth."

If the woman wasn't crying, Angela would have had a hard time not laughing at the ridiculousness of what she'd said. But she held it together and asked, "What brought him to believe that Kushiel was on Earth? We all know he fell from Dingir, and it's been *fifteen* years. If he survived, we would have found him years ago."

Sarosha wiped underneath her eyes. "I agree, but the moment a report came in for an older man wearing Anunnaki armor, Ja'noel just felt compelled to go off searching for him. I tried to talk him out of it, but he left that very day."

Angela exhaled slowly as her mind digested the news. "All right, so where was Ja'noel last seen?"

She sorted through the papers on her desk, dropping tears on a few, and placed some in front of Angela. "These here are the last reports I received. Nearly two weeks ago he sent for a translator, and I received this very brief report. Something about how Ja'noel was leading a search through some woods outside one of our camps."

Angela furrowed her brow. "Did you send someone else out to find him? Maybe get an update since then?"

Sarosha's teeth clenched. "Don't think I'm stupid. Of course I did. I sent men after him a week ago, but I haven't heard anything from them, either."

Angela bit her lip. She was fairly accustomed to dealing with Ja'noel, considering he had been the Grand of the Uri Gallus for many years. Kushiel would have been her favored choice, as the man always listened to what she had to say. But Sarosha was a different beast entirely. Angela heard rumors years ago that she was a true spitfire when angered, but only time would tell how she would react when Angela told her why she was really there.

Sarosha wiped at her tears again and sniffed once or twice. With a few deep breaths, she calmed herself again and said, "I know that this isn't why you came. I take it you've dispatched the councilman you were after? No more crystal thieves?"

Angela's gaze dropped. "No, Maulkatu is still alive and well, and I'm afraid that the fight will follow me wherever I go."

She narrowed her eyes, leaning in ever so slightly. Even though Angela was sure she already knew what she was there for, Sarosha at least had the courtesy to ask, "What does that mean?" She was a smart woman, no doubt, quick to catch on to the true reason she had come back to Dingir. So Angela figured it would just be best to get it out of the way.

Angela let out a long sigh. "I-I guess I've come here for a different reason, as I'm sure you're suspecting right now. To make the story short, two councilmen were involved in an uprising of power in Kur. While I don't have proof they were the ones stealing crystals from Dingir, I can't imagine it was anyone else. They've released ancient creatures that've been trapped in the lower tunnels for thousands of years. Shedim, Udug's pupil, is dead by my hands, which leaves Maulkatu, who seems bent on harassing me and believes that the Nephilim will become the leaders of all races and worlds."

"Nephilim?" Sarosha scoffed. "Ja'noel was going on about them and the ancient Anunnaki before his report about Kushiel distracted him. I'll believe such ancient beasts still exist when I see them for myself."

Angela held out open palms in front of her. "Sarosha, I need you to believe what I'm saying. Maulkatu is talking about teaching them how to teleport between the worlds. They won't be just a problem for Kur, and you cannot underestimate them in battle. You think fighting the Dalkhu alone is tough? The Nephilim are *animals*. They don't care if you are a woman, man, human, Anunnaki, or even a child. They will spread their control over anything and everything they can."

Sarosha clacked her nails against the desk as she thought. After a few moments, she said, "You still have not answered my question: what is your purpose here?"

Angela's gaze fell to her hands. "I need Dingir's help. Maulkatu is leading the Nephilim to finish me off in three days' time. He has access to spells beyond your imagination and will know exactly where I am no matter where I go." She looked up at Sarosha. "My time is running out, and if this isn't stopped now, it won't ever be." Guilt rippled through her. She knew what she was asking of Sarosha and of Dingir. It would be no small thing for them to fight with her. It reminded her of Neti. "If you help me," she said, "I promise I will never call upon Dingir again. I know it's not fair."

Sarosha's eyes were calm as she searched Angela's expression for every detail she could perceive. She sighed. "If you say the Nephilim are a threat to worlds beyond Kur, very well. I will be honest: I am not a fan of you or your desertion of this city, but I also have no reason to suspect you would be lying to me."

"Thank you," Angela said, putting her hands together.

Sarosha held up a hand. "Hold on now. I did not say I, or Dingir, would help. With Ja'noel missing, I am the acting Ensi, and I'm hesitant to allow you to bring your fight here. You know the city's condition is terrible. We never recovered from the last time the Council attacked."

Angela nodded. She remembered her agreement with Maulkatu; the loser would take a knee and accept defeat, not flee. Angela figured it would be best to leave that part out. "I know, but it will be different this time. If things go wrong, I'll lead the fight to Earth or even to Kur. It's me Maulkatu wants most. I promise I won't let things get so out of control that Dingir is destroyed beyond the point it cannot return."

Sarosha sighed and stared at the ceiling for a moment, thinking. "I will allow you to use Dingir as your battlefield, consume what little resources the city has left, and use its forces on one condition." Sarosha's eyes stared coldly at Angela. "When it's finished, you will take the role of Ensi and immediately begin a search for Ja'noel yourself. You will swear to find him and will search for him until your life expires or we find that his already has. And when you do find him, you will stay in Dingir and take on the title of Grand Etlu. Furthermore, you will help train a new squad called the Bui'du, and you will serve and never forbid this city again."

Angela stuttered, unsure how to say that her fight was

so much larger than Dingir alone. Seating herself in a position of authority here would make it harder for her to protect humanity.

Sarosha did not let her speak. "This is my only offer. Take it or leave."

CHAPTER TWENTY-SIX

A kick to his bed frame rattled Neti awake. Sunlight streamed in the window, splashing prisms of colors against the row of white-sheeted beds. A silhouette stood between the foot of his bed and the light beyond. He groaned and rubbed at his eyes, then threw his blanket off himself in anger.

"Angela told me to wake you," the woman said. He couldn't remember her name...

Her boots clacked against the floor as she walked, and the weapon at her waist clinked as she sat on the bed next to his. He noticed her hands first. The soft skin had cracked open, and the flames spread underneath her bracers, up her arm and neck, then across her face. As the woman spoke, her voice began to change. "She told me you could help me understand what we're up against."

Neti groaned and sat upright. His waking soul was beginning to realize their aetherical differences, so he stood and walked to the window to help calm his visions. "What's Angela doing, then?" he asked.

"Off looking for someone, as far as I know."

Neti scoffed. "Using people again... That's where her strength truly lies."

"It's also what's going to cost her."

He turned back to her, surprised, and for a moment he could see her frizzled black hair and green eyes. They were just like Angela's. "There's truth to that."

She shrugged. "We've struck a deal. Dingir will fight with her in exchange for her service as Grand Etlu. Ja'noel and I can't keep running this city by ourselves. It'll never heal."

Sarosha... That's her name. Neti leaned back against the wall and crossed his arms. When the flames of her soul began to make it uncomfortable again, he cast his gaze to the wall across the room. "To be realistic, I'm quite certain we won't win this. It's not just going to be the Nephilim and Maulkatu. There will be others from the Council and lower-ranked fighters."

"You're probably right about the other soldiers, which is why you'll wear Anunnaki armor from here on out. It'll be the only way my soldiers will be able to differentiate you from the enemy." Sarosha sighed. "We will also have to keep someone with you at all times. No offense meant, but people will have a hard time trusting a flame-headed Dalkhu that's walking around unaccompanied in a battle."

Neti rolled his eyes and hated how she was trying to come off like *she* wasn't personally invested in the idea of an armed escort. "Whatever, fire-breath." He pushed off the wall and walked a few feet away, his back to her. Even a dozen feet away he could feel the heat of her soul irradiating his skin. He strained to see through another stained-glass window and stretched. "If we're really going to do this, we will need all the luck we can get. I'm not sure what Angela's told you, but the Nephilim are nothing to joke about. They are *strong*, and not just their bodies."

Sarosha huffed behind him. "Let's be real, Neti. My soldiers aren't able to do anything to them on a spiritual level, spell- or projection-wise. So just tell me how I can kill their bodies."

Neti turned. "Their scales are as hard as any metal. Same with their teeth. They can spit fire if they really want to, but I don't think it's easy for them." He shook his head, exasperated just at the thought of fighting them. And then there was Maulkatu's black energy. How were they going to defeat that?

He remembered Angela's last fight in the valley on Earth. *It must have been terrible.* He probably should have tried to get her out of there sooner, but he had been frozen with fear until the moment he charged in. When the guilt began to grip him, he shoved it away. Things wouldn't be better until it was over with and he could leave this all behind.

He shrugged. "Honestly, just find a way to keep them on the ground."

ANGELA WASN'T SURE WHERE TO BEGIN. SHE ALMOST knelt and placed a hand on his lap as she spoke with him, but this man wasn't the same Donny she knew before. Not only had he lost an incredible amount of body weight, but his smile wasn't the same, and the twinkle in his eyes was dull.

She watched the soldiers remove the shocking helm from his head and lift him from his death trap. He groaned as his legs straightened for the first time in a long while. As the men helped him leave his cell, she said, "I never had a chance to thank you for everything you did for me. This whole time, I-I thought you were dead. If I had known you were alive, I would have—"

Donny raised a finger and cut her off, his eyes solemn and serious behind his shoulder-length blond hair. "You didn't know any better. It's all right. There's not a piece of me that regrets stepping up to help you, if that's what you're wondering."

"Well, I still feel bad for it," Angela said. When they reached the stairs, she took one of the soldier's places so she could help Donny walk. He groaned as he lifted his leg up each one, but they took it slow. "You've been imprisoned for the last fifteen years. I'm not going to forget that price you paid. It's my fault. And don't say it wasn't. You didn't have to break me out of Dingir."

"You're right. I didn't have to." Tears welled in his eyes, probably from the pain. "But I wanted to save you from the agony you carried in your chest every day. I saw it in your eyes, and while I didn't know how to fix it, I couldn't let you suffer in a cell."

Angela took a deep breath. This man was far from the Donny she knew. No jokes. Just pain. "Well, I'm thanking you now. For everything you did for me. If you can't tell, I got my soul back." She smiled.

Donny leaned against the wall for a moment as she opened a door for them to pass. "Yeah. I still heard some news: the attack on Dingir after I woke up, what happened to you, and—" He paused, eying her cautiously.

"Go ahead," Angela said, letting him lean on her again.

"I know what happened to Michael."

Angela hurt when she heard his name, but she steeled herself.

"I'm so sorry. I wish things would have worked out better for the two of you."

She nodded and took his words to heart. He was consistently kind, and she only wished it hadn't cost him so much. She missed his strange mannerisms and the way he acted quirky in seemingly normal tasks. A snicker almost left her lips when she remembered the "brown hail." But now his words were somber, his face bleak, and the lines around his forehead were heavy.

"In a weird way of looking at it, I probably wouldn't have found the motivation to push on and keep fighting for my soul if Michael hadn't died. I wouldn't be in the position I am now, and the worlds would be in worse shape if things didn't go how they did."

"Still, it's a shame you've been beaten down as much as you have."

Angela half-shrugged under his weight. They rounded the corner on their way to the infirmary. "It doesn't matter. You saved me, Donny, and I can't thank you enough. I mean that. It would have taken me a lot longer to break myself free and I never would have met Teshub without your guidance. I just wish it wasn't so hard on you, too."

A soldier held the infirmary door open, and they passed through. She sat him down onto a bed, and he was quick to lie on his back and stretch, his eyes looking sleepy already. With a half-smile, Donny said, "We all have times to grow and change, but sometimes we have to hurt first. But enough dread. I've had my fill. Tell me about Teshub. How has he been?"

Angela exhaled slowly. "Teshub isn't with us any longer."

"Oh... I always thought Teshub was a great man."

"He was. But since we're on the subject..." She pulled

at the grip over her shoulder and extended the ex-council-man's last token. The silver blade shimmered in the window's colored light. "Do you know anything about this sword? Teshub said his son made it. It belongs to him."

Donny opened his eyes and glanced at it, then sighed. "Sarruma died a long time ago."

A pit opened up in her chest. "Are you sure?"

He nodded. "Unfortunately."

"That's…" Angela trailed off as she put the sword away. "That's disappointing. I'd been hoping to give it to him in Teshub's honor."

The room grew quiet for a minute, and Angela became worried that Donny was going to fall asleep on her. She knew what she had to ask of him. The final fight was coming her way, and she'd pushed away so many people in her efforts to control something bigger than her. Every person she'd ever loved, hated, or hurt had been affected by her decisions thus far. It hurt her pride to admit it, but she knew she needed help.

"The Council has sided with the ancient Nephilim," she said, "and they are coming for me soon. I plan on being in Dingir when they do. It's the best chance I have, even though it's slim." She turned to face him. "I could use your help preparing the town, but don't think for a second you'll be involved in the fighting."

Donny lifted his head and examined her for a moment. "You know, I think I remind you of the past, what you used to have: the old Dingir and a house full of books and love. You don't want to lose that. If you lose me, you lose your last connection to that time when you were the most happy."

Angela sighed. "Maybe. I won't deny that, but I can't help holding onto the things that made my life worth living.

Now I'm clinging onto the last things I have. Dingir. Neti. My life. Even though I signed up to fight for my city in the beginning, so much of my life has revolved around violence I don't know what I'll do if we win. I am just so tired of fighting."

"You are a new woman, Angela. I can see it. A much more tender, relatable person who's learned something from her mistakes. And to this new Angela I say I'm honored to stand by you once more. I may contribute only in small ways, but you are, and always will be, a friend of mine."

ANGELA PUSHED HER SHOULDER THROUGH THE DOORWAY and entered Ja'noel's old office. Sarosha was pacing behind the desk. She turned to face Angela and let out a long sigh. Her hair was frizzled and unkempt. Preparations had begun, and no one had been sleeping.

"How much time do you think we have left?" Sarosha asked.

"A day and a half, maybe." Angela pulled back a chair, sat with a *thud*, and propped her head on her hand. "Did you get the reports? I gave Donny to Barrat."

Sarosha held up a finger and slid a stack of handwritten sheets across the desk. "That's a count of the alchemical resources, where they are in the city, and what kind of extra equipment we have in the armory." She shrugged. "I have no idea what good a tether gun will do if these things are truly as impenetrable as Neti says."

Angela picked them up and thumbed through the pages. There were at least twenty, and she wondered what good charcoal and salt would do against the Nephilim. Maybe they were allergic and would break into hives and leave due to annoyance. She chuckled to herself. "They aren't invincible. I killed one of the smaller ones, just barely, with a thrust to the eye, but that's such a small target. You are right to be concerned." She pointed to the report in her hand. "Can we have the alchemists transmute any of this into something useful?"

Sarosha dropped into her chair, sighing in exhaustion as she rubbed her eyes. "Unfortunately, it would take too long. We have enough explosives for at least a dozen charges, but the amount of damage those things cause makes me question if they're worth it." She scanned the desk again, mulling over the reports that seemed to suck all hope from her soul.

Angela bit her lip. "You're probably right. No point in blasting ourselves to pieces."

"I wish we would have thought that way when we dropped a third of our city..." Glum took over her strong face.

While Angela was grateful she had gotten her soul back that day, a lot more bad had happened than good. "What about armor?" she asked, changing the subject.

A sigh escaped her lips, but she lifted her heavy head. "We'll be all right, with some to spare. I've sent men to Earth to bring back supplies and more soldiers. Those spares will probably go to the alchemists and metalworkers so we have people of skill when we rebuild."

"I hate that word. You act like we're going to be crushed into a pile of rubble." Angela stood and walked to the stained-glass window behind Sarosha. Of course, they were going to lose a lot, but she needed to instill a little faith and help the others believe there was a chance they could win.

The sun was on the other side of the Ascendancy, casting its light onto the buildings across the lawn, although the moisture tower's shadow was gone. They'd begun cannibalizing and dismantling it the night before to make weapons.

"What exactly do you have Barrat doing?" Angela asked.

Sarosha spun in her chair, a long pointer rubbing at her temple and her eyelids nearly slamming shut against her will. "Running pipes down to the boilers below the city right now, but I think they'll make time well enough. We need to concern ourselves with the citizens now." She turned her chair back to her desk, sorted through reports in a drawer, and said, "There were 622 people in Dingir at our last census five years ago."

So few? Angela thought. When she served, there was always at least double that, but things were a lot better in Dingir back then, so it made sense. *How could you bring a child into a time and place like this?*

"The prisons are full, unfortunately," Sarosha continued. "Otherwise I'd harbor citizens down there. But I suppose it's better the prisoners are down there than out in the world."

Angela held her breath for a moment as an idea came to her mind. "No... I think I'll take care of that problem."

CHAPTER TWENTY-SEVEN

Angela led the party through the sturdy metal door and down the spiral staircase. Sarosha and two of the Uri Gallus followed close behind, their feet sounding like a barrel crashing its way down the steps as the bolted panels on the wall reverberated with every step. At the bottom, she paused at the T-intersection and glanced down both of the hallways lined with prison cells and storage rooms. A jailer she'd never met walked toward her hesitantly. A ring of keys hung at his waist. He seemed nervous until he noticed Sarosha.

"Are you sure you want to do this?" she asked.

Angela nodded confidently and turned to the guard. "Open the cells."

He was a squat man with light lines of age underneath his eyes, a potted belly, and a forked beard. His lips twitched as he stammered in confusion. "W-What did you say?"

"Do as she says," Sarosha said. "All of them."

He glanced at Sarosha and Angela in turn, eyes full of disbelief. "You can't be serious."

Sarosha folded her arms in silence.

"You aren't worried they will try to escape? Kill us?" he asked. "What's the meaning behind this, ma'am? I've half a mind to question your authority here."

Angela shook her head. "They won't try anything. Most of them know me, and they all have powered anklets to keep them anchored, correct?"

The guard blubbered something, but Sarosha cut him off with a wave of her arms. "Open the cells or leave us the keys on your way out."

His brow tightened, but he spun around without another word and walked to the closest cell. With the ring of keys from his waist, he unlocked cell after cell, swinging them open and announcing, "Someone's here to speak. Get out."

The Uri Gallu soldiers stood post before the stairs, their brass knuckles drawn and ready to shock anyone who tried to push into the Ascendancy. One by one, disgruntled prisoners dressed in stinking, ragged clothes gathered in the hallway. They shivered and clutched their arms for warmth as the hallway flooded with nearly fifty people.

Some prisoners looked angry, others afraid, but most confided among each other when they saw Angela. She had put a good number of them into these cells in the first place, and she wasn't surprised by most of their reactions. They were the scum she'd removed from all over the Earth. Slavers, traffickers, pirates, and more. But hopefully they would turn their lives around now.

When a small crowd of about forty people filled the halls to both sides of her, Angela began: "I'll make this short and easy for all of you. I know at least half of you here, but I ask that you put our past encounters behind us. I'm here today because something far worse is going to happen if we don't stop it. In a day and a half, a Dalkhu councilman is coming for our city again, but this time, he has a weapon we cannot withstand alone: ancient creatures called the Nephilim. Beasts so old they say they're from another world entirely."

Someone laughed to her left, and she turned to the sea of faces in front of her. A grizzled man with a scar across his forehead and a curl to his lower lip pushed his way from the crowd. "Don't play us stupid, Angela," he said with clenched fists. "There's no such thing as Nephilim. These three worlds are what we've got, and you took *all* of them away from us."

Angela had forgotten about him and did her best to remain calm as the commotion grew. The other prisoners liked what they had heard and shuffled, rambunctious. "Believe me, Farcus, I wouldn't be here to offer you freedom if I wasn't serious."

The halls went silent. All ears were now listening to her.

"You won't—in any way—be required to fight beyond where you're posted. You'll be our eyes and ears atop buildings. Run supplies and usher citizens while the soldiers who signed up to die for this city do the majority of the fighting."

Sarosha stepped forward and said, "Some of you may be asked to man guns, but the reward will be your freedom. If you take part in defending this city, the place where you were born and raised—your home—Dingir will owe you that. You can consider any wrongdoings that put you here forgiven and will be free to leave for Earth without fear of being hunted down. You may even remain in the city if you wish."

The hallway filled with murmurs again while Farcus crossed his arms.

Angela let a minute pass and said, "You can either do your part up there, hoping that we win and that we all survive, or you can die down here if we lose."

Farcus held up a hand and took a step forward. "So just how much of a target will we be? Will we be armored? Armed? None of us have a lick of Dalkhu training. We'll die in the blink of an eye if we run into one of the Council members."

Angela crossed her arms and wondered if it would be better to lie. She said, "No. You won't be given any weapons to defend yourself, but you'll wear whatever armor we can spare."

He shook his head and turned his back to her. "See? They give us scraps. Meat shields is what we are."

The halls filled with chatter again. A few had taken to shouting and pointing as the prisoners began to ebb and flow like the ocean, pushing and shoving against one another.

The jailer next to Angela looked to her anxiously and said, "I told you we're gonna get killed."

The Uri Gallus gripped their knuckles tighter as the crowds edged closer and tensions rose.

Sarosha clapped her hands together once. "Stop! I've rigged the stairs above to blow at my command. Settle!" she screamed, and when they did, her fury carried out on every word: "All right. Those of you who can't see this opportunity for the kindness that it is, go back to your cells and dissolve into the pasty shit piles you are on the inside. Those of you who want to be a part of something bigger than yourselves will be moved into a vacant apartment complex a few blocks from the Ascendancy, where you will be monitored under the guard of two dozen armed soldiers until you're called upon."

People turned their backs, muttering to one another and scoffing as they returned to their cells one by one until the hallway had lost nearly half its number.

"Once your cell door closes behind you, that's it," Angela added, but few seemed to regard her.

The jailer walked past Angela, then glanced back at her with a shrug. "It might not be as many as you wanted, but at least we aren't dead." He turned to lock the cells again.

The prisoners returned to their cells until there were only fourteen out of what should have been twenty or thirty. It was dishearteningly less than she'd hoped for, but it couldn't be helped. Those that remained were quiet until given orders to begin climbing the stairs, and Angela watched each of them pass her on the way up. Farcus's glare was the hardest of them all.

A BLAST OF AIR DISPLACED THE LOWER HALLWAYS JUST before she took her first step up toward the surface. An unfamiliar Uri Gallu approached Sarosha on long strides. Curious, she cocked her head to the side and asked what he needed.

"Ma'am," the guard began, throwing a salute across his chest. He was panting, like he'd just ran a marathon. "On the lawn—there's a Dalkhu."

"It's probably Neti," Sarosha said, rolling her eyes. "I already sent notices out to both wings of the Ascendancy."

He shook his head frantically. "No, it's not Neti. This one's not armored." There was genuine panic in his eyes.

Angela didn't need to know more; she disappeared from the prison below the city. Quickly, with a strong focus, she tore through the white expanse and shoved herself back into reality just outside the Ascendancy.

A mob of Uri Gallus and Etlus shouted angrily on the grass. Even common people had joined in on the circle surrounding the Dalkhu—shoving one another as chaos erupted. Angela plowed toward the epicenter until she found the inner ring of soldiers with their tether guns raised and sparking. The black-robed figure stood still, a short brown staff in one hand and completely silent to the soldiers' demands. When the councilman removed his hood, she relaxed so quickly she felt dizzy. Toth nodded to her without a word.

"Put down your weapons," Angela said, grabbing the nearest tether gun and pushing it toward the ground. "He's with us."

The soldiers looked to her, confused and angry, but she ignored them and stepped to Toth. "So you came to help?"

"No, not you," Toth said indifferently. "My people. I know that this resistance is likely the best chance we have to defeat the Nephilim. I cannot imagine what chaos they would bring if they learned how to walk the veils. Besides," he said, a grin on his face, "I want that amulet back when this is finished."

Angela smiled. "I'll be happy to give it over to you, but I want to know, what is Maulkatu doing to prepare? Do you know?"

His expression turned sour. "He's been meditating almost constantly, but he approached me today. I was afraid he would finally ask me to join him and kill me when I refused, but he did not take offense."

Angela furrowed her brow. "He just agreed to leave you out of it?"

Toth shrugged. "It seems that way. He was feeling me

out for something, and I cannot say if he got what he was searching for. I wonder if he expected me to stay out of the fight entirely, not side with you. Daevas has confided in me that he will not be joining the fight, so that's two fewer councilmen Dingir is up against."

Angela half-laughed. "So, what, that gives us Maulkatu, Melech, and Kanu we're up against?" She sighed. "At least it's fewer than last time."

"Yes, but replaced with something far worse," Toth said grimly. He was referring to the Nephilim. "But together, we may have a chance."

Angela smiled and outstretched her hand. "Together," she said. "I like the sound of that."

Toth took her hand in his and shook. "Maybe the Nephilim's return marks the beginning of an era of peace between Dingir and Kur. Fighting a universal threat may unite us in a way we never have been before."

The Ascendancy's doors swung wide open. Sarosha stormed down the steps, shouting orders for the crowd to disperse. Angry citizens tried to stop her warpath and question her, but she disregarded all of them as she shoved her way to Angela and Toth. She put her hands on her hips and made an expression like she was waiting for an answer.

"This is the Council's Virtuoso, Toth," Angela said, motioning to him. "One of the newest councilmen but their most gifted in deciphering old languages and spells."

Sarosha and Toth exchanged short bows instead of shaking—neither of them were wearing gloves and Toth had to be seeing the wildfire of soul flames.

"I'll get him some armor to wear, but do you think there will be anyone else joining us?" Sarosha asked. "We're getting close to running out of supplies, and we have no time to make more."

Toth seemed to immediately understand the purpose of wearing Anunnaki armor and thanked her.

"No," Angela said. "I think we've just about exhausted every friend available to us."

Nearby, men shouted as they heaved a bundle of pipes up a pulley system. Atop buildings scattered around the city, people worked together, filling every street with the clanging and pounding of hammers. The wind was chilling, and the sun had reached the last quarter of its revolution for the day. If the moisture towers were still standing, they would have been covered in a spectacle of colored light.

"There's still a lot to do," Sarosha said, "but I think we're going to have to call it a day for you." She dove her hand into her pocket and held out a key.

Angela hesitated to take it. "What? Why? I'm going to help out with the last of the preparations. Maulkatu will be here tomorrow."

Sarosha shook her head. "I need my best fighters rested. Those who are keener to using their souls will have the greatest impact on the battlefield, and I need you all at your best." She shook the key in her hand, begging Angela to take it. "I've been holding onto this for you for a long time, Angela. Take all of your Dalkhu companions with you." Sarosha stepped forward and forced the key into her hand. "It's the key to your home. No one has lived in it since you and Michael."

ANGELA WALKED AHEAD OF TOTH AND NETI, DOWN THE gold-brick streets lined with shops and apartments. As they passed the tea shop where Donny had once shared a mug with her, she remembered how loud the trading areas of

Dingir had been. They passed the bookstore she used to trade at, now defunct and closed by old wooden boards. The bakery Michael had loved was still open, but glancing through the glass, she saw it was grimy and the wares half-stocked inside.

The feeling Dingir gave her now was vastly different than the last time she'd been there, let alone how it felt before her life had been turned upside down. Seeing familiar shops and homes of people she had known, now dead or gone, filled her with sadness. She couldn't bear to look anymore and watched her feet and the growing fog as she walked. Her breath drifted into the cold air, but there was also a warmth that enveloped her. A *good* feeling of familiarity. It seemed she could lie to herself no more. *This* was her home.

And suddenly, she was there. Yellow sandstone stacked and mortared with clay shingles on the roof. Two steps up and a small patio. The empty pot next to the big red door. The white fence surrounding their section of metal platform from the neighbors.

Angela sucked in a deep breath of air and opened the gate. The metal plating clanked underneath her feet as she walked to the door. The pot that once held her pine tree was entirely devoid of dirt and plant. She didn't mind if someone had taken it; it wasn't like she had been taking care of it.

With shaking hands, she inserted the key and opened the door. The kitchen and living room were the first things she saw, but it didn't smell how she remembered it. There was no warmth of fireplace heat or anything that made her home feel welcoming. There was something foreign about it now, and it was her own fault.

Her books were still stacked in neat alphabetical rows

on the shelves next to the fireplace. The wooden bench with cushioned seats sat in the living room. As did her rocking chair. There wasn't any food in the cupboards, to Neti's dismay, but he would survive.

She sighed before she left the kitchen and walked down the hallway to the back of the home. There were clothes still on the bathroom floor. She ran the shower for a few minutes, testing for hot water, then left. The room Michael had used for his tinkering was still as messy as she remembered, and nothing seemed amiss. It hurt to be in there, so she turned to the bedroom.

When she entered, she felt stupid that she'd expected to feel better there. The bed was covered in dust and more clothes, and a brass figurine was sitting atop a sealed envelope on the dresser. It was Michael's work, no doubt.

She lifted the paperweight—an abstract view of a woman with long hair—and set it to the side. After breaking the seal, she pulled the old letter out and immediately put it down and turned away from it.

Dear Angela, was the first line.

She stood there biting her lip as she contemplated if she should read it or not. Would it do her any good to be thrown down memory lane before tomorrow? So much had happened since she'd been there, and who knew when Michael had written the letter? She took a deep breath and turned. She had to know what it said.

This is the last letter, the last string of words, I'll ever say to you, because I know that you're no longer with me even when I speak with you. You are possessed. I know it must hurt, but what I really want to know is, do you hurt as much as I do? I love the thought of being with you forever, or maybe it's the thought of not being alone, yet the only thing I can't get through is a life without you.

When we held hands on the city's edge, kicking cans so we could watch them fall, and we talked about this and that and everything we wanted in life, one of those times I realized that the only thing neither of us had growing up was someone genuine by our sides. And when you realized it, and from that point on, we fell into each other and filled the roles both of us needed in our lives.

You're smart, caring, and strong, and I don't know what to tell you when I try to confess that I have failed you. They say it takes years to come back, but I don't know how to do that. Maybe that's the answer to this great big riddle: when you find someone that loves you for you, you have to keep being with them. That's what really matters in life.

So maybe what I'm trying to say is that I can't do this without you. I know it must hurt you more, and I'm sorry for the things I did behind your back, but it can't hurt like I do right now. I'll find a way to fight through this. Next chance I get, I'll put your body to sleep, then my own. I don't know if there's another life beyond this one, but maybe our souls have the kind of love that will pull us back together in the end, or maybe we'll just sleep.

Michael.

CHAPTER TWENTY-EIGHT

The mud grabbed Ja'noel's boots like hungry hands, but he carried onward. He had slogged through slop for the last two hours. His legs ached and his eyes were heavy from when he slept on the ground last night. They'd combed through the woods a dozen times, it seemed—up and down and back and forth on the river's banks, searching for anything: a footprint, a dagger, a tether gun, any sign that Kushiel was alive or had been there. And while Ja'noel knew that it would take time for his men to find a translator and then bring the human to him—since they could not survive the effects of teleportation—he was incredibly irate that three days had already passed.

He remembered telling Sarosha that he wouldn't be in any danger, but the more time that passed, the more he worried that he'd inevitably get into some kind of trouble. What the trouble would be was anyone's guess, but a few of the men had murmured about hearing blasts of teleportation the night before and had witnessed a Dalkhu's fire. *Only rumors*, Ja'noel hoped.

The stream they followed widened, pushing back the trees and shrubs as it bent to the left. Ja'noel stopped and put his hands on his hips, irritated as he turned to Durian and asked, "You're absolutely certain this is the area you found the man?"

Durian stuttered and pointed across the river. "Either here or over there, sir. I was pissing into the water at this exact bend."

"Well, why haven't we found anything, then?"

Ja'noel cursed under his breath and was just about to tear into Durian for the second time that day when the sound of half a dozen mechanical wings and the whimper of a single man came from somewhere overhead. Durian and the other soldiers called up to them, and they veered down toward them like a flock of geese, folding up their wings and crashing through treetops to thud onto the forest floor.

The human they'd mistaken for Kushiel squirmed free of the Etlu that held him, panting and panicking as he ran. He was easy to detain a second time, and Ja'noel saluted the first soldier who spotted his approach.

"Ja'noel, sir," the soldier said, throwing up his own salute. "Per your commands, the entire camp's been searching for a translator. First Etlu Dagan has taken extensive testing in many human languages and claims to understand Kushiel's look-alike."

The soldier turned and motioned to the Etlu holding onto the human's wrist. No matter how the human pulled and shook, screamed and hit, the soldier did not let go. He only bowed his head and said, "Ja'noel. Pleasure to be of service." He reached out with his other hand and shook Ja'noel's. "I am Dagan, First Etlu of the 22nd Order," he said in a low voice.

Dagan was wide and muscular under his armor, as far as Ja'noel could tell. His eyes were hard and brown, his gaze pressing like heavy boulders, and his single hand was strong enough to hold onto the thrashing human.

"It is wonderful to meet you, Dagan. Now, if you don't mind, please forgive any shortness I may seem to have. As you can see, we've all been searching through the mud and thorns for answers with little luck. I hope you will be able to provide some."

Dagan nodded and asked, "What would you have from him?" Even his neck was thick with muscle. If this man could speak multiple human languages, then Ja'noel was certainly in for a surprise. At first glance, he never would have guessed he was multilingual.

"Ask him if he remembers the armor he was wearing when he was captured," Ja'noel said.

Dagan, the brute, shook the human by the arm violently to get his attention, then said something in a guttural language. When the human responded in turn, Ja'noel knew Dagan wasn't kidding. His command of the language was very impressive.

"The man remembers," Dagan said, his heavy eyes shifting back to Ja'noel.

"How long has he had it? I need a time frame. A month? A day? Not the last ten years, I hope."

The two spoke for a moment, and Dagan shook his head. "He owned that armor for three days, he says."

Ja'noel's heart beat a little faster. The chance that Kushiel was alive kept growing and growing. "And why did he have the armor?"

"The man says he found it cast to the side on the ground, like someone had taken it off and just laid it there. He thought it would be worth something to someone, so he took it and was making his way to the nearest city to try to sell it. He says he got sidetracked and was trying to find a way around the river when he ran into who I must assume was Durian."

"It was just lying on the ground?" Ja'noel asked again.

Dagan nodded without asking the human again, confident. "That is what he said. 'Discarded.'"

"Tell him to take me to where he found the armor and I will see that he has more wealth than anyone in his family."

The Etlu turned to the human, and Ja'noel watched the simple man's eyes grow more energetic.

"He'll show us," Dagan said.

Ja'noel nodded to both of them and turned to the others standing behind him. "We're taking flight."

DAGAN'S VOICE CARRIED WELL OVER THE SOUND OF A dozen flying soldiers. By his instruction, they began their descent toward a clearing in the forest. The party had been flying for the better part of the afternoon and covered at least two dozen kilometers. The farther they went, the more streams and rivers split out and the wider the forest on the horizon grew. But finally, they reached the place where the human had found Kushiel's armor.

Limbs and branches snapped as the company landed. When everyone was settled, Ja'noel approached the translator. He rubbed the fatigue from his eyes and asked, "This is it then?"

The hulk of a soldier nodded and pointed to a tree Ja'noel hadn't noticed before. Its bark was white, and it loomed at least forty feet into the air with gnarled, leafless branches. "The human recognizes that dead tree. The armor was on the ground just on the other side of it."

"He traveled quite a way, didn't he?"

Dagan shrugged his massive shoulders. "He did say it took him three days of travel before he ran into Durian."

Ja'noel nodded and walked to it before it was too dark to see. He stepped around piles of cracked white bark that had fallen from the tree. It must have been at least ten feet in circumference and much older than him. He scanned it up and down but hesitated when he reached the other side. A hole, nearly perfectly circular, had been cut into its roots. The strangest part about the hole was that it was lighter beneath the ground than it was above. The sun was bright in the middle of the sky, but that did not explain the sheer bright white some twenty feet beneath his feet. He crouched, picked up a piece of bark, and dropped it, only for it to fade out of sight.

A hand touched his shoulder. Durian looked down at him with weary eyes. "I don't like this. Something's off."

Ja'noel turned back to the hole in front of him. "Agreed."

"Could be Dalkhu magic," Durian said from somewhere behind him. "We should turn back while we can."

Finding honest, hardworking, and self-sacrificing soldiers was hard now. They'd sooner save their own skin than give their lives for Dingir. It disgusted him. Kushiel needed them.

"I'll go myself," Ja'noel said. He threw his feet into the hole and scooted off the edge. The shouts of the soldiers he left behind faded as he hit the white wall. It washed over him like water, covering everything in sight. As seconds seemed to linger for an eternity, he wondered if he was going to crash into a cavern floor and break his legs. He closed his eyes and felt tempted to activate his shifter and leave, but a freezing cold took over him almost as though he was already traveling through the...

His stomach lurched, like his guts realized he'd stopped falling, or maybe his body wasn't even sure what was going on. He opened his eyes and looked at his feet. They were still, and he could jump and walk on an invisible barrier that kept him from falling into the expanse of color-lessness below him. The emptiness spread out in every direction and swallowed the horizon except for a single speck in the distance.

He squinted at it, yelled at it, and tried his best to deter-mine what it was, but eventually he began walking toward it. The dot remained where it was, and while it felt like he walked for hours, he came to realize the perfectly still spot was a person. Dressed in a gray cloak, leather riding breeches, and a green tunic, the stranger never moved until Ja'noel was only ten feet from him.

When Kushiel opened his eyes, revealing shimmering black pools, Ja'noel froze. "What—" Ja'noel started but tripped over his own tongue. He wanted to believe that his mind was playing tricks on him, but now he was close enough to know better. "How are you alive? After all this time?"

Kushiel chuckled. "I suppose I cannot let you leave now," he said. His voice was two-toned like a woman was speaking with him. "This is not what it may seem, Ja'noel. Kushiel did not stay here by choice, so he has not aban-doned you."

Ja'noel felt the air around him tighten, almost as though the atmosphere was pressing in to crush him.

"Take solace," Kushiel said, his black eyes radiating a glow Ja'noel had never seen before. "You'll understand soon enough."

CHAPTER TWENTY-NINE

A ngela rolled onto her stomach, groaning. When the call came, her limbs still felt completely sapped of all their energy, but the bed was shaking and she knew what that had to mean.

"Get up," Sarosha said softly, but the words were urgent.

All too quickly, a rushing blur of anxiety swarmed over her as she woke into a nightmare. Her dry eyes stung when she opened them, her muscles stiff and painful. When she threw her legs off the bed and stood, a million tiny pins stabbed her guts, flooding her with the feeling that she was about to throw up.

Sarosha was standing at the foot of the bed, arms crossed when she said, "They're here."

A few breaths later, all Angela could manage to say was, "Shit... This is it."

And it was. Already, the third day had come, and while there were so many more preparations they wanted to make, there was nothing they could do now. Time was up.

This was the final fight where either she or Maulkatu would die.

"How long have I been asleep?" Angela asked as she walked to the dresser for her mug of water.

"About four hours," Sarosha said.

She drained what was left in the cup, swished, then swallowed. "And you?"

"I got five, but I've been up a while longer than you."

"Are the others awake?"

Sarosha shook her head. "I snuck in and woke you first."

"Good," Angela said. "I'll wake them."

As she walked toward the door, Sarosha grabbed her arm and stopped her. "Here," she said, motioning to a pile of clothes on the foot of the bed. "You'll want these."

Angela wasn't sure what to say. Even just at a glance, she could tell that the brown and green armor was hers. It had been so long since she wore the armor of Dingir that it almost felt taboo to consider putting it on.

"I'll meet you at the Ascendancy," Sarosha said as she left the room.

There was still dirt and mud embedded in the creases, confirming that the armor really was hers. Neti must have returned to the sinkhole and grabbed it when she was busy the other day. With a sigh to shake off the nerves, she slipped her arms through the cuirass and fastened the buckles and snaps along her side. The greaves seemed loose around the ankles, but the heavy boots took care of that. The pauldrons locked into place on her shoulders, and the gauntlets strapped to her forearms.

The tether gun was heavier than she remembered, but looking at it closely, she could tell it had been cleaned, tested, and filled with water again. The batteries were brand new, too, and she contemplated if she was really going to carry all that gear again. Nonlethal wasn't really her aim, but maybe it would have some use, so she stashed it at her waist. The brass knuckles were an obvious choice, as was Teshub's sword, but she left the clamp there on the bed.

With the wing-pack from the floor slung onto her back, Angela paused to look in the mirror before she left. It was a strange feeling, without a doubt. For being so far detached from home for so long, it felt right to dress like this. Comfortable, reminiscent of a time long gone, when things were simpler and she didn't have to worry about the balance between dimensions, councilmen, and giant ancient beasts threatening everything. That reminded her of the emerald amulet tucked under her pillow.

Maybe now is my time to use it. Or maybe it would make it worse, distract me from a truth I can't handle...

She scooped it up from the bed and tucked it into a pocket on her cuirass until she had to decide.

Stepping into the hallway, she found Toth asleep on the floor next to Neti, who lay on the padded bench. Toth woke up gently enough, but when Angela woke Neti, he groaned and flung the blanket off himself in a tizzy. He clenched his fists and sat upright quickly, grinding his teeth and angry that she had woken him. He looked up at her and said, "It's finally time, huh? Thank the worlds. Once this is over, I'll never have to look at your face again. Won't have to feel myself tear in half."

It killed her inside, but Angela held her tongue; everyone was exhausted and on edge. To give him space, she walked out the front door and slammed it behind her. The cold air washing over her helped calm her nerves while she waited. The Dalkhu were behind her within a few minutes, and Angela took their hands and they disappeared from her home.

The lawn in front of the Ascendancy was not as quiet as the street her home sat on. Shouts carried from the rooftops all around, over the wind's gale, but the only people Angela saw were Anunnaki. A trickle of alchemists and metal-workers were ushered inside the double doors, but Sarosha was nowhere to be seen.

A large wooden platform straddled the peak of the Ascendancy's roof, where the steep inclines of both sides met. On it, a large mess of steel pipes and rotating rings was connected to the boilers below the city, giving them the largest gun ever made. Silver rods the size of spears had been ground to points and set along the side of the platform in racks. They'd stationed four men there to operate each gun in case they lost at least one or two. Farcus glared down at her, his eyes like those of a hawk.

Sarosha stood next to him, pointing off into the sky as though she needed to see it. Angela followed her gesture and saw three massive winged figures in the air. They circled like vultures, but luckily, the wind was blowing them around constantly, forcing them to fight the air's currents. That would help.

One of the Nephilim roared distantly, as though it was officially announcing their presence, and they grew larger as they dove toward the city. Soon, Basmu's golden scales were glimmering in the sunlight. He was the easiest to see, but not seconds later, green and red stars twinkled above, too.

Next to her, Neti and Toth were standing as stiff as boards. She was nervous as well, but it seemed a little over the top at first. Then she felt it: a strong presence brushed against her mind and soul, prodding lightly at her and testing her strength. As soon as she tried to reach back out and grab him, the presence retreated beyond her grasp.

"That was Maulkatu," Angela announced.

Neti took a deep breath. "That's a strong soul."

The Nephilim's great black wings beat the air as they came over the top of her. The green one, Kishar, was the first to stumble to the ground. Her claws dug into the earth, tearing up the grass not thirty feet from her, followed by her father, Lahmu the Red. Both creatures had saddles strapped to their backs, and Melech and Kanu rode atop Kishar and Lahmu, respectively. The councilmen looked weary, maybe even nervous, and Angela wondered if Maulkatu had forced them to come.

Not far off, blasts of teleportation filled the air as more and more Dalkhu cloaked in black appeared atop the roofs of homes and businesses. They would be the ones looting and stealing, catching Dingir's soldiers off guard while they focused on the Nephilim. There was no way to be certain how many were now hidden throughout the city.

Neti cursed under his breath. "With councilmen on them, the Nephilim are going to be a lot faster than we anticipated."

Then Basmu's massive golden body came zipping down onto the platform, shaking the ground as each of his trunk-sized paws slammed into the ground. He was nearly as large as the apartments and stores behind him, and Angela swore she saw the buildings flex and bob. The creature roared and began to walk closer. Maulkatu sat atop the Nephilim's back. He lowered his hood, revealing his tattooed scalp, piercings, and smug smile.

Hopefully Angela would be able to smack it off him. She turned to Neti and Toth beside her and said, "First things first, we have to separate rider from Nephilim, and we need to take out the foot soldiers. If we can't do either of those, we might as well give up."

Toth wrung his hands on his staff and nodded. "I will handle the latter."

Angela took three strides closer to the Nephilim and stopped. For a moment, the air vibrated in silent tension. The gunners all around gripped their handles, ready to fire at Sarosha's command. The Dalkhu behind them prodded at their own souls, waking them, and prepared to weaponize the veil. The soldiers of the Ascendancy were lined up in front of the building, ready to protect those that now hid inside. Everyone was terrified.

Maulkatu spoke from atop Basmu's back. "I'm impressed by the number of people you've convinced to join your side."

"What do you expect when you threaten their way of life?" Angela asked.

Maulkatu laughed. "Oh, round and round we go. The never-ending debate of wrong and right. Moral and amoral. The battle of perspective never ends, but we both agree that it should. We aren't that different, you know."

"We both want peace more than anything, but beyond that, we differ. I seek to free those who are enslaved, feeling that it would be better for people to learn from their mistakes and move on toward a better future. You use your power to pressure, judge, and take control of people's lives before they've even done anything wrong."

"Sure," Maulkatu said, shrugging, "but it seems to me that the only way to stop the fighting that plagues our existence is by a final, decisive victory. Peace will spread throughout all three worlds because Dingir will be the pedestal from which the Nephilim rule everything below—all three worlds."

"Peace can't be achieved when you force it," Angela said. "Fighting begets more fighting."

He sneered and rolled his eyes. "Think what you want. There's no order to any of the worlds, only chaos and prejudice further enforced by the flames of our souls. Even our very souls—Dalkhu and Anunnaki—embody this nature. You should know, after seeing your city burn before your eyes, we can reduce it to this: it's *people* who create conflict, prejudices, and hatred for one another, and it doesn't have to be this way."

"You're right." With one fluid motion, she drew the sword over her shoulder and took the fool's stance. The Nephilim shifted their weight onto their back legs, readying to launch toward her. Neti drew his long knife from its sheath on his belt, and Toth tensed next to her as the soul in his chest began to glow and expand.

Maulkatu shook his head and looked down on the three of them in pity. "You all must realize that in the grand scheme of things there is nothing important about any of us. We're all lost, pointless people. Except for you, Angela." His lips twitched into a smile, and those black eyes stared down at her. "You have a touch of fate about you. So come, show me your best fight and take one step closer to it."

Maulkatu and Basmu disappeared in a flash, the air slamming back together and crashing over the wind. The concussive clap bashed Angela's skull as Basmu appeared above, his great clawed hand falling toward her. Toth and Neti were quick to disappear, but Angela dove to the side as Basmu collided with the ground.

"Fire, now!" Sarosha commanded from somewhere behind her.

A dull *thud* came from a steam-powered harpoon atop

the buildings surrounding the Ascendancy's front lawn. Steel spikes four feet long smacked into Basmu's scales, cracking them before deflecting into the distance. The Nephilim reared and bellowed, his deep voice shaking Dingir to its core.

Destroy them, he shouted.

Lahmu the Red shifted his attention to the closest turret and charged, taking his rider, Kanu, with him. The beast lunged and grabbed hold of the building's windowsills, fire escape, and finally the roof as he climbed his way up to them. The soldiers wailed as his snapping jaw came up and snatched the first prisoner and tossed him to the ground below.

Next to Angela, Kishar the Green was trying to pin Neti down, but he was too fast for Melech to keep up with. Nephilim were big and hard to teleport through the veils. They would tire, and that was a relief, because the others would have to keep them busy while she focused on Basmu and Maulkatu.

He smiled, then disappeared in a *bang*. The sudden flux of such a large amount of air pressure made her head spin. A second later, the giant creature appeared behind her, displacing the air even more and pushing her to the ground. But she was not out of it, not entirely; she rolled, whipped herself around, and lurched to the side just in time to avoid Basmu's claws. She rolled out of the way of a stomp, then warped ten feet back to give herself some breathing room and time to think.

Maulkatu was smiling from ear to ear, his black eyes reflecting in the sunlight. With the councilman strapped to the creature, Angela knew there was no easy way she could win. With his strength, he could move as fast as she could, and with Basmu, he could hit harder and fly longer. The

Nephilim was nigh-invincible, too, and neither of them had even projected his soul's energy yet.

"Thinking of giving up, already?" Maulkatu asked, noticing her hesitation.

"Wouldn't dream of it," Angela said, and she plunged herself into the icy, cold space between worlds.

Reappearing in the air, she spun and dove, slashing at Maulkatu as she passed him. Basmu caught on quickly and stepped to the side at the last second; the tip of her blade only grazed the side of Maulkatu's arm. She tried again and managed a paper-thin cut along the other side of his temple but knew he would catch her if she tried again. Warping twenty feet into the air, she pulled the controller from the bottom of her backpack, and the mechanical wings burst out. When the wind of her fall filled the linen membrane, it only took a few thrusts to begin hovering above them.

To the skies, then? Basmu asked in her mind.

Angela hoped that her smaller size would give her more maneuverability and that she wasn't a fool for saying, "Yes."

TOTH TURNED TO NETI BESIDE HIM. SWEAT WAS ALREADY beading on his forehead, and the fight hadn't even started yet. The boy was nervous, and the ex-councilman wondered if he would make it through the day. He was the least practiced Dalkhu in Dingir, but he would have to hold his own.

"Keep Melech busy," Toth demanded.

Neti raised his brows. "Sure. Easy."

And with that, Toth teleported to a nearby roof in a blast of air, sat atop the clay shingles, and expanded his mind. There was a reason his people considered him the most skilled at controlling his soul, and he aimed to show it. From up there, he could reach out and touch the lesser soldiers while remaining safe from the Nephilim long enough to—

A mind brushed against his. Quickly, Toth latched himself to the presence like a snake's fangs and wrapped himself around it. The mind was soft under his pressure, and its attempts to wiggle free were in vain. The young Dalkhu disappeared from the adjacent roof with little challenge. Toth held him in the fire for a few seconds to ensure little misery as his body was incinerated into dust.

One down, at least a dozen more to go.

Angela was still standing in the yard below, unsure of what to do next, it seemed, while Neti was teleporting around the green Nephilim and Melech, trying to confuse the creature. Toth didn't have much time. Definitely not enough to do what he needed to.

He reached out across the rooftops, feeling for any presence that wasn't an Anunnaki. When he found his next Dalkhu, who must have known what Toth had done to the first, his would-be victim steeled his mind like an iron dome. Toth prodded and pushed at it, visualized his mind into a spear, and slammed against it to no avail. This one was stronger.

A second presence rushed at him like a tiger from somewhere behind him. Toth retreated to his own body, then teleported to a different rooftop and stood. Scanning the buildings around him, he watched sunlight gleam against the gold-brick streets, which sparked and created rolling fires that billowed in the wind. There was no smoke, so he knew it was only soul flame.

Blocks down, a figure in black moved behind a chimney, and the soldier's mind tried to grab hold of him. Toth warped again, and when he reappeared next to the boy, he said, "I'm sorry, brother," and swung his staff into his head. The green-corded soldier groaned as he tumbled over the edge of the building. The *thud* of his body hitting the ground three stories below came a few seconds after.

They are too young for this... too young to die for Maulkatu and the Nephilim. What a waste.

In front of the Ascendancy, Angela had taken to the air and the green Nephilim was pinned to the ground with a silver harpoon straight through her leg. He watched Kishar struggle to grab the spear with her teeth and pull it from her leg. Lahmu the Red had destroyed his first turret and was now back on the ground, circling around Neti in the yard. Melech was missing from her back as well. Toth did not have to wonder where the councilman was for long.

A robed man appeared atop a far-off roof, then disappeared a second later. Blast after blast cascaded through the city as Melech vanished and appeared closer each time. Toth gripped his staff tightly and waited until a mind jabbed *past* him and pierced the veil. If anything, Melech's mind was fast, but not as strong. A pillar of stone erupted from the thin air behind him, crushing into Toth's back and plowing him onto his stomach.

His face scraped against the shingles as he slid to a stop not a foot from the edge of the roof. Rolling onto his back, he winced and saw that his finger had been disjointed in his fall. With a pull, he straightened it and began rising to his feet. Thunder came from behind him, blowing his hair into his face.

"This isn't how it should be," Melech said, stepping to the peak of the roof. A thin red cut from temple to jawline was new and bleeding. "You shouldn't be fighting against us."

Toth leaned on his staff to support himself against the roof's slope. "I didn't know it was customary for a Dalkhu to bend the knee."

Melech scoffed. "You think I *want* the Nephilim to rule over us? Judge us all? I want Angela *dead*. She's overstepped her boundaries countless times and I cannot have it any longer. Maulkatu's right, and you know it, Toth, with all your glorious wisdom. When she's finished with one of us, she puts her sights on another councilman. It is only a matter of time before she picks us down to nothing. Then what of the Dalkhu? She's an Anunnaki at heart, and you need to remember that. She will always harbor a hatred for us. It is her nature."

Toth took a deep breath. "You are right in her hatred for us: it may always exist. But its origin stems from what our people have done to her and the Anunnaki. Mainly, we may thank Udug for making her what she is, but it is also the war we refuse to stand down from. I think we all should heed what Ruchin said, or this fight will never end."

Melech shook his head and said, "Brother, I wish we saw things the same way."

"As do I," Toth said, and he pushed his mind toward Melech's.

Toth's mind connected with his like a battering ram, bending and warping its point of contact. But quickly, Melech squirmed to the side and out of the way, then raced toward him to counterattack. In a split-second decision, instead of retreating as he usually did, Toth re-aimed and pushed harder. He spread himself out over Melech like a blanket, then snared him tighter. At the same time, Melech gained a grasp on Toth and pushed. They vanished from the rooftop.

They floated between the worlds, staring at one another as their minds battled. Each time Toth pushed them toward one dimension or another, Melech would counter and pull them somewhere else. They were draining their energy, even in a place where time did not affect them. What was once a race was now a challenge of stamina. Neither of them wanted to expend everything they had, lest they be stuck in that never-ending expanse.

So they jested against one another with light, peppering blows, neither letting the other go. With as fast as Melech was, Toth knew his chances were slim in the long run. He would expend his energy and strength faster trying to keep ahold of Melech rather than simply moving around and dodging.

Toth changed tactics. He pulled himself away from Melech, releasing his grip and retracting himself. He hardened the forefront of his mind to keep the situation from getting worse, then pushed himself through the veil. While Melech didn't let go of him entirely, he relaxed and hesitated in his confusion.

It had felt as though a week had passed, but Dingir was still alive with fighting when Toth fell to his knees. He leaned against his staff, taking heavy breaths and trying to save the last of his energy. Melech's shadow cast over him, and his eyes narrowed.

"Tired already?" he asked.

Toth panted.

"Too bad you gave Angela your amulet. I know how long you searched for it, especially when no one believed your adamant claims that it existed." He shrugged. "Oh well. History will know it as a mistake that cost you your life."

Melech pulled a dagger with a silver pommel and cross guard from his robe, removed the sheath, and tossed the leather to the ground, revealing the serrated black blade. He gripped the handle firmly and said, "When all this is finished, I will make sure you are laid to rest with the others under the Kissum."

Toth glanced up as Melech's shadow grew larger. He poured his soul's energy into his arms and swung. The staff plowed into the back of Melech's knee, kicking his legs out from under him and sending him to the ground, where he landed on his back. A quick jab with the end of the staff to Melech's temple jerked his head to the side. The councilman's eyes fluttered, and he fell asleep, the dagger loose in his hand.

Toth rose slowly. He'd already expended half of his soul's energy to get this far, and he had another decision to make. Melech truly did not want the Nephilim to rule and only wanted Angela out of the picture. He could kill him, or he could let him go and send him somewhere else. Would he return to the battle when he awoke?

Toth had no way of knowing. He bent his knees and took the dagger from Melech's hand, weighed it, and stuffed it into its leather sheath. He rested a hand on his brother's forehead, then pushed him out of Dingir.

Sarosha jumped in fright. The Uri Gallu standing next to her burst into flames. He screamed as his skin bubbled and he flailed from the rooftop in an attempt to extinguish himself. Bile rose in her throat as she watched him on the ground below, only to be sure the Ascendancy didn't catch fire.

"Etlus and Uri Gallus, shifters on!" Sarosha yelled. The prisoners were wearing their anchoring anklets so they did not have to worry about the Dalkhu. She pointed across the grass lawn below. "Focus fire on the red Nephilim. It's going for the other turrets!"

The men working the gun next to her aimed the barrel and fired. The cannon blasted a plume of steam into the air, shaking the hastily constructed platform they stood on. The steel spear soared, but Sarosha turned her back as the cloud of hot water blew past her. She could barely feel its sting. When it passed, she looked and saw that the spear had embedded itself into the side of the wrong building across the alleyway.

"Reload and fire at will," Sarosha commanded, disgusted at the shot's inaccuracy.

What were we thinking? she wondered. *I should have expected this. They aren't trained soldiers, and I don't have what it takes to do this, either. I need Ja'noel...*

The half dozen prisoners scurried about the platform nervously. Two worked on shoving a new spear down the barrel while Donny and a few others worked cranks that adjusted the gun's horizontal and vertical position. A brass dial on the side slowly crept upward as the boiler assembly below the Ascendancy built up pressure again.

The next spear launched into the air and soared over to the next city block. It clattered against the rooftop, right at the creature's feet. Their aim was better that time, but Sarosha still had to watch the Nephilim tear apart the last two men stationed at the other gun. When the screaming stopped and the creature was satisfied, it shifted its attention to a different turret a block down. It was lucky for her, but bad for them.

That gun team was firing downward at the green beast Neti was dealing with rather than paying attention to the Nephilim leaping across rooftops toward them. She tried to recall who led that gun team but couldn't remember whom she'd appointed.

It wasn't the most self-preserving choice, but Neti needed her assistance more than the other gun team did. He'd grown sluggish already and had taken three long cuts from a claw through his robes and across his chest. The councilman that was atop the Nephilim was missing, and Sarosha wondered if the boy had taken care of him by himself.

With a single order, Donny and her other men began pointing the cannon toward the lawn down below. Every ratchet and crank signaled another passing second as Sarosha watched the beast get closer and closer to Neti. He warped five feet at a time, narrowly avoiding blows and lashing out with his dagger in a dizzying fury. Then he staggered, and the beast was on him.

The gun behind her fired, launching a spike. It flew through the air with an accuracy Sarosha couldn't have hoped for and punched through the green Nephilim's hind leg. The creature screamed like a mixture of a beaten horse and a lion and tried to pull itself free but couldn't lift its leg. The spear had plowed into the ground, pinning it there. What seemed like gallons of thick blood colored the grass red.

Dagger in hand, Neti was inching his way closer to the creature when Sarosha felt something pulling at the gun at her side. She jerked away and swatted for whoever was grabbing at her weapon, but the assailant's grip on her gun was tight. A soldier behind her shouted something. The cannon fired again, shrouding her in stinging mist. Her foot caught, and she toppled over, crashing onto the platform. She was on her back when the fog cleared, and Farcus loomed over her with her own barrel pointed down at her.

A million thoughts ran through her mind. She'd never led a battle before, so why did she think she could do it now, when so much was at stake? Maybe her love for Ja'noel was blinding her. What had she done so wrong, or so right, to deserve this role? She was not ready for this.

Farcus's hand shook the gun wildly. His lungs were out of breath. His eyes darted from her, on the ground beneath him, and the Uri Gallu on the other side of the wooden platform. When the soldier took a step forward, Farcus shook the gun.

"Don't move an inch closer or I'll kill her," he screamed.

"Why... What are you doing?" Sarosha asked, trembling and wanting to sit up but too afraid to try.

"Give me your shifter. Now," he demanded. "Give it to me or I'll take it from your corpse."

Despite all the chaos around them, everyone on the platform had stopped working the gun. Donny's eyes bounced between Farcus and her. Behind the menace's back, he bent and picked up a silver spear from the ground.

Ever so slightly, Sarosha bent her wrist and held up her hand. "You... You don't want to do this," she said, both to Farcus and to Donny. He must have gotten the message; Donny paused, a confused look on his face.

She continued. "What do you think will happen even if you get out of Dingir? Angela will come for you."

Farcus stepped over her, straddled her between his legs, then bent at the waist. "Angela's not going to survive this,

Sarosha. Thought you were smarter than that." He ripped the shifter from its holster at her waist, then the leather bag with crystals of every color next to it. Lastly, he took the battery from its pouch and stood upright. With one final smirk, he pressed the button and vanished into thin air.

Immediately, Donny stormed over to Sarosha, jerked her up by her arm, and asked, "Now why did you let him go? I could have taken him. Now you have no shifter, and we're down a gunman."

Sarosha's hands were shaking, everything was spinning, and she was so weak. So irredeemably *weak*. All she could muster to say was, "It's... It's not worth it... None of this is."

Donny's lip curled and he shook his head. "It might not be worth the price we're paying, but dammit, someone has to, Sarosha. Look at those people out there, trying to fight for their way of life." Donny pointed over the edge of the platform, over the lawn torn by the claws of ancient beasts and the spreading fires atop buildings.

He grabbed her by the shoulders and looked her in the eyes. "Those people are fighting for what they love. Steady yourself and do the same."

Sarosha took a deep breath as she tried to shake the fear.

Where are you, Ja'noel?

She followed Donny on wobbling legs, taking Farcus's place at the turret.

ALL AT ONCE, BASMU JUMPED WITH HIS MASSIVE HIND LEGS and launched into the air, jaw snapping at her feet. The mechanical wings that kept her above ground barely pushed her fast enough to slip away from razor-sharp fangs. Angela felt sick when she imagined Basmu's teeth tearing off her kneecaps and calves.

The wind blew both of them as the golden Nephilim rose to catch up with her. Normally, she wouldn't be too worried. Being in the air gave her a distinct advantage very few had, but already, a sinking feeling grew in her belly; she was at a severe disadvantage now. She was stupid to think that her mechanical wings would beat a winged creature's maneuverability. Basmu was gaining on her, and as terrifying as it was to twist and dive headfirst toward him, she reminded herself that Maulkatu was her true target.

Passing her wing-pack's controller to her right hand, she drew the sword from over her shoulder and pointed it at the ground below and at Basmu's shimmering mass. The creature swerved, lined its neck up with her falling path, and opened his mouth to catch her.

Angela ground her teeth and *pushed*. They were set to collide, faster than she expected. A scream escaped her lips. She slashed out with her mind and disappeared before Basmu's mouth snapped shut around her.

Appearing only a few feet away, sword flashing, Angela roared as she zipped past Maulkatu. It happened so fast she wasn't able to see if she actually hit him, but the sword pushed back in her hand like she'd hit something soft.

She continued falling toward the ground, without glancing back, in hopes that she could use the extra speed she gained. Nearly a hundred feet above the city, where she could see the battle raging below in greater detail, she extended her wings and straightened her descent.

Rushing over the city faster than she ever had before, she reached the edge and turned to circle it. Maulkatu and

Basmu were hovering in place above her still, and she wondered if that was a sign she'd hit Maulkatu harder than she'd thought.

Better take advantage of this opportunity, Angela thought, and she pushed into the veils again. Keeping her forward momentum, she broke back into Dingir and leveled herself with Maulkatu. The councilman turned, yellow teeth bared and a deep, bleeding cut stretching from his cheekbone to the back of his head. She had separated his ear into two disgusting flaps of skin.

Angela folded her wings and braced herself as she crashed her shoulder against his frame. They both groaned as their weight impacted one another, but she had misgauged just how tightly the councilman was strapped to the saddle. When she righted herself and glanced back, he'd only shifted in his seat slightly.

Her speed had already slowed down incredibly, but something felt wrong within the first few flaps of her wings. Looking over her shoulder, she noticed a tear through the membrane of the right one. It wasn't severe enough that she couldn't fly, but she had to manually correct for the damage. The few lucky blows she'd managed justified a short retreat so she could survey the rest of the city.

Below, Kishar the Green was pinned to the ground by a steam cannon's spear through her rear leg. One turret was on fire, as well as a few other buildings throughout the city. Toth was nowhere to be seen, but she could make out Neti where she'd left him. He was on the ground, and the way he moved seemed off and unusual, like he was badly injured, so she set her sights to land next to—

A crushing blast of air rammed into her side, blowing her off target and into a roll. As she spun, a golden paw the size of her entire torso flashed in front of her. Then talons scraped against her back, tore the fabric of her wings, and bent the metal frame.

Angela mashed the controller, but only smoke poured from the backpack in a long black stream behind her as she fell faster and faster. A quick jump through the veils returned her to a higher altitude and bought her more time, but no matter what she tried, she could not get the wings to respond or slow her spinning. Holding herself tightly, she shut out everything as she fell and pushed the fear from her racing mind, desperate for a solution. Inside, an instinctual urge to panic *screamed*.

Outspreading her arms to try to stabilize herself, she warped again. Blurring visions of gold and blue whizzed past. The air was knocked from her lungs as something gold crashed into her chest, and for a second, she wasn't sure if she was right-side up or upside down, but the spinning had stopped, and just below her was Basmu's wing coming up to flap again.

His great head turned to face her, but before he could roll away or attack, Angela slashed out with her sword, cutting a gash in the leathery membrane of his left wing. He bellowed, and she teleported to the other side of his body. Timing her arrival just right to catch his right wing on its upstroke, she sliced another hole. Compared to the size of his entire wing, the hole was like a watermelon to a wagon, but she hoped it would tire him faster.

Teleporting just behind Maulkatu on his saddle, Angela appeared on Basmu's back and took hold of a spike along his spine. The councilman noticed immediately and twisted to face her. He gripped the saddle with white-knuckled rage, watching as Angela straddled the Nephilim's back and reached for the tether gun at her waist. A short grunt escaped his lips, and she felt the veil between them ripple. A stream of dark red flame burst from the air. Almost throwing herself into the air again, Angela shifted her weight to the side and avoided it.

Basmu's nose dipped. His wings folded into his side as he broke into a dive, and Angela's legs began to float. She held onto the spike in front of her and squeezed for life as the creature drove them straight toward Dingir.

Tether gun in hand, she aimed and fired. The steam came back at her on the wind, but when it cleared, she saw the cabled spike in Maulkatu's back. Angela smiled and pressed the button. The tattooed councilman screamed and clutched at his back as he tried to fight his own spasming body.

Suddenly, Basmu tilted upright before they crashed into the ground. Thrust into a horizontal flight, Angela felt her hand slip from the smooth spike and she dropped toward the ground like a stone thrown from a catapult.

NETI'S HEART POUNDED AS HE TOOK A STEP CLOSER TO THE injured green Nephilim. The cuts on his chest stung. There was so much blood and sweat he had to wipe his hand and dagger on his breeches to get a good grip. He wondered if he should retreat and look for a healer, but the spear that pinned Kishar to the ground had her complete attention. If there was ever a chance he could finish her off, it was now. The councilman, Melech, had disappeared after spotting Toth taking out his men, leaving only the two of them on the Ascendancy's lawn.

To his relief, the icy wind numbed his exposed, wet skin, and he took another step forward, but the beast noticed him and chomped at the air. He bounded out of the way easily enough.

Curse you! she shouted in his mind. *You die! You die! You die!*

No matter how hard she pulled at her gimp leg or how many times she tried to grab hold of the slick metal spear with her teeth, she could not free herself. Even for a younger Nephilim, she had a reach of at least four feet and was extremely ferocious. But a small part of Neti didn't care. He wanted all of this over with. He wanted to be alone.

Tiptoeing on the edge of her reach as she snapped and hissed, Neti rolled out of the way on his ankles. Within seconds, the creature turned back to the spear in its legs, trying again to pull her leg free. Neti watched the spear move and wiggle from the dirt ever so slightly and knew that his time was running out.

He took a step closer, to within her reach, and said, "Hey."

The green Nephilim's head turned and snapped for him again. He thrust out with his dagger, the tip of it glancing up the bridge of her nose and burrowing into her left eye. She wailed and jerked her head back, but Neti's grip failed him and the dirk went with her. Kishar shook and screamed. The blow had been well-placed, but it wasn't enough.

He circled her flailing frame for a few steps, then lurched forward in a leap to push the dagger in just a little bit more, but he found his ribcage landing between her jaws. Kishar clamped down, teeth tearing into his flesh as she whipped him around like a toy. He felt ribs crack and screamed. Through the pain, he bent, reached up to her eye, and slammed his fist against the pommel of his dagger. It sank farther into her skull and she released him, sending him down onto the grass as her throat rumbled weakly.

Neti clutched his side as he lay on the ground. The pain seized him, forced him to stay immobile, but if he didn't move, he'd be an easy target. He lifted his head to see Kishar lying lifeless at his feet, then spat coppery blood. The sight would have been a relief it not for Lahmu the Red clambering his way down a building toward him. Neti could not sit up, stand, or fight any longer. It had been a long time coming, he knew. He didn't deserve to have won against the first Nephilim, and now her father was going to kill him.

Lahmu bounded across the grass to his dead daughter and prodded her with his nose, a sad rumbling in his throat. Kanu noticed Neti lying on the ground first, then the red Nephilim. Lahmu howled, and Neti knew all the anger and rage that existed in the beast was about to surface. He'd be lucky if the creature only tore him to pieces or lit him on fire. Yet just before he was certainly going to die, a body dropped onto the grass between them in a blur of yellow and brown, a trail of smoke following behind it.

EVERYTHING WAS NUMB FOR A MINUTE, AND THEN THERE was pain. A dull throbbing pain in her head, chest, legs, and pretty much everywhere. But when she finally opened her eyes and saw Neti clutching his bloody side next to her, it all went away in a surge of adrenaline.

With a groan, she pushed herself to her hands and knees, saw Basmu and Maulkatu looming over them, she lurched in a surge of panic. Grabbing hold of him by the arm, she scurried through the grass, pulling him along. She stumbled, mind still spinning from her impact. Maulkatu laughed at her from behind.

When she turned to look again, the councilman and the golden Nephilim hadn't moved. He was grinning from ear to ear, likely because she was struggling just to walk. "Is this it, Angela?" he asked. "Is this that moment where you bend the knee?"

Angela's common sense, her rationality, and her memory of what had happened so far returned to her slowly. Her breathing evened and the panic lessened. She looked down at Neti and realized that he was unconscious, and this was the most dire hour of her life.

Smoke billowed into Dingir's clear skies from raging fires. Every last turret was quiet and unmanned, and all around her were the scattered bodies of prisoners and soldiers. Lahmu the Red had retired to his daughter's side to weep while Kanu still sat atop him.

How long have I been out?

Legs shaking beneath her, she said, "No." Sluggishly, she unclasped the backpack and let it fall onto the ground. Her teeth hurt and she tasted blood, her back screamed, and her head pounded. Pulling energy from her souls to reinvigorate her body helped, but she wouldn't have enough time to get back into shape. A part of her knew what she needed —knew it was the time to use it—but half of her was still afraid of using the ancient trinket.

What if I find something in me that doesn't help? What if the guilt, the hopelessness, eats me up?

Maulkatu seemed to notice her hesitation and asked, "Do you need a moment? Can I get you a cup of tea or a blanket?" He laughed.

Basmu shook the ground as he took a step closer. *There needs be no fear. Accept.*

"You brought this on yourself, you know," Maulkatu said as they came closer.

Her mind raced. She'd promised that, when the end was near, she'd stop struggling and accept her fate, but she didn't want to believe that the time was now. It couldn't be the end. She still had energy in her souls—still felt a will to live, to keep fighting—but how was there a chance in the slightest that she could win?

Four Nephilim and the most powerful councilman I've ever met. Was I a fool for thinking I could beat them?

Soon, she would be forgotten. A faded memory lost to the annals of time. The Nephilim would raze Dingir and settle there. They'd be taught how to move between the worlds, and they would spread to Earth. Sarosha would never see Ja'noel again. Neti's life would end here and he'd never be able to find himself. The people who had invested in her and showed her the way, like Toth and Teshub, would have wasted their time. And all the countless others whose fate now fell on her shoulders filled her with sorrow.

What made it worse was that, deep in her core, she knew it was true: she had brought all this on herself. If she would have stayed in the sinkhole and kept to herself, she wouldn't have hurt Shedim's brother, and he wouldn't have sought revenge. In turn, she'd brought the hammer down onto all those she loved. Every single person involved with her would pay because they were affiliated with her and she'd opened a door she could not close. At least not by herself.

Her thoughts drifted back to memories of the good days when she served Dingir. Back then, not only was following orders and just doing what was required of her simple, it was simpler to just *live, too*. Things weren't as complicated. Sometime after she'd gotten her soul back from Udug, she'd lost something she couldn't put a name to.

I remember the moment I took back my soul. It felt like the floodgates opened inside me. I had so much energy that I could bend to my will. What did I have that day, fifteen years ago, that I do not have today? How did I manifest my wings?

Sure, she'd just pulled her own soul back out of Udug's body, but she'd had it ever since and never harnessed her energy in the same way again, so that couldn't have been the reason. Having two souls didn't matter—the Nephilim only had one complete soul. They were good at complicated spells, too, so maybe...

Maybe it was more like a spell and had more to do with her ability to control and *shape* her own energy and less to do with the amount of it she possessed. That aura, that feeling of *fullness,* and that complete command she'd had over her souls disappeared after she took Neti to Earth with her.

And why is that? Why is it that I only held my wings for a few days? What changed, and how?

The answer snuck up on her silently, and she smiled.

My grief. Within hours of taking Neti from Kur, I began to wonder if I was doing the right thing and felt I owed him so much more than I could ever give him. I'd never had a kid, didn't know what I'd just jumped into, and I felt so guilty for what I'd done to his parents. I still do, and I never forgave myself for what I did.

Angela looked to Maulkatu, his black eyes staring down at her with curiosity when she smiled. "It's just like Gor told me: there's no balance."

Maulkatu raised an eyebrow, shifted in his seat, and didn't seem to grasp what she was getting at.

"The biggest thing that holds me back is myself."

Angela had made terrible choices, lost control, and struck others down in rage, and she had always regretted it and never let herself forget—never let herself move on from those mistakes—and it was crippling her. She had never forgiven herself for what she did to Neti, let alone accept that her anger was a part of her and that she had to learn how to control it. And when she cleared the slate and dismissed the panic, the worry, and the guilt, all the pain, the fear, and the emotion was removed. Her heart and mind relaxed, and the light inside her bloomed.

Accepting herself, she shaped her energy once more.

Lines of purple-blue light emerged from the thin air between her shoulder blades. They grew in length and branched off in a hundred different directions in just as many places. The energy from her souls warped and bent, manifesting in the glowing outline of the wings she'd so desperately craved for the last fifteen years. It felt as if she'd gone from drinking through the neck of a bottle to drowning herself in a bucket.

Like a complex spell, she pushed the energy inside her to apply its force downward. With a smile, Angela lifted from the ground in a streaking flash of blue and red lines. The air around her crackled and vibrated, and she willed stark purple light to form around her fists as she collided with Maulkatu's chest. He blew over like a page in the wind, grunting and bending backward to let her pass over him. When she turned back around, she saw that his robes were singed and smoking where she hit him.

Maulkatu was gasping for air, but he recovered more quickly than she'd expected. "There. There it is, huh, Angela?" He straightened his back and took a deep breath. "I knew you still had it in you." He reached down to his ankles, unclasped the straps at his legs, then stood in his stirrups and pointed at her. His black eyes flashed when he smiled. "Every step you rise in strength brings us closer to the end."

"What does that mean?"

Maulkatu vanished from the saddle and appeared inches in front of her with a smile, no wings, and no means to fly. Wrapping a hand around her throat with one hand, he clubbed her with the other, harder than he had before. The edge of Dingir, brass and gleaming sunlight below her, seemed to shift and flow like water.

She lost concentration as they fell toward the city in a fury of kicks and punches. She grabbed his throat and kicked at his groin, but she couldn't land a hit hard enough to get him off. In their tangled mess of entwined limbs, they dissolved from Dingir's sky in a bang.

The councilman was in control, guiding their destination by the strength of his black soul, which matched his black eyes. Their gazes were locked onto the space between worlds for only a second or two, unusually, and they crashed back into a different reality. Maulkatu released her neck, and crystal blue water flooded her lungs in a sudden rush. Her body told her to cough, but she bit down on her lips to fight it. Every breath—maybe even her *last* breath —counted.

As sudden as it was to be in the dimension of water, the cold seemed to snap her head back into place. She focused on her souls, the energy sparking between them, then gathered it around her knuckles again. Zipping forward with a thrust, the light boiled the water, creating a trail of bubbles as she swung and connected a blow with his jaw. His head cracked back at the force, but he regained himself and sneered as he drew the two short daggers from his robes.

Even in the flowing water, which made moving so much harder, they still attacked and maneuvered with speed. The light around her fists parried and deflected Maulkatu's blades well enough, but as they fought on, she began to lose her breath. She did not want to be the one who gave up, and to her surprise and luck, Maulkatu touched her with his mind and pulled them into the void.

Fueled by his outside source of energy, Maulkatu pulled them through the veil once more with a speed Angela had never experienced before. In seconds, something crashed into her cheekbone, and the first thing she saw was red, porous rock. Three orange suns glared down at her, and the heat of them warped the air and created mirages against the endless fields of boulders and stone. The ground rumbled beneath her feet, and magma and fire billowed into the air like a geyser. This was the surface of Kur, she knew.

As she pushed to her feet, something rammed into her side and knocked her onto her back. Maulkatu stood above her, steam rising from his tattooed head and his black robes.

He flipped the daggers in his hands and said, "Do not disappoint us." He threw his weight down on top of her to slam his blades into her chest.

Without thought, she channeled nearly a third of her souls into her fists and sent him twenty feet into the air as his daggers glanced off her light harmlessly. Spinning uncontrollably, he landed on the stones with a grunt. Before he could get upright and take control of the situation again, she latched onto him with her mind and pushed them both into the veil.

The cold air pounded against them when they reappeared in Dingir, out in front of the Ascendancy where they had left. Angela plucked her sword from the grass and stood ready as Maulkatu rose from the ground with a sneer.

"A good hit," he muttered, wiping the blood from his chin. "But I suppose like all good hits, they must be followed by a better one. A final test before the destiny right in front of you is revealed. When it comes, don't try to run. Don't try to hide from it. She thinks you'll make it."

"Who is—"

Maulkatu looked toward the sky, and the veils trembled like heavy rain on a lake. The very fabric of that dimension rumbled like an earthquake. A line of brown and red streaked across the sky like a comet. Then a second line stretched across it, forming an X, and the veil *crumbled*. Beyond the ends of Dingir, into the horizon and blocking the sun, a meteor cut from another world descended toward the city.

Everything froze. Her breath. Her heart. The entire city stopped to look up at the catastrophic moon-sized chunk of rock growing bigger as it fell toward them. It was dark now, like a sunset on Earth, with only a ring of light and reddish sky around the city. Terror and panic rippled through her, but she could not move, couldn't fathom the size of it or what she could do about the incoming impact.

The resounding *boom* slammed down onto the city, shoving Angela to her knees and snapping people out of their mesmerized horror. The purple energy from her souls faded; the sudden concussive blast gave her a headache and shattered her balance. Screams and shouts came from distant blocks, women cried, and the remaining soldiers wailed. In moments, some began to disappear in teleportation rather than trying to rescue whom they could.

"Dingir will be consumed because of you!" Maulkatu sneered, breaking into a run. But everything seemed to be moving in slow motion as he came barreling toward her. His knives flashed in the twilight as his arms pumped. Sweat beaded on his tattooed scalp, and he smirked in triumph. He leapt into the air, daggers aimed to stab her shoulders.

It was now or never.

Purple light traced the curved edge of her sword as she rose. Twisting her frame, she stepped clear of his knives and flicked her blade downward. Maulkatu was screaming before he hit the ground. He rolled onto his back, bloody stumps where his wrists used to be. He groaned in pain and slobbered like an injured animal, rocking back and forth below her. As his blood left him, the blackness in his eyes faded back to yellow. Then tears streaked his cheeks and he began to smile and laugh hysterically.

She held the edge of the glowing blade to his throat and said, "I don't know what changed you, gave you this power, but no one deserves it."

The purple energy from her soul faded as she closed her eyes; she needed it elsewhere. Maulkatu was no longer a threat. With a great heave, Angela thrust her mind upward. Leaving behind her body, she judged the meteor's distance from Dingir and began to carve away at the veils between them. Her mind, a dagger to the barrier between worlds, sliced through and dragged along the sky as Maulkatu had. Instead of brown and red rock, sparkling blue appeared.

When her cross appeared in the sky, she grabbed hold of the opening in the middle and peeled back the veil. A great wall of water rose above the city, shimmering and blue as it crashed into the moon above. As the rock fell, she tore at the veils and stretched them. A presence brushed against her mind, and she knew that someone else out there was helping her. The portal into the blue watery expanse swallowed the meteor above, and it began to rain.

When Angela closed the hole she'd created and returned to her body, Maulkatu was still lying beneath her blade. He beamed and said, "I'm so happy for you. You have no clue what's coming."

Angela's eyes narrowed, but she did not speak.

His voice was cool and calm. "Slay me, then kill the Nephilim. Take the leap toward fate and the worlds will be reunited!"

Angela's grip on the sword tightened. Then she shook her head. "Trying to control you and your people is what created you." She motioned to the stumps he now had for arms. The heat of her souls' energy had cauterized them with black and red gunk. "You have your shame," she said. "I have mine."

A roar filled the air. The ground shook. As she turned to see that Basmu was upon her, his massive claw scraped against her side, tossing her into the air. When she recovered and the swirling picture of Basmu's golden figure standing over Maulkatu stilled, the Nephilim's voice permeated all their minds.

I knew you draw from the weyline, but reunite the worlds? Was it the plan all along?

Maulkatu seemed like an ant underneath Basmu, but he was not afraid. "Yes." He laughed. "These worlds are too chaotic, too unruly! I have looked into the black and seen Vi'dinor! She's come back!"

Basmu rumbled in his throat in disappointment. *Fool. What have you woken?*

The councilman lifted his head and smiled at Angela, his yellow eyes glimmering in tears. "She has been awake for some time but has only now begun to act. You have no idea how—"

Basmu roared. The golden beast's maw snapped down on Maulkatu. His bones crunched, but the councilman was laughing as he was lifted into the air. In seconds, he was sliding down the Nephilim's throat.

CHAPTER THIRTY

Basmu bellowed into the sky when the lump in his throat reached his torso. Something was clearly wrong, more so than it was before, if one of Maulkatu's Nephilim had just *eaten* him.

Angela was afraid, but she stepped closer and asked, "What is going on?"

The golden creature ignored her and instead turned to Lahmu the Red, who was still mourning over his daughter's body.

Instead of keeping the conversation between him and Lahmu, Basmu allowed his voice to rattle her mind, too.

Did you know that Maulkatu had found her, Lahmu? he asked. *It is clear that they have spoken. Did you know that she's returned?*

Lahmu's red head slunk low to the ground, almost like he was intimidated by Basmu's size or anger. *I suspected, but I did not know for certain. Our time may be up. Perhaps we, too, should seek to return to grace.*

Basmu grumbled. *There will be no forgiveness for me, nor do I seek it.*

Lahmu's head turned to the side in curiosity. *But you can feel it now, can't you? It has already begun in this world. We should seek her while we still can. If you remain so steeled against her again, there will be no place for you in the new world.*

Basmu's step shook the ground. He lowered on his front legs, threatening to pounce. *I warn you: forget this notion and leave. Take sons of Dalkhu with, before I lose my temper again.*

The red Nephilim huffed once, then dipped his head. He turned to Kanu, who was still on his back, and said, *Flee.*

The councilman nodded, then took one last glance at Angela before they both disappeared in a blast of air. Only a few moments passed before the other Dalkhu around the city realized that the fight was over and entered the veils. One by one, throughout Dingir, the sound of their departure surrounded them and cascaded through the city as Angela looked up at Basmu.

"Who is this 'she' and 'her' I keep hearing about?" Angela asked.

The golden Nephilim turned away from her, looking toward the horizon in thought. *Leave me. I need to think.*

So many questions ran through her mind, but the great-bodied creature only looked over the city in silence. Like him, she contemplated what his next step was and where the two now stood in relation to one another. But Angela knew that the other questions she had were far larger than his. That ancient creature understood something that she did not, and she would have to wait for her chance to understand.

Sarosha shouted behind her. "Get this Dalkhu to the infirmary, stat!"

Angela turned. She'd forgotten about Neti and rushed to him. His eyes were closed, yet when she placed a finger to his cold skin, she did still feel a faint heartbeat. Sarosha knelt next to him. A new, thin cut ran along her temple. While Angela was grateful the Grand was alive, she didn't have the time to say so.

"I'll carry him," Angela said, and she scooped the boy into her arms. Before she led the way into the Ascendancy, she turned to Basmu and said, "Don't go anywhere."

The golden Nephilim only blinked.

Soldiers rushed through the double doors ahead of her, and some, stationed on rooftops, shouted down as they prepared to begin extinguishing fires. There were more survivors than she had thought, and one held the double doors open for her as she entered the lobby. Citizens had begun pouring into the Ascendancy after being released from prison cells below. Angela had to twist, push, and shout her way through the crowded halls to the infirmary.

Once she was through the door, a frantic woman with red hair shook her head and sighed in exasperation. She wore a long red gown and a leather belt that held her medical tools.

"He needs to be looked at," Angela said, stepping up to her. "He has several lacerations across his chest and has lost a lot of blood. He needs to be warmed and—"

The healer pointed to the farthest bed in a sea of injured men and women. "You came just in time to get him a bed. These things are filling up faster than I can look at them."

Before Angela could explain Neti's significance, Sarosha nudged her toward the back of the room. While she wanted to resist, she continued on. They placed Neti next to an Etlu woman who was biting down on a gag and moaning in pain. There was a tourniquet around her stump of a leg.

Angela had to look away, and instead of waiting for the healer to come, she and Sarosha found medical equipment and sanitized the wounds on his chest and bandaged him themselves. When the woman took over, Sarosha laid a hand on Angela's shoulder and said, "Let's leave him be for now. I have something for you to sign."

A rock formed in her gut. "I know I have a promise to fulfill," Angela said, "but I don't want to leave his side until he awakes. I know he will be leaving me soon, and I may never see him again."

Sarosha sighed. "He'll be all right. Promise. And he's not going anywhere for a while. You made a promise to me."

Angela grumbled but said, "I know," and turned away from Neti.

They walked through the Ascendancy's halls, which had already begun to empty. The commoners had left to see the city's damage, most likely. Soldiers still jogged up and down the halls as they ran messages and ordered the repair of city buildings and public services. They even walked past the squat jailer, who bent and released the shard anklets of prisoners that had survived the battle.

Sarosha took her to Ja'noel's office and settled behind the desk. Within moments, she pulled three pre-drafted papers from the desk and placed them in front of Angela. The first was a declaration of intent. By signing it, she swore to Sarosha and the rest of Dingir that she would begin her search for Ja'noel once the city was re-stabilized from the day's events. The second page was an acknowledgment of the temporary transition of power. When she signed it, Angela was officially the Ensi of the Ascendancy, and all soldiers of the Etlus and Uri Gallus would answer to her until Ja'noel returned to power. Even though everything she was signing mattered to her heavily, Angela only really listened when Sarosha told her about the final page.

"This is another acknowledgment," she said, sliding the page in front of Angela. "This one states that you understand the newly formed Bui'dus do *not* fall under your jurisdiction. They remain independent of—"

Angela shook her head and raised a hand. "Wait a second. What did you say? The Bui'du?"

Sarosha paused, tapped her bottom lip, and said, "Yes, I told you before we even entered into this arrangement. The Bui'du are Ja'noel's new squad of soldiers. You are to train them in 'natural' teleportation and spells. This document states that you understand their position in Dingir and your promise to train them for a minimum of five years."

"Right," Angela said, shaking the fog from her mind. "Sorry. I forgot about them. But five years? That's a long time, and I'd like to meet them first."

Sarosha frowned. "You will, and these terms are not negotiable, Angela."

She sighed. "Yeah, I know. I promised." Angela picked up the pen again and signed.

A look of relief washed over the woman who was now only the Grand Dubah. She leaned back in her chair and pushed her hair aside, revealing the bloody cut on the side of her face.

It was hard to think that just half an hour ago they were all fighting for their lives. It ended so quickly, and it still felt like there was something out there looming on the horizon. Even though they'd been granted a reprieve, something didn't sit right.

"It's strange," Angela said after a moment of silence. "It doesn't feel like I've won, even though it's over. Maybe

I just don't believe that it *is* over, and I never imagined I would actually be replacing Kushiel as Grand Etlu."

Sarosha shrugged. "It could be because you weren't the one to deal the finishing blow, or maybe it's just surreal that we survived. Who knows what the future holds for Dingir, but I think it will be a pleasure working with you and Ja'noel." She rose to her feet and extended a hand.

Angela took it in hers and shook, smiling. A part of her was happy to be back, fulfilling a childhood dream. "If we are done signing my life away for a second time, I need to talk some sense out of Basmu, if he's still here."

Sarosha's eyes widened in interest as she nodded. "Yes, I would like to join you in doing that, if that's all right."

With Angela leading, they walked the Ascendancy's hallway on long strides, passing soldiers that were technically under her command now, Angela realized. It almost made her feel sad. Becoming a Grand meant that she had a responsibility to protect Dingir now, and that would keep her from defending humanity as she had been before.

Humans were practically defenseless, but becoming the Grand Etlu of Dingir didn't *have* to mean that they were ignored. Why couldn't she fight for both? She smiled. A small part of her was giddy. Becoming a Grand was something she'd dreamed of for a long time, and to now be a part of her people's defense again made her happy.

They turned into the main lobby, past the attendant with the thick-rimmed glasses, when Sarosha pulled Angela to a stop and pointed to the other hallway. Coming toward them from the Etlu wing of the building was the crumpled and bandaged form of a Dalkhu boy she cared very much for. At Neti's side, and attentively helping him walk with a gloved hand, was Donny, who looked as though he had only taken a few minor scrapes and cuts during the fight.

Toth was walking alongside him, too, letting Neti use his staff as a cane to lean against.

Angela took a deep breath and stepped to the group. From a pocket in her cuirass, she pulled out the copper and emerald amulet and handed it to Toth. "Even though I didn't need it, thank you for letting me have it and joining us today, Councilman. I'm not sure how things would have ended without your help."

Toth smiled from behind his frazzled red hair. "You are most welcome, but I'm not sure if I'm a councilman any longer. I'll find that out soon enough, though. From here, I'll see if I can find Kanu and Lahmu. Maybe my peers will be wiser now. I hope I played a part in forming a lasting peace."

Angela thanked Toth one last time before turning to Neti. She was nervous but asked what was on her mind: "How long do you figure you'll stay?"

Neti shook Donny's hand off his shoulder, eyes burning with anger. "Are you that eager to be rid of me?"

She shook her head, unsure if she could convince him to stay or if she should even try. "The truth is, I'm scared to lose you, but if you think you have to leave, I will support you in any way you need it. Supplies, food, whatever it is, just ask. You're like a son to me, Neti, and I'll try my best to start over if you want."

Neti cringed and looked to his feet. His black bangs covered his eyes, and he said, "I can't live that way, Angela. Not anymore." He sighed and seemed to force himself to relax. "I can't remember the last time you even thanked me, and I know that you would try your best, but I'm going to make my own path. Like you." He lifted his chin into the air. "Besides, you still pick your boogers."

Angela's jaw dropped. "I do not!"

A smirk stretched across his face. "I've seen you do it, and it's not cool. No Dalkhu would be caught dead in the sight of Grand Etlu Booger-Picker."

"You little—" She raised an open hand. He flinched and scooted back. Then the others laughed.

When things settled and Angela realized she'd have to live with the title, her gaze turned to the floor. "I have no choice but to respect your wish. But know that I will miss—"

The wooden doors of the Ascendancy burst open, slamming into the stone wall with a loud *crack*. An Etlu charged in, his eyes curiously scanning the room until they settled on them.

"What's the matter?" Sarosha asked.

The soldier approached swiftly and said, "It's the Nephilim."

"What about him?" Angela demanded.

"Something's wrong with it," the nervous soldier said.

Angela's eyes grew narrow. Without another question, she stormed ahead of the others and pushed her way out of the building and onto the grass lawn. Basmu's massive body made him easy to spot, but it also made it clear that he was lying on his side with his head resting on the ground. Angela ran to him. His heavy breaths rattled deep in his lungs as his chest rose and fell furiously.

"What's the matter?" she asked.

The Nephilim lifted his head just enough so that his black eyes could look at her. When she thought of putting a hand on his nose to feel him, she wondered if he was feigning sickness to get her close so he could snap her in two.

I will not live much longer, he said.

Sarosha, Donny, Toth, and Neti joined her at the

Nephilim's side. Everyone looked as genuinely concerned as she was.

"Is he all right?" Sarosha asked.

Angela shook her head and turned back to Basmu. Confused and in disbelief, she asked, "How could you be dying, and how do you know? Has Lahmu cast a spell on you?"

Basmu's throat thrummed. *No. That would be from the outside, and I would know. This… This feeling is from the inside, so I must tell you while I can. The key to her is in the deepest memories of—*

A single crash of thunder boomed across the city, and the strangest sensation came over Angela. An urge, quiet and humble, grew inside her. A premonition commanded her to move, not out of fear but of a wanting to go *home*. From somewhere above, a beam of black light plowed into Basmu's side. The ultraviolet glow of energy filled the air with a queer vibration as it burned through scales and flesh. It punched through his ribcage and into his chest cavity until he was still and breathless.

Everyone was quiet, dazzled and confused by what they had seen. Angela guessed the angle of the energy beam and saw a silhouette standing on an adjacent rooftop. The stranger was dressed in a ragged gray tunic, a black cloak, and thick brown breeches. Burlap sacks were fastened to his feet by strands of thinning twine on his ankles. The man closed his outstretched hand, and the glow in his palm faded.

"That is quite enough, I believe." The man's voice carried as unnaturally as the light he had cast from his soul. He jumped from the flat roof above and landed gracefully with a slight bend in his knees. He glided forward on long, relaxed strides. His shoulders were wide but slightly hunched. Fear bubbled in her gut as her suspicions grew.

"Take off the hood," Angela demanded.

Yellow teeth flashed from behind his white beard. He dipped his head and said, "As you wish," then pulled it to his shoulders. Thinning gray hair on top of his head and the wrinkles beneath his eyes told her that he was an older man. But even though two things about him were new, the beard and the blackness of his eyes, Angela could see Udug underneath. The pull to move that she'd felt in her chest suddenly made sense. It was his soul pointing her toward its original host.

"H-How are you alive?"

"So surprised to see me?" he asked with a smile. "The body did not die, and I have you to thank for that. If I had not fallen from this city's edge, I would never have seen how much greater the true scope of things really is." He must have sensed her confusion; he leaned closer and tilted his head. "Did you not consider that I was still alive? Has word of Kushiel's survival not caused you to come to the same conclusion for me?" He clacked his tongue and wagged a finger. "I assumed one of you would have put the pieces together, but it seems not."

Angela reached out with her mind and lightly brushed against him. His whole aura was *wrong* and uncannily similar to Maulkatu's. Somewhere inside him was an immense soul, a source of the energy that radiated unfathomable strength. It resonated loudly and shook her to her bones.

But how could he have a soul when I took it from him?

Almost as though he knew her thoughts, he smiled. "But enough of this drivel from Udug. I know this whole situation—and even I—must confuse you, but understand I could not tolerate Basmu ruining the surprise or the journey you have ahead of you. You and I have a history to resolve, Angela—a history you do not remember. Allow me to introduce myself..." He tapped on the side of his face, pointing at his eyes like he wanted her to look *past* Udug and into the black abyss that was his soul. "*My* name is Ti'amat."

Someone tugged Angela's shoulder. Neti cleared his throat and whispered in her ear: "Something's not right with this guy. Is it really Udug?"

She shook her head. "I-I don't know."

The stranger straightened and said confidently, "I am Udug, as I am Kushiel and Kuda. I am nearly everyone, but Ti'amat is my true name."

Angela clenched a fist, her temper rising. "I don't understand what you're blabbering about, but you better start explaining a little bit clearer. Your clock is ticking. When it stops, I'm going to beat your face in."

Udug crossed his arms over his stomach and chuckled. "That fury has not left you, has it? Perhaps I should call you by the last name I knew you by: Antum. But that was such a long time ago. A whole different era and existence that I doubt you can recall now. You see, Angela, I have been around for a very long time. Trapped, even, but I have always watched what I could focus on. Still, I had not realized that half of your soul had left the weyline and was reincarnated until fifteen years ago when you used a crystal to pull the soul out of this man. And I believe you did not know of me until you searched the void between the worlds for your husband's soul. That's where you found me, remember?"

Terror froze her heart. "What do you mean?" Angela

asked softly. She was afraid she already knew the answer, but she wanted to hear it.

"Would you like to speak with Michael again, no strings attached?" Ti'amat chuckled.

Angela swallowed. Ti'amat was the tendrils in the void, holding onto her husband's soul between the worlds. Bridging the gap in her thoughts, she realized that the aura in front of her now was the exact same as the black in the void. Somehow, the entity she found there was possessing Udug's body and it had been possessing Maulkatu. Black eyes were the mark of Ti'amat's presence.

"You only need to take my hand and I can show you everything from the world before," he said, extending a wrinkled hand. "You will see Vi'dinor and even worlds before that. Most importantly, you will understand what you did to me. What you destroyed." Ti'amat's lip curled as he spoke, chilling her.

A whole different incarnation of my soul did something in a whole different world to Ti'amat? Even as fear made her heart race, more than anything, Angela wanted to understand. She began to reach and take the stranger's hand when someone grabbed her by the elbow.

"Don't do it." It was Neti. Sweat beaded on his forehead, despite the cold. "I don't trust him."

Ti'amat snickered and said, "Maybe you would like to see as well, Neti." He extended his hand to him for a moment, then tucked it back away into his cloak. "Thinking again, flee while you still have the chance, boy. You play no part in our destinies and are, in turn, quite useless."

"Enough of this," Neti sneered. He drew his dirk from his sash, then teleported not a foot from Udug. The old man was spry, twisting his body and sidestepping Neti's swing entirely.

Like a snake, he struck Neti with an open palm to the side of his head. Neti staggered for a brief second, then stood motionless with his back to Angela. His fingers twitched, and slowly, he turned, his eyes as black as the night sky.

Ti'amat smiled. "Do not worry about him. He won't intrude any longer."

Angela's lip quivered. *Stupid, stupid kid!* She drew her sword as her blood began to boil. Fear had kept her from moving, but she would not let it now. "What did you do to him?" she asked.

"He has peace now. His soul was a small part of me, and now he has returned home. Do you understand, Angela? I am something of a god."

She could not accept any of it. Fire burned through her veins like nothing she'd ever experienced. An anger so strong she could not dream of holding it back bubbled to the surface. With rage, she screamed, "I don't believe you," and vanished from where she stood. When she reappeared, swinging down at Udug, Neti's pale, expressionless face was there, taking his place, just before her blade planted into his neck. She'd buried the edge halfway through. Dark red blood ran down Neti's chest.

Angela let go of the sword, covered her mouth, and stumbled back, horrified, as Neti dropped to his knees in front of her. He coughed once and, without a word, fell to the ground.

"No, no, no, Neti. No... What... What were you doing? Don't... I can't..." She collapsed next to him with shaking hands, unsure if she should remove the blade or leave it until she could get him to a healer. The air felt colder than it had a moment ago, the ground less stable. Everything spun.

Ti'amat's shadow loomed over her. "I don't require your faith, Angela. Your soul twitches just before you use it. You see, life can exist without a soul. Both humans and Udug's body are prime examples. But souls are my currency with which I manipulate, extort, and inspire. They are my gateway into people. Sometimes I walk the worlds with this face or countless others. I can take—"

A loud *snap* came from behind him, and a sweeping cloud of steam billowed on the wind. Udug stood over her, eyes blinking as he twitched uncontrollably, then fell to the ground next to her. The prong of a tether gun protruded from the back of his skull, and the cable led to the gun in Sarosha's hand.

She let out an exasperated sigh and said, "Now, let's get Neti inside the—"

Donny wailed and clutched the sides of his head. His chest heaved heavily as tears ran down his cheeks and his eyes turned black. He mumbled something Angela couldn't understand, then straightened like nothing had even happened. Then Ti'amat turned to Sarosha. "My qualm is not with you. If you dare lay another hand on me, I'll see that what little time you have left will be in misery." He faced Angela. "Now, I'm becoming rather impatient, so answer me quickly and truly. Where do souls come from?"

Angela's eyes burned as tears streamed down her cheeks. "What did you do to Donny?"

"Answer the question," he said. To think that someone else was using Donny's voice horrified her.

"I don't... I don't know," she sobbed.

"Every soul is a small piece of me. For the last age, I've been so broken and spread out that I could not control my energies. My souls have reincarnated into other bodies without my permission. But now, I am coming back together again. The crystals that have been disappearing from Dingir and Kur are fragments of my being, and as I regain them, my reach grows."

Ti'amat smiled through Donny. "Do you think it was by your strength alone that you ripped Udug's soul from his body? I was there, in that crystal shard you held between your fingers. I am the weyline that holds onto your dear Michael. I am the voice that spoke to Kuda when you were injured and instructed him to save your life so I could see you rise to the strength you needed to pass this test and defeat the Nephilim. I am a circle within a circle—with no beginning and never ending. I am the Anchor Crystal, and I am your god."

Angela stilled herself for a moment and asked, "But why now? Why me?"

Ti'amat took two steps closer, hand extended for her to take it. "You and I have a history. In another body, you betrayed me. All I want is a second fight—a *fair* one. I want to see you become my equal, and we will settle this once and for all. Just touch my skin and I'll show you everything from Vi'dinor and even worlds earlier. You'll understand."

Angela bit her quivering lip, then took his hand in hers.

EPILOGUE

The breeze on the mountaintop was pleasant that day. Not enough to counteract the heat of the sunlight, but just enough to keep it from getting uncomfortable. The cavern was cramped, and Gor would have much preferred to be out of it.

As he lay basking in the warmth, the sound of footsteps approaching woke him. A cloaked man approached, and it was not the human that usually kept him company. With a reach of his mind, he felt the person in earnest and rose to his feet.

My lord! I did as you requested and pointed the woman to where she might recognize her greatest weakness and how she could strengthen herself.

Ti'amat sighed, threw down his hood, and walked across the stone to him, then sat on Gor's leg. This time he was in the form of a human Gor had never seen before.

It is the perfect height for a seat, Gor thought.

They sat in silence for a few moments. Gor knew better than to interrupt, so he watched the sun setting on the horizon, casting oranges and reds in the sky. Finally, Ti'amat said, "I am aware of what you did, Gor. She did well against Maulkatu's Nephilim, and by her own strength, too. Enough progress was made that I felt it was good timing to reveal myself. I made contact and she is sleeping now."

Praises, then! Gor exclaimed. *What must we do next?*

"There is still much progress to be made. For the both of us. I will need more time to gather the pieces of myself, and Antum will need time to rejoin her other half. But, Gor, my trusted friend, I must ask, if I lose this fight and she takes my place, will you serve her like you do me?"

Gor thought about it. Any being capable of defeating Ti'amat likely deserved to be followed, but in the present, Gor could not admit that. *No,* he said. *And you forget all you took from the others of your ilk. I have faith you will restore Vi'dinor.*

A LETTER FROM THE AUTHOR

W ow. Book two is out of my hands and out there in the universe. I really hope that you've enjoyed Angela's story so far, and I would sincerely appreciate it if you posted a review on your favorite retailer's website. It's been a long ride getting it this far, but there's still a bit further it has to go.

It's been years since I've started this journey, and book three is going to be the ultimate conclusion to the series. The things I've been leading up to are finally right on the brink of happening.

ABOUT THE AUTHOR

Austen Rodgers is a science fiction and fantasy author living his best (and only) life in Waterloo, Iowa. He spends his free time painting miniatures for D&D and other role-playing games and dabbles with fantasy maps of his own creation.

Wait, you're still reading? Cool. This is the paragraph where I tell you about all of my accomplishments. But, to be honest, I hate talking about myself. So, here's the quick and dirty version: In 2015 I published my apocalyptic novel *The Book of a Few*, and earned my BFA in Creative Writing from Full Sail University in 2016. In 2019 I launched the first two books in my fantasy series, *The Flame Seer* and *The Fire's Scar*, and completed the trilogy with *The Fire's Soul* in 2020.

Slaying warlocks isn't an issue, either.

Find my other works on my website:
www.austenrodgers.com

www.ingramcontent.com/pod-product-compliance
Lightning Source LLC
Chambersburg PA
CBHW030545180626
46816CB00005B/1410